BREATHE

ME

IN

Other Titles by J.L. Drake

BROKEN TRILOGY

Broken

Shattered

Mended

BLACKSTONE SERIES

Honor

Escape

Freedom

Courage

DEVIL'S REACH TRILOGY

Trigger

Demons

Unleashed

QUIET MAFIA SERIES

Quiet Wealth

Quiet Secrets

Quiet Power

Quiet Empire

DARK WATER SERIES

Shadows

Whiskey

Alpha

Tango

HAVOC OF SINS TRILOGY

Grim

Havoc

Sins

DARKNESS TRILOGY

Darkness Lurks

Darkness Follows

Darkness Falls

STONEWALL TRILOGY

Extraction

Embedded

Breached

STAND-ALONE BOOKS

Behind My Words

Christmas at the Cabin

Omerta

BREATHE ME IN

J.L. DRAKE

Published by Montlake, Seattle

www.apub.com

Amazon, the Amazon logo, and Montlake are trademarks of Amazon.com, Inc., or its affiliates.

EU product safety contact:
Amazon Media EU S. à r.l.
38, avenue John F. Kennedy, L-1855 Luxembourg
amazonpublishing-gpsr@amazon.com

ISBN-13: 9781662539879 (paperback)
ISBN-13: 9781662539862 (digital)

Cover design by Hang Le
Cover image: © KinoMasterskaya, © Melinda Nagy / Shutterstock; © Svetlana Repnitskaya / Getty Images

Printed in the United States of America

To my sweet friends, Rachel and Lyle Womack.
Thank you for all your time, research, and unbelievable
kindness you've shown me over the years.
I'm so grateful that books brought us together but even
more thrilled that our real bond is rooted in friendship.
Jx

Chapter One

BREE

Sheffield, New York

When they're little, most kids fear the monster under their bed or in their closet. When I was nine, I hid in the kitchen and spied as my brother watched a movie with his friends about monsters that lived in the shadows of your room. It didn't take him long to discover I had seen the movie, and for years he tortured me with it. I hated him for it, but it also helped me see that monsters were all in my head. Eventually I got over my fear. Until the baseball game.

"And it's outa here!" Robert screamed. The crack of the bat against the ball left no one in doubt that it was a homer. Robert's scream came from the bottom of his lungs, and my feet pounded against the damp grass as I raced into the woods after the ball. I was determined to beat Brad, who was right on my heels.

"Go, Bree!" Brad's best friend, Kennedy, called out. As I glanced over my shoulder, I saw Brad turn around and flip him off with a laugh.

The trees were thick, and the forest closed in around us as we ran blindly, our eyes intent on locating that little white ball. I'd watched where it had arched down and had an idea of which direction to go.

"Bree," Brad called, "don't go too far in. They'll throw out a new one."

"You scared?" I shouted.

"Don't be ridiculous—I'm not five," he shot back. I saw the bushes move as he wove his way toward me through the scratchy grass. "Ha! I found it." His grin looked suspicious, and when he didn't run back toward the field to brag about it, I challenged him.

"Sure you did."

Bradley Stone was a year older than me and was arguably one of the best people in town. He was on the hockey team and a really good athlete, but he wasn't like the other jocks—he was nice. On the weekends we'd play baseball at the school field with some other friends until we got hot, and then we'd all head down to the river to our favorite swimming hole.

"You don't think I got it?"

I laughed. I could read his face like an open book. "You got shit."

"Maybe not, but I got swagger with the ladies." He tucked his shaggy brown hair behind his ear as we wandered deeper into the woods, neither of us wanting to give up.

"Speaking for all the ladies out there, ya got jack shit." My voice dripped with sarcasm.

He made a noise and shoved my shoulder. "Sherry Cummings thinks I do."

I hated how that bothered me, but, typical me, I deflected with an asshole comment. "When you get some standards, add that to your list of shit to forget." We continued on, and soon the roar of the river that ran through our town became louder. "You know she's expecting you to ask her to homecoming?" I slipped on a rock but managed not to fall. "She wants the whole grand gesture." I eyed him hard.

"I got something planned."

"Let me guess, a Sharpie, a whiteboard, and a bag of Doritos?" I jumped when he swatted my hip. "I know they're her favorite, but jeez,

her mouth must be like the inside of your jockstrap when you kiss her."
I gagged on my own words.

"You're such an ass."

"The way that chick inhales a bag of them, oh wait—" I stopped
myself and acted like I just realized something. "Oh, now I see it, it's the
Hoover mouth." I smirked. "All right, I get that, I see that."

He gave me a side glance. "Finished?"

"No, but you better—"

He snagged my waist and pressed down. I stopped as the pressure
made me buck with a laugh. I had one ticklish spot, and I hated that he
knew about it. He went still suddenly, and I was able to wiggle free. As
I fixed my shirt, I realized his expression had changed. "What?"

"There's something in the water." The ball forgotten, he moved
down the bank to the water's edge. "Here." He reached back and lifted
me down before I could protest the help. We headed for the old tree
that had fallen across the water a few years ago. It was the only way
across this part of the waterway. The river was a good twelve feet across,
and this area was well known to be the deepest part before the waterfall
just a mile or so down. A friend of ours had fallen into the river once
near this spot. A whirlpool had nearly sucked him under just before
the waterfall. If his brother hadn't been with him at the time, he would
have drowned and maybe never been found, thanks to the underwater
caves below.

"It looks like something's caught up in the branches. I can see white
fabric floating around it." I tried to see clearly, but the boulders made it
tricky. "We need to cross." I jumped up onto the tree and slowly made
my way over. Brad gave me a warning to be careful, but I'd crossed at
that spot lots of times. You just had to go slowly and watch the center
where it had begun to rot. The water beat against the trunk and made
me question when it might finally let go. I wondered who'd be on it
when it finally gave out. I kept my focus toward the bump on the shore
end. I'd never admit it, but I was scared.

"You good?" He'd noticed I'd slowed my pace.

"Yup." *One foot in front of the other*, I told myself and was more than relieved when I hit solid ground.

He hopped down next to me. "Come on."

I wasn't sure what we were going to see, but there was no way I'd chicken out now.

"Shit." Brad fell behind when his shoe got wedged between two rocks. I went back and helped him.

"Hurry, Brad." My curiosity had gotten the best of me. I grabbed his hand, and we hurried along the riverbank to get a better look.

"Jeez, what's the rush?" he complained. As we got close, I stopped short, and he stumbled into my back.

"Brad," I whispered, and I took a step back. A set of lifeless green eyes stared up at me. One eye was just below the waterline, where her blond hair swirled around as if she were alive. Her white dress was caught up around her legs and exposed her bare hip.

"Holy shit." He bent down and reached out his hand but stopped himself. "Look at her neck."

I ripped my gaze from her eyes and saw the barbed wire that was wrapped around her throat. Her wrists and hands were covered in cuts like she'd been trying to pull it off her. "What kind of a person would—" Something made a sound, and we both whirled around to scan the tree line.

My brain fired off all kinds of possibilities, and I could barely swallow my own spit. Then I spotted him as he spotted us. He dragged a woman by a barbed wire leash around her neck. The way she hung from his hands, it was obvious she was dead. He wore gloves to protect his hands, but there was no doubt he would feel the pricks of that wire from the pressure of her hanging body. In a flash of a second, the realization took hold that he was the killer and he was getting rid of the bodies.

"Bree." Brad slid his hand into mine. "Don't move." A strange calmness flooded my body even as my head screamed at me to run.

The killer's head tilted to one side as he studied us. I wondered if he was trying to figure out how he was going to deal with the situation.

As we stood there, frozen, I noticed things about him. I was sure it was a "him" mainly because he had a man's build and wore a gray zip-up jumpsuit like a janitor would wear. He had on white sneakers and had a black winter hat pulled down over his ears. A cotton scarf was tied around his neck, and he'd pulled it up over his face so only his eyes showed under the brim of the hat.

Brad and I both flinched when the man dropped the woman and her lifeless body jolted at the impact. He stood there and looked at us for another bit, then he just stepped back and faded into the thick brush.

"Go, Bree!" Brad's words broke through my trance, and I suddenly felt my body come alive as fear burst through me like electricity. His fingers dug into my hand as we raced back toward the log. Terror made me hang on to Brad's hand like a lifeline. Pure fear seemed to put wings on my feet at the thought that the murderer was on our heels and could grab us at any moment. Brad pulled his hand out of mine when my Converse sneakers suddenly slipped on a wet rock. He grabbed my arm so I wouldn't fall and then hoisted me up onto the log ahead of him. "Hurry!" he urged, and he gave my butt a push.

"Not without you." I waited for him to jump up and follow.

"Keep your eyes on the log," he instructed. I felt the log move and looked over my shoulder. "Don't look back," he cried. "I got you. I promise." I focused on my footing, and once we crossed, we both hit the ground running. The uneven terrain made my shoes slip, and I desperately grabbed at trees so I wouldn't fall. We finally reached the beaten path, and just as we hit the opening to the field, Brad grabbed my arm and swung me around.

"Wait." His eyes were wild, and I was sure they mirrored mine. "Just hang on a second." He quickly scanned around, and it made my heart beat even harder at my need to escape. He cupped my face as we both fought to catch our breath. "I need to know you're okay. Are you okay?"

"I'm okay," I managed to say.

"All hell's going to break loose soon." He shook his head in disbelief. "Once we tell what we saw, all kinds of shit's gonna happen."

"Yes, I know. Come on, he might be watching. We need to tell the police!" I cried and tried to pull away, but he leaned down close to my face, and his own barely controlled panic showed.

"Just"—he took a breath—"just promise me if things get real bad, you'll tell me. I've seen this stuff on TV."

I felt the killer was on our heels and couldn't understand how he could even form a thought at a moment like this.

"Okay," I agreed. I just wanted to get to safety.

Brad's words that day couldn't have been truer. The whole town became a circus, and we were pointed at and questioned for months about what we'd seen that day. Our lives were never the same. But the fact that he was never found was the worst part. The Barbed Wire Killer was still out there.

That was the day I learned that some monsters were real.

Chapter Two

My feet beat the pavement as I fought to pick up speed. It was hard to run with one hand holding a cell phone, but I needed to talk down the store clerk before the opportunity was lost.

"You got this, Zahid. I get your frustration, but please do this for me." I nearly took out a kid who stepped out of a barbershop. His angry shout followed me as I ran. "What's she doing?" I gasped.

He sighed. "She's currently stuffing a week's worth of food in her book bag."

"Whatever it is, I'll square up with you."

"I know you will. That's not where my frustration lies, Bree." I whirled around the corner and stopped just outside his food mart. "It's just these kids. They're getting out of control, and I've my own kids to feed—"

"I understand." I bent at the waist and took a couple of deep breaths to right my head. "And that's what I'm trying to fix."

"I know." He cleared his throat. "Can I help you?" His voice changed, and I knew exactly what was happening. One of the girls was distracting him so the other could run out. I hung up and raced down the alleyway between the store and the next building and arrived just in time to see the young girl dip out the back door.

"Justine, wait!" I called out her name, and it only made her run faster. "Shit!" Already tired from my run, I headed back to the main road and took a shortcut. Luckily, I knew the area, and soon she'd be faced with only one direction to go. "Stop!" I yelled at a man as he pulled a rug from his car, and he froze but gave me the finger as I raced by him. The sidewalk was so crowded. I hated New York sometimes; it was so busy and loud, and it made my job a hell of a lot harder than it needed to be.

I came to a stop and glanced around the corner. I saw the girl's reflection in a window, but she spotted me at the same time and skidded to a stop on the sidewalk. She lost her footing, and it gained me a few seconds on her. She jumped up and headed back where she came from, only this time she tossed her book bag and tried to spider monkey her way up a fire escape. It gave me the chance to grab her leg and pull her to the ground. She hit hard and yelped as the air was smacked from her lungs.

"Christ, kid!" I leaned over and heaved in a deep breath. "You're fast."

"Just arrest me already!" she cried, and it was evident that street life had already rubbed off on her.

"Arrest you? I'm not a cop, for Christ's sake." I held out a hand, and she looked at me funny but pulled back. "I was hired by your dad and stepmom."

"What?" Her eyes softened a little with surprise, then she looked at my hand and, to my delight, took it. I pulled her to her feet and snagged her book bag off the ground. "You sure you're not a cop?" Mistrust was written all over her face.

I grinned and lifted my sweater. "Look, no badge, no gun, no hand-cuffs. Much like you, I don't do well with rules." I heard her stomach complain. "If you hear me out, I'll feed you."

"Yeah?" Her eyes lit up.

"Yeah"—I pointed toward the road—"but if you run, no food and I keep your book bag." I slipped it over my shoulder and started to walk.

"Deal." She slowly walked behind me.

Two hours later, I had convinced Justine to let me call her father, and they were soon reunited. Her dad gave me a bag to put the stolen food in, and I gave him his daughter's book bag as promised. It wouldn't be a quick fix, but at least he could see she was all right and hadn't been trafficked somewhere. The city was a cruel place for a young girl alone. Especially one without any direction or guidance. I was glad to turn her over to his care. Now, it was up to the two of them to figure shit out.

"As promised." I set the bag on Zahid's counter, and he looked relieved. "Check it. If anything's missing, I'll square up."

"Thanks, Bree." He pulled out the bags of chips, canned soups, and whatever else she'd been able to grab in two minutes. "It looks to be all here." He eyed me. "You're a good person, you know that?" His eyes softened. "Someone's"—he pointed to the sky—"watching over you. He knows you do good things."

I pulled out a stick of gum. "Someone's watching over me, Zahid, but it sure as hell ain't that guy." I smiled at him before heading back out to the street.

"Wait, Bree, your camera." He held up my beloved Canon, and I swiveled on my heel to retrieve it. That old camera had been by my side since Quantico. I missed the days of working toward becoming an FBI agent, and it turned out I was really good at it. I'd taken a class about how the human eye couldn't catch as much as a photo could. I didn't necessarily agree, because I felt the human eye caught all the things, it's just that the brain didn't necessarily hold up its end in remembering it all. Pictures taken at a crime scene often revealed clues that changed the direction of a case.

I'd discovered that I loved to capture stills in a given moment to enjoy later when I had the time. A simple flower, the face of a loved one. I captured everything I could, and it had served me well over the years.

"Thanks." I waved and stepped outside with my camera in hand.

I swiveled as some loud taps on a window drew my attention. I'd been deep in thought as I walked down the street. It was Dale, my ex, waving at me to join him inside the coffee shop. I forced a nod and headed to join him.

Dale stood as I approached his table. He towered over me and leaned in for a hug. It was awkward, as we hadn't seen each other for a while. We sat down across from one another.

"You look good." He shook his head after he said it like he wished he hadn't. "I saw you running by earlier and figured you were working one of your cases. Runaway kid?"

"Yeah. Another happy ending." I loved my job, and I knew he could tell. He always said my eyes lit up whenever I talked about it. There was nothing better than reuniting a parent with their child.

"Remember when you told me about that boy you were tracking down and how he slipped up by buying a pack of cigarettes at a gas station? Little did he know he was also up against an FBI agent."

"I was never a full agent," I reminded him and felt that stab to the gut that always came with this conversation. If only things hadn't taken the turn they had at Quantico. If only he'd left me alone.

"You could've been. Hell, you still can be. You just can't up and leave without warning, that's all."

I looked away. Did he think that was what I'd wanted? I'd worked damn hard to get into Quantico, and he knew that. It was where I'd wanted to be. I'd had no choice. When I found all four of my tires flattened that day in the parking garage, I knew the Barbed Wire Killer was still out there—watching me.

Dale leaned over and put his hand over mine. "Whenever you get that far-off look and your jaw locks in place, you seem so lost. Let me in. Bree, please, it's hard looking in from the outside at the woman you love. I've tried to be patient with you over this past year. I hate us being apart."

I stared down at the jagged marks that ran along his wrist, then pulled my hand away. "I'm not what you need, Dale. I've got too much going on inside, and it's not fair for you to be kept on the outside." I pulled out my vibrating phone from my pocket. "I have to take this. I have to go. Goodbye, Dale." I hurried toward the door and took a breath as I hit the street. He deserved more, and the faster he accepted that, the better we'd both be.

"Jaminson," I answered as I walked back in the direction of my old Chevy truck. Having a truck to use in the city was one of the perks of the job that I really appreciated. It allowed me to head off in any direction when parents got a lead on where their child might be.

"Hey, Bree, it's Robert." His voice made me sharpen my focus as I wondered why my childhood friend, now the Sheffield police captain, was calling me.

"Hey, Captain, how are ya?" I held up a hand as I jaywalked through the slow-moving traffic.

"Truth, I need your help."

"Gimme a sec." I pulled out my keys and raced down to the parking garage, hoping my reception wouldn't fail. I hopped inside and started the engine.

"You've got my attention." I used my teeth to pull the cap off a pen and got out my notebook, ready to take notes.

He wasted no time. "It's been a few years since we've had a murder in Sheffield, and this past month, we've had two." I spat the cap out and sat straighter. "I've got people breathing down my neck who want answers, but my hands are tied." He paused. "I know you worked with Detective Monroe at the NYPD a few times as a consultant, and when I reached out to him, he said you have a real eye for detail and don't cut any corners with research. You're one of the best PIs I know, and frankly, I could really use you here."

"You need *me* there?" I repeated as I glanced quickly at the number he'd used to contact me. "Is that why you're not calling from the station? Why is it a different number?"

"Yeah, we'll go with that." He made a noise that told me there was a lot more to this whole thing than he was saying. "Our detectives are stretched thin, and . . ."

"And you need someone not bound by the law to dig?"

"I wouldn't exactly say that." He went silent for a moment. "I need you, Bree. It's no secret that you have a way with people, and like I've said before, if you ever decide to wear the badge, you just let me know. Anyone in their right mind would hire you. Look"—he sighed heavily—"I'll make it worth your while. I'll bring you on as a consultant, and I would never ask you to relive what you—"

I cut him off. "I know." If he was calling me in, it was for something big. A strange tightening in my chest brought a displaced feeling. Years might have passed, but I wasn't ready to see *him*. "Is Detective Stone still working there?" I managed to speak in spite of a dry mouth.

"He's over in Rochester," he answered, and I nodded like he could see me. *Okay, yeah, I can handle that.*

"When do you need me?"

"Last week." He attempted to laugh, but there was a heaviness to his voice. "Look, at the risk of crossing a line, I'm going to say this one time, and you can take or leave it."

"I'm listening."

"I'll give you everything that our department has from *that* day."

A coldness spread through my bones, and I felt the blood drain from my face. I had so many questions that still haunted my thoughts, and Robert knew that. Questions I knew could possibly be answered if I could get access to those dusty boxes in their basement.

"We both would get something from this deal." He was right, and he knew it.

"Send me what you can on the case, and I'll be there tomorrow." I squeezed my eyes shut as I admitted to myself that this couldn't have come at a better time.

Sheffield, New York

I leaned over the steering wheel and stared up at the pounded metal sign. **Cedar Creek Ranch.** The afternoon sun shone through the cut-outs in the sign and cast a cedar-tree shadow onto the hood of my '76 Silverado.

I closed my eyes for a moment as I gave myself a mental pep talk, then slipped the truck into drive and followed the tree-covered driveway. I had been home only three times since I packed my bags after high school graduation, and I hadn't looked back. A lot had happened in that time period, and I wondered where I'd have ended up if I'd stuck with my original plan. I pressed my hands into the steering wheel and pushed that curiosity down deep. *You can't go back in time. What's done is done.*

Five years into my hiatus, my dad made a trip to New York City and shamed me into a trip home, as my mom needed hip surgery. Thankfully, she bounced back quickly, and I'd tried my hardest to visit ever since. But was it my hardest? Because I only visited two more times in less than ten years and knew it was a pretty shitty thing to do to them. But this time was different. I eyed the pile of suitcases that I'd slung into the back of my truck and made a face. My nerves were frayed enough.

I downed my coffee as I refocused my head.

October was my favorite time of the year. A zillion different oranges, yellows, and reds framed the beaten road with the promise that the humidity would go back into hiding as the months grew cooler.

I wrinkled my nose at a new sign that reads SLOW DOWN FOR HORSES and fought the string of curse words that wanted to flow. So much had changed, but did I have any right to question it?

I rounded the corner and felt my stomach coil into a ball as I spotted my childhood home. It was breathtaking. The eight-bedroom log cabin had been featured several times in *Country Living* magazine. My parents had worked hard to keep our slice of paradise up and running as a functioning cattle ranch, but when the economy tanked and then Mom was out of commission for a bit, my sister and her husband took over with a new idea to bring in much-needed cash flow. A dude ranch for those who wanted a taste of country life. I tried not to shudder.

I parked behind Dad's truck, slipped off my sneakers, and replaced them with boots.

My phone vibrated on the dash, and I swiped it up.

Dale: I don't like how we ended things at the café. Can we talk?

I bit my lip as I opened the glove box and reached to the far back corner, where I felt it. Its sharp barb pricked my finger. A tiny piece of wire hidden away from the world. A cold, deep-rooted shiver went through me, and I slammed the box shut.

I tossed my phone into my purse and forced myself to clear my head as I sucked the tiny drop of blood from my fingertip.

As I hopped down, I spotted my twin brother. He carried a saddle over his arm. He slowed when he saw me, and his lips went into a thin line.

"Hey, Patrick." I forced a smile, but I knew he saw through it and that he knew that if it was up to me, I'd never return to this town.

"Trail ride starts in fifteen." He eyed me, then shoved the saddle into my arms. "Toby needs to be tacked." He brushed by me, and I awkwardly shifted the hunk of leather in my arms.

"Right," I huffed and headed off to the barn where Toby waited patiently. The place looked great. The cedar stall doors and their black hinges complemented each other. I was surprised to see skylights had been installed—the natural light they allowed in would be appreciated by the horses as well as the stable hands, especially in winter, when they craved it. Even the tack room had been given a facelift and sported a wagon wheel table and a couch. I had to chuckle when I saw everything had been well labeled *for the idiots of the world who can't follow simple instructions.* I could hear Patrick's voice in my head.

"Hey, boy." I rubbed Toby's head as he pushed into me as a greeting. I slid the bar back to release the door and walked him out to the cross tie. "I see Patrick is as grumpy as usual." I spoke quietly to the horse as I clipped his ties on either side, then flipped the saddle pad up over his back and settled it into place. I grunted as I swung the heavy saddle up on top.

"Can you blame him for being grumpy?" When I heard a deeper voice, my lips stretched wide, and I turned to find my brother-in-law polishing a set of reins.

"Hi, Charley." I moved around Toby and wrapped my arms around him, and he hugged me back. "God, it's good to see you."

"You too, stranger." He settled back, and I saw him glance at me a few times as I continued to tack up Toby. I tapped the horse's belly, and he sucked it in so I could pull the girth tight. I could feel Charley's questions as they probed my silence. "How long you back for?"

I pulled the stirrups free and let them hang to be adjusted to the rider's length later. "Not sure. Few weeks, maybe."

"Do Jacob and Nina know you're back?"

"They do." At the mention of my parents, I avoided eye contact. We both knew this wouldn't have been the first time I had flaked on a promise to stay awhile. "They most likely didn't think it was true." He chuckled, and I turned to stare at him.

"What?"

"You act like we don't love you." He hooked the reins back into their place and pushed off the stool. "Lower your defenses, Bree. We're just happy you're here." He swatted my back playfully as he skirted past me.

"Yeah." I shrugged and knew he was right. A lot of my problems with returning home were my own.

I finished with Toby and led him out to a group of women who looked to be straight out of New York City.

"How fast do these things go?" one woman asked as she cringed at Lucky, the horse Patrick brought up to her. He held out the reins, but when she didn't take them, he pursed his lips and let them drop.

"Well, that depends"—Patrick grabbed the woman by the waist and hiked her up and over the horse—"on how loud you are." He handed her the reins as he winked at Charley, who made an effort to hide his grin.

"Oh." She lowered her voice. "Yeah, okay."

I took pity on the terrified woman and reached for the reins she held awkwardly in her hand. "Hold them both in one hand and hold the horn to keep yourself stable. Squeeze your thighs to move forward, and the horse will do the rest."

"Squeeze, horn, stay quiet," she reassured herself. "Got it."

I helped the rest of the riders and waited as Patrick rode to take the lead of the group while one of the ranch hands took the rear. Cedar Creek Ranch was now known far and wide for its country adventures on horseback, for weekend camping trips, and as a place to go for a break from people's normal lives, all because of Lainey's vision.

"Are we ready?" Patrick called out. They all answered with a thumbs-up. "Great, now remember, the most important thing is never ever—" His phone rang, and he pulled it free. "Hello?" He turned and started down the path, and the rest of the horses started to follow.

"Never what?" they all called nervously. Charley chuckled as he tucked his phone away.

I laughed. "That's messed up."

"Maybe, but after three tours a day for five days a week, you hear the same complaints, and guess what." He urged me to follow him toward the house. "They all come back with smiles on their faces, and they can't wait to rebook."

"Good." I looked over my shoulder and watched the last horse disappear into the tree line. "So, business is doing well, then?"

"Yes, and now that we got our new buggy, the winter bookings have taken off." He patted Finley, one of the border collies, as he raced around our feet.

Charley was family and had been since he married my older sister, Lainey, a year after I graduated from high school. Lainey was ten years older, and they had plans to live in New York, but when the ranch fell on hard times, they decided to live with my parents to help save the property. I admired Charley for that. My sister told me he'd given up a corporate job for this.

"Nina," he greeted Mom warmly as we walked into the house, "look who I found." He stepped back, and I saw my mother's face light up.

"Sweetheart, you're really here!" She pulled me into a warm hug, then held me by my shoulders. "Gosh, look at you. You're so beautiful."

"Thanks, Mom." I tried to push my guilt away. "Is that Grandma's gingerbread I'm smelling?"

"Yes, three loaves, to be exact." She moved toward the kitchen, and I followed as my stomach grumbled. "It's a big hit with the guests."

"It's a hit with me too." I took a seat on the high-back chair by the island, and she cut me a steaming slice and topped it with vanilla ice cream. "Christ, this is so good." I moaned at the comforting feeling it brought me.

"So gingerbread is what it takes to get you home?" Lainey stood by the doorway with her arms crossed. She was a clone of Mom, with short, dark, wavy hair to her shoulders, a slim nose, and deep-brown eyes.

"Be nice." Charley kissed her cheek. "She's here now—that's what matters."

I leaned back and pulled a bag of her favorite cookies from my purse. They were from a famous bakery in the city that she loved. "I brought a peace offering." I handed it to her.

"Oh, yum!" She snagged the bag and dug one out.

"See?" I shrugged at Mom. "I'm not the only one who can be bought with sweets."

She hugged me again, a little longer this time, and planted a noisy kiss on my head. "Why don't you get your things and get settled in your room? Once the trail ride is over and Patrick is back, we'll have dinner."

"Sounds good." I washed my plate and headed out to get my belongings.

Dad had obviously beaten me to it and had loaded my suitcases into a wheelbarrow. It was parked at the bottom of the porch steps.

"You're back," he said from where he sat on the porch chair. His still-handsome face was weathered from the sun and hard work. His faded Weber-grill ball cap was pushed up like it often was when his day was nearing the end.

"I am."

"For how long?"

"Few weeks."

He nodded but made a point to look at the heap of luggage that had come with me this time. "Doesn't look like a few weeks."

I leaned my shoulder into a post and took in the gorgeous sunset that could be seen through the colorful trees. "Robert called me."

"Oh yeah?" Dad sipped his coffee. "What does the good old captain have to say?"

"Guess there's been a couple homicides in Sheffield. His boss is breathing down his neck about making things right, and he asked me to officially lend a hand." Dad's eyebrow arched as he took another sip and patted Finley, who was happily draped over his lap. I knew what he was thinking, but thankfully he didn't go there.

"Doesn't surprise me—you're one of the best PIs in the state." He shifted, and Finley jumped down. "You stay for as long as you want." He stood up and kissed my cheek. "All I ask is no drinking in the loft."

"Sure, Dad."

I swung my legs over the end of the loft door and handed Patrick a cold beer, which he happily took. With a full stomach thanks to a delicious dinner, I felt it was time to check in with my twin. We sat there above the barn like we'd done as kids and looked out together at our property. There was a great view of the fields lined with fences, the lake, and the trees. I breathed deeply. I really loved this place, and I knew my brother did too.

"Where's Maxine?" My brother had married my childhood best friend. It was a little strange at first, but Maxine was an amazing person, and after a love-filled summer I knew she was perfect for him.

"She picked up a shift at the hospital. I guess they were short staffed again, and we could use the overtime."

I nodded. I knew Maxine was a hard worker, and if they were short staffed for nurses, she'd give up her day off to help out.

"You were quiet over dinner." He twisted the cap and took a swig. "Must feel strange to be back after all these years." His dig hit hard in the center of my chest. I deserved it.

"You could have visited," I whispered.

"So could you."

"I did."

He made a wry face and shook his head. "Right, three times in twelve years. It's a long time to leave your family." When I didn't respond, he sighed, and I could see he fought to let his hurt go. "At the risk of driving you off, can I ask you something?"

I shot him a cautious look. "Depends."

"Do you think it's a wise idea working a homicide case? You know . . ."

I looked away and cleared my throat. "It's my job."

"No, missing runaways is your job. Real investigator work could have been, though." He stopped himself when he realized he was being a dick. "Sorry, I know you do more than work with missing teens. And I know you work sometimes with the NYPD. That last case must have been pretty cool to be a part of." When I looked surprised, he grinned. "Cap filled me in." I nodded with a rueful smile. "Can you just explain why someone as smart as you would drop out of the FBI program?" His gaze moved to my white-knuckled grip on the beer bottle. "Okay." He shook his head. "I'll drop it."

"Good."

He was right that I hadn't dropped out because I couldn't hack it, though. But I had found a place for myself after I quit the FBI. It happened quite by accident when I heard about a missing kid and decided to try to help after the police had given up on him. It didn't take that long to figure it out. I found I was good at thinking like a troubled teen. Runaways became my thing, and word got out, and I soon was getting calls from desperate parents who had nowhere else to turn. My heart was full when I brought their children back to them, and I lived for it. "I know, it's not my usual gig, but I need a change." I hesitated. "A challenge. The fact that Robert asked me personally means something. He knows I have an eye for detail. Besides, sometimes a person like me can dig around on the outside without the boundaries of law. Carefully, so as not to mess up the case, of course."

"Sure, and that's cool and all, but don't you think it'll dig up past—"

I cut him off. "Nope." I didn't want to even go near that thought with him.

"One more thing"—he eyed me as he drank—"I know you said you wanted your files you kept after—"

"I did." I didn't want him to finish the sentence.

"I didn't realize there were potentially three more Barbed Wire victims."

"You went through my files?" I'm not sure why that bothered me. Patrick knew pretty much everything that had happened.

"Of course I did." He brushed me off. "Guess I blocked that part of it out."

"Lucky. Look"—I leaned my head against the wood frame—"I just want my family right now. I need this." I waved my hands around at the horses that grazed in the field. "I need to reset and reboot. Is that okay with you?"

I felt a little guilt seep in at the thought of my family. My parents, who were getting older but both still had to work hard. My sister, Lainey, and her husband, Charley, one of my favorite people. My twin brother and his beautiful wife. They were all dedicated to keeping this place going.

He looked away and finished off his beer, then reached for another. "Promise you'll let me know this time before you leave?"

"Yes."

"You'll take over some of the barn work." He tilted his head at me. "Yes."

"You'll let me drive your sweet truck?" My brother's smile returned.

"No." I laughed, and he joined in. "Yeah, sure." I relaxed a little and thought how good it would feel to be in my own bed.

A high-pitched squeal drew my attention, and we both looked in the direction of the truck that had just pulled up. I turned to my brother. "What the—"

"That's Kevin, the noisy pig. He's got a serious love affair goin' for Finley and Dad." The pig in question had jumped out of the passenger side of Dad's truck and was headed straight across the driveway toward the border collie pup.

"Christ, he's fast for such little legs." I smiled around the mouth of the beer.

He chuckled. "Wait for it. Dad takes that little potbelly everywhere. People know Kevin." He snorted.

"Jesus." I shook my head with a laugh. "What did I come home to?"

"For fuck's sake"—Dad looked up at the two of us—"are you two drinkin' up there?" he called from below.

"No," we said in unison.

Chapter Three

My blades cut into the ice as I tore down the outside with the puck between my skates. I passed it quickly from foot to foot, while the goalie's eyes flicked and followed its movement. I spotted the defenseman in my peripheral vision as he raced toward me, and I let him think he had me, but at the last second, I twisted and did a quick little side hop and stepped around him. I could hear his body slam into the boards.

I tapped the puck up to my stick and quickly flipped it over the goalie's shoulder. The sound of the beloved siren filled my ears as the third period ended. I circled around the net and fist-bumped a few of my teammates. God, I loved my hockey. It was one of the few things that calmed my brain and allowed me some peace.

"Nice goal." My buddy and fellow detective, Kennedy, slapped me on the back as we headed off the ice. I awkwardly went off balance and almost got a skate blade to my face.

"Whoa there!" Hank, a guy who sharpened our skates, quickly caught me. "Last thing you need is an injury, Bradley. I just finished sharpening these."

"Jeez, sorry about that," Kennedy apologized. "We sure don't want this guy's pretty face messed up."

"Yeah, sorry, Hank." I whistled. "Kennedy's face might need a little scar, but I don't need anything to draw the ladies." I turned to show my profile, and we all laughed. I snatched up my roll of Savage tape from the bench, and we headed to the locker room. I wanted to retape my stick.

After I showered and changed, I gathered my stuff and headed out toward my car. My schedule was busy between playing on the Sheffield Police Department hockey team, coaching the university team, and being the lead detective on two new murder cases.

I checked my watch as I pulled into my driveway and hurried inside the house. I was going to be late for Captain's meeting if I didn't get a move on. I had only a few minutes to get ready.

I tapped the light and stepped into my color-coordinated closet. I took a moment to scan the perfectly aligned dress shirts, all within an inch of each other. My shoes were lined up, toes faced forward, so I could easily see which would work with the shirt I chose. I chucked my wet towel into the laundry hamper—I knew my housekeeper would be by within the hour—then spun the rack to choose a tie. I decided on the one with silver specks.

Satisfied, I headed to the kitchen and poured myself a coffee to go. I ran my hand through my dark, shaggy hair and tucked a piece behind my ear. Cap didn't give me shit for keeping my hair long. Mind you, it helped that I'd known the guy since the sandbox, and he had bigger things to deal with than my hair.

The phone in my pocket rang. "Stone," I answered without a thought, then corrected myself. "Hello?"

"I don't think I'll have time to drop her off this afternoon." Sherry sighed through the speaker. My frustration flared, but I swallowed it back and rolled my eyes. "I'm heading to my sister's, and I'm not sure there's enough time."

"Sherry, you always make the point that there should be a specific time to drop her off when I bring her to you," I reminded her. The whole shared-custody thing wasn't working. "Please try and drop her off on time. I'll talk to you later." I hung up with an exasperated huff. Eight months into our divorce, and we still hadn't gotten the hang of it. Life with Sherry had ended because of the darkness I held inside. I desperately needed to get to a better place.

My trusty alarm went off on my work phone, and I grabbed my things and headed out.

The Sheffield Police Department had been on edge since the first murder popped up two weeks before, and with a second murder just two days ago, in the same general spot, and with the same MO, everyone was sweating. We'd had our fair share of homicides, but these were different. They were not the domestic blowups or bar fights gone bad we usually dealt with. Two young women, both dead on the floor of a nightclub, with no apparent reason for their deaths. No stab wounds, no gunshots, no sign of strangulation. Just dropped dead. Another victim, a bartender, had been sent to the hospital on the night of the second murder. They had to be some type of poisoning, but the medical examiner was still working on it. I only hoped this was the end of it, but something about the whole thing made me worry more homicides might be coming.

Normally, I'd stop by Captain's office and check in, but as I was already late, I went directly to the conference room and took a seat in the back. I nodded at a few faces and focused on what was being presented.

"So, here's what we've got." Captain shared photos of a few possible suspects. "It's not much, just smoke and mirrors really, to buy us time, but if you spot any of these guys, you have a warrant to bring 'em in. They're all known criminals, and chances are, it'll lead to nuttin', but we have to start somewhere."

"Why do I feel like we're chasing ghosts here?" My old partner, Ray, shook his head and leaned over to whisper as Cap continued. "I've seen this stuff before, never around here. This ain't your average domestic dispute," Ray cautioned. We all knew that already. I kept my eyes on Cap as he continued to speak but gave a nod to Ray. He had a temper, and I sure as hell didn't want to feed the embers that always seemed to smolder in the guy's belly. Ray was a great detective, and he'd taught me a lot, but he did things that I didn't always agree with.

Ray was a year away from retirement and hated the idea of being pushed out by the department. Sadly, he needed to go. He was old school and often got us into trouble. We had rules, and Ray only chose to respect them when they worked in his favor. After being his partner for six years, I'd asked to be reassigned. I don't think the old man even noticed the change.

"The Velvet Nightclub wants us front and center when they open. We need to show the public that we're taking the murders of Shelly White and Maggie Deloitte very seriously." Captain turned and pointed to a schedule taped on the whiteboard. "I'm assigning a few of you inside the club"—he stabbed a finger to the schedule—"and I want uniforms outside the doors as well."

He stared around the room. "You see anything, and I mean any-damn-thing, you call it in. Do not approach."

"Or they could simply close the club." Kennedy sounded exasperated. "At least till we catch the killer. Or killers." He was right: How could we know for sure it was just one person?

Captain huffed as he tossed a file onto the table. "In a perfect world, maybe, but let's face it, it's all about the almighty dollar. Their reasoning is they don't have to close since the two victims weren't employees, and now we're finished processing the scene, they want the doors open."

What a reckless way of thinking. "But those women were killed there. We have no concrete idea how or why, or who could be next. Two of their customers are dead. I mean, call me crazy, but that sounds bad for business."

"I agree, Stone, but I don't own the place." He shook himself as though to throw off his stress. "All right, dismissed."

I closed my notebook and tucked the pen neatly away in the spine.

"Detective Stone?" I swung around to see Officer Adam Smith, the newest rookie at the SPD. He stood there, looking nervous as he held out a file. "I was asked to give this to you."

"Thanks." As I slid the file from his fingers, his expression made me hesitate. "Anything else?"

"No, I mean, yes, actually," he said, stumbling on his words. "I was wondering if maybe you'd let me help out."

"Oh." I knew Smith was one of the more eager young officers, and I respected that.

He looked worried when I didn't respond right away. "I love connecting the dots to things, and I've got a pretty good eye for detail, so I thought if there's anything I can do, like grunt work, making copies, et cetera . . . I'd be more than happy to do it. I want as much hands-on experience as I can get. I'd like to make detective someday."

"You need to be the best cop you can first, Officer Smith." I smiled. "But yeah, I'll keep that in mind." I bumped his arm on the way out, then had a thought and stopped myself. "Hey, yeah, maybe there is something."

His happy, wide-eyed face lit up. "As you know, we can't find any connection between the two dead girls. If you want to cross-reference all the people who were at the club on both nights of the murders, that would be a huge help." I had the list already, but I wanted to see what he'd come up with. Fresh eyes on a case were always a smart idea. Couldn't hurt.

"Of course!" He beamed as I waved him off so I could answer my ringing phone.

"Detective Stone"—I recognized the voice of the owner of the Velvet Nightclub—"it's Donald Longboard. I was hoping you could come down for a chat."

"I was just about to do that, sir. I'll head right over." I hoped he might have something to tell me. At this point any leads were first priority. As I made my way through the station, I picked up the file again to take with me. I noted the blood work had come back on the bartender. He'd gotten sick the same night Maggie Deloitte, the second victim, was killed. I was surprised to see they had found a small trace of the same mystery substance in his blood work. Whatever it was, it had to be some kind of poison. It wasn't any kind of street drug. How come he wasn't dead? Interesting . . .

I hurried outside, slid behind the wheel of my Genesis GV80, and turned onto the street in the club's direction. It didn't take me long to arrive.

"Mr. Longboard." I joined him at the bar top. "Do you have something for me?"

"Nice to see you guys are taking things seriously enough to send two detectives." I let his words sink in. I wondered if Kennedy had come by after the game. "Well, like I was telling the other detective, my bartender who was working the night of the second murder—" He grimaced. "Guess what his blood work showed."

"Traces of something unknown. Yes, we know." I held up the file.

"Yeah, poison."

"That hasn't been confirmed. I suppose it's possible he could somehow have ingested something, and that same something could have been what killed the victim." I decided to give him that much.

"I see." He studied my face, and I knew he wanted this storm to be cleared up fast. "I heard a rumor the first woman had traces of it, too, right?"

I wasn't about to give out any information on the case. I ignored him as I thought.

"Detective Stone, I get this is just a nightclub to you, but it's my business, and when word gets out women are dying here—"

I finally looked up, and I saw him swallow. I knew that behind that expensive shirt, which no doubt cost half my salary, he was terrified of losing business.

"Where is the bartender now?"

"Resting at home, but he's willing to help."

"Call him."

His face brightened. "I'll make the call." He whistled at a busboy to move as he whisked by him. I leaned into the bar and watched while the rest of the staff prepared the place before they opened for the night.

I snatched up one of the menus . . . My eye caught the beer ads on the side. East Dog Brewery and Sea Foam Brew. I wondered who came up with the names. I did recognize Sea Foam Brew. I'd never tried it, but I often noticed cases of it kicking around in the dressing room at the local college where I coached.

"They said you'd be here." The captain waltzed into the room. I pushed off the counter and went to meet him. "Need to talk to you about something."

"Sure." I looked around at a few people who had stopped to look at us. "What about?"

"Not what, but who. I brought someone with me from the station." His face twisted as he stepped back and indicated whom he referred to. I saw him steal a quick glance at me as he ran a hand over his face. I knew he would be unsure what my reaction would be as I took in the very fit brunette in tight jeans and a T-shirt with a flannel shirt wrapped around her waist. She stood with her back to me as she spoke to one of the bouncers. "Don't kill me, Stone," he breathed.

I stood frozen as I looked at her. I saw her shirt lift when she raised her hands to explain something to the bouncer, and my gaze slipped down her small curves to the bare skin that showed. The guy smiled at her, and she tossed her head back and laughed as she put a camera back into a bag that was slung around her neck. Her long, glossy brown hair tumbled around her midsection.

"Why would I kill . . ." My words faltered when she turned, and her dark eyes found mine. So many things ran through me at once. The box I had tucked deep inside cracked open for a moment, but I shut it down fast. I knew she'd feel uneasy to see me again too. It had been years. Her neck contracted, and she reached for the table next to her. I hated that she was still unbelievably gorgeous. It was as though time had stopped with her.

"Excuse me," she whispered to the man and headed toward us, shooting daggers at Captain.

"I see no introductions are needed," Captain said and gave a nervous chuckle. "Shit, guys, how long's it been?"

"Twelve years," we both said within a half beat of one another.

Captain's eyes bugged out as he absorbed what we'd just said. "Well, nothing like ripping the BAND-AID off."

"What are you doin' here?" I sounded rude. I didn't mean to be. I also couldn't help but feel a little lighter at the sight of her.

"Saving your ass, apparently," she fired back, and I smirked.

"I see nothing's changed."

"Fuck, I hope it has." She sank onto the chair next to a table, and Captain joined us. "Robert here asked me to come." I glanced at the captain, who nodded.

"Our hands are tied at every corner, Stone." He explained what I already knew. "I need these murders solved. I'm getting zero help from above."

"So you bring me on as the lead, and you want to play dirty?"

"The hell you say!" Bree snapped, and I fought a grin; she was just as feisty as the girl I once knew. "I know there've been some issues with the public not trusting cops. It's not my problem some assholes 'tarnish the badge,' but I hardly think my being here means we play dirty."

"I didn't mean it like that." I hated that she was right. A few bad cops, and we all got labeled as crooked.

"I just work the system a different way and get what needs to be done." She stood defiantly and stared me down.

"Come on, you two. We're all professionals here." Captain held a hand between us. "We're also all friends. At least we used to be. Stone, I got you lead on this case, but if one of the others got it, I'd be pulling the same card. We need this case wrapped up." He took a long breath to calm down. "Surely, we can come to a level playing field and get this mess cleared up?"

"I wasn't the one that ran," I muttered and eyed Bree hard, and she sank back down onto the chair. I remembered that day very well.

She just up and left without a word. It was the same day I asked Sherry to marry me.

"Could you blame me?"

Silence blanketed the room while years of pent-up hurt and damage from that long-ago day pricked at my core.

"If anything, Bree, you'll bring fire to this PD." Captain chuckled. "All right, well, here's the cherry on top: Bree starts today, and you two will be working together."

You could have bounced a ball off the tension as we swallowed that little tidbit.

"If anyone asks, you're a consultant on this case, Bree. Stone brought you on," he added and shot me a shit-eating smirk that faded fast as he took in my expressionless face. "Stone, get her up to speed."

"Understood, Robert." I used his name on purpose, and he looked at the two of us and let out a long puff of air as he clapped his hands together.

"Well, this is incredibly awkward. I'm leavin'."

Once the door shut behind him, we both broke into big smiles at his reaction.

I tossed the menu back into its place, needing something to do. "That was fun." I laughed.

"Yeah." She tucked her long, wavy hair behind her ear. "Making Robert uncomfortable used to be our thing." She gave that throaty chuckle I remembered, and it felt so good.

"Easy target." I gathered my things, but her words about not being able to stay bothered me. We could pretend it was all an act, but we were far from being okay together. I still struggled with my decision to choose Sherry over trying things with Bree back then. In spite of how close I'd been with Bree, I'd felt Sherry was who I needed after all the trauma I'd been through.

"Detective Stone." Mr. Longboard hurried toward us, and I pulled my head out of my memories. "He's on his way." His gaze shifted to Bree. "Hello again, Detective Jaminson."

"It's not *detective*," Bree said. "I'm a PI, and a consultant on this case. Hope my captain didn't confuse you." He shrugged. "Please call me Bree." She turned her pearly whites on him, and I gave her a slit-eyed look.

Longboard whistled. "First name basis already." He grinned at her. "Perhaps by the end of all this, we'll do dinner." I fought not to roll my eyes. The guy might be worried about his business, but it was clear he thought he had a way with the ladies.

"Well"—she checked her phone—"that depends on what you've got for me."

Longboard turned his grin on me, but I glared back at him; I had no time for this. The bartender arrived, and I was glad we could focus on him instead. We settled onto barstools to wait.

"Hi." I shook his hand to ease his nerves. "I'm Detective Stone, and this is our consultant, Ms. Jaminson. I know you gave a statement before at the hospital, but given what's come to light, I was hoping you could walk me through your night and any interaction with the second victim, Maggie Deloitte."

"Nice to meet you both." He pulled out a barstool and sat next to us. "I work the weekends—it's the busiest time of the week. I got bumped pretty quickly to bar manager because of my BA in hospitality management."

"How well did your quick promotion sit with your fellow workers?" Bree cut in.

He shrugged. "I didn't get much time to make friends before they gave me the position. Probably for the best." He paused. "If you think one of my staff members did this, you're wrong."

"Everyone's a person of interest," I reminded him. "Keep going."

"My shift was like every other night. Nothing stood out. All the regulars were there. I wasn't working the night the first girl, Shelly something, was killed."

Bree opened the file she was holding and scanned staff photos. "Shelly White?" She made sure to confirm the name. "All right, so where was Maggie when you took her drink order?"

"Right there. She was standing close to that jar of olives." He pointed at a large olive jar that sat on the bar top. "I'd just finished serving a guy who ordered five Stellas for his table." He pointed at a table.

I noted that he used a lot of detail. "That's a good memory." His face twisted, and I could see I'd hit a nerve there. *Interesting.*

"Here's the thing." Bree perched on the stool next to him. "The first forty-eight hours are the most crucial when it comes to a case like this. The detectives only have a small window to collect the evidence. They have a bit more time to form relationships with the witnesses to help paint a picture. We're now on the start of day three." Her face flinched. "They've ruled out some of the more obvious people that Maggie knew. So, now we're here following a new lead. Thanks to your coming forward." His shoulders lowered as he nodded.

"Look." He opened his hands. "I served the man, then her. I had to read her lips—it's noisy in here when we're busy. Then I repeated her drink order back to her."

"Which was?" I asked.

"Lemon martini." His eyes rolled up as he thought. "I turned away to make her drink, so I had my back to her, then when I turned to hand it to her, she immediately took a quick sip. I remember she didn't really look at me. She kind of scanned the room."

"Like she was watching for someone?"

"Maybe." He shrugged, and the fatigue of the last two days was evident by the way his shoulders sagged forward. "Anyway, since she didn't go for her purse right away, I took the person's order next to her. When I looked at her to wait for her to pay, I noticed her eyes were watering, like she'd just stopped a sneeze. I didn't think anything of it, just slid a napkin over in case she needed it. She paid, took her drink, and left without her card. I figured she'd come back for it.

"It was more than a minute or so later that I felt funny. I went downhill fast, and I ended up at the hospital. The doctor said I must have gotten drugged or something, but they had no idea what it was.

After what happened, I feel lucky to be alive." Bree gave me a small glance when he lowered his head. "Am I in trouble here?"

"Did you kill anyone?" I asked.

"No."

"Then you shouldn't be in any trouble."

"No, we just want justice for the girls' families, and with what you provided, it gets us partway there." Bree's soft voice seemed to soothe his tension again. She pulled out a card. "If you think of anything else, give me a call."

"Okay, yeah." He stood, and we joined him. "I will, thank you." He gave me a look, and I stepped back to dismiss him.

"You know you're a big man, right?" Bree's odd comment threw me, and I moved my attention to her now that the bartender was gone. "You're six foot, what, three?" She put her hands on her hips.

"Your point?"

"Brad, you're built like an NHL defenseman. You have a resting brooding face, and look at the size of your hands." She pointed at one. "You're intimidating. Tone down the whole *I'm a detective, therefore I have knowledge on how I can hide a dead body* thing."

"It's Bradley or Detective Stone," I said, and she rolled her eyes. I grabbed my notebook while Bree hooked her purse over her shoulder, and we moved to a table. I waved at Longboard to join us.

Longboard lowered his phone a minute or so later, then joined us at the table. "Everything okay with my bartender?"

"Yes, we just need a few more minutes, then we'll be on our way." As he spoke to Bree, I took a moment to study the place. The room was all dark wood with vinyl black-studded chairs around high tables. More standing tables were scattered about. The ceiling held bars of strobe lights above the dance floor. The hallway that led to the restrooms was across from the bar. I noted where the entrance was in relation to the rest of the room. Satisfied, I looked at Bree.

"So, how about that dinner?" Longboard pressed again.

"How about you take my card, and if you think of anything else, you give me a call?" Bree handed it to him, then joined my side as Longboard scurried away.

"Jerk," I muttered.

"So"—Bree ignored me and thought out loud—"I read through the information Cap sent me on the case. Let's start from the beginning. From what we know, the first victim, Shelly White, age twenty-four, ordered a drink here." She stepped up to the bar top. "She orders a piña colada, a drink that requires the bartender to turn his back to make it. Shelly takes the drink, starts to feel funny. Her friend said she sloshed the drink as she put it on the high-top table they were at." She walked to the table and mimicked putting down a drink. "Then she heads to the restroom"—she pointed to the restroom door—"where she drops to the floor. The other women in the restroom freak out, and moments later a bouncer is giving her CPR, but it's too late. She's gone."

"Okay, yeah, that's about right," I agreed. I enjoyed watching her work. She was a quick study, always had been. She went back to the bar top and took three steps down from where Shelly had stood, then pulled out her camera and took a couple of photos as if from the victim's point of view.

"The second victim, Maggie Deloitte, age twenty-two, orders her drink here, another drink the bartender turns away to make. He gives her the drink, then helps another customer. When he turns back, he notices her eyes are glossy. According to a different witness statement, she hands him her card to pay, and before the bartender is back from running the card, she pushes away from the bar and stumbles through the crowd. She heads outside toward her car, gets about five feet, and collapses."

"That autopsy will be ready by tonight," I commented.

"Come here." She waved me over, and I stood next to her. "Closer." She pushed into my side as she looked at the file the captain must have given her. "Shelly was a little taller than me; I'm five eight." She leaned her body over the bar like she was giving her order to the bartender.

"She was in jeans and a tank like mine, and Maggie was in a short dress—she was more my height." She moved the flannel shirt that was wrapped around her waist to look like a mini skirt, then leaned over the bar top. "I assume this is roughly where the attack happens." She ran her hands along the bar. "Maybe one step back." She looked up at me then and tilted her head to the side. "Flirt with me," she ordered, and I chuckled.

"What?"

"Work with me here. We're jammed in like sardines, and both girls were gorgeous. I'm sure they were being hit on the entire night."

"The place was packed." I followed her thoughts as she got close to me again. "He could have leaned over to speak." I leaned down, trying to think how he could make contact without it looking like he was. "He slips something into her drink." I made the motion of doing it. "But nowhere on the tapes does Maggie Deloitte talk to anyone other than the bartender, and no one really seemed to be trying to grab her attention. Also, both bartenders were cleared thanks to that little camera right there." I pointed to a staged tequila bottle that I'd been told had a hidden camera. It pointed straight down to where they mixed their drinks. "Not that I plan to rule out anyone just yet, but they're in the clear as of right now."

"Okay." She pressed her lips together. "And we know for sure they weren't into drugs or affiliated with drug dealers?"

"No, and no drugs were found in their systems. At least none of the usual ones. We checked that angle multiple times from the start. According to their families and friends, these two young women were focused, had drive, and Maggie often had to do drug tests for her job."

"Good." Bree's brows went up. "It makes sense it had to be a poison, though. One passes out in the bathroom and one out in the parking lot. The timing is about the same between when they ordered their drinks and when they collapsed."

"Correct."

"He just lets them die. Doesn't do a thing to them."

"Seems so, yeah." I flipped a page in the folder and scanned the page. "Nothing stolen, no assault—they just drop and die."

"Then why kill them?" She stepped back and looked around the room. "For sport?" She cringed at how monstrous that sounded. "Maybe this guy hits on girls, and whoever rejects him becomes his target?"

My phone rang, and I held up a hand. "Hi, Cap."

"Stone, I need you and Bree to swing by Maggie Deloitte's house and speak to her parents. They've put together some stuff for us. I want you to pick it up and go over it with them."

"All right."

"It'll be good for Bree to have a look around too," he quickly said before he hung up. I could kill him for not giving me a heads-up about her.

"Captain wants us to swing by Maggie Deloitte's house. Her parents have something for us." I filled her in as we headed out. "And heads up, they're carrying a lot of anger, given she's the second victim."

"Understandable." She hesitated when she saw my car.

"What?"

"Nothing." I caught her smile in the mirror as she slipped inside. "Nice."

The hum of my car was entirely too quiet for two people who shared a past like we did. One moment I was watching the red light, and the next I was back at the river holding Bree's hand, staring down a killer. It still burned me that the Barbed Wire Killer was never found and that he probably had more victims out there. But more than anything, it drove me crazy that he let us go. Why spare us and not those two innocent women he murdered?

"It's green." Bree pointed to the light, and I shook my thoughts clear.

Bree was thorough as we met with Maggie Deloitte's parents. They walked us through some ex-boyfriends and a coworker she seemed to have a beef with. Bree snapped her photos, and once she got what she felt was all they could give, she thanked them and reassured them they'd hear the moment we had anything. I didn't speak much; she had an easier way with people, and, apparently, I was intimidating. We headed back to the car.

"Want to go get your truck, or do you want a ride home?" I glanced at her in my front seat as she studied a photo. When she didn't answer, I made the decision for her and headed for her place.

"Why did these murders happen? On paper Shelly's boyfriend, Oliver, seemed wonderful, and Maggie's ex-boyfriend appeared to be fine with the split. They both seemed like level-headed guys. Even Shelly's coworker moved on to a different company and sounded fine about it. According to her family, Maggie was a nice young woman with a good job, good friends, yet she died in the public parking lot of a nightclub. It just feels so unnecessary. Neither of them was robbed or assaulted. The whole thing just seems off." She sighed, then looked at me. "You're quiet."

"You're me two weeks ago." I shrugged. "I've run through every detail you are. I've come up with zilch. No clue as to the killer or motive."

She frowned.

"Don't worry, something will show itself in time."

"Mm-hmm. Gotta love the waiting game." She chewed on her pen cap. "So how pissed were you today when you saw me?" She grinned, but it didn't last long.

"I wasn't pissed."

"Yes, you were." She called me out. "You never forgave me for leaving when I did and not going to your wedding."

I felt the lash of that old scar. "I wasn't pissed that you missed my wedding—I was pissed that you left without a word and just disappeared. Yes, I was just shocked to see you standing in front of me. The captain didn't share his plan with me, and from the look on your face when you saw me, I take it he didn't with you either."

"Nope." She puffed her cheeks out. "He specifically told me you were over in Rochester. I took that to mean you had transferred. Clearly, I misunderstood."

I grunted when I realized what Cap had done. "I was in Rochester but visiting a friend for two days. He's tricky like that."

"And my being here, stepping in on the case, is that going to be a problem for you?"

I flicked my finger on the signal light before I crossed traffic and eased into the far-left lane.

"I'm confident enough at this stage of my career to admit when we need another set of eyes on a case. I'm fine with us working together, but you should know that I don't bend the rules for anyone, so whatever happens during your stay here is on you. Just be sure whatever you do find, we can use it in court."

"Understood." She didn't miss a beat, and the awkward silence settled between us again. Thankfully, I had just pulled into her driveway, but then a rush of memories flooded me from back when we were in high school together.

"I appreciate the drive home." She gathered her things and opened the door. "I'll drive myself home tomorrow, so you don't need to put yourself out."

She wasn't putting me out. "I'll text an hour before I leave in the morning."

"Okay. See you then."

"All right." I waited for her to shut the door so I was concealed behind the tinted windows. I tipped my head back and took my first real breath of the day. Everything inside me had jolted alive at her familiar perfume. It lingered in the car and sent my memory back to when I first met Bree in Spanish class. Her beautiful smile had lit up the room, and when her gaze had found mine, her eyes had done this twinkling thing that had made my stomach flip.

I'd kept Bree at arm's length after things took a bad turn that afternoon by the river. I'd pushed any thought of her away and hung on to the one constant thing in my life—Sherry Cummings.

"Stop." I slapped the heel of my palm against my eyes in a bad attempt to stop my spiral. I slammed the car into reverse and headed home.

Chapter Four

I stretched out on the dock and dangled my legs over the edge into the chilly water. The cold felt good on my tired feet. The moment I had arrived home, Patrick had given me endless chores to do. I wasn't complaining—I knew I had to show my brother I was sorry for leaving, and he was going to use me until he felt better.

"I can't believe you're back." Maxine plunked a heavy cooler down, then sat next to me and gave me a huge hug. "I forgot how much I missed you."

"Me too." It felt good that Maxine and I could pick up right where we left off. "You're looking really good." I studied her short raven-black bob above her perfectly arched brows. She looked happy.

"Thanks." She cracked open a bottle of something homemade and cocked a brow as she poured out some for each of us. "A toast to having you back home."

"Cheers." I tapped the little plastic cup against hers and downed the smooth, fruity drink. Crickets and an owl came out to join us, and their comforting sounds could be heard across the water.

"Is it true?" She studied my face, and I looked at her, confused. "You're working at the SPD?"

"Yes, as a consultant." I sighed. "Captain Robert totally lied to me." I shook my head and sipped some more of her delicious cocktail. "The bugger told me Brad was in a different town."

"Well, you can thank your sister for that one."

"What do you mean?"

She handed me a slice of apple. "It was her idea to have you come back and work here."

"Is that so?"

Her mouth stretched out like she realized she shouldn't have said anything. "Yes, it's so." She lifted a brow. "But what I really want to know is what is Bradley like now? Because that guy had a body on him. I remember Kennedy even bragging about how fit Bradley was in high school."

"I should be asking you that." I bumped her shoulder. "I'm the one who's been gone."

We laughed and went back to watching the river as it spilled into the lake.

"It's going to be painful." A smile broke across my lips as I remembered when I laid eyes on Brad at the nightclub. "When I saw him today"—I fanned myself with my hand—"it was like I was in high school all over again." She tossed her head back with a laugh while I took another long drink. "He hasn't changed a bit, still very sexy, and smart, and he still gets that look in his eye where you can't tell what he's thinking but you know it's all kinds of dirty." My stomach coiled into a painful knot as I remembered how hard it had been when I first moved away. I missed him so much, I physically hurt. I'd never wish that feeling on my worst enemy. I covered my face as I moaned. "God did not play fair when he made that man."

"Ha! That's for sure." She patted my arm and sighed. "Well, Dale seemed nice that time I met him. How are things there?"

"Hmm." I wasn't overly pleased about that. I'd kept Dale from my family because I wasn't ready to take that next step. "We broke up. It wasn't meant to be."

Her face fell. "That's too bad."

"I loved him, but not enough. He's wonderful in a lot of ways, but my heart wouldn't let him in." I looked across the lake to where Brad's parents' house was, then pulled my eyes away. I noticed the corners of Maxine's mouth had gone up.

"Well, it's great that Robert asked you to come, and bonus, you get to work with Bradley Stone." She chuckled, and I appreciated that she steered the conversation away from Dale.

"Yeah, and speaking of which." I stumbled to my feet as a surge of anger went through me.

Maxine was on my heels as my confidence grew. Mom and Dad were across the way working with one of the horses, and they called out to me, but I ignored them—I needed to speak with my sister. I whisked through the tall grass, across the driveway, and up the stairs into the house.

"Lainey, where are you?" I burst through the door and blinked to get my eyes adjusted to the light. Finley jumped up from his bed by the door and followed on my heels as I tore into the kitchen. "Maxine told me you suggested I work at the SPD. How could you not give me a heads-up that I'd be working with Detective Sexy?" I chuckled drunkenly at my own words; that was a great name for him. He was even more sexy as an adult. My heart fluttered as I thought of him. I made my way across the room as I spoke. "Seriously, it was like a drum going off between my legs the entire day. What do you think that's like for someone who doesn't have a designated penis on hand like you do?" I came to a dead stop, and Maxine bumped into me. I swore my heart dove for cover behind my stomach.

"Autopsy report came in." Bradley held up a file from where he sat in the corner of the room, and I think I turned about eight shades of red. "Thought you might like to go over it." I noticed he wouldn't make eye contact.

"I have never been happier about living at our parents' house than in this very moment," my fucking brother drawled as he stepped into view. He eyed his wife, who seemed to be frozen. "Were you two into the happy juice without me?" He raised his hands. "You know what, it's fine. That moment, right there, well and truly makes up for it. Bree, you were saying something about a drum?" He snorted, and I shot him a death glare. I was repaid with an expression of enjoyment.

I looked at Brad and pointed at the table. "Yeah, I'd like to see it."

"I'm sure you would." Patrick snickered. Maxine came back to reality and slapped his arm, then hauled him out of the room.

Brad picked up the file and flipped it open in front of me, then took a seat next to me and pointed at the report. Why was he so close? I swore he could feel my body heat from where he sat. I picked up the report and scanned it and tried hard to absorb what I could with a less-than-sober head.

I read the words out loud. "Some kind of poison."

"Yup, what we thought. Apparently it's not native to the US, but they're working out whether or not it's possible to buy it here. They're seeing what they can drum up." I could've sworn he drew out the word "drum."

"So, both victims were killed in the same way, but when the second victim was targeted, the drug somehow got to the bartender as well. Do you think we have a serial killer on our hands?"

"I do." He followed my thinking. "But we can't jump to any conclusions yet. Tomorrow, we get the tapes from the businesses across the street, then we'll see if there's anything there. We could get lucky, maybe catch someone watching people as they go inside."

"Great." I closed the file and handed it back to him. My skin was still hot from embarrassment when he looked over at me. He held my gaze for a beat, and something next to a lightning spark zinged between us. Or maybe it was just the liquor, but the way his throat contracted let me know he felt it too.

"Mom asked if you'd stop out and visit tomorrow morning. I'll be spending the night at their place so we can drive in together."

"Right, about that. If I don't have my truck, I can't drive myself home, and it's not fair to ask you to drive me back here when you have a place in town."

"I'm coming back here tomorrow night, too, so it's no trouble." He stood. "Just don't flake, okay?" If he didn't mean to hit a nerve with that comment, he wasn't successful. I knew most people knew I'd run away after what happened. I did, but shit, could anyone blame me?

"What time?" I bit back as I built my walls up even higher.

"Eight thirty." He checked his watch. "From there, we'll get the footage, and I'd also like to talk to Maggie's modeling agent."

"All right." I stood and wrapped my arms around myself. "Thanks for coming by."

He nodded and left. I relived the embarrassment all over again as Charley laughed from the doorway. I could tell he'd been listening from the living room.

"You're such an ass." I glared at him.

"Lainey's here too," he said, tossing his wife under the bus and laughing harder while Lainey tried to smooth over the situation.

"Sorry for not saying anything." She poked her head around the corner. "But look, you're here now, and it's going well."

"Why did I have to say anything?" I groaned as I sank into a chair and tipped my head back to look up at the cathedral ceiling. "Kill me now."

She stepped into the room with Charley right behind her wearing a wide grin. She gave him a hand flip, but he just rolled his eyes and sat down across from me. Everyone went to Charley for advice—he kept shit real and had an easy way with people.

"Listen, Bree"—he removed his ball cap and tossed it onto the table—"you want the upper hand back?"

I flipped my head over to him. "I do."

"Just be yourself. If you act like there's something there, it'll only make things worse. Men don't dwell on this stuff. If you act cool, he will too."

I mulled over his words, and they made sense. "I can do that."

"Good." He pushed to his feet and grabbed an apple from a bowl on the table as he left the room.

"Although there's nothing to say you couldn't wear something a little tight." Lainey winked. "Dad put your things in cabin three."

"Wait, I'm not sleeping in the house?"

"He seems to have it in his head that if you feel like you have your own place, you might stay longer." She shrugged. "And maybe it's because I need your room for a party that's coming tomorrow for four days. If it helps, even Mom and Dad are being kicked out." She showed her teeth in a fake smile.

"Where are they staying?"

"The north cabins." She removed her earrings. "You're in one of the west ones. There're some businessmen staying over there too. I want them far away from the houseguests." She stretched.

"Right." I was fine with that. The west cabins would make my coming and going at all hours a little easier.

"I love you, baby Sis. I'm glad you're home." She kissed my head, then followed Charley upstairs.

I spent the next few hours getting settled away in my cabin, then meandered back over to the main house.

"Nightcap?" Maxine shook the half-full pitcher of happy juice. "I heard it cures embarrassing moments with sexy detectives." I grinned, and we headed down to the dock. We lasted till eleven o'clock, then we both turned in, knowing tomorrow would come soon enough.

Sleep hadn't been my friend in years. I could fall asleep no problem, but I usually woke at the same time every night, just after midnight. It was always the same—no matter what I dreamed about, it had the same ending. *I was running out of a forest, and when I reached a clearing, I turned back to see who was following me, and he was standing there. His eyes were locked on mine, only in the dream he didn't fade back into the tree line the way he did in real life. Instead, he walked toward me. I wanted to run, but I couldn't; I was frozen in terror. "Bree."* His eerie voice jolted me awake right as his hands connected with my neck.

"Jesus!" I sat straight up, my heart pounding in my throat so hard my dinner threatened to resurface. "I'm okay." I flicked the light on, and it pushed the shadows back. "Everything's fine, everything's fine." I took in the little cabin. It had a small kitchenette, a bathroom with a shower tub, and a log fireplace that I was tempted to light. Instead, I crossed the room, grabbed a stack of files from my bag, and stood in front of the massive whiteboard my dad had bought for me.

Like countless times before, I studied the file I had put together over the years on the Barbed Wire Killer. I started at the top of the board and taped on the photos of three other women who had gone missing in Sheffield before Brad and I had our encounter at the river. They were cold cases, but I knew they were connected. I could feel it. Next I posted the photos of the two women who were killed when we stumbled upon the killer. In the center I taped a photo of a black square to represent the killer. Next to it, I put a close-up photo of a piece of barbed wire that had been left for me in my car tire. I leaned in to look at it. I could just make out the tiny spots of red paint at the ends of the spikes. I knew he wanted me to know it was him. It was his signature and his warning.

A while later my board was plastered with every little thing that was ever discovered, any witness who came forward to claim they saw something, the aerial view of the river and ball field—nothing was spared. I had used a Sharpie to draw lines to connect things. Then I added my top questions: *Why were we spared? Where did he go? Did he stop killing after we almost caught him? Where was he now?* Then I huffed out a grounding breath, and in red marker I added my own encounters I was sure I had with him since. I put the dates, the times, the locations, and what had happened at the time.

Some might call me obsessed, but no one had gone through what I had, and until they did, they'd never understand the desperation inside. I continued working until the wee hours, until I was satisfied. Then, exhausted, I turned the board to face the wall and prepared for another night of restless sleep.

I woke with a stiff neck and decided a warm shower would help. I fought back the fog of not enough sleep with a couple of cups of Lainey's coffee. I appreciated that she made regular morning runs to the cabins with trays of coffee carafes. I chuckled at the picture of a potbellied pig on my mug as I topped off my cup with a heaping spoonful of sugar and a generous shot of thick cream.

I felt like I was ready to tackle my day. It was just after eight o'clock when I finished hanging up my clothes in the closet, then hurried outside and looked over at the Stones' property across the lake. I took the path toward it. It was well beaten down by the trail rides. I smiled when I saw that the old sign my brother and I had made years before was still there. It gave directions at the fork in the path so the trail riders knew which way to go and didn't end up face-to-face with another rider coming back. It was before it had become a dude ranch, but the sign still made sense, and it was nice that Lainey had kept it.

A strange sound like a cross between a grunt and heavy breathing caught my attention. I looked over my shoulder, but the path was empty. I scanned the tree line and heard that strange noise again. Fear nipped at me and begged my head to go to all those forbidden places.

"It's nothing," I spoke out loud. I often talked myself down from a panic attack.

"*Squee!*" An ear-piercing shriek came from behind me, and I nearly jumped out of my skin. I whirled around with a scream to find Kevin the fucking pig. He'd come out of nowhere and stood his ground as he squealed again.

"Kevin!" I yelled. "Don't ever do that to me again!" My heart nearly beat out of my chest. "You know what a smoker is?" I threatened him. All I got was a short curly tail twitch as he stared at me with his little beady eyes. "God!" I spun on my heel and began to jog until I rounded the bend. I slowed a little as I neared the edge of the lake and veered off to the right of the trail. The Stones' beautiful log cabin sat on the edge of the water, and a little farther down, Bradley's brother Ronnie had a place. From here, I could see our dock, where Maxine and I had been the previous night. We really did have the best place to grow up in.

"If I didn't know any better, I'd still think you were that gorgeous girl heading over to ask where Bradley was." His father stood near his shed with a pitchfork in his hand. He put it against the wall, then leaned over and gave me an enormous hug. "But I see now it's a gorgeous woman."

"Who's still looking for Brad," I said, playing along with a warm smile and noted the hay stuck to his hand-knitted sweater. "Hi, Jerry, how are you?" I hugged him like he was my own father.

"I'm well, thanks." He pointed for me to follow him over to the family cabin. "I was mighty surprised to hear that the SPD picked you up as a consultant. Never thought you'd come back here to work."

"Not as surprised as I was." I chuckled. Brad's mother put her dish-cloth down as I came inside. "Hi, Kim."

"Bree, honey, it's so nice to see you again." She stepped back to look at me. "Still such a pretty face."

I bypassed her comment and moved in to hug her.

"Are you hungry?"

"Always." I grinned and let my gaze wander over toward Brad and his older brother, who had just come in the door.

"Wow." His brother, Ronnie, whistled as he came up to me. "You haven't changed a bit."

"Wish I could say the same about you," I joked, and he swatted my arm as he brushed past me. Ever since he was young, Ronnie had been all about the military, and his body reflected that lifestyle. He looked super fit.

"Morning." Brad pretended not to check me out, but I'd caught his look while I spoke to his brother. After all, I had just done the same to him.

His mother called us over to the table. "Let's go sit. Everything's ready." Brad pulled out my chair, and just as I sat, something soft brushed by my legs, and I jerked back at the intrusion.

"Oh!" A big golden retriever sat between Brad and me. "Well, hello there."

Brad reached down and gave the pup a pat. "This is Ginger—she's five but still thinks she's a puppy thanks to certain people." He tilted his head at his father.

"Oh, yeah." Jerry laughed playfully as he handed me a plate of waffles. "I'm the problem."

"Well, the first step is recognizing it," I bantered back, making Kim chuckle. It was so comfortable how we all fell back into our old pattern.

I caught Ronnie's face when a chime went off in the kitchen. His smile slipped, and his expression took on a distant look. He must have felt my eyes on him because he looked at me suddenly and seemed to blink the thoughts away. Ronnie suffered from PTSD, and I knew that there were times for him that were better than others.

Jerry set the syrup down in front of me. "Your parents must be pleased to have you home."

"They are."

"Has much changed?" Ronnie asked through a mouthful.

"Hmm." I thought as I swallowed a bit of warm pastry. "Aside from the city guests, who all want that *real ranch experience*"—I finger quoted—"and the fact that my father's best friend is a hefty pig named Kevin, things are pretty much the same."

"Ah, yes, that little porker's pretty funny." Ronnie smirked at Brad. "Has your brother shared that he hired us to haunt the deep wood trail in October?"

"Seriously?" I laughed.

"The riders love it." He stuck a fork in my direction. "One year we even did the Barbed Wire Killer." The moment he said it, my soul dropped from my body.

"Ronnie," Kim hissed. "Inappropriate."

"Like I said then"—Brad's pissed voice broke through my discomfort—"and like I say now, we don't talk about that."

"Sorry." Ronnie smacked his brother's arm, then looked at me. I looked away. "So, Bree, do you carry a gun?"

Brad choked on his coffee, and I glared at him. "No, and I don't like to carry one."

"Yeah, good thing." Brad spit-laughed into his napkin. "If history has taught me anything, it's that you have the worst aim."

"No, I don't." My mouth dropped open as the memory came back to me. "You know I hit that squirrel."

"No, I saw the slingshot veer so far left the squirrel went flying but only because the tree trunk next to it vibrated from your rock."

"That's such crap!" I waved a hand at him. "Please, you just sit there all up in your lies till you're ready to tell the truth."

Brad leaned back and rested his arm along the back of my chair. "Sit here like this?" I rolled my eyes. "'Cause I'm comfortable sitting in the truth."

I caught his mother smiling at his father. "I see nothing's changed between these two."

We both sat up straight and went back to our food. It felt so good to slip back into our old banter. To feel like my old self again, the one who hung out here years ago. I caught Brad's eye for a split second and read his expression. We both knew what was there. We'd always had an attraction toward each other back in high school. It was mostly physical, not that we ever acted on it, but also intellectual, as we were both on the debate team. It was a strong connection that couldn't be denied, but we were young, and he was dating Sherry.

I always wondered if we might have eventually ended up together if we hadn't stumbled upon the Barbed Wire Killer that day. I always thought Sherry wouldn't last. Even Kennedy joked about *ole Doritos breath*. Yet here we were, years and a lot of pain later, with the same chemistry crackling between us. Too bad it was too late for us. I loved my job back in New York, and I had no intention of staying.

We finished eating, cleaned up and said goodbye, then hopped into his car.

"That was really nice." I felt like something needed to be said because neither of us had said a word all the way to the main highway. "Your brother seems a little different."

"Yeah." He cleared his throat. "A lot has changed since you left."

I looked away as his comment ate at me. I left because I had to. It had been the decision I'd felt I had to make at the time, and I shouldn't have been punished for it. We rode in silence the rest of the way.

We spent most of the day running through videos from the nearby businesses, but nothing stood out. Officer Smith joined us partway through and offered some theories, but they didn't lead to anything. "Can I see the club videos again?" I asked Brad in spite of the fact that my butt was numb from sitting. We'd been in the office for ages, and I looked forward to a bit of sunshine, but we had a job to do, however tedious it might be.

"Yeah." Brad pushed a few buttons, and the club videos came up. "What are you thinking?"

"Nothing yet." I stretched my neck and squinted to see the screen.

But the sheer volume of people in the frame made it nearly impossible to pinpoint any one person. Even though we knew roughly when the attacks had happened.

"Well, if Shelly died in the bathroom," Officer Smith asked, "wouldn't you just follow her steps and question anyone that had contact with her?" He scratched his leg absently, then got up and pushed his back up against the doorframe. Like me, he needed a stretch. It was wonderful that he'd offered his help, and it was a good experience for him.

"That's a lot of people." Brad tapped his fingers on the table as he thought. "And because we don't know what the actual substance is, we're not sure how quickly it takes effect." He paused. "We have a rough timeline of how long the substance may take to attack the system thanks to the surveillance videos, but what we really need is to be able to pinpoint any possible suspects. There're just too many."

"Right." I leaned forward and pointed to Shelly on the screen. "She interacted with at least seven people since she arrived at the club, another six as she walked up to the bar top, three at the bar, and one on the way to the bathroom. And that's just men—it doesn't include the entire party of women she showed up with."

"We'll still question them," Brad added, "but narrowing it down is the hard part."

Smith tossed his sandwich wrapper into the trash. "Okay, yeah, that makes sense. It's just, all this sitting around is hard. I hope I can learn the patience you two have."

"Always nice when they're interested in learning," I commented to Brad as the young officer slipped away. I grinned as I heard his groan when he reached his desk just outside the room. I'd seen the pile of paperwork on it. "I need more coffee." I yawned and stretched my arms out and heard my elbow snap. "Why don't you keep watching, and I'll grab us some?"

"We just had coffee."

"And?" I blinked at him.

"So why do you need more coffee?"

I squinted, confused. "I'm sorry. I don't follow."

Brad shook his head and pulled out his phone. He scratched the shadow of a beard on his chin as he took in the time. Seven thirty. "Fine, I'll go check in with Cap, and I'll meet you in there when you're done being an addict."

"We all have our thing, Brad." I hooked my bag over my arm. "I'll find out what yours is soon enough."

"It's Bradley or Detective Stone," he grumbled and made me laugh.

"Bye, Brad." I waved over my head.

The next four days, we ate, slept, and breathed the case. We hunkered down and went over every single piece of evidence till I could see everything in my head when I closed my eyes at night. I felt like I was going squirrelly at one point. My old job as a PI had a lot more action than being hunched over a table rereading statements and rewatching videos over and over.

"I feel like I should take up yoga if this position is to be my new normal." I plucked my coffee off the table, took a sip. I wrinkled my nose as I realized it had gone cold.

"That I'd like to see," he snickered, and as I went to swat him, Captain Robert appeared.

"Brad, a word?" He head-pointed toward his office.

"Sure thing." Brad shot me a quick glance, scooped up his phone, and left. I took the opportunity to feed my addiction without his judgy eyes following me to the elevator.

The coffee shop was busy, so I ordered and sat in a chair by the window while I waited. I scanned the faces and fell into my routine of watching teens. I always looked for something in their expression that might indicate they were in trouble. Old habits were hard to break. I wondered if one of them might somehow be connected to a runaway case I'd never solved. I found myself wondering which one of them might die next. *Whoa! That took a dark turn.* Then I saw a young woman who had her phone on a tripod across the street. She was pointing to the bakery sign as she bit into a pastry of some kind. I watched her for a bit.

Two young girls kept giggling over something they were watching on a phone. It was irritating. Lord, social media was always in our face. I wasn't from the generation that saw its potential to make an income; I just viewed it as invasive. The giggling girls also watched the one outside with the tripod. Then one of them held up her coffee and pointed to the brand on her cup as she spoke into the camera lens. "This is the best coffee in town! I highly recommend it. Oh my god, we're influencers!" Her shrill voice made me cringe, but her friend just giggled more.

I leaned back in my chair and shook my head as I tried to shut them out. I looked down at the file I had in front of me and noticed advertisements for both Sea Foam Brew and East Dog Brewery from the photos I had taken at the nightclub. I wondered if either company had influencers too. If so, maybe they'd have some footage from the nights of the murders. Not bad. *Thanks, girls.* I grabbed my coffee and called Brad on my way back to the station. It went straight to voicemail. I called Adam, curious if maybe he was still stuck in paperwork.

"Hello?"

"Hey, Adam. I mean, Officer Smith. It's Bree." I was pleased now that we'd exchanged numbers. "Do you know where Brad is?"

"It's okay for you to call me Adam." I could almost see his eager smile. "He's still in his closed-door meeting with the captain, and the chief of homicide just went in with them."

"Okay." I slowed my pace and looked down at my bag. "I'm going to follow a possible lead. Will you tell Detective Stone to call me, and I'll fill him in?"

"Sure thing."

I unlocked my truck and climbed into the cab. I let out a breath as I settled in. "Ahhhh." It felt good to be back in my office. The cab of the truck was quiet and cozy and had everything I needed.

I searched social media like a champ. Hashtags were a PI's best friend—well, that and people who didn't have their accounts set to private. East Dog seemed to do just fine without any influencers, but to my delight, Sea Foam Brew was brewed locally, and it hired college kids to promote the products through their accounts. The company paid them per post. I clicked on one girl's account, and there must have been over a hundred videos posted there for the company. It didn't take long watching her videos to see she spent a lot of time at the Velvet Nightclub, and a lot of her posts were recent. It made me wonder how much footage she had versus what she posted as a rep.

"You'll do just fine," I happily said out loud. I felt hopeful as I direct messaged her. I shouldn't have been surprised she answered me back almost immediately. I had, after all, said I was looking for exclusive footage and would pay for it. I was surprised she wanted to meet in person. We could have done it over email, but I went along with it. She told me to meet her at the city library. We agreed on five minutes. Good for her, she chose somewhere public. Maybe there was hope for the next generation. I grabbed my things, refilled my coffee, and headed out to meet her.

"What are you looking for exactly?" Sophia McKinnon asked as she pulled out her laptop. She relaxed a little once I showed her my ID and told her I was a consultant with the police department.

"Any footage from the Velvet Nightclub on the nights those two girls got killed." I gave her the dates.

"Oh my god, I know, it's so tragic."

"Mm-hmm." I leaned forward when she brought up her videos.

Sophia swung her finger around the trackpad and brought up the days I asked about.

"I just leave my body cam on, so there's hours of footage." She hesitated. "I guess I could send it to you."

I pulled out my wallet and dropped three hundred on the table. I knew Sea Foam Brew offered twenty-five per video, so I knew I was being more than fair.

"Sold." She clicked a few buttons, and the footage was sent to my email. "Here." She handed me a card. "If I can ever help again, contact me."

I took the card and tucked it into my notebook. "Thanks, Sophia."

Once she left, I called Brad, but again, it went to voicemail. I headed back to the station and set up in the parking lot, not wanting to head inside. My stomach rumbled, and I knew I'd need something to eat soon. I huffed in frustration that Brad hadn't picked up but licked my lips and set myself up to study a bunch of drunk people party and dance. I lost track of how many times I jumped forward on the videos. She interacted a lot, and though it was her job, I wouldn't have the energy to do what she did each night. I had to admit Sophia was engaging as she carried around her beer samples on a tray. I rubbed my temples and blinked my dry eyes to moisten them. I was glad I was past the nightlife scene. It was exhausting.

Later, she switched to handing out brewery merch. At one point she jumped up on the bar top and started tossing T-shirts into the crowd. She was friendly and made sure to have fun with the regulars who knew her.

Hours later, my eyes were dry and I had a slight headache, but sheer stubbornness wouldn't let me stop. I'm glad I didn't, because a few moments later, something caught my eye. I tapped a button and backed the video up. I couldn't see a face, but an arm blocked the camera for a second, then I saw some fingers reach toward Sophia. They took hold of the cuff of her shirt for a second before she shook the hand away and tossed another T-shirt. I paused the video and backed it up, then enhanced it the best I could with my computer program. Something was odd about it. A deep-green color lined the thumbnail, and the skin seemed like it was irritated.

"Shit, now I'm imagining some kid's slime making it look like Daddy is a murderer." I laughed at myself and gave my head a shake.

I reached over for the autopsy report and sent the papers sliding down to the passenger-side door.

"Really?" I leaned over and gathered the disorganized mess and tossed it onto the seat. When I pulled back, I saw the time stamp of each murder side by side.

I read out loud from Shelly's paperwork and then slid my eyes over to Maggie's. "'Time of death, approximately one thirty a.m.'" I read it out loud again.

I closed my eyes and remembered the two women who had been killed at the river that awful day. I now knew they were Hazel Morgan and Eve Scott. It was Hazel in her white dress that stayed with me. The way she lay in the water. I shook off the terrible vision of those blank, open eyes and tried to focus. Hazel's time of death had been the same as Shelly's, and it was determined that Eve Scott, the second victim that night, had been killed only a very short time after that.

As my mind often did, it jumped back to the Barbed Wire Killer. Someone with very little imagination had dubbed him the Barbed Wire

Killer because he'd used barbed wire to strangle both women. One thing always bothered me about those killings—why had he waited so long to dispose of the bodies? If their deaths had happened in the early morning, why wait till the next day to drag them to the river? What happened in that frame of time?

I stopped my train of thought. I needed to remind myself that not every case was connected to the murders at the river. I knew the fact that he could still be out there was what made my skin crawl and my mind always wonder if he was involved.

My hands shook, and my heart raced as I pushed the memory away. "You're okay." I breathed through my nose and exhaled to try to get rid of the fear. "In and out." I coached myself until the ringing in my ears faded away and the urge to pass out subsided. "Good job." I hated that I was so fascinated with anything that reminded me of the Barbed Wire Killer, but I also used it as a crutch to fight the fear.

Something tugged at me, and I refocused my head and went back to the time those slimy green fingers touched Sophia's shirt. The time stamp on the video read 1:15 a.m. *Another young life snuffed out before the sun came up on the rest of us.*

Knock, knock! I jumped at the sound and looked up. Kennedy stood there, and he looked freshly showered. I rolled my window down. "Jesus, Kennedy, you scared me!" I ran a hand over my face. "It's nice to see you again."

"I heard you were working here. Sorry, I just wanted to apologize that it took me nearly a week to finally see you."

I smiled. Kennedy had always been a nice guy and a good friend to Brad. "I dove headfirst into the case trying to catch up." I grabbed a handful of papers and made a tired face. "I don't know how you guys do this."

"Well, we start with not working late on a Friday." I glanced at the time and saw it was past dinnertime. He reached through the window and closed my laptop. "We get lots of exercise." He took the keys out of the truck ignition and opened my door and nodded for me to hop out. "And we blow off steam by joining friends at the local pub." He pulled out my purse and dropped my keys inside. "If you want to be a part of this department, you need to get to know us."

As much as I wanted to keep digging into the videos, he had a point. Besides, I needed to find my place here, and what better time to get to know people than when their defenses were lowered by alcohol?

The Wicked Goose was only two blocks away from the station and was a popular hangout for off-duty cops. It was busy when we arrived.

"Everyone, listen up," Kennedy called and put an arm on my shoulder as he introduced them. "Ellis, my partner"—he pointed to a tall woman with a super short haircut and a kind smile—"and that's Ginny, Bostwick, Marcot, and Ray. This here's Bree Jaminson." He turned to me. "Bree, everyone."

"Nice to meet you all." I waved as I tried like hell to remember their names. *Ellis, Ginny, Bostwick, Marcot, and Ray,* I chanted inside. The two females were going to be the easiest to remember because Ellis had tracks buzzed into the side of her head and Ginny reminded me of Maxine with her adorable thick red glasses. The others I'd need to work on.

"Bree's our new consultant at the department and once was a local like me, so no hazing, or Stone will kick your ass, and I'll be right behind him," Kennedy warned as he pulled out a chair for me.

"Thanks." I slipped into the seat just as the waiter came over. I ordered a beer and a round of pitchers for the table. I figured I might as well start earning my place.

"Where's Stone?" Ellis called.

Kennedy poured himself a beer. "Custody battle."

"Wait." That nearly sucked the air right from me. "Brad has a kid?" How had I not heard this? My head went cold at the thought. More importantly why did I have that reaction? What did I care? *Maybe because you're in love with him.*

"Not exactly." Kennedy studied my shocked face. "His ex and him share custody of their dog, Ginger."

I shook my head as I tried to process what he'd said. "He and Sherry share custody of a dog?"

"Yes. Not just any dog, though. A cute little floppy-eared golden retriever."

"Okay." My lungs filled as a little air found its way inside. "So, not a small human?"

Ellis laughed, chiming in, "God no. The man needs to get away from her—she's nothing but an anchor."

"But that's nothing we talk about in front of Bradley," Kennedy cut in, and I appreciated that he was looking out for his friend. "It's his life, and we only want what's best for him. But yes, a large part of me would love to see him with someone not so . . . different."

"Mm-hmm, different." Ellis smirked as she took a drink. "That's a real kind way of saying it."

"Okay." I laughed along with her in relief that he didn't have a kid, but it quickly faded when I caught Kennedy's expression.

"It's okay. I blush too whenever I think of Brad," he teased, and I glared at him.

"Kennedy, you still comin' over to play at my place?" Bostwick asked.

"Wouldn't miss it."

I looked at Ellis, confused. She rolled her eyes and leaned over the table so I could hear her better. "Poker. They have a whole casino-night thing."

"That sounds fun."

"It is." Kennedy flipped his partner off. Ellis just laughed; clearly their relationship was strong. "It's just something to do. Keep the mind busy with friends." His eyes were bright with excitement.

"I get that."

"Don't encourage, Bree," Ellis laughed. "I really think they get together to play an adult game of *D&D*."

Kennedy shook his head. "Have you ever played *D&D*?"

"No, that's why I'm super cool." That sent the table into laughter.

"So, Bree"—a familiar face at the next table pulled my attention—"how's the Velvet Nightclub case going?"

"You remember Stanley?" Kennedy asked.

I nodded, leaned back in my chair as Stanley joined us. He had been a year below me in grade school, so I knew of him, but we never ran in the same circles. These guys were all police officers, so I let myself go a bit. "Things are moving along. We're combing through everything, camera footage and all that. Interviewing everyone we can."

Ray, the older detective, spoke up. "So, why'd they bring you in? Stone doesn't usually need hand-holding." He sniffed. "Need to bring in a *consultant*." He finger quoted. "The department payin' you for what, lookin' over our shoulder?"

"Fresh eyes on a case like this can't hurt. Two murders in such a short time can cause panic if people think a serial killer is out there." I didn't want to get into it, especially with one of the more experienced guys. "Captain just felt more hands on deck were needed, and I was happy to oblige." I went for a smile.

"So, what have you come up with so far?" He seemed determined to poke at me.

"Well, I'm pretty sure the same guy killed both women. He got in and out both times without being noticed. He's smart, probably familiar with the club's layout. He waited until the place was busy, the alcohol had been flowing, and the sea of bodies was tuned in to the loud music. Everyone pressed in close both on the dance floor and at the bar. He's probably decent looking, hits on the women, and they talk."

"That's a stretch." He made a face. I noticed the others watched us.

"I disagree." I looked at him. "Straight women dancing and enjoying a few drinks are always open to a nice-looking guy. It's why many of them are there."

"She's right," Ginny chimed in. "I see it all the time when we go out. It's nothing personal, but a girl's got standards, just like men. A nice-lookin' guy's always welcome." She laughed, and the others joined in.

"Race, age, height, and motive?" Ray cut through the noise of the table, shutting everyone up. He shrugged and waited for me to take the bait.

"That's not something I want to comment on right now." I turned to Ginny, but Ray held up a hand.

"No, let the newbie answer the question. You're here as our consultant, so consult."

I licked the inside of my mouth. I often ran into cops who had a problem with the fact that I didn't wear a badge or that I didn't have to follow their rules. "I'm not gonna speculate on that." I hoped someone would change the subject again.

"So, what is it that you *do* speculate?"

"The facts." I was tired but knew this was a test. "But if you insist." I shifted my weight in my chair and looked at Ray. "White male, forties, medium height."

"And that's based on?"

"Nothing, because we don't have all the facts yet. These facts are based on the average serial killer in America."

"Motive?"

"To kill." I lifted a shoulder. "His motive was probably to simply just kill someone, women. It probably wasn't premeditated. He didn't have any specific target in mind, but who knows at this point."

"I could have told you that," Ray scoffed.

"Of course you would have, because that's really the only thing we've got so far." I turned my glass in my hands.

"Weren't you training to be an FBI agent?" Bostwick held up his phone. "I googled you." He grinned as he scrolled through the page, and I knew the moment he read it. "No shit, you're her?" His eyes lit up, and mine dimmed. "Oh my god."

"What?" Ellis strained to see the screen, and Ray squinted at me like he distrusted me even more.

"She's the girl Bradley was with when they stumbled onto the Barbed Wire Killer when they were just teens." Bostwick grinned like he'd just met a celebrity. My stomach rolled, and I did everything in my power not to show how much that topic affected me. Though I saw Kennedy's pissed expression when he saw my face fall at the mention of it. "What was it like? You got in a stare-down with a killer. You must've shit your pants wondering what he'd do to you."

I refused to comment. People always wanted to know the details, like when you see a car wreck.

"The case was never solved," Bostwick said, filling in for the others who hadn't heard of it. "The guy wrapped barbed wire around his victims' necks and choked them with it. Threw their bodies in the river. Bradley and Bree just escaped by the skin of their teeth. Ran like hell and got out of there."

"Just like *you* should," Kennedy muttered. "Read the room."

"So, you didn't solve *that* case?" Ray's mouth twisted as he folded his arms and sat back.

I could feel the sweat break along my forehead and swallowed hard as my head shot back to that day. I could see the eyes of the killer boring into mine, and I imagined the wire was around my own neck. Fear hit me in a wave. I took a moment to try to get myself under control so I could speak without emotion.

"I think you'd agree the department would hardly let a teen solve a murder." I gave Ray a wry look. Kennedy pressed his hands against the table, and I could see he was trying to hold back. It wouldn't do for him to get into it with them over me. I knew he could see how hard this was for me.

The walls seemed to close in on me, and I could feel my heart pound in my chest. "I think I should go." I grabbed my purse and headed for the door against their protests. I pushed it so hard I nearly hit someone in the face.

"Wow, where's the fire?" Brad dipped down low to catch my expression when I tried to hide it.

"No fire." I plastered on a smile. "Kennedy thought it'd be nice for me to meet some of the guys. He invited me for drinks, but I really need to get some sleep."

"You want me to drive you home?"

I pointed over his shoulder. "No, thanks, I've got my truck."

"You sure you're okay?"

"Yeah . . . yes, I'm just mentally fried. Go enjoy your friends. I'll catch up with you tomorrow." I didn't wait for a response—I hurried across the street and down the two blocks to my truck. Once I was safe in my steel box, I flopped my head forward against the wheel and let fear simmer its way to the surface. Tears burned down my cheeks, and my heart began to race to the point of pain. Thoughts of that awful day at the river swirled in my head, and I knew I just needed to ride out this panic attack, then I could pull myself back together again. Maybe being back in Sheffield really was a bad decision.

"Oh my god," I whispered as the tremors set in and rooted to my bones.

What I wouldn't do to feel safe for one day.

Chapter Five

"You know what Ray's like." Kennedy tugged hard on the laces of his skates as he filled me in on the details of the previous night at the Wicked Goose. "He was giving her some newbie hazing, but it was Bostwick that drove her off."

"Why's that?"

"He googled her while we were all there. You can imagine how that went."

He gave me a face, and I closed my eyes and shook my head. I was thankful for the cold air in the rink as my temperature rose.

"He sure as hell didn't read her body language, if you know what I mean. Gotta give her credit—she held her own for a bit, but after Bostwick's big reveal she skipped out the second she could. That's when she bumped into you."

I wriggled the jersey over my pads and grabbed my gloves and stick. "Shit." I was pissed.

"At the risk of overstepping, especially on something I promised you I'd never ask and want zero to know about"—he gave me a look—"I know everyone processes trauma in different ways, my friend, but I could practically smell her fear. I kid you not, she went white as a ghost when Bostwick brought it up." He leaned closer when the ref popped his head through the door to see if we were ready. "All I'm saying is maybe check in with her."

"Ready?" the ref asked.

"Yeah." I tried to push Kennedy's words out of my head. Ever since Bree came back, all sorts of mixed and twisted feelings about so many things had come out of hiding. I'd tried to make a life with Sherry, but I'd failed miserably. The darkness inside me finished us. But in the short time since Bree had returned, I felt better—lighter actually. I just didn't know what to do with that.

"Come on, let's go kick NY's ass." Kennedy slapped my shoulder. We hurried onto the ice and skated over to where the rest of the team warmed up.

"Drinks tonight?" Kennedy asked as we were about to split up to head for our cars. "I mean, these quick hands"—he wiggled his fingers at me—"basically won the game." He grinned.

I waved him off with a laugh as my phone vibrated, and I wondered if it was Bree. I hoped last night didn't play too hard in her head. "I'll get back to ya," I called out to him as I tossed my hockey bag into the SUV and slid into the driver's seat.

Sherry: Thought maybe we could have dinner tonight and talk.

I started the engine and thought about her text. She'd been keeping her distance from me, and I was happy with that.

Bradley: Not a good day. Rain check?
Sherry: I know how your days get. Dinner will be ready at six.
Bradley: Another day.

Another text came through, and I switched over to that chat.

Bree: I think I might have found something.
Bradley: Where are you?
Bree: Just got to Velvet Nightclub

I was just down the road from her, so it would be easy.

Bradley: Stay there, I'll come to you.

I took the next turn and headed in her direction. With my arm on the edge of the open window, I felt the cool northeastern autumn day refresh my hot skin. I squeezed my water bottle and sucked some Gatorade down my throat, then tossed back some peanuts for protein.

My phone rang, and I saw it was Mom.

"Hey."

"Hi, honey." Her voice rang through the speaker. "Sherry just confirmed she's picking Ginger up tonight. Okay?"

Fuck me.

"No, I have Gin for three more days." Was that why she wanted to have dinner, so she could pick up Ginger early? Ginger wasn't even her dog to begin with. I had gotten her when I knew I was spiraling, and I was only being nice by sharing her.

"Must be a misunderstanding, hon. Maybe just give her a call."

"Yeah, I'll do that later. Thanks, Mom. I'll see you."

As I drove, my mood took a dive. Sherry knew what Ginger did for my head. She was my buddy, the one that never judged or cared if my day sucked. She was just there for me. The past week I'd noticed that Sherry had been messing with me through her. I had no idea why, but I wasn't going to let her get away with it.

When I spotted Bree's truck, I parked as close as I could. I couldn't help but slam the door as I left. It made me feel a little better, but the anger still simmered as I met Bree outside the nightclub. "Tell me you actually got something and are not just chasing some bullshit lead."

"Wow." She shifted her bag on her shoulder. "So, you're in a good mood." She studied my face and whistled.

"Sorry." I rubbed my head. "Been a day."

"I thought hockey helped you de-stress?"

"How did you know I played today?"

She smiled wide. "Because you smell like hockey."

I did? I sniffed my arm. "Is it a bad smell?"

"No." She pulled out her phone. "It's just your hockey smell."

"I didn't know that," I muttered and wondered what else I had that I wasn't aware of. "Why are you here, anyway?"

"I was just poking around. I could have met you somewhere else, but since you're here . . ." She opened the door, and I followed behind, taking a moment to enjoy her backside, and all thoughts of Sherry went out of my head. "What do you see?"

"I see the coat room, the ID checkpoint, today's shipment of"—I turned the box around—"GREY GOOSE." I looked at her, not sure what she was getting at.

"I see this." She pointed to the wall, at all the beer advertisements. "Which made me think about marketing, which led me to think about social media and how beer sponsors online are huge right now. I looked into some of the breweries, and, for example, East Dog increased their sales thanks to a deal with some local college pubs. Then I went to this beer's"—she pointed to the Sea Foam Brew—"social media pages." She stepped close and held her phone up so I could see it over her shoulder. Her scent filled my nostrils, and I inhaled deeply. She smelled fresh and had a hint of something sweet I couldn't quite pinpoint. "This is Sophia." She pointed at the screen. "She's one of their top influencers. She was here both nights the girls were murdered."

"Really?" That's something.

"And she works the club from open to close wearing a body cam." She tapped on a video, and the girl popped up. She was talking about the upcoming night's events. Then the camera flipped around as she clipped it back into place on her chest. It showed a great view of everyone's faces.

"Holy shit, Bree." I leaned down to study the footage better. "How did you get this, or is all this on her social page?"

"Detectives." The bartender we interviewed before gave us a wave, and we approached. "Can I get you a drink?" He polished a glass, and I noticed his hand shook slightly. "Or maybe something for dinner? The staff orders from next door."

"No thanks, we're good." Bree smiled.

"Your hand okay?" I asked.

"Yeah, just tired. Hazard of the job, I guess." He held up the glass.

"Where was I?" Bree went on. "Oh yes. There was a lot on her page but only small snippets, so I contacted her and got the entire two nights' worth of footage."

"Wow." That impressed me. "Did you go through it? Did you find anything? Any leads?"

"I watched a lot, but there's a ton of footage, and I was tired last night. However, I did catch this." She switched to her camera roll and brought up a screen-recorded video. "Sophia jumped up on the bar and this guy"—she gave a light shrug—"reaches for her cuff. Look at his thumb." She looked over her shoulder at me. "It might be nothing, but this was about fifteen minutes before the actual murder. Just the way he touches her, how he rubs her cuff . . . I don't know, but it gives me creepy vibes."

"Creepy vibes?" I raised a playful brow at her, and she scoffed at me.

"It's a real thing."

"Right." I laughed, impressed at what she'd found. "Any chance you can get this Sophia and maybe some of her friends together so we can interview them?"

"One step ahead of you." She waved her phone at me. "They're already waiting for us at Sophia's apartment."

"Great."

She turned and walked backward toward the exit. When she opened the door, it revealed the sun was almost down. "I *am* kinda great, aren't I?" She laughed as I followed her out, but I stopped when she climbed into her truck. "What?"

"Let's take my car."

She squinted at me. "Something wrong with my truck?"

"No." I unlocked my car. "But mine has heat—does yours?"

Her mouth dropped open. "That's incredibly offensive to her." She made a face at me but hauled out her big purse that doubled as a work bag. "Just because she doesn't always produce the warmest of air doesn't mean she's not as classy as this thing." She looked at my car funny. "What the hell kinda space car is this thing anyway?"

"A reliable one." I slid her bag off her shoulder and opened the front passenger door. "Don't argue—I'm going to win every time." I couldn't resist getting under her skin like old times. Her eyes narrowed in on me, and her mouth pressed into a fine line. *There she is.* "Isn't Sophia waiting for us?" I reminded her and held her murderous gaze as I struggled not to grin. I knew she could see the twinkle of amusement in my eye.

"All right." She nodded a few times. "I see the old Brad is still just below that corporate tie and crisp dress shirt." She slipped inside and closed the door. I hurried around to my side, and we headed across town.

Leaves fell around the town and cast a colorful palette for the tourists who often drove for miles to see them. There was a reason I'd never left this place—we had the best of the four seasons, and though the winters were intense, the rest of the year was perfect. Bree's phone rang, and she answered it. She hit the speaker button as she steadied the computer on her lap. "Hi, Mom." I listened for a moment as her mother spoke about her twin brother and his wife having some problems. It wasn't meant for my ears, so I tuned them out to give them some privacy. After a few minutes she hung up and seemed lost in thought.

As we sat in companionable silence, I pulled into the driveway of the Terrace Court apartments and looked up at the notorious college hangout. I remembered patrolling there a lot with Ray.

Bree opened the door and stepped out. I followed, waiting for her to round the car. She was still lost in her thoughts as we headed inside to visit Sophia.

I knew people liked swag, but Sophia's apartment looked like a swag warehouse with all the products she endorsed.

"Pretty impressive, right?" The cute, bubbly thing beamed up at me as I admired her Sea Foam Brew award. "I won a thousand dollars that year. Who knew a pretty face, big chest, and bright eyes would be what could help pay for my schooling?"

"Better than stripping," Bree chimed in, and I laughed. She was right.

"Oh please." Sophia draped herself over her couch and looked up at me. "Stripping's so nineties—besides, my friend does it, and she's got men following her home all the time."

"And you don't?" I meant that every other way but the way she took it.

"Detective Brad." She waved me off with a flirtatious giggle. "You sure know how to make a girl blush."

"It's Detective Bradley or Stone," I said with a straight face. "I just meant, given that your job is to influence people to drink beer, and I can see by your videos you're flirty, doesn't that sometimes make men follow you home? I know it shouldn't be that way, but it's taking an awful risk."

"Maybe?" She gave a lazy nod. "Well, yes, sometimes, but they're mostly all losers. You know, middle-aged men who still live in their parents' basement. I just call the police, and they go away." Apparently, the idea of being stalked by men who may or may not have plans for her didn't faze her. Christ, twenty-year-olds had no idea what the real world was like.

"Sophia." Bree studied a photo on her bookshelf. "Why do these girls look familiar?"

Sophia bounced off the couch and joined her. "That's my squad." She pointed to the girls and gave her their names while I slipped a glove on and sifted through her huge pile of mail.

"And the guys behind you?"

"Jeremy, Josh, and Jordon. They're the brew reps. They like to keep an eye on us." I caught her eye roll. She was sweet, but I imagined she'd be high maintenance. There must have been a few months' worth of mail in front of me. "You'd have seen my girls in my videos. We work the same hours, leave at the same time, have breakfast at Tony's, then head home to bed before going to class." *I miss having that kind of energy.* I guess I still did, I rationalized, it just came out differently, like when I played hockey or chased down a killer.

"I know Maria's on her way over, but can you call the rest and ask if they'd give me copies of their footage?" Bree asked, and Sophia grabbed her phone and started to text them.

I stopped sifting the mail when I noticed a green smudge on an envelope. I held it up to Bree, who joined my side. "That shade of green looks familiar."

She pulled my arm down to see it better and was careful not to touch the paper. "It sure does." She turned to Sophia. "Do you mind if we take—"

"Take whatever." She shrugged. Someone knocked on the door, and she walked over and opened it without even checking to see who it was. "Hey, girl." Her voice went high pitched, and I cringed. "Maria, this here's Detective Brad and PI Bree." She pointed to us.

"Detective Bradley." I licked my mouth with frustration. "We just have a few questions for you."

"Sure." She seemed a little more uneasy with us than Sophia but nonetheless was a good sport about answering our questions. "Is this about the double murders at the club?"

"Yes." Bree moved to the chair across from her and pulled their attention off me while I bagged the envelope.

Maria handed her a piece of paper. "I uploaded all my footage to the account like you asked. I probably added way more than you need, but I'd be lying if I didn't share that this stuff is getting crazy."

I turned, and Bree shifted closer to the girl. "What do you mean?"

"Look, Longboard's the owner of the club. He's a good guy, but he's hardly ever there, and we're paid by a secondary company that wants us to flaunt ourselves around all night in skimpy outfits and give out free tasters. We have to stop and talk—"

"Flirt, you mean," Sophia said.

"Yeah, flirt. We stop and flirt with whoever's interested, and we're supposed to give them a few minutes of our time and then move on. We're literally a wet dream for freaks and geeks."

"All right." Bree waited for her to go on.

"But some guys don't think a few minutes is enough. They think it's an open invitation to take it a step further. I had this one guy follow me around the entire night, all the way to my car, and when I arrived at Tony's for breakfast, I saw him in a car in the parking lot. I had to call the cops. I stayed here that night 'cause I was too scared to go home. I mean, all that shit that's going down."

"Did you ever get his name?"

"Ron Jackson." She sniffed as she answered Bree. "But I haven't seen him in about a month. I'm hoping he's in jail or something."

I sent a quick text to Officer Smith to run that name, and a moment later he came back.

Smith: County Jail. Got picked up about a month ago on B and E. Also charged with resistance.

"He's in jail," I let her know.

"For how long, and what'd he do?" Maria seemed to relax some.

I shook my head. "Breaking and entering charge." I fought an inward sigh. "If he's in county, he's not our guy." I went back to the mail while Bree dug some more.

"All right"—Bree took a deep breath—"if it wasn't Ron, is there anyone else that you noticed hanging around, or watching you girls, or just anyone that stood out? Christ, what about the staff?"

"No, the staff are all good people. Minus Jeremy Law."

"Who's that?" Bree asked before I could.

"He's the beer delivery guy—strange, but whatever. I just use him to get what I want."

Bree shot me a quick look as she jotted down his name. Everyone was worth looking into, especially since Maria called him strange.

"Anyway," Sophia went on, "they're always looking out for us. It helps that we share our tips with them, but it's worth it. They've pulled us out of flash mobs or fights before."

"That's good to hear." Bree spoke gently, and I could tell she was digging like she did with the kids she used to search for. I'd done a little homework on Bree, and the number of kids she'd rescued from the streets was impressive. "Any of those times happen within the last three weeks?"

"Um." I watched in the reflection as Maria tilted her head back as she thought. "Well, yeah, actually." She sat straight when she looked at Sophia. "Remember that guy with the ninja fingers?" That made me turn around.

"Oh yeah, ninja-turtle guy." Sophia made a disgusted face. "I hate that guy. I tried to get him banned."

"Name?" I asked.

"That's the problem," they both said at the same time. Sophia held up a hand to speak.

"He's a blender."

"Meaning?" I hated expressions.

Bree filled me in. "It means he's hard to spot because he blends in so well."

"Yeah." Sophia nodded. "I think he uses a different ID sometimes. He always seems to get past the bouncers. He wears dull colors, so he doesn't stand out. Simple haircut, probably drinks Coors Light, or something light, anyway, so he appears to be having a good time, but he's never drunk or anything."

"Well, what's the issue with him then? What'd he do?" I tried to understand better. "Try to get too close and personal or something?"

"Exactly." Sophia sat down next to her friend. "And he's all touchy."

"Yeah, it's so strange." Maria rubbed her head. "He's got these creepy hands."

I pushed the stack of never-ending mail to the side. "You said ninja turtle. Why?"

"It's a nickname we gave him because he has green stains on his thumb and fingers, like food coloring or something." Maria looked at Bree when she pulled out her phone and turned it around so they could see the photo of the green fingers on the hem of Sophia's sleeve.

"Gross." Sophia made a face at Maria. "Yup, that's ninja turtle's gross fingers all right."

"Any chance you guys have a still shot of his face? Or at least more of him than his hand," I asked.

"Maybe, I mean, we could dig," Maria offered.

I scratched my chin as I thought. "How long have you noticed this guy hanging around?"

"Um?" Sophia looked at her friend. "I'd say a week or so before the first girl was murdered."

"Yeah, I agree with that." Maria nodded at her. I threw a quick glance at Bree. She obviously was as happy as I was at that answer. Maybe we'd just caught a new lead.

"Anything you find, big or small, call me." I held out my card to Maria.

Sophia slipped the card from her fingers. "Do I get one of these?"

"Share." I stretched my lips in an attempt at a smile, and Bree arched a brow at my coldness toward Sophia.

Bree stood and pulled out her own card. "Send me what you find, and if you think of anything else, just let me know." She gave her card to Sophia. "Also, the PD has officers at the nightclub every night, so there's added protection. But you ladies might want to think about switching careers—men like these can get infatuated, and shaking a stalker these days isn't as easy as it once was, what with the internet and all." Bree glanced at me quickly, then headed for the door.

Sophia tried to justify herself. "It's just such good money, and school is so expensive. Why do weirdos have to ruin it for people like us?"

"Maybe you should ask those girls who were murdered just for trying to have a good time." My voice dripped with sarcasm, and both the girls' faces dropped.

I didn't remember being that reckless when I was their age. You'd think a double homicide at a place they worked would shake them up and make them rethink their actions. I caught Bree's face and shut my mouth.

"Okay." Bree stepped forward. "Thank you, ladies, for your time and help. If you find any shots of him, that would be very helpful. We've got another interview, so we have to get going." She headed for the door, and I followed.

Once we were down at the car, she turned and folded her arms as I unlocked the door for her. "You were pretty hard on them."

I got inside. "I just get frustrated when young adults can't see how reckless they're being. It's an unforgiving world out there." I waited for her to get settled and fasten her seat belt. I took a moment to study her pretty face and the curve of her jaw. When she looked up, I moved my gaze to the wheel, tossed the car in reverse, and headed out to the street with my headlights leading the way.

"I understand how tricky it can be to try to connect with these young adults. They think they're untouchable, but that's when they need us the most."

"I see," I muttered and tuned her out as a truck behind me with blacked-out windows caught my attention.

Out of the corner of my eye, I saw her shake her head at me. "Don't patronize me, Brad. I'm good with kids and young adults. I know better than you how to connect."

"I—" I started to say more but stopped when I switched lanes and the truck did as well. I swung quickly into the far-right lane and pulled off the highway as Bree yelped and grabbed the side handle. I reached for my radio but pulled my hand back when he didn't follow.

"Well, my soul just slipped out my ass. Thanks for that." Bree rubbed her hands over her shirt. "I could use some coffee." She started to look around for her favorite, Starbucks, when I noticed the truck again. When it drove under the streetlight, I spotted the front grill in my side mirror and took note that it was a Ram.

"Bree." I reached for her hand and gave it a light squeeze when the light turned red. "Stop moving for a second."

"Why?" She tuned into my tone and looked at me. Then I noticed she looked down at my hand on hers but didn't pull away. She leaned back in the seat. "What did I not catch?"

"Hang on." The light turned green, and I went through the intersection, then turned onto a surface street. I tried my best to get a look through the Ram's windshield. I couldn't see anything, and his tinted windows made it almost impossible to see the driver, but before I could try to get a better look, the driver pulled into the traffic and started to follow us again. I grabbed the radio and held it low.

"Dispatch, this is Detective Stone, badge number five five seven nine. I need you to run a plate for a Ram."

"Copy that, Detective Stone. What's the plate number?"

I rattled it off.

A second later the car that was between us pulled into the left lane, and the Ram moved up on my bumper.

"I think we're being followed." I knew he couldn't see us just as we couldn't see him—that was the downfall of the deep-tinted windows on both of our vehicles.

"Okay." She took a deep breath. "When did you notice?"

"Not long after we left Sophia's." I slowed at the next light and just as the left arrow turned green, I swung over and tore down an old country road. The Ram didn't miss a beat and did the same. I hit a button on the steering wheel, and Captain picked up, and his voice flooded the car.

"What's going on, Stone?"

"We were questioning a couple girls from the club, and after we left, I noticed a truck on our tail. It still is and not hiding the fact. I'm on Lisbon and Old School Road."

Dispatch crackled over the radio. "Detective Stone, the plates you gave are not registered to a Ram, but to a gray Toyota Corolla that was filed as a missing vehicle three weeks ago."

Dammit! "Copy that."

"I'm sending backup now," Cap said.

"Copy that." I hung up and took a quick glance over at Bree, who held herself very still. "Glove box." She opened it, but her hands retracted at the sight of the gun. "It's a TASER, not an actual gun. See the little red button on the side, click that." She awkwardly turned it on. "If you have to use it, you need to hold it tight and point, shoot, and don't hit me," I instructed. "But you have to wait until he gets close enough, within twenty feet." Not that I planned to let anyone get that close to her.

"I don't really like these things." She held the TASER like it was going to bite her.

The truck came closer, and I picked up speed. "Well, when it comes down to you or him, you'd better choose you."

"I don't disagree." She carefully pointed it toward the floor, between her legs. "I've just had a few bad experiences with weapons," she whispered as I concentrated on the road and my mirror until I spotted Old Mill Road up ahead.

"Did you have this problem when you were at Quantico?" When she didn't answer, I let the topic go. We had bigger shit to deal with. "Hold on." I waited for the last possible second before I turned down the side road. I hit a bump, and my car jumped, and it sent a dust storm up around us that settled on the trees that lined the road on one side.

"I can't see him!" She held on to the dash and seat as she watched behind us. "Maybe we lost him?" She tried to sound hopeful. "Wait, Brad, am I wrong to say this road leads to a—"

I slammed on my brakes and spun the car around to face the way we came. I quickly cut the engine and the lights. The bright-yellow DEAD END sign was all that was visible as my eyes adjusted to the darkness. Bree's heavy breathing as she looked around told me she was all right.

"I can definitely say, I prefer being the predator." She tried to joke, but fear made her voice quiver.

"Agreed." I scanned the dark trees, but it was nearly impossible to see anything.

Suddenly, a bright light illuminated the entire forest around us like someone had turned the sun into a giant flashlight and pointed it in our faces. The power of it was blinding.

"Get down!" I grabbed her head and shoved it down and bent over top of her as I waited for the shots. I heard the stun gun fall to the floor. *Thank God it's not a real gun* flashed through my brain.

Her body shook under me as we waited for something to happen. I raised myself enough to peek over the dash as the light suddenly went out. Slowly, I lifted my head and tried to adjust my eyes, which were still trying to recover from the blinding light. I could see flashing lights from police cars through the trees. "I think he's gone."

She sat up, and we both looked around. There was no sign of the truck.

"Shit." She ran a shaky hand through her hair and looked at me. "That was intense. Those lights were crazy bright."

"He must have some sort of light bar or spotlight." A loud bang made her jump, and she grabbed a fistful of my jacket.

"It's okay," I whispered close to her ear. "It's one of the officers' cars hitting that same bump as we did."

"Okay." She shook her head a few times. "Same bump," she repeated as she slowly eased back, but her death grip stayed on my jacket.

"I got you—I promise." As soon as the words were out of my mouth, I knew. Her eyes widened, and the sadness that passed through them pierced my chest like a knife. "He's gone." I tried to pretend I hadn't felt that moment from the river between us.

"Right." She straightened, and her hold on my jacket loosened. "Well, this is why you chase the bad guys and I deal with finding kids." She picked up the stun gun, quickly turned it off, and returned it to the glove box.

An officer jumped out of his car and rushed over to us. I saw it was Bostwick, and I got out to join him. Smith was right on his heels.

"You guys all right?"

"Yeah."

Bostwick quickly filled me in. "Cap's got an APB out on the truck, but the plates were stolen, and we didn't see anything as we drove down here."

I went back to my car and removed a high-powered flashlight as Bree stepped out. She kept a hand on the door like her legs were shaky. I turned on the flashlight and swept it across the tree trunks, but I couldn't see anything.

"Christ, this place gives me the creeps." Bostwick rubbed his hand along the back of his neck as he looked at Bree. "You okay, Miss Bree?"

"Oh yeah." She forced a smile. "This shit happens daily for me." He chuckled, but Bree didn't join in.

"Must stir up some memories." He tilted his head at her.

Bree shot me a quick look before she turned away.

"Bostwick, you're an asshole," I growled. He hadn't been around much longer than Smith, but at least Smith had the ability to read peo-ple. I knew Bostwick had been warned not to mention the Barbed Wire Killer around me, but he should have smartened up after his Google search at the bar.

"Sorry." Bostwick shrugged. "You guys ready to go?" He looked around. "I've seen *Blair Witch* one too many times for my subconscious to be cool with this place."

"Yeah, but first, do me a favor and drop this off to Wes." I handed him an evidence bag containing the envelope with the green substance. He didn't question it. He knew better. "All right, let's get out of here." I pointed for Bree to get back into the car. "Thanks, guys."

"Sure thing." Bostwick waved, and we all drove back out to the main road. Bree's eyes were as big as saucers, and she kept her head on a swivel until we hit the city limit.

"Home is that way."

"I don't think it's a good idea to head to the ranch." I didn't trust we weren't still being watched. "Whoever that was wanted to make a point, and I don't know about you, but I don't need them knowing where our families live."

She sat back and thought about what I said. "Okay, that makes sense. My truck's not far from the station. I can sleep there tonight."

"No. Are you crazy? You think I'm gonna leave you alone in your truck in the middle of a parking lot in town?"

"No?" She peered over at me.

I wasn't having it. "You'll come back to my place, and I'll drive you to your truck in the morning, then you can go home."

"No, Brad, really, I'm fine. I've spent plenty of nights in my truck."

"Great, but you're not tonight." I ignored her huff and drove. I pulled down my street and parked in the driveway.

"I see nothing's changed." She grabbed her bag and opened the door. "You're still the same old Brad, bossy as ever."

"And you're still the same old Bree." I got out, and we walked to the front door. I stopped before I opened it and looked down at the girl who used to stop my heart whenever she smiled at me. "Pain in my ass, fights me at every turn."

"Like you'd want it any other way." She arched a brow, and her eyes twinkled like they used to. Something inside me sparked, and I was taken aback by it. "You've never been a man that liked the woman in your life to be a doormat." Bree knew me well, and I found it comforting.

"I like the women in my life to listen." I poked at her feisty personality because it was fun with Bree. She made me feel youthful again, and that was something I'd suppressed for a long time.

"Give me a reason to listen, then." She barely got the last word out when I stepped toward her, and she stepped back so her back hit the wall by the door. I hovered over her as she raised her chin to look straight into my eyes. Her smell engulfed me, and I gave in to it and bent down and pressed my lips just below her ear. Her breathing fluttered when I gently brushed my lips over her skin, giving in to a long-ago teenage crush. She didn't pull away nor seem to care that we were on my front porch for all to see.

"I'm not a teenager anymore, Bree. I'm different from how I once was." I pulled back a little and looked into her eyes.

She flattened her hands against my chest, and I closed my eyes, relishing how good her touch felt. "Do tell." She grinned and gave me a sexy look.

"Don't tempt me." I darted my tongue and stole a quick taste of her sweet skin. She sucked in a sharp breath. Just as I was about to surrender to her, my front door swung open and there was my ex-wife shooting daggers at both of us.

"Sherry"—my voice fell flat—"I told you tonight wasn't a good night, and where the hell is your car?"

"Down the street." She lifted a shoulder as if it wasn't a strange place for her to park instead of in the driveway. "I thought I heard someone out here." She made a point of looking at Bree's hands on me, so I stepped back and let them fall away. I didn't want Bree on Sherry's radar. "I made dinner for you." She pointed over her shoulder, then moved her attention over to Bree.

"Sherry, I don't appreciate you coming over like this."

"Well look here, the rumor is true." She ignored me. "Bree Jaminson is back in Sheffield."

"Sherry Cummings." Bree never could hide her dislike for Sherry. "I should get going."

"No." I took her bag from her arm and walked by Sherry, who gave me a confused look. "We have work to do, Sherry. Like I said on the phone, I'm very busy right now." I didn't miss the fact that Ginger lay on a mat near the door instead of her usual place on the couch.

"Busy doing what exactly?" Sherry tossed her words at Bree, then seemed to pull herself together. "Okay, okay." She lifted her hands, not wanting to fight. "I'll just set an extra spot for Bree."

"No, really, I just called a ride. My truck's only a couple streets away from the station." Bree stood in the doorway looking beyond uncomfortable.

"Bree, get your ass inside the house before I bring it in myself," I commanded, and she jumped inside. I hid my smirk. *See? She can listen.*

Chapter Six

Well, this is awkward as hell. I sat next to Sherry, who had made sure my place was set as far away from Brad as possible. My mind still raced with what had happened on the front porch. I didn't say a word as she dumped a heaping pile of tuna casserole onto my plate like a prison cook. *Ew.*

"Bradley loves my cooking," she said, filling the painful silence, and I moved the pile around and hoped she wouldn't notice I wasn't hungry. I took a tiny taste and felt my organs shrivel to dehydrated hockey pucks. "So"—her elbows landed on the table—"Bree, when did you get back in town?"

Brad spoke first. "A few days ago. She was asked to work with us on this new case. So remove your claws." He shoved his chair back and took his plate in his hand. "I need salt." *Salt? The whole casserole is salty, with a questionable topping of tuna.* I smirked when Brad tossed more than half of his serving into the compost bin, then covered it up with some carrot peelings. *Wait! Is there carrot in this thing? I call bullshit on that.*

"Oh, how lucky for the department to have you so ready to return." She gave me a forced smile.

I cleared my throat, as my tolerance for this woman was nonexistent. "Yes, they are very lucky. I'm very good at my job."

"I heard from Kennedy that you work with runaway kids. That's actually really cool."

I stared at her for a moment and questioned her kindness. Sherry was never kind to me. "Thank you, I do love my job."

"And you primarily work in New York City?"

"Yes."

"Must be hard coming back here." At my look she rephrased. "I mean, you know, going from such a busy, beautiful city to quiet little Sheffield."

I rolled my eyes internally. That was the Sherry I remembered. It was classic—she would say something, then try to cover it up with innocence. "Well, it's home."

Something crossed her face, and I knew what was coming. I braced for the impact.

"Gosh, Bree, I'm trying to recall when I saw you last."

"Barn dance at Lucky's, the same night Brad proposed to you." I wasn't going to give her the satisfaction of saying it. That night had also been the tipping point when I knew Sheffield wasn't for me anymore. It had been the night I left.

"Was that it?" She tossed back her shoulder-length hair. "That night was such a blur, yet I remember it like yesterday." Her fake smile wavered when Brad plunked back down. "I swore it was way before that."

Oh, there it is. Like all the locals she just wanted to bring up what I wanted to forget. I only wish I could.

"Enough," Brad cut in. "Time for you to leave, Sherry. Bree and I have a case to work on."

"Oh." Sherry's face dropped. "I wanted to discuss Ginger's schedule," she pushed. I saw the pup's ears perk up at her name, and she came over to sit at Brad's feet. Sherry reached out to awkwardly pat her, but the dog inched closer to Brad.

"There's no need for discussion." He reached down and gave Ginger's head a scratch. "Her schedule remains the same. Look, Sherry,

Cap is breathing down our necks with this case. We have two bodies and no real witnesses or leads. Every second counts." Brad tossed his napkin onto the table and stood.

"Bradley, I'm not even finished." She laughed and glanced at me for help like we were good friends. I pulled in my chin and gave her a wry look. Brad didn't bite, and she slowly rose. "Maybe I could help. It wouldn't be the first time I've done that."

"No." He walked her to the door.

"Why, because she's here?" she whispered loudly enough for me to hear.

"Yes."

I took the opportunity to slide the mess off my plate into the compost bin. Out of the corner of my eye, I could see her fold her arms. "Bradley—"

"Good night, Sherry." He stepped back and watched her leave.

I started to wash the dishes for something to do. I pretended not to notice the dishwasher. If I hadn't done something, I'd have left. Then again, maybe I should have left. I'd let myself slip with Brad on the porch. *So stupid, Bree.* Old desires were hard to fight.

"I'm sorry about that." He stood next to me and looked out the window. "She has a key because of Ginger, but I'm starting to regret that decision."

"It's fine." I rinsed the plate and placed it on the drying rack. "I really think I should be the one leaving, though. This might be a mistake."

"I disagree." He lowered his head with a sigh, then stood straighter. "Look, Bree, about outside."

I stopped him. "Let's not. You've got lots on your plate, and Lord knows I do too. Let's not complicate life any more than it already is."

When he didn't respond, I glanced up and found him watching me. His dark eyes held on to mine, and I resisted the urge to run my hands through his hair and push my lips to his. My eyes slipped from his and lowered to his mouth, which begged me to taste it. I could feel the heat in my chest spread up my neck and lighten my head.

A phone rang and broke the moment. I stepped back and dried my hands on the dish towel when I realized it was mine. The caller ID read *Dale*, so I sent it to voicemail.

"I'll order us a pizza," he suggested. "I'm starving. Then we can look at the case."

"Good idea." A text message made my phone screen light up.

Dale: I gave you some space, but no communication is ridiculous Bree. I just want to see if you're okay.

We started to pull out all the paperwork and spread it across the living room table. Once the pizza arrived, I grabbed some napkins. Brad popped us each a beer and got to work.

"Thanks to Smith"—Brad pulled out a stapled clump of papers—"we have a list of everyone who was at the club on both nights the girls were killed. Seems we have an overlap of twelve people. Doesn't include staff—they're over here." He pointed at a separate stack.

"I can start there." I took the papers from him, snagged a second slice of pizza, and started to familiarize myself with the names and faces. I appreciated Adam's careful notes on each person. He'd done a good job pulling their ages, their professions, and if they had a record or not. I also appreciated that he pulled both males and females, as there was zero room to assume at that point. I checked each person's social media pages to get to know them better. One guy was creepy as hell and had a serious hand fetish. I got excited for a few minutes, but a time stamp on a few of the videos didn't work, and when I dug even deeper, I found a few of his buddies had posted him at the same time as the murders—and the timing was correct because one of his friends' smartwatch displayed the date and time. So he must have left early.

Brad stood up and stretched his back. "I'd never wish ill on our victims, but I do wish they could have at least scratched the killer so we'd have some DNA."

"Well, I've got plenty of questions." I pulled off my heels, kicked my feet up, and sank farther into his unbelievably comfy couch. "Does he kill for sport? For a sick thrill? Does he do it and just watch them die slowly from a distance? Did he plan on doing more to them, but people got in the way?"

Brad rubbed his head, then undid his shirt midway down his chest. His smooth skin caught the light above him, and I felt a stab of heat. I hated that he was built like an athlete. Why couldn't carbs find him? Why wasn't he at least bald?

"I think he just likes the idea of killing someone in public, seeing if he can get away with it. He's smart and obviously knows how to keep under the radar. If he wanted to play with his victims, he'd use the woods or somewhere private, then dispose of them somewhere like the lake or, hell, the river."

I sat up as his words brought back that day at the river. "Got anything stronger?" I wiggled my beer bottle at him.

"Yeah." He disappeared into the kitchen and returned with a bottle of scotch. "Will this work?"

"Sure." I poured myself just enough to line the bottom of the glass and tossed it back. I couldn't afford a hangover, but I needed a little help being in my own skin right now.

"Can I ask you something?" Brad broke through my thoughts, and I nodded, not wanting to do personal. "For someone who was a badass through school and again through Quantico, why do you seem so scared?" All the doors slammed shut in my head, and the sound of the dead bolts being locked echoed through my brain. "Is it because of what we saw that day?"

"I have my reasons." I waved a hand and moved over to the whiteboard we'd been using to track people's whereabouts. I pushed back a memory from the day in the Quantico parking lot, but I couldn't fight it off, and it flooded my head.

I'd been halfway through my training for the FBI. Eventually I wanted to become a profiler. I wanted to learn everything I could about what made people the way they were. I knew the Barbed Wire Killer had shaped me into who I was, so why not turn it around? It was fascinating, and my scores were high, and my instructors were so impressed, I'd been offered a job when I was finished training. I was going to be sent to Paris to work at the US embassy. I was so excited, I called my dad and told him the great news. My life was about to change for good.

Two days later, still riding my high, I splurged on a couple of dresses for the trip. When I got back to my truck, all four of my tires had been slashed. Shocked, I bent down to examine the rubber and discovered a piece of barbed wire had been stuck into each tire. My immediate reaction had been anger. *Who would do such a thing?* But when I pulled one out and looked closely, I saw the barbs had been dipped in red paint. It looked like blood. Just like the wire around the necks of those poor murdered girls in the river. My veins froze, and my knees went weak as black spots floated about my vision. I turned and pressed my back to the car and slid to the ground with my heart pounding out of my chest. It wasn't the first time I'd experienced a panic attack, and sadly, it wouldn't be my last.

That was the day I knew deep inside that he was still out there.

When I was finally able to stand and found a postcard for Paris, with a black *X* across it under my windshield, there was no mistaking it. It was a warning not to leave. It screwed my head up so badly that I couldn't sleep and began to have a whole new set of nightmares. I weighed all my options and thought about ignoring what I was sure was a warning, and the next morning I knew I couldn't go. If it really was him, I knew what he was capable of, and I wasn't going to tempt fate twice. I had quit the FBI the next day.

I only wished that was the last time I'd gotten a sign from him.

"This just came in." Brad's words brought me back to the present, and I saw him post something on the board. "You said in the car you had some bad experiences with weapons. What happened?"

I scanned the board and fingered the note card he'd just posted—it read POISON and was from the autopsy report. I turned around and snagged the full printout from both autopsies.

"'Butterfly root moss,'" I read out loud as something tugged at my memory. *Where have I heard of that before?* "Huh. My mom is always in the garden, and her hands often get dyed green when she works with Miracle-Gro."

He let out a small sigh, no doubt because I'd ignored his question. "All right. Go on."

"As we know, there were traces of poison found in both victims, but we still don't know how much."

"Yes."

"Moss and gardening go together?" I tried to find a connection.

Brad reached for a different file. "'Butterfly root moss is found in the Netherlands,'" he read aloud. "'It's highly poisonous when it's broken down into powder or liquid form.'"

I quickly typed that information into YouTube and scrolled through a few videos.

"Look." I stopped at a guy who held out his hands. His fingers were green. He explained how they got that way from working with the dangerous moss. "So, maybe *slimy green fingers* from the videos is our guy?"

"It's a start." He rubbed his eyes. He looked beat. "I'll fill Captain in tomorrow, and we also should hear from the lab on that piece of mail we found at Sophia's house."

"Good. You look tired. We both are." I dropped the file onto the table and hoped like hell we were onto something worthwhile. I shrugged off my sweater and wished I had some extra clothes. My dress was comfortable but not for sleeping. "Any chance I could borrow something to sleep in?"

"Yeah, of course." He disappeared and returned a moment later with a T-shirt and sweatpants. "Bathroom is right down that hallway."

"Thanks." I grabbed my bag. I changed quickly and thought about skipping the pants because the shirt was like a dress on me, but I wasn't sure what kind of message that would send. Thank God for the drawstring. I pulled it tight and tied a bow in the front. The strings hung down to my knees, so I doubled the bow. Whatever, they were comfortable. When I returned to the living room, he had changed into a T-shirt and sweats as well and was studying the whiteboard.

Headlights filled the window, and I quickly moved over and hid myself behind the window frame. I peeked through the edge of the curtain. What if our stalker followed us here and was watching the house? "Who do you think it was tonight in the truck?" I knew my voice was shaky. My usual nervousness had heightened since I'd come back to Sheffield. This was where I'd witnessed such horror all those years ago. Maybe my fears of him watching me were true and he wanted me back here.

"Don't worry, whoever it was just wanted our attention." Brad's voice was calm as he looked me over. "If he wanted us dead, we'd be dead, so I don't think he'll bother us tonight."

"But I couldn't go home?"

"Wasn't worth the risk."

"But we came here, so now you're at risk."

"It's fine." He moved across the room until he, too, was standing next to the window.

I took a deep breath. "Are we fine though?"

"That's a loaded question." He smiled.

I ignored him and looked away. That constant fear was always just below the surface. It was why I had come to realize I needed to be here. I wanted those files the captain offered. I think I knew, deep down, I had to find out who he was. Maybe this new role as a consultant would give me the opportunity to find more clues. I needed answers no matter how hard I had to fight against my fear. I licked my dry lips.

"Are you okay?" he asked.

"Yeah, I am." I ran both hands through my hair and tried to rein myself back in. "Tonight just stirred something up inside me."

He muttered something I couldn't hear.

"Look, I'm sorry. I'll get my head back in the game and focus on this." I went to move close to the couch, but he grabbed my arm and turned me to face him.

"Come here." He pulled me into a hug at first.

I stiffened from the contact but then soon relaxed. He was wonderfully warm, and I felt so safe with his strong arms around me. I found myself nuzzling against his chest to seek all the comfort it brought me. I never once felt like that with Dale. Being in Brad's arms reminded me of how much I'd missed him, and I had a burning urge to press myself against him so badly.

"I don't know what's going through your head, but whatever it is, it looks exhausting," he said.

"It is." I moaned and let my guard down for a moment.

He pulled back slightly, and I hoped he wouldn't see what I felt. His chin brushed my jaw, then his lips hovered over mine the way they had earlier. My gaze jumped from his eyes to his lips again, and I was sucked into his vortex just as I always was since we met years ago. "Brad."

"What is it with you?" he said, more to himself than to me. "It's like witchcraft, the way I'm pulled to you." *Yeah, ditto.* It could be just untamed lust from those younger days. Maybe if we'd slept together before he'd married Sherry, that pull wouldn't be so strong. But in that moment I didn't care. Brad brought a hunger out in me like no man ever had. My body ached for him, and the way his hand flexed on my lower back told me he felt it too.

His thumb brushed over my bottom lip, and I closed my eyes to savor our moment of weakness.

"I just want a little taste," he whispered, and the heat from his breath made my heart pound harder. "Just a taste."

The moment his lips connected with mine, something wild and unhinged ignited between us. His hands were in my hair as he deepened the kiss with his tongue. He kissed just like I imagined, strong and dominating. I molded my body to his need, to feel him against me. His arm hooked under my bottom and lifted me into the air. I wrapped my legs around his waist as my back hit the wall. One hand slid up my shirt and cupped my breast through my bra. His erection rubbed all the right places, and I wanted to cry with how much I wanted him. My body hummed, and my legs squeezed to draw him in closer. I wanted this so badly. Suddenly, he ripped his lips from mine and buried his face in my neck. His chest heaved with mine as we both let what just happened sink in.

"Christ," he huffed, still holding me in place against the wall. "I just lost control with you."

I wasn't complaining, but one of us had to point out the obvious. "But we work together, so . . ."

"Right." He thumbed my nipple through the lace, and my body pulsed with need. "We work together."

"Yes," I shamelessly panted in agreement.

"Don't do that," he growled. "I'll be inside you so quick if you keep making sounds like that." I closed my eyes and cried internally at the idea as he slowly lowered me to the floor. My knees were shaky as I stood there. "Take my bed—I'll take the couch."

"No, please let me take the couch."

"Bree." His voice told me not to push him. "Come on." He led me down the hallway and into his room. He brushed a hand down my cheek, and I fought to not melt into his touch. "Good night."

"Night." I slowly closed the door on him and sank into the cool wood bench. *What the hell was that? You can't let this happen, Bree. You love your job in New York.*

I crossed the neatly organized room and slid under the covers, too tired to do any bedtime prep. I didn't even let the fact I was in Brad's bed enter my subconscious. I closed my eyes and in seconds drifted off into a hot and bothered sleep.

I knew I was dreaming, but I couldn't stop it. My throat hurt as I swallowed around the barbed wire that cut into my skin. Terror coursed through my insides, and I tried to move, but my legs and arms were bound to a pipe. Confusion swept over me like it often did. Why me, why now? What did he want from me?

"Bree," the Barbed Wire Killer yelled in my face as he grabbed hold of the tops of my arms and shook me hard. All I could see were his red glowing eyes. They seemed to bulge out and spin about like a kaleidoscope. Barbed wire tore at my flesh and sent pain everywhere. "It's time."

"No!" I jolted straight up from a dead sleep and tried to remember where I was. He was always in my dreams, every night. I was at his mercy, and he was playing with me. Only that part wasn't a dream. The Barbed Wire Killer *had* contacted me on several occasions over the years—Quantico wasn't even the half of it—but being back in this town made all the night terrors and horrific daydreams feel much more real.

I flipped on the light and licked around my cotton mouth. There was no way I could ever fall back to sleep after he visited me; I never could. The clock read five, and I eyed Brad's bathroom. *Screw it.* I showered, redressed in yesterday's outfit, grabbed my bag, and hurried out to the living room, where Brad was passed out cold on the couch. I snagged my phone and scribbled a thanks on the whiteboard and left.

The walk to the station felt good. The cool autumn air helped fight off the fog that always lingered in my head in the mornings. The only thing different was I watched every single truck that went by or was parked to see if they had a light bar on the roof.

I made it back to my truck and changed into one of my spare outfits that I always kept on hand. In the last year, I'd spent more time in my truck than in my apartment, so I kept my life in a bag on the back seat.

I hopped out with my little bag and made sure no one was around, then squeezed a small line of toothpaste onto my travel brush and cleaned my teeth. I rinsed with a swig from my water bottle and spat carefully by the tire. I checked out my reflection in the back window to review my outfit. I shrugged on my long coat and light scarf and did my makeup in record time. I felt human again.

My brain begged for hot coffee, and who was I to disagree with myself? So I grabbed my bag and headed out of the parking lot.

When I arrived at the station with two cups of yummy coffee in my hand, I spotted Brad through the door of his office. He sat at his desk with his legs stretched out. I could see the slight bulge where his gun rested in a shoulder holster.

Images of last night sent a wave of goose bumps down my arms, then warmed me on the inside. We'd crossed a line that we simply couldn't cross again. It was totally unprofessional. Who knew what the future held, but I couldn't risk my career or my reputation. If word ever got out, it would spread like wildfire. I knew a lot of people in this town, and so did Brad. It wouldn't do to become the subject of gossip when we had an important job to do. Besides, I didn't have plans to stay here for long.

"Good morning, Kennedy." I smiled warmly as I passed his desk in the open office space, then I entered Brad's office and held out a coffee. "Morning."

"Why can't my partner bring me coffee?" I heard Kennedy yell at Ellis.

"When you're as cute as Stone, I'll bring you coffee," she yelled, turning the room on Kennedy.

"You see what you started?" he playfully called out to me.

"Thank you." Brad held up the coffee. "I wondered if you'd show up this morning."

I sipped the heavenly brew. "I couldn't sleep, so I figured a walk would do me some good."

"Was that before or after you remembered that we were almost run off the road last night by some unknown person or persons, who, by the way, we didn't catch?"

I pressed my lips together and used my long hair as a curtain to shield my face. "I wasn't worried. It was broad daylight, and I watched my surroundings."

"Seems to me you were terrified last night." He raised a brow, and I looked away.

"That was different."

"Mm-hmm." He laughed darkly and took a sip of his coffee, then he pulled out his phone. "We have court soon."

"That explains the suit." His gaze shifted over to mine, and something ran across his face, but I couldn't figure it out. "Hold on." I remembered his words. "You said 'we.'"

"Yeah." He checked the time on his phone. "I need to testify on a case that happened about six months back, and the courthouse is close to where Shelly's mother lives. She called me this morning—seems she found something she thought we might want to see."

"Which is?"

"A piece of mail." He waved for me to follow. "Let's go."

Brad was impressive in court, and I watched in awe as he answered every question with ease and confidence. A few times he glanced over at me, and I felt a sudden surge of excitement just from having his eyes on me. How I'd missed that feeling; it took me back to our days on the debate team at school.

Once he was released, we walked back to the car and headed toward Mrs. White's house. Our noses were assaulted when she opened the door. The whole place smelled like Bath & Body Works. She must have had every kind of scented candle known to man lit and placed in every nook and cranny. I couldn't tell if it was to hide the smell of her twenty-odd cats who lay on every flat surface or to hide the smell of whatever she'd been cooking. Chili? Either way it was a great challenge not to put a hand over my nose.

"I'm sorry to bring you here just for this. I didn't think to ask for the mail from the landlord when he stopped by before—things have been . . ." She hesitated and held a tissue to her cheek. "Things are hard right now."

"Of course they are," Brad agreed and gave her an understanding look. He removed a latex glove from his pocket and pulled it on, then carefully placed the envelope into an evidence bag. "Was this the only one that had any green smudges on it?"

"Yes, and when you asked me to look through Shelly's mail, that's when I remembered she'd asked the landlord to collect it for her while she was on vacation. I sorted through it all, and as soon as I found it, I called you. But please, you can go through it all if you want." She placed a heap of mail in front of him, and as he sifted through it, I took the opportunity to look around the house a little.

"Do you mind if I use your restroom?"

"Not at all. The main one is broken, so please use the other—it's just up the stairs on your left." She motioned toward the stairs.

I climbed the stairs up to the landing and admired the photos on the wall as I went. They painted a picture of a small, loving family with a daughter who was an obvious overachiever and seemed to share a love of soccer with her father. I smiled when I saw the mother as she held up an award that read **WORLD'S WORST COOK**; her daughter laughed next to her. *Maybe Sherry has one too.* I almost laughed at the thought—until the realization that I was staring at a family that had been ripped apart by some monster hit hard. My heart squeezed at the thought of their loss. Their beautiful daughter taken from them at a time when she should have been living her best life.

I moved on and saw the parents' bedroom on my right, so I headed left and peeked into what looked like a guest room, then moved down the hall and pushed open the door to a room that had obviously belonged to the young woman. Shades of soft pink and purple with white curtains and a matching bed skirt clashed with the vanity that overflowed with brightly colored jars and stacks of small plastic boxes. I stepped inside and did a quick scan of the room. A couple of gray cats raised their heads from where they were entwined on a soft beanbag chair. They both lost interest in me in seconds and curled themselves up and went back to sleep.

I studied the room and used the skills I'd honed from my past work trying to locate kids to see if anything stood out here. I raised my camera and started to document the room my way. A few photo strips from her senior year lined her vanity mirror. She was a cheerleader, and I spotted her among her teammates in the base position. The brightly colored lipsticks were stacked neatly in clear jars with lip marks showing each color on a paper next to it.

"I'm impressed. You were organized," I whispered as I pulled on a pair of gloves and sorted through the stack of papers and notebooks on the vanity. I pulled a photo off the mirror. It was a picture of Shelly and some friends out at dinner. There were a few men staring at them in the background. I snapped a photo of it so we could study it later and slipped the original into my pocket.

"Hello there." I studied a Velvet Nightclub napkin that had a phone number scribbled on it. If I were to guess, I'd say the handwriting was male. Thick and scrawly. I carefully tucked it into an evidence bag. The perks of not wearing the badge meant I didn't have to document things, but I handled it carefully for DNA. I moved to the drawers and felt around. Something smooth hit my fingers, and I found an iPad Mini. Slowly, I sank onto the vanity stool as I tried to turn it on. Nothing—it was dead. I did a quick scan of the wall and around me and found a cord that had slid in behind the vanity. I plugged it in and waited until I saw the apple appear.

"What else you got for me, Shelly?" I left it to charge and headed over to her bed. "Give me a direction," I whispered as I respectfully sat on the edge of the mattress and looked around. "What happened that made you catch this guy's eye?" Shelly was smart, pretty, young, athletic. She seemed like a really good friend and girlfriend. A beep pulled my attention to the iPad.

Shockingly, there wasn't a password on the device. I swiped through the icons and noticed one was a simple, faded gray color. "There you are." One thing I had learned quickly about young adults was where they hid things. Fake icons were often used to hide their social media platforms. "Of course, TikTok strikes again." I had a love-hate relationship with that particular platform. In this case, the victim's outcome had already been decided, so I needed to look at this as a win. "Let's see who you've been interacting with."

My phone pinged, and I quickly pulled it free from my pocket.

Patrick: You've been gone from the ranch almost all week, and your chores are piling up.

I rolled my eyes but then reminded myself that I knew I needed to do damage control with my family, and part of that was following through on my word that I'd help out more.

Bree: What can I do to make it up to you?
Patrick: Give me and Max the weekend and do the trail rides with the new company coming in today.
Bree: Deal.
Patrick: And lend me your truck.

I laughed. I'd be happy to lend him the beast for the weekend. Looked like I'd be sitting on a whole different seat for a couple of days anyway.

Bree: Deal.

I got a thumbs-up, and I instantly felt better.

"Where was I?" I quickly tapped the app and stopped when I came across Shelly's posts. I saw the newest post, then her second and the one after that. "Well, hello there." I shut the iPad, returned it to her drawer, and pocketed my gloves.

Chapter Seven

BRAD

When Mrs. White turned away, I used the toe of my shoe to flick the mangy little cat, who now had my shoelace in its teeth, back into its bed next to me. The little bugger was impossible to shake and seemed to think it was a game. I grimaced as I tried to brush some cat hair from my pant leg. I'd picked a bad day to wear a suit.

I saw Bree as she reached the bottom of the stairs and quickly stood up to say my goodbyes. If I needed to stall any further, the little feline was going to end up as a hat.

"Excuse me." Bree touched Mrs. White tenderly on the arm as she joined us. "I'm wondering if you'd mind if we had a quick look through Shelly's room? You never know what we might turn up that could help."

"Of course."

"Thank you." Bree smiled and stepped back to let Mrs. White lead the way. I followed, curious what she might have already discovered.

Holy shit, the girl's room certainly screamed *female*. Who knew there were so many shades of pink and purple to put on your face? Between this cotton candy nightmare and Lord of the Cats up- and downstairs, I really needed a shower. That and some bleach on a Q-tip to scrub out my nostrils. I wondered briefly if I'd ever get my sense of smell back.

"I'm not sure what you're looking for"—Mrs. White waved around with a sniff—"but you're welcome to look around. She only came home on weekends since she started working."

"You'd be surprised what a daughter will keep at home instead of her own place." Bree wiggled a pair of gloves on and headed straight for the vanity.

I moved around some books to seem busy, when really, I was watching Bree dig through the top drawer.

"When I was younger, I used to keep this journal tucked between two floorboards. I kept all my deepest secrets in there, and when I moved"—she closed the drawer and moved on to the bottom one—"I left it. The idea of moving it from the safety of my childhood home was scary. Home is safe." Her voice trailed off, then she held up a small iPad that was tucked between some notebooks. "Time may pass, but girls' habits are still the same. Any chance you know about this?"

"Of course." Mrs. White nodded. "That's her iPad. When her father picked her up from the airport after her trip, she had it with her. She wanted to spend the night here, then go out with her friends. She was going to come by to pick it up with the rest of her things before"—she suddenly choked up—"before work. Only she never . . ." We gave her a minute. Then she pulled open the closet to show us Shelly's unpacked suitcase.

"May I take this?" Bree asked, holding up the iPad. "Detective Stone has a great IT guy that can get past the password. As soon as we're finished, I'll make sure it gets returned to you."

Mrs. White covered her chest and nodded a few times. "Sure. At this point it's only stuff, and I'd give up my own life just to find out what really happened."

Bree removed her gloves and moved to stand in front of the grieving mother. "I can't imagine what you're going through. We're"—she waved a hand between the two of us—"usually on the other side of things, but as a human and someone with a big old heart, can I offer you something for comfort?" Mrs. White nodded as Bree stepped in and wrapped her arms around her. "My mom always says that a daughter's hug can be felt through anyone. On behalf of your daughter, this is her." I held my breath, worried that Bree had gotten too personal, but Mrs. White held on to Bree, squeezed her eyes shut, and let her tears flow. With a painful expression, Mrs. White whispered something to her, then kissed her cheek.

"Sorry to interrupt, but, Bree, we are due back at the station." I knew we needed to get moving.

"Okay." Bree smiled warmly at Mrs. White, and they walked arm in arm down to the front door, where she asked us to stop by anytime. Of course, that was directed at Bree, and I was happy with that. You couldn't pay me to return to this house of feline horror unless a fat raise and free dry cleaning were involved.

"You were really good with her," I said as soon as we left the drive-way and I was far away from those cats. "I can see why parents would choose you to find their children."

"I appreciate that." She smiled as she pulled out the iPad and rested it on her lap. "And I think you'll appreciate what I found too." She started to tap away on the screen, and I grinned when I saw there wasn't a passcode. She was good. "When we went through her social media on her watch, phone, and laptop, we found three platforms she was on—Instagram, Facebook, and Snapchat. What was odd was she didn't have a TikTok account. Everyone her age has TikTok. Hell, even I do. So when I found this guy"—she held up the iPad—"and saw this funny-looking icon and clicked it, look what popped up." I pulled over and took the device from her.

"Why hide it?"

"I'm not sure, but"—she leaned over, and I was instantly enveloped in her perfume—"she has a follower that likes and comments on her posts a lot." She pointed at a name. "Puff the Magic." She rolled her eyes at the ridiculous name. "But more importantly look at what they wrote here." She leaned over farther, and I fought the urge to touch her.

"Hang on, that's the outfit she was wearing when she was killed."

"Yes, and look what Puff wrote."

"'Hope to see you tonight, maybe you should wear velvet.'" She read out loud. "So, it's probably a he, and he knew she was going to be there, and from what I can see on here, he was pretty obsessed."

"Interesting, considering she never posted on any of her other sites that she was going to be there." I tapped my finger on the wheel as I thought. "Does her boyfriend follow her on there?"

"Um . . ." She tapped around, and I watched her fingers play with her chain as she concentrated. "It doesn't look like it, unless he uses a fake name and background."

"I think maybe we question him on that."

"Agreed."

"Two for two, Bree." I turned, and our faces were inches apart. She didn't move. She just stared at me, then her gorgeous brown eyes moved down to my lips, and that same crackle of electricity zinged through me as it had the other night. "Nice job."

"Thanks." She smiled, and I felt my jeans tighten. She pulled back, and I finally relaxed my body and breathed in deep. "We should get to the lab. Oh, and I need Smith to look into this as well." She showed me an evidence bag that held a napkin with a phone number on it.

"And that's the part I don't want to know about, but for what it's worth, nice find."

"Thanks." She grinned.

"Yeah." I checked my blind spots and eased back onto the road. I wished I didn't love it so much when I made her smile like that.

The lab was white, cold, and sterile, but despite the overall feel, my buddy Wes loved his rock music, so when we walked in the door and Chickenfoot blasted at us through his speakers, I just grinned at Bree.

"This wasn't what I expected." She laughed.

"Just wait." I opened an inner door for her, and she stepped into the smaller lab, and her face lit up. "Yeah, Wes loves his music." One wall was covered from floor to ceiling with posters of rock bands.

"And this is allowed?"

"When you're as smart as Wes, yes, they leave him alone to do what he does best. Music and science."

Suddenly the door swung open, and Wes, in his white lab coat and goggles, held up the envelope I'd given Bostwick to give to him the other day. "My favorite detective's here." He beamed as he turned down the music. "And he brought me a treat?"

"This is Bree Jaminson, our newest consultant. She's also a PI."

"Consultant?" He eyed Bree playfully.

"Let's go with PI."

"Yes, let's." He peeled off his eyewear and looked Bree up and down. "So, does this PI carry cuffs?"

"No." Bree smiled. "No gun either."

"What?" Wes's eyes popped. "So, what does a pretty thing like you do when you catch someone or you're attacked?"

"I've been lucky enough not to have dealt with that yet, but if the moment arises, I have pepper spray."

Wes looked at me. "*Yet*," he repeated grimly. "Good God, man, you'd better stick to this little thing like glue or get her a weapon. Now I say that, maybe you're on the right track." He smirked and wiggled his brows.

"Don't worry, Wes, I'm on it." I shook my head at his sly grin and had to laugh. "So, you said you found something?"

"I did." He turned his playful expression on Bree again, and I rolled my eyes—he was such a flirt. "The substance found on the envelope is the very same that was found in your two victims. It's butterfly root moss, like you said." He nodded at me. "It has a very special quality. Highly concentrated and very poisonous."

"So, chances are this one"—I handed him the envelope, now sealed in a plastic evidence bag, that we'd gotten from Mrs. White—"will test the same."

He held it up and studied the coloring. "I'd put down good money that it's the same. I'll run tests regardless, but your killer risked a lot to send these."

"But there wasn't any DNA found?"

"No." Wes shook his head. "And to be honest, the fact that there was a green smudge on both envelopes leads me to think he did it on purpose to screw with you guys. There's no return address, and they were mailed from the main post office in town. You could check the cameras, but it would be nearly impossible to pinpoint who actually mailed them." His mouth dipped like he wished he had more for us to go on. "The postmark doesn't really make sense on the timing of the death, and why send one to Sophia, who is alive? Though this was obviously done purposefully, I can't see the point of it."

"I agree." I added, "It feels a bit like an afterthought."

Bree studied the envelope. "So why do it?"

"To play with us." I shrugged. "Which means these girls are more than likely not his first kills. He's too cocky." I rubbed my head. "Tell me there was something inside we could run with."

Wes pulled the letter out through the tear on the side of the envelope and held it up. "Nothing but traces of the butterfly root."

"Why go through the work of mailing it? What's the point?"

I let that swirl around my head. "Like I said, he's playing with us." Wes grunted in agreement.

"Oh, Wes, could you check for DNA on this napkin?" She handed him the bag, and he gladly took it.

"Of course."

"Thanks." Bree turned away as she answered a call, and Wes wiggled his brows at me.

"She single?"

"No." I pinched the bridge of my nose. "Never in a million years did I expect my new partner to attract so much attention."

"Have you looked at her? She's gorgeous." Wes lowered his voice. "All I can picture is her in a pair of lab glasses, a white coat, and her hair pinned up with a pen."

"Fuck," I huffed and tried to push the idea of her with her hair up in a messy bun that exposed her neck out of my head. Flashbacks to my mouth there didn't help.

"What's wrong?" Bree was suddenly at my side.

I shot Wes a look to behave. "Nothing."

"All right. Well, Oliver, Shelly's boyfriend, is at work at the gym just round the corner, and he said he's got time to talk with us in between clients."

"Great." I waved at Wes. "Thanks as always. Enjoy your day."

"I'm sure you will," he teased, and Bree looked at him, confused, but I pulled her along.

"Bree?" Officer Smith met us at the front doors. "You mentioned you had something for me to look into?"

"Yes, thanks, Adam. Can you maybe ID the guys in the background of this photo and find me a name to go with this phone number?" She handed him a photo and a copy of the phone number she'd found.

"Anything for you guys!" He smiled and whisked them away.

We didn't need the car, so we walked down the road toward Muscle Gym. I was glad we didn't drive, as it was hard to park there at the best of times.

Bree filled the silence as we walked. "Wes seems nice. You two seem close."

"We go back a long way."

"I got that impression." She tucked her hair behind her ear as she fished through her bag for her ringing phone. After she read the caller ID, she sent it to voicemail.

"Everything good?"

"Yes." She wouldn't look at me and slipped her sunglasses on in a poor attempt to shield her face from me.

"Remember Wilson Saunders?"

She shook her head with a laugh. "Now, that name takes me back."

"Remember how he asked you out, and when I asked you about it, you denied it?"

"I plead the Fifth on that one." She chuckled. I didn't say anything, and she looked up. "What was that trip down memory lane for?"

"I'm just pointing out that I know when you lie. You did then, and you're doing it now." I waved toward her bag.

"Pff." She held up a hand as we slowed to cross the street. "You know jack shit."

I stood behind her and lowered my lips to her ear. "When it comes to you, Bree Jaminson, I know more than you think." I tapped her arm to get her to walk when the light turned.

"Is that so?" She tried to play it cool, but I could see that faint blush she got when she was excited. "You think you know me so well?"

"I know I do." Bree and I had been good friends, and I'd always had feelings for her, but they were complicated. What if I made a move on her and it didn't work out? I'd lose her altogether. I hated when guys would flirt with her. She was pretty and smart. She had a self-confidence most girls didn't. She attracted a lot of attention, including from me, but she was the girl next door, the kind of forbidden fruit that I wanted to taste, but I was scared to go for the whole thing. I was protective of her and always made sure she was okay and no one messed with her.

Over the years in high school, I had learned a lot about her reactions to things. Like where she blushed or how she dipped her head to the side and used her hair as a curtain when she was unsure of her own feelings. I had known back then I wanted her, and I had been sure she wanted me too.

My head slipped back to the times we'd given in to our attraction back in high school. Once when we were in the basement watching a horror movie, the power went out, and she grabbed for me. I pulled her close, and our lips touched, but just as I started to deepen the kiss, the power flickered back on, and the moment was lost.

Another time, we rode horses way up into the hills to watch the sunset. A coyote spooked the horses, and they ran off and left us. We spent the night up there together. I made a fire, but with no sleeping bags, I wrapped myself around her body and held her all night long. It was a moment I'd never forget. It would have been the perfect time to move things forward, and I hadn't taken it.

All that stopped after we stumbled on that double homicide. Things changed between us. We both pulled back from one another, and, I realized later, I'd thrown myself at Sherry and shut Bree out. Sherry had been my safety net back then. I hated the attention and desperately needed to be anyone but that boy who witnessed that terrible event with that girl.

"Well, I guess we'll see how much you think you know about that, won't we?" Bree turned to look at me over her shoulder.

"What does that mean?" I held open the door, and she marched through with the police-issued ID badge Captain had given her held up to the front desk. "We're here to see your personal trainer, Oliver. He knows we're coming."

"Yes, okay." The young guy behind the desk nodded and made a quick call. "He said he'll be right over and that you can wait in that room right there." He pointed across the hall.

"Thanks." I nodded, and we headed to the glass room to wait. I was glad to have the nice, quiet place to chat. The fewer people who knew what was going on, the better. I couldn't help but take a moment to tease Bree some more. It was entertaining to see her squirm, and the playful flirting made me feel young again. "I know you very well," I went on. "One of my favorite things I notice is how you get this little bit of pink that spreads across your chest whenever you get excited or"—I hesitated—"turned on."

"I haven't had sex in almost two months, if you must know." She folded her arms.

I liked that answer. The sudden thought of her being intimate with someone else bothered me.

"Well, that's a lot of info." I jumped out of the way when she swatted me.

"Don't blame me for being wound up," she scoffed. "I'm only human."

"A horny human, you mean."

Her face lit up. "Not after tonight."

That caught my attention. "You got a date?"

"I do." That hit me in the stomach like a dumbbell, not that I'd show it. "Something like that."

"Well, I'm happy for you." I ground my teeth. I sat up straight as Oliver opened the door.

"Sorry, my client got tangled in the ropes." He tried to hide his amusement. "It's a thing. I know why you're here." The weight of what happened to his girlfriend grew evident on his face. "Ms. Jaminson, you said you only wanted to ask a few questions, so I've got ten minutes before my next client. Whatever you need to ask, ask. I want to help you find this sicko."

Bree took the lead. "Great. I'll get right to the point." As she was the one who'd found the iPad, it was right that she would run the show here—plus she had a way with people that I didn't. I enjoyed watching her work. "I appreciate you taking the time to talk with us. Excuse me if I'm blunt, but does Shelly have a TikTok account?"

His head dropped forward, and he let out a sigh. "She did have an account, but after an argument she promised to get rid of it when we were six months into us dating."

"Why?" I asked.

"Because she was talking to a guy on there, and when I found out, I was pissed."

"She was cheating?" Bree pulled out her phone.

"Not physically, but emotionally she was, yes." He sank into a chair. "It was her professor." He licked his lips. "Look, I want to sit here and toss that shithead under the bus. I'd like to point a finger and say he killed her, but it'd be a lie. It wasn't him."

I leaned forward. "How are you so sure?"

"Because he died three months ago from complicated surgery or something. The guy was like in his forties. If you ask me, fate just stepped in."

Bree closed her eyes, and I could see she was frustrated that her lead might have just gone cold.

With one last effort to save the lead, I pulled out the iPad from Bree's purse. I clicked it on and opened the app before I turned it around so he could see it.

"At the risk of upsetting you further, I have to ask you something."

"Brad." Bree bit her lip, clearly unsure of what Oliver's reaction would be. "Maybe we . . ."

I looked back to Oliver, who squinted at the screen. "I see." His face went through a series of painful emotions.

"Do you have any idea who this is?" I pointed at the Puff the Magic guy's name. "Or why he'd be all over her page?"

"No, but I'm not on that platform. All that is like a different world to me. I use Instagram for work, because I have to. I'm not much for posting."

"I get it." Bree reached over and turned off the screen. "I'm sorry. I'm sure that's hard to see."

"I should have known she still had that account. She gave it up too easily." He looked at his watch and stood to show he needed to go. "Shelly was in her prime and had everything going for her. Things came easy to her. I'm here working overtime just trying to make it through school without any help."

Bree squeezed his forearm. "That's admirable, Oliver, and will count to the right person. Again, thanks for meeting with us. Just keep faith we'll find this guy."

"Thanks." He shook my hand and smiled warmly at Bree. "You know where to find me."

He left, and Bree groaned as the door closed. "Dammit."

I understood the feeling of thinking you were onto something and then having the door slammed shut in your face. "I saw a coffee shop next door."

"You trying to make me feel better?"

"Maybe." I held the door open. "Is it working?"

"Maybe." She shrugged, and we headed toward her addiction and ordered our treats.

As we drove toward my parents' place, the car soon smelled like a bakery, and I eyed her extra-large coffee and warm cinnamon bun and wished I'd caved and gotten one. She licked her slim fingers, and my stomach clenched. My appetite suddenly went from a warm bun to a much warmer feeling inside. *Get yourself together.* I pretended not to notice when she looked over and forced myself to focus on the road and not how much I wanted to taste the sweetness from her lips.

I spent as much time as I could at my parents' place now that Ronnie was back home for good. My brother's PTSD made me worry. His time overseas in the service might have been over, but he still carried a lot of it with him. I knew it was hard on my mom and dad to see him slip in and out of *the dark places*, as he called them. By being there, I acted as a buffer. The fact that Dad was fixing the fence around the property gave me a good reason to be there, and I liked to help.

"Another dead end." Bree pulled me from my thoughts as she held up her phone. "Smith said the guys in the photo were her friends who all have an alibi for Shelly's murder, and the phone number was to a dry cleaner."

"On to the next lead." I squeezed her arm to let her know it was all right.

"Yeah, I guess so."

It started to rain when we hit the highway, and we were in the middle of a good downpour. Bree angled the vents in her direction.

"It's cold," she explained as I looked at her. "And I don't like leaving my truck in town," she grumbled. I smirked at her. I loved that she was still pissed I'd convinced her to leave her hunk of a truck at the station. I liked having her with me. She wasn't the girl next door anymore. I had to be honest with myself, it felt good to just be with her.

"But it worked out for Patrick."

"Mm-hmm." She knew I was right. He was already in town with Maxine and wanted to borrow Bree's truck to haul some stuff home from the feedstore. "He'd better be careful with my truck. She's touchy at times." I turned off the road and headed down her long driveway.

"That I believe." I laughed and ran a hand through my hair when I caught her glare. "You know, you're still cute when you're mad."

She glared harder.

"Oh, not the main house." She pointed for me to swing around and head toward the cabins. "I'm living over there now. Number three." She tucked her coat around herself as I pulled in, then reached for her bag. "Thanks to Lainey, I'm now bunking with a bunch of businessmen who thought this place was better than a hotel. I really like it, actually. I like my space, and this allows it."

I didn't like it, but I couldn't say much. I turned off the car and looked at the cozy cabin.

"Wait here." I opened my umbrella and got out into the pouring rain and hurried to her side. "Come on." I walked her to the covered porch and waited for her to open the door, though not before glancing at the other cabins around her, wondering what kind of men were just a few steps away from her.

As I stepped inside, I immediately felt comfortable. Her cabin was nice and homey with a bit of country living woven through. It was a big open room with a fireplace straight ahead and a door off to the right that led to what I assumed was a bathroom. She had set up a big whiteboard where she had written some thoughts on our case. She bent to quickly light the fireplace that was all laid for her and hung her jacket from a peg on the wall.

"This is home." She waved.

I looked around and admired the place again, before spotting cookies on the table. "Are these . . . ?" I lifted the glass dome on the cake display and snagged one. I'd forgotten that her mom could bake a mean cookie. "Oh my god, they are!" I let the chocolate melt in my mouth and fought the urge to groan. Her mother always used to have them for us after school when we were kids. I leaned on the table and watched her plug in her phone and laptop. "So, when's your date arriving?"

She reached around me and held up a package. "He's already here."

She barely had time to blink as I grabbed the package and tore it open. I pulled in my chin, and my brows shot up as I eyed the sex toy in my hand.

"Hey!" She grabbed it from me and tossed it onto the bed, where it turned on and did a little flop and a wiggle motion, then died. "That's not for you."

"No, it's not." I laughed, and she gave me the finger. "Seriously, you don't need a fake—you can get the real thing from almost any guy we met today."

"Right." She sipped her coffee and looked out the window as the rain pelted it. "I'm not really into dating strangers right now. So, he'll"—she pointed to her bed—"have to do." She slowly turned, and I saw an expression I didn't recognize cross her face. "Hey, Brad?" I felt my insides twist with heat. "You still know how to ride?"

"A horse, you mean?" I grinned.

"Yes, you idiot." She laughed.

I side-eyed her. "Yeah."

"Great." She beamed. "Meet me here tomorrow at noon."

"Why?" I swallowed hard as I watched her reach back to undo her damp dress. The zipper was partway down when she grabbed something silk from the dresser drawer, then headed into what I assumed was the restroom. "Hey, you never answered me."

"Sec," she called, and I began to heat up, not sure where this was going. "I need your help tomorrow around twelve thirty."

"Surrre." The word fizzled away when she came back dressed in a PJ set of a silk shirt and shorts. "Is that your date outfit?" I rubbed my hot hands on my thighs and shamelessly let my eyes roam all over her.

"Yes, it is." She smiled, then headed for the door and held it open for me to leave. "Good night, Brad, and remember, if you're late, I still know how to unlock your bedroom window and get to you."

I stood in front of her and kissed her cheek, lingering there for a moment. I had to force my hands to stay at my sides when all I wanted to do was grab hold of her, press my body into hers, and ravish her. But that whole thing about us being coworkers was hard to navigate . . . so I'd behave, at least for a bit. "Good to know. Night, Bree." I kissed her one more time just to witness the sprinkle of pink go across her chest, then with a light chuckle, I headed out into the wet night. I needed a cold shower after that.

Mornings on a farm came way too early. When the sun was up, you were up. Farm life waited for no one. Just as the morning light peeked over the Cedar Creek Ranch across the lake, my boots touched down on the dirt and I called to Ginger to follow. She bounded after me with a big old smile. We crossed the property to where I had stacked the pine boards. I tossed my hoodie onto a hay bale in case I needed it later. The temperature often took a drop at that time of year without warning.

Ginger loved being out here even more than at my place in town. I knew she was spoiled rotten, mostly thanks to my father. She was rarely alone and always had someone or some other animal for company. Here she had all the space in the world to run free and swim. Her best friend, Finley, the Jaminsons' border collie, lived at the ranch, and the two were often spotted swimming around the dock. I grabbed a stick and tossed it into the air. "Go get it, girl!" She raced off to find it.

With my tool belt in place, I grabbed a piece of board and began to nail it to another. The old fence needed a lot of boards replaced, and the physical labor felt good. It was just what I needed. Maybe it was because I didn't get as much action in my job as I used to, or maybe it was because I'd been a little pent up lately.

I worked away until my muscles screamed at me to stop, and I knew I needed a break and some water. It felt so good. I leaned back against a tree and listened to the world wake up around me. It did wonders for the head.

A short while later, Dad walked into my line of vision and helped hold a board in place, then he gave Ginger a pat on the head. "Morning, girl."

"We're out of lumber." I swung the hammer and smacked the nail into place. "You want me to go pick up some more?"

"I have a few things to grab—I'll head in." He stepped back and admired my job. "Looks really good, Son." His smile showed below his cowboy hat as he handed me a fresh bottle of water Mom must have sent out with him. "How's it going?" He jerked his chin toward the ranch as I downed the water, gaining myself a moment to think. "Must be strange having her back in town."

"Yeah" was all I offered.

"Heard you, Sherry, and Bree had dinner the other night." He looked away as I looked at him, confused about how he knew. "Bree told Nina, who told your mother."

"Christ." I chuckled at the phone tree of gossip. "It was awkward," I admitted. Dad and I were close, and I'd leaned heavily on him for advice during the divorce. "I don't know." I mopped my face and let the cool breeze pass over me. "Bree's back in town, and now suddenly Sherry seems to want to talk." I looked away, knowing I still didn't have my head 100 percent in the game, but it was straight-ish. If I wanted a relationship with Bree, it had to be handled carefully, no matter how badly I wanted her.

"And?" Dad prompted.

"And nothing. We're done. Sherry's always wanted what she can't have."

Dad's face twisted, and he looked over at the lake. He went to say something but seemed to change his mind and coughed. "You and Sherry were together a long time. You have history. But like you said back when you divorced, you weren't happy in your marriage."

"No, I wasn't." I shook my head and let out a long, heavy breath, hoping to shed some tension.

He leaned against the fence next to me. "So, what's on your mind? You seem to be struggling with something. Is it Sherry?"

"It's not about Sherry. She just feels threatened now Bree's back. She was always jealous of my friendship with Bree. I'm struggling with the fact that old feelings are surfacing for Bree. I think she's always been the one I wanted. I just don't know if it's too late to act on them now. I've pushed her away so many times." I dropped my head and closed my eyes. "When I married Sherry, I thought it was what I needed, but now I know that wasn't the case. I just don't want to mess up." I let out a heavy sigh, feeling drained. "Man, life's timing is interesting, isn't it?"

The wood creaked when he pushed off the fence. "It is."

"If you were me, Dad, what would you do?"

Dad removed his hat and ran his hand along the brim. "Son, you have some healing you need to do before you let your heart decide on anything. But only you can decide if you're ready to try again." He swatted his leg with his hat. "Just remember what the two of you have been through. That girl's gone and created another life for herself elsewhere. She might not be willing to give that up."

"Yeah, I know. It's one of the things I'm worried about." I huffed as I swatted at a horsefly. We began to slowly walk back toward his pickup truck.

"At the risk of overstepping." He jammed his hat on his head and opened the driver's door. He laughed as Ginger didn't miss a beat and jumped in and settled on the front seat with a big, jerky, tongue-lolling grin. "Just don't let Sherry wiggle her way back in. We both know she's good at getting what she wants." He was right. Sherry had a side of her that could be vindictive at times, and her best friend, Anna, was worse. "It's your life, and it's okay not to know what the right call is right away."

"Yeah." I hit my glove on his open window as he started the truck. "Thanks, Dad."

"Anytime." He patted Ginger's head, then headed out toward town.

I put my tools away and checked the time. I had forty-five minutes before I needed to meet Bree. I eased myself down onto a pile of hay bales, tucked my arms under my head, and stared up at the gloomy gray sky. It wasn't long before I drifted off to sleep.

Hot, wet air shot across my face, and my eyes jerked open as a big soft white nose touched my cheek, then flared its nostrils at me.

"Rise and shine, cowboy." Bree smiled down at me from her saddle. "Hope you stretched, because you and I got a job to do." I stood and blinked away the fog as I registered the rope in her hand. She led another, fully tacked horse.

"What the hell, Bree! No."

"Partners are supposed to have each other's backs." She untied a black cowboy hat and tossed it at me. "And I owe my brother this."

"And?" I grabbed my hoodie and took the lead for the horse she wanted me to ride and started walking back to her place, where I fully intended to leave the horse.

She crossed an arm over her lap as she pressed her lips together. "Are you really going to make me take this group out on my own?"

"You're not on your own." I looked across the lake and saw a group of horses and riders. I squinted to see the two young guys who worked for the Jaminsons. "There are at least two ranch hands with you."

"Yes, two guys I don't know, and look at who I have to entertain." She waved ahead of us as she rode next to me. I saw four men all on their phones and a woman who looked like she'd just stepped out of a fashion show. "They're from New York and are being forced by their boss to be here as a *bonding experience*." She air quoted for emphasis. "Let me tell you, there's no bonding happening whatsoever." She shrugged and pursed her lips.

"Are they the guys who are staying in the cabins near yours?"

"Yeah." She stuck her bottom lip out. "And you owe me."

"What do I owe you?"

She raised a brow. "You made me eat dinner with Sherry, and that was awkward as hell."

Christ, she was right. That was bad. Finley came running down to greet us. "Sorry, bud, Ginger went into town." I rubbed between his ears. "She'll be back later."

"Brad, please." She sighed. "Patrick is off today, and I honestly don't want to be alone in the woods by myself and even less so with strangers."

Shit, she had me there. "Fine." I tossed the hat back at her. "But I'm wearing my ball hat."

Chapter Eight

"Pull your reins to the left to go left, same with the right. Pull gently back to stop. Squeeze your thighs to go forward, and use your loose reins to swat the horseflies. Really, the horse will just be following the one in front of him, so you won't have to do too much," I instructed the less-than-interested group. I glanced at Brad, who sat on his horse comfortably with a grin on his face. He obviously enjoyed this way too much. "Most importantly, don't forget to—" My cell phone rang. "Hello?" I answered and waved as I turned and spotted Charley up near the barn.

"Sorry, Sis, but I couldn't resist." He let out a belly laugh, then hung up. I didn't miss Brad's grin as he moved his horse toward the front of the riders.

"Most importantly, what?" the woman called out, and I ignored her and started to move the group forward.

About forty minutes into the ride, when the trail opened up, Brad moved up to be next to me.

"How was your date?" He kept his horse at the same pace as mine.

"Eventful," I lied, not at all pleased that my new friend had needed batteries—the cheap ones that had come with it had only lasted about five minutes, and there had been none to be found in the main house.

"As long as he treats you well." He smirked.

"*Very* well." I sighed deeply, as though it had been a great night between us. "He even spent the night."

"Sounds serious," he teased.

I steered the horse around a stump. "I think this could be the real thing."

"I hope to be at the wedding." He chuckled.

I looked away at the sudden memory of the day Brad's wedding invitation had arrived in the mail. My mother had forwarded it to me in New York. I'd felt so lost when I looked at it, at an already lost time.

"So." Brad must have felt my mood change. "Where are we headed, anyway?"

"Lucky's Canyon." I nodded ahead of us. "Lainey has a whole setup there for dinner with firepits and sleeping tents."

Several hours later, with a few breaks along the way, we finally came to the edge of the lake, where everything was set up.

"Oh wow," the woman cooed, "when you said *tent*, I thought you meant camping, not glamping."

"We don't do things halfway here at Cedar Creek Ranch." I beamed at what Lainey had created. It was spectacular. There was a huge fire-pit with smoothed-out log benches and chairs surrounding it. Old-fashioned lanterns hung from tall poles staked in the ground, and some even hung from the trees, helping light the pathways to the off-white canvas tents. The tents were huge, high enough so you could stand inside comfortably. I knew from Lainey that most of them had two double beds, chairs, and coolers filled with water, booze, and snacks. The nice part was they were spread out and nestled between the trees, so the guests weren't right on top of each other.

"Okay, everyone, take a little time here to choose which tent you want and get settled in."

Confident everything was under control, I grabbed my bag and headed to the far tent. I pulled off my flannel, then gathered my hair up into a messy bun.

"And which one of these fine-looking tents is mine for the evening?" Brad came in and looked around. "Actually." He flopped onto the bed across from mine. "I think I'll just take this one."

I pulled out my silk PJs and set them on my pillow. They were my favorite. "Don't get too comfy—your tent is the one next to mine. Out there."

"Nope, this one suits me just fine." He ignored me. "So, what's next on the schedule?"

"You're not sleeping in this tent. So get that right out of your head. We're coworkers, remember that."

"I know how to be discreet." He flashed his perfect teeth at me. I internally groaned and hoped he'd stay close. I hated to be alone, especially out here. I eyed my PJs and wondered what he wore to bed. I looked away and brushed off the thought.

"Not happening, Brad."

Later, that night, as we sat around the firepit with full bellies, one of the male guests leaned toward me. "All right, camp leader, you can ride, you can cook, you can make a mean dessert, so where's our spooky story? Isn't that part of the whole campfire thing?"

I laughed, and my eyes searched for the two ranch hands, but they were down with the horses and had their own little fire. I stalled for time. "Ahh."

Trish, the female of the group, nodded. "Yes, bring me back to my childhood. I love a good scare."

I took a deep breath through my nose and knew Patrick would kill me if we came back with anything less than five stars on their exit review.

"Okay, ahh, give me a sec." I wasn't very creative at making up stories, but one idea came to me. "When I moved to New York, I went to school with this girl, Amanda. It was our first year, and we knew nothing about what we were doing." I tugged at the hem of my sleeve. "She was young, bright, and had her whole future ahead of her. She made friends quickly, fell into classes like a champ, professors were impressed with her grades—she seemed happy. One day, toward the end of her first year, she had an opportunity to travel with her professor and some other students to visit the US embassy in Baghdad.

"She would work side by side with some very powerful people who could help launch her career. An offer like that rarely happened to first-year students like us." I stared into the fire and saw the story play out in front of me like a movie. "The night before she was supposed to leave, she told me she'd had a goodbye dinner with friends but when she got back to her place, something didn't feel right. The hair on her arms stood up, and a strange feeling in the pit of her stomach made her want to turn and run. But she said she just shook it off and forced herself to look around.

"She slowly entered her bedroom and saw her window was open. Now, Amanda was a very careful girl. Her parents had taught her to be watchful, and she would never have left the house without every window being locked. She said she felt a shiver run through her as she stood there in her room, because she saw . . ."

"Saw what?" Trish whispered, her face a study in concentration.

"Her itinerary. It was taped to her mirror, and not only that—there was a warning attached."

"What kind of warning?" one of the men asked, as entranced in the story as Trish seemed to be.

I looked around at the circle of faces in the firelight and then let my eyes adjust to the darkness again. "It was a warning not to leave. The next day, Amanda headed to the airport and stared at the board that listed the departures while she battled the storm inside. With the warning clenched in her hand, she went to the counter and switched her flight from Baghdad to another state. She never contacted her professor; she just wanted to find a new city, to slink away into the crowd. She never told a soul what she found that night in her room, not even me. Well, until several years later."

"Someone sure wanted her to stay." One of the guys snorted a laugh. "I mean, it would take something big to make me miss a trip like that. So, then what?"

"Or a death threat," the guy with the yellow hat added. "Must have been a major warning." He shrugged when I looked at him.

"You could say that." I looked at them again. "Anyway, it happened two more times. Each time, it was when she tried to change her life in some way. A warning would be left somewhere for her to find. Not always in the same way. Sometimes the warnings were worse than others. She knew she was being manipulated, played by someone for a reason she never understood, but she was always too afraid not to pay attention." I felt something cold go up my back, and I looked around at the shadows where the fire couldn't reach. Was something out there?

"Okay." Trish looked around. "Then what?" I spotted Brad as he leaned against a tree just behind the others. He was watching me, his face in shadow. I took a breath and blew it out. It was just him.

"No clue." I pressed my hands between my knees and let out a puff of air and watched my breath dissolve in the cold air. "I haven't seen Amanda in a while."

"Wow, I wonder what makes psychological stories scarier than those bump-in-the-night stories." Trish shivered and pulled her jacket around her.

"It's one thing for someone to jump out at you," Brad said as he made his way over to us. "You know they're the bad guy. Your brain can understand that type of fear. It's another to have someone mess with your head. Because you don't know if maybe that person you're sitting right next to is the one who's calling the shots. Faceless fear is the worst of all."

"Spoken like a true detective." The woman winked, then stood and rubbed her arms. "And on that note, I think it's time to call my kids and head to bed."

After the good nights were said, I did a quick once-over of Lainey's to-do list and headed back up to the tent.

"Hey, roomie." Brad appeared suddenly in the doorway.

"Shit, crap!" I jumped about a foot as he flashed me a killer smile.

"Sorry to scare ya—must have been your campfire story." He looked at me as he kicked off his boots and reached back to pull his T-shirt off.

I tipped my head back and looked up at the roof as my heart fought to stay in my chest. Then I cried internally. *Seriously, fate? This is what you toss at me?* His gorgeous body screamed *hockey player.*

I cleared my throat. "Your tent is next door."

"No one saw me come in, I promise." He tucked his hands under his head as he lay back in his bed. "The lumbar support in this one is spot on too," he teased and grinned at me, then his face softened. "I know you don't really want to be alone out here."

"Whatever." I pulled my blankets up to my chin, not addressing what he'd just stated, because he was right. "Just stay over there." I waited to see what he'd do. I wasn't sure what I wanted him to do. My stomach clenched at the thought of him above me, and my body heated with desire. I could hear him breathing, but as I lay there and argued with myself over what I wanted, I felt my own eyes grow heavy.

I slipped off to an uneasy sleep.

The frozen ground pained my feet. The branches ripped at my skin as I whirled around to see if he still followed me. Condensation puffed a misty cloud in front of my face as I tried to catch my breath. I knew he was there; I could feel him. I strained to listen, but the ringing in my ears blocked out my ability to hear.

Keep moving! *I screamed at myself and suddenly tuned into what I was wearing. I was in* her *white dress. The woman from the river. I could see her open, unblinking eyes even as the water flowed over one of them. My hands were covered in blood, then I felt the warmth from the blood on my neck. Wait, what?*

"Bree!" The Barbed Wire Killer hissed at me like a snake, and I jolted awake with a yelp.

Arms reached out to touch me, and I fought back, still consumed by my dream. "No!" I screamed, but a hand clamped over my mouth and pushed me back into the bed. I squeezed my eyes shut and prayed that whatever was about to happen would happen quickly.

"Hey," Brad's voice cut through my panic. "Stop. It's me." Slowly, his words registered, and I felt my heart's rhythm break its wild pace. "Bree, look at me." He pushed my flailing arms above my head and pinned me there as he eased onto my bed.

"Yeah." I blinked away the horrific dream and let the tears of relief flow. "Sorry."

"Sorry?" He looked at me, confused, as he kept a tight hold on my wrists. "Sorry you had a nightmare?" He spoke quietly. "You've nothing to be sorry about except maybe for giving me a black eye." He smiled in the low light and slowly released my wrists. I brushed my hair off my face. "Want to talk about it?"

"No," I whispered.

"Okay." He reached down and pulled the blanket up over me. Then, to my surprise, he leaned over me to turn down the lantern to a soft glow, then settled in next to me.

I forced the painful lump down my throat as the darkness crept back in around us. "I don't . . ." I barely had a voice. "I don't normally sleep after this point," I confessed. I could feel the warmth of him where he lay against my frozen body, and I fought not to roll over into him.

"Is this an every-night thing?"

I tensed up again because I'd lived alone with the truth for so long. I'd tried to even keep it from Dale—not that it ever helped. It only caused more problems in the long run. The unsteady breath that shot from deep inside gave him the answer.

"Christ, Bree, you must be exhausted." The bed shook as he turned on his side toward me. I could feel his warm breath in my face, and his bare chest touched my arm. "Can I ask you something at the risk of upsetting you?"

I didn't answer; I didn't want to. I realized it was the first time since that day at the river that I didn't feel completely alone. It was so nice to have him there when I woke from that terrible nightmare.

"Kennedy told me that the guys brought up the whole Barbed Wire Killer thing." Brad's voice sounded tentative.

I studied him for a moment. "Don't you struggle with it?"

"Well, no, I've found a way to deal with it."

"By marrying Sherry?" I snapped but instantly regretted it when he looked away. "Sorry."

He leaned his weight on his elbow. "By playing hockey." His tone was less than impressed with my insult. "Are you all right? Bree? Kennedy said—"

"I'm fine."

"Sure." He just cleared his throat, and it pissed me off.

I let myself ask before I could stop the one question that had been on my mind for years. "Have you ever heard from him?"

"Him, who? The killer?" His eyes widened out of his head. "No! Why? Have you?"

"No." I pulled my chin in. "I only ask because he got a good look at us, and I always wondered if he followed us that day. You know, followed us home."

"No," he repeated, "I've never seen him since that day. Same goes for you, right?"

"Right."

"You sure?"

"Yes, Brad, it was just a curiosity thing. Let it go." I felt myself shut down. This was the reason I never spoke about the topic, because look where it got me. Now he'd doubt me and wonder if I was all messed up. And why did I have to bring up fucking Sherry? She'd always been a sore spot for me, a wound that had never healed. Here I was in bed with a man I'd loved nearly my entire life, and I brought *her* up.

"I wish I could read your mind sometimes." He flopped back on the bed with a heavy puff. "Because you're maddening, woman."

"I know."

"You're such a stubborn woman," I heard him whisper, then he suddenly reached out and pulled me into him, then wrapped his leg over mine as his arm went around my waist. "You can push me away emotionally, but you'll have to fight me physically if you want me to leave you alone." He chuckled because we both knew he could pin me down and I couldn't wiggle free. He moved his hand into my hair and held my head in place. "I will break you down, Bree." He was serious, but his eyes softened in low light. "Because I don't want you living with all that fear."

"I'm really okay." I pulled myself together. "I think it's just you and me here, where we are—it's just bringing back all those emotions and memories."

"I can understand that." He yawned and moved his warm hand to my hip. "Let's see about getting some sleep."

"Okay," I whispered. I tried not to focus on the heat caused by his touch and let my gaze drift to the side walls of the tent. The shadows from the branches were dancing around the canvas when suddenly, they morphed into a silhouette of a man, and I squeezed my eyes shut tight and wrapped my fingers around Brad's arm. *You're fine, Bree. He's not out there . . .*

The next morning, I was happy to overhear a few comments about how much fun the guests had had. I knew my sister would want satisfied customers who'd give good reviews.

"Storm's coming in, quick." One of the ranch hands pointed to the dark sky. "I think we should head back."

"I agree." He went to tell the others while I quickly gathered my things and went to get my horse. Brad was already mounted as I drew close.

"Morning."

"Morning." I avoided eye contact, feeling a little uncomfortable about him witnessing my night terrors.

He pulled back on his reins as his horse started to move. "Don't pull away from me, Bree, just because you were vulnerable."

I didn't answer, but he was right. I was good at keeping people at a safe distance. I put my foot in the stirrup and hiked myself into the saddle as the others joined us.

"Ready?" I asked. "We're going to go a little faster to make it back before the storm." I led the way, and they fell in behind me.

Once we got home, the ranch hands gathered the horses, and the guests raced to get out of the wind that had picked up. Brad and I quickly helped Charley and the others put the horses away.

I finished up and headed outside. "You feel like working?" I whirled around to see Brad's fit body as he leaned against the door. Why did his T-shirt have to be so tight on his arms? Nothing was left to the imagination, and I was totally all right with that.

"I feel like a shower more than working."

"All right." He pushed off the wall. "Let's get cleaned up then, and I'll meet you back at your cabin in, say, an hour."

"Okay."

He moved to stand in front of me and tucked a loose strand of hair behind my ear. I resisted the urge to lean into him.

"If you overthink things and don't answer the door, I might be inclined to come looking for you. So unless you want some company in that shower . . ." He winked playfully, and I let out a light laugh and started to walk backward as my heart thumped against my rib cage.

"I'll see you soon, Brad."

Chapter Nine

"Heading out already? Didn't you just get home?" Ronnie asked as I tucked in my T-shirt, then glanced in the hall mirror and adjusted my hat to fit just right over my wet hair. "Damn, I love that goal!" Ronnie was in the La-Z-Boy watching a rerun of last year's Stanley Cup Finals, with his buddy Hayne on the sofa across the room. Though he had his own place, he spent almost all his time with Mom and Dad. They loved it, and I think he needed it.

"Hey." Hayne waved a beer at me.

Christ, it's barely noon. "Hey." I didn't like Hayne, but he'd been overseas with Ronnie, and they shared a bond. He just rubbed me the wrong way. He was sleazy and had a way of gaslighting people without them realizing it. "Heard you got lead detective on that nightclub case."

"I did."

"Anything new?"

I checked the time. "Nothing I can talk about."

"That's what you have to say, but when you're talking to someone like me . . ." He leaned his head to the side like he was more important. I fought not to roll my eyes.

"What puts you above everyone else?" I shot back, and Ronnie gave him a look to lay off.

"Brad." Bree was suddenly in the entryway of the house. "Why aren't you answering your phone?" Ginger ran over and nearly jumped into her arms. Ginger had never behaved like that with Sherry. Bree bent down and showered her with rubs and kisses.

"Has it been an hour? I thought we were meeting at your place." I replayed her words in my head. "My phone? Sorry, it's on the charger."

Hayne drained the rest of his beer, and I saw him glance at Bree. "Who's that?" he asked my brother.

"Brad's coworker." Ronnie raised his voice. "Hey, Bree," he called, "how are ya?"

"Good, thanks." She stepped up into the house and stopped for a second as she saw Hayne. I snagged my phone off the charger in the hall and held it up for her to see. I tapped the screen and saw she'd called twice. There were also a few text messages from her, plus one from Wes and one from Captain.

"Bree, is it?" Hayne came over and offered a hand. "I'm Hayne."

"Hi." Bree flipped her glossy brown hair over her shoulder. "Are you a friend of the family's?"

"Ronnie and I did a couple tours together," he answered her. "Seen a lot over there. Makes you wanna stick with each other once you're back." He shook his leg when Ginger moved to sniff at his boot.

"Here, girl." Bree had picked up on Hayne's body language and pulled my pup back to her. She kept her hand on Ginger's back as she leaned her hip into the doorway. "I could only imagine. If it counts, thank you for your service."

"It counts." Hayne grinned. I rolled my eyes at his flirty tone as I held my phone to my ear. The ringing stopped, and Captain's voicemail kicked in.

Hayne continued to talk to Bree. "So, what brings you knock-ing today?"

"Need to see Brad and apparently Ginger." She babied my pup, then looked at me, and I held up a finger while I tried Wes. "Why are you calling them when I know what the news is?" Her hand went to her hip, and Hayne seemed entertained at her sass. Ginger sat at her feet and looked at me too.

"They called, and I was returning their calls," I muttered, then left a quick voicemail for Wes that I'd get the details from Bree.

"We need to go." I rushed over and snagged her arm and practically dragged her out the front door. I didn't need Hayne sinking his claws into someone like Bree.

"What the hell, Brad!" She fought to find her footing as I hurried us down the walk. I felt raindrops hit my face, and I knew a downpour was coming.

"Do we need to head into town, or can we work with whatever Wes gave us from here?" I ignored her pissed-off expression.

"He emailed us everything." She looked over her shoulder. "I have some paperwork laid out in my cabin that'll help us."

"Good." I steered her toward the path, and we sped up as a clap of thunder shook the ground. Suddenly, a shriek from the bushes made Bree jump right into my arms as we both had a collective heart attack—until a familiar snout and set of beady eyes appeared.

"Kevin!" Bree screamed at the pig and quickly tore herself from my arms. "Damn you, little porker. You'd look mighty fine on a sandwich, you little shit!" The little shit in question just squealed again and raced off. The last thing I saw was his little curly tail as he disappeared. "I know he gets some sick thrill out of trying to stop my heart." She positively fumed. I had to turn away so she wouldn't see how funny I found the whole situation.

"Come on, the rain's coming." I took her hand and pulled her along. Just as we reached her cabin's covered porch, the rain began. "Phew." Bree blew out a breath. "That was close. I'd hate to have to change again."

Kevin suddenly appeared as the rain eased a little, and I swore he had a grin on his face.

"Is it bad to wish that the heavens would open and rain so heavy it'd sweep that little sucker into the lake?" Bree whispered hopefully. We watched as he strutted up the drive toward the sound of a truck. Bree's dad, Jacob, rolled up and opened the door. The little porker made a run for it and jumped inside with Jacob's help. "That right there's the problem. He thinks he's a dog."

I couldn't help but laugh out loud at her expression.

"Bradley." Jacob waved. "How are you?"

"Well, sir, and how about you?"

"Good." He squinted at the sky. "Gonna rain heavy here soon. You two working?"

"Yes, sir."

Her father looked at Bree, who had her arms folded tightly around her. "Who pissed in your cereal, darlin'?"

She scoffed. "Your demon sidekick is determined to give me a heart attack." I pressed my lips together when Kevin put his hooves up on the car window to look out at us. "Why can't you just love our Finley and not waste it on that soon-to-be appetizer?"

"I'll have you know Kevin's won two county fairs and one state." He reached over and patted the ugly thing. "Maybe if you gave him a chance, you'd see he's not that bad."

"Hang out with Kevin Bacon? Unless he can teach me some dance moves from *Footloose*, I'm not interested." Bree shivered as the wind blew across us.

"Well, up to you. I'm glad to see you two together again. You best get inside now." He looked up at the sky, and I saw Bree scowl at the pig.

The heavens opened, and the rain came down in a sudden sheet, and with the help of the wind, we were soaked. I grabbed Bree's hand, and we raced inside.

Bree went to grab a towel as I peeled off my wet shirt and hung it on the back of a chair to dry. I put my shoulder holster on the side table.

I'd learned to carry it with me at all times, as I was really never off duty. I bent down and began to build a fire.

"No," I heard Bree exclaim behind me. I turned and caught her glare. "No way, I can't do this again."

"Do what?" I stepped back as the flame took off on the kindling.

"We need to find you a shirt." She opened up a drawer and started to dig. "There is only so much a woman can take, and because the world hates me and decided that double-A batteries can't be stocked here, I need to set boundaries."

"Boundaries?"

"Yes, boundaries with you and"—she raked her gaze down my front—"all that."

I joined her as she pulled out a tube top. "That's funny." I took it from her and tossed it back in the drawer. "Can we talk about Wes now?"

"Brad," she groaned. "All right, fine." She pulled back the curtains to expose her giant whiteboard. She had put up the photos of both victims, Shelly and Maggie, and had notes beneath them.

"Someone's been busy." I went over to examine her work, as she had done a lot since the last time I'd seen it. "And Wes?" I plucked one of the markers off the ledge and added a few more things I knew about the case.

"Right." She pulled her phone from her purse. "Wes said"—she swiped the screen a few times—"that the drug found in both victims was confirmed to be butterfly root moss."

"Okay, we knew that already, but we don't know how much or how deadly."

She nodded. "Right, and he said there was four milligrams in each victim. It's as potent as fentanyl." She glanced at me. "You don't need more than a few grains of fentanyl to take a person out, so it's like major overkill."

"Interesting." I let my head go with it.

"I agree, and Wes said that they found traces of it in their noses, throats, and lungs."

"They're inhaling it, not ingesting it." I studied the girls' photos and internally played out what I thought had happened.

"Seems that way." Bree squinted at her phone. "Wes said that, given the amount in their systems, the girls had only seconds before they felt the effects and minutes before they died."

"Okay, so he's comparing it to fentanyl, which is a hundred times stronger than morphine and fifty times stronger than heroin," I thought out loud. "If these women are being blasted with that much butterfly root moss, he made it a quick death."

She scoffed. "How big of him."

"Mm-hmm." I added Wes's findings to the board and stood back, letting it all sink in. "But what this gives us is a time between an inhale and death." She turned on her TV. I saw it was connected to her laptop. "Nice setup." I smiled. "Can you bring up the footage? Maybe we can start to eliminate those from outside those two minutes."

"Okay." Bree hit a few buttons on her laptop, and the surveillance video of Shelly White popped up.

"Fast forward to just before she gets to the bar." She did, and we watched. "Somewhere around here, she'd be inhaling it." I leaned forward on the couch and studied everyone who was close to her.

"Nothing stands out." Bree backed the video up, and we rewatched frame by frame all of Shelly's interactions. "All right, let me switch to Maggie Deloitte." I watched as her video popped up, and again, nothing seemed to stand out. "Is it possible he's got it in his mouth? Like something that shoots out as he speaks?"

"No." I couldn't see that happening. "It's too dangerous—he'd risk ingesting it himself." I rubbed my head. "All right, let's study the videos we got from Sophia and Maria."

Again, not one person stood out. Not even an eye shift. It was frustrating. I had been sure we'd get something. I leaned in closer to the TV as I watched Maria pass right by Maggie as she stumbled toward the entrance. "Go back to that," I called to Bree, "right there." She skipped the video back and hit play again. On the screen, someone reached for a free sample of the beer she was offering.

"Wait." I tilted my head and scratched my chin. "Back up like fifteen seconds." She did, and I saw it. There was a definite green color on the thumbnail that reached for the drink.

"Ha!" I slapped my knee and pointed at the screen.

"Son of a bitch." Bree leaned forward. "Given the angle, he watched her leave."

"Assuming that's him." I didn't want to get ahead of myself.

"It is, Brad, I know it!" Bree sounded certain.

"I agree." I moved to the whiteboard and drew two lines from both girls to the center and wrote *green thumbnail*. "If anything, it's a strong lead."

"Now what?"

"Now we talk to Cap and show him what we know, and hope Mr. Greenthumb shows himself again." I stepped back to take in the board as a whole. "And we start to dig on exactly where that butterfly root moss is sold here in the US."

"Isn't it strange—" She leaned back and pressed her lips into a straight line as she thought. "Somethin' bothers me here."

"What?" I liked how Bree's head worked. She was smart and thought everything through thoroughly.

She twisted toward me on the couch as I sat down next to her. "If this powder is inhaled, wouldn't that be risky? Other people around his victim might get sick, or at least have symptoms. Or even die."

"I thought of that, too, when you were reading off Wes's notes. I believe if this guy is spraying it right in his victims' faces, it sure lines up with the bartender's story and how he also got sick. He just got the tiniest bit."

"If that's the case, does it change anything?"

I rubbed my chin. "It gives us a whole new series of questions to ask the clubbers who were there those nights."

"Wouldn't that risk the killer finding out we're onto him?"

"Yeah, and it might even flush him out. More than anything, I'd like to hear everyone's answer. People who have something to hide either say too little or too much."

Her gaze drifted back to the board as we let this new direction sink in. "What about—"

Bang!

Bree nearly jumped right out of her skin as a gunshot echoed into the night. "I hope that was thunder!" Her eyes were like saucers as I grabbed my gun from the table and moved to the window and carefully peeked out. It was too dark and stormy to see much. "Can you see anything?"

"No." I squinted into the stormy darkness, and a lightning strike jolted across the sky and lit up our property across the way. *Oh no!* My stomach sank like a bowling ball, and I grabbed my boots and rushed toward the door. I didn't have to see to know what the hell was probably going on. I had been through this a few times now since he'd been back. "Stay here, and lock the door behind me," I ordered and closed the door as Bree said something. I jumped into ankle-deep mud and beat my arms at my sides as I sprinted across the property. Another shot rang into the storm. As I got closer, lightning lit up the entire place, and I saw him. I could only imagine what was going through his head. I swiped the rain from my face as I picked up speed and headed into the field toward him.

"Ronnie!" I yelled, but the storm was too wild, and he was clearly not in this world. He was in a whole other universe, facing God only knew what. As I got closer, I saw his face. His eyes were wild as he whipped his head around. Then he put Dad's hunting rifle up to his eye and expertly moved it around as he looked for the enemy. The cords in his neck stood out like thick ropes in his torment.

I quickly assessed the situation and figured the safest play was to join him in his moment rather than try to pull him back.

"Captain Stone!" I yelled as I army crawled toward him. I acted as if I was staying low for cover. "The eagle's en route. Hold your position."

"Identify yourself!" he yelled back and pointed the weapon at me.

"Corporal Brad Stone, sir. Alpha Company."

My brother wavered slightly as he glanced at me. Then he dropped down next to me. It was hard to see him this way. My older brother, whom I'd looked up to my whole life, was now a victim of PTSD. The demons that lived inside his head dragged him back in time to when his unit had been attacked one awful night. Out of the six guys, only he and Hayne had survived. The incident had screwed him up badly, and he'd been sent home. There'd been offers of help from the military, but the system was just so bogged down with similar cases that he was left languishing on a waiting list.

"I see them." Rain sprayed from his mouth. "Ten o'clock." He steadied his rifle. "There's two."

"Hold fire, Captain," I commanded, hoping like hell he'd listen. "Eagle is almost—"

He suddenly flipped around onto his back and pointed the rifle at Bree, who looked down at us.

"No, Ronnie!" I grabbed the gun as I threw myself on top of him, and we rolled together. The rifle pointed toward the sky. "It's me, Bradley! You're home, Ronnie. You're home!"

Bang! It went off again, and the look on his face was pure terror as the realization came to him that it was me. He threw his arms over his face and suddenly went limp. Quickly, I unloaded the gun and tossed it as far from us as I could.

I hopped to my feet and went to Bree.

"What the hell were you thinking?" I tried not to yell out of my own fear.

"I was worried about you." She looked over at Ronnie. "Are you guys okay?"

Ronnie sat up, pulled his knees up close to his chest, and dropped his head. "I'm sorry, I'm sorry, Bradley."

"Don't be." I bent down in front of him. "It's not your fault."

"Don't." He closed his eyes, and I knew my brother lived in a world of pain. "I could have killed you." He looked over at Bree, his face white. "I could have killed you both."

"But you didn't." She came close and rubbed his arm as I quickly called my dad to come outside. "Brad was here."

I was thankful that Dad came so quickly. He pulled Ronnie to his feet and shot me a look. "It's okay, Bradley. I've got him. Take Bree home." He squeezed my arm. "It'll be okay."

Without another word, I took Bree by the hand, and we jogged back toward her cabin. We were sopping wet when we burst through the door. I shook myself and took a deep inhale. My head was in a tailspin. My concern for my brother had grown more intense.

"What just happened, Brad?" I turned around and saw her wild eyes.

I reached for her and pulled her to me and slammed my lips to hers to shut out the horror of it all. I needed grounding, and I needed it from her. Her body molded into mine, mirroring every ounce of my intensity. We couldn't get enough; our kisses were deep and passionate. I took her in my arms and lifted her onto the table, and she wrapped her legs around my waist as we ravished each other's mouths. My erection pressed into her belly, and I let out a growl from deep within my throat.

"Brad." I barely heard her speak. Then she pressed a hand against my chest, and I pulled back. She eyed my chest and stomach with such hunger that I lost myself again. "Christ, Brad, I think—"

I slammed my mouth back to hers to swallow her words. Her hands ran over my bare shoulders and into my hair, deepening the kiss.

Her touch soothed the storm inside. All thoughts of my brother had gone from my head. I ran my hands up under her shirt and palmed her wet breasts.

"Oh my god, you're making this hard," she groaned.

I lowered her hand and brushed it over my erection, and the feeling was unreal. "You're telling me." I broke free for a moment, pressed my forehead to hers, and tried to slow myself down. I moved my lips to her neck and devoured her smooth skin, as her hips ground against me.

"I want you to be with me, Bree. I've always wanted you." The words slipped from my lips, and I felt her go stiff.

"Brad," she put a hand on my chest and pushed me back gently. "Brad, I've wanted this too. But we work together now, and—"

"I know." I caught her lips again, then spoke against them. "I don't care about that."

She pulled away again. "It's not just that. My life's in New York City, and I can't see myself living back here." I knew she had a life in the city, but this was home. This was where she needed to be, here and with me. "Damn, I can't think straight. Look, Brad, I'm not denying I want you, but there's a lot going on right now, and everything's up in the air. Besides, being back has opened old wounds."

"Wounds," I whispered. I knew her words weren't just about that day at the river. Bree had left the day I asked Sherry to marry me, and I knew I'd hurt her.

"Yeah." She brushed her hair back from her face. "Look, Brad, can we just get through this case and see what happens?"

I nodded. She was right. We had a case to work on, and I had a lot to figure out. I leaned down so we were at eye level. "I understand what you're saying." I gently tugged at her nipple, and her lips parted with a silent moan. "I guess I'll just have to convince you to stay."

She smiled weakly.

"I do love a good challenge." I moved in slowly and kissed her jaw. "I'll call you later." Somehow I ripped myself away from her and let myself out the door. If I'd looked back, I wouldn't have been able to leave.

Chapter Ten

BREE

The process of interviewing thirteen people who might have inhaled the drug cocktail was utterly exhausting. It literally took all day. No one had come forward before we asked the question about not feeling well, but suddenly we had about ten hypochondriacs to deal with and only a few solid nos.

One man spoke about his possible exposure to the poison: "I felt like this lump in my throat, and then I think I had a fever."

Brad glanced at me, and I closed my eyes. It was almost seven o'clock at night, and my patience was growing thin. I knew I couldn't deal with these people much longer.

"I thought I was going to have to call 911," the man continued, "but after I threw up, I felt better."

"Is it possible you were just hungover?" Brad tried not to roll his eyes.

"Ah," the man stumbled, like he had never thought of that.

"Three beers and"—Brad lifted the paperwork—"six shots would make me want to vomit."

The man's face reddened as Brad's suspicions hit hard. "Yeah, I'm not sure, Detective, but I think I had a good dose of whatever took those two women down."

"I don't think so," Brad said and licked his lips, "because if you had a good dose, you'd be dead."

"Oh, I'm not dead."

I had to hold back my laughter at that response.

Brad stood and ran a hand through his hair. "That's all for now. Thanks for stopping by."

"If you need anything else, you've got my number." The guy nearly tripped over his chair on the way out. Brad leaned his weight onto the table and chuckled.

"We have one possible person who actually felt something." I tried to look at the positive side of this crapshoot. "But it's still not enough."

"Nope." Brad pulled out his phone, and his jaw ticced. "Shit, I have to go. Are you okay to head back home without me?"

"I think I'll manage." I gave him a wry look and started to gather my things. Brad stopped at the door.

"Look Bree, about Ronnie." His face said it all.

"He didn't do any damage," I assured him. "I'm just sorry that he's going through that."

"Yeah." Brad tapped the doorframe with his fist. "Hard to see him like that."

"It is." I slipped my bag over my shoulder and squeezed his arm as I passed. "He's lucky to have you."

"And I'm lucky to have you." He gave me a playful smirk.

"As partners, you mean." I slit my eyes at him even as I felt my own regret.

"That too. I'll call you later," Brad called out.

"Sounds good." I waved over my shoulder.

I stepped outside the station and breathed in the fresh air, happy to be away from everyone's sudden syndromes. Lord, people could be heavy at times. I thought of Brad and wondered if it was Sherry who'd pulled him away. I was sure it was. A movement caught my attention, and I quickly turned to see Hayne.

"I was hoping to catch you." He leaned against his car with a smile. "So, I heard you like Italian food?"

I hesitated and looked at the time. I wasn't overly hungry yet, and I wanted to go home and shower and change.

He pushed off the car when he saw my hesitation. "All right"—he tucked his hands into his pockets—"if you're not feeling that, how about coffee then?"

Ugh, my weakness. "I can do coffee." I shifted my bag on my shoulder and headed toward his car and hopped in.

"How was your day?" He couldn't hide the fact that he was pleased that he'd gotten me to agree to join him.

I let out a long-tired breath. "Why don't we talk about your day instead?"

"Sounds good to me." He tipped his head in agreement, and we headed toward the coffee shop.

We got our respective brews and sat in a booth together. He entertained me with talk about his struggles in the army, and I tried to keep up, but a few yawns escaped before I could stifle them.

"You're tired." He studied my face.

"Yeah, it's been a day for sure. I'm really sorry, Hayne. I guess I shouldn't have accepted your invite."

"Hey, not a problem at all. I kind of caught you off guard. So, Friday, Italian?"

"Oh, gosh, I'm not sure. My days change from one to the next. And to be truthful, Hayne, I'm not looking for any kind of relationship right now. I'm not sure how long I'm staying in town."

His face fell with disappointment. "That's too bad, but a girl's got to eat. Surely you can fit one dinner into your busy schedule for a *friend.*" He emphasized the word. "I'll pick you up at six."

"I'll have to get back to you on that."

"You know I've got a good feeling about this, so six o'clock it is. Come on, I'll run you back to your car." I was too tired to argue.

When I got home, I found my mother in the kitchen, making some of her famous muffins. I dropped my bag on the floor and sank onto the stool at the island.

"Hi, sweetie." She grinned at me. "How was your day?"

I shrugged. "I'm exhausted," I groaned. "We interviewed a bunch of hypochondriacs that got us nowhere."

"People want to help," Mom said as she slid the batter into the oven, "and sometimes they go about it the wrong way."

"It was the power of suggestion." I grimaced.

"I know." She kissed my cheek and placed a warm muffin in front of me. "You missed dinner, but I put leftovers in the fridge in your cabin. These are for the morning, but try one and give me your thoughts."

"With pleasure." My stomach grumbled painfully.

I popped a piece of the pastry into my mouth and moaned. "Mom, these are amazing. The guests are going to love them."

"I'm glad," she sighed. "It's nice to know I'm useful for something." That caught my attention.

"Mom?"

She turned with an apologetic look. "Sorry, just feeling sorry for myself, I guess." She sat on a stool and looked at me. "Now I'm getting older, I'm floundering a bit. Not sure where I fit."

"Not sure where you fit?" I repeated. "I've only been back for a bit, but I can see how much this place needs you. You're a major cog in the wheel. Without you, Lainey wouldn't have helped with all the food, and Patrick wouldn't have all those homemade blankets you make and sell on the website. I might add, by the way, you've gotten over six hundred reviews as of yesterday."

"Really?" She raised a brow.

"Yes, and jeez, Mom, Charley would be stuck handling all the guest check-ins himself if you weren't here. Not only that, but you also put cookies and leftovers and yummy stuff in my fridge to keep me from starving. We couldn't possibly have all this without you."

She smiled then and tossed the dish towel onto the counter. "Thank you, sweetie. I think sometimes I just feel that since my hip problems, I'm not as useful as I once was. Add age on top of it and my children all grown up . . . Sometimes you just wonder what your purpose is anymore."

"You're more than just a great cook, Ma. Utilize that." I hopped off the stool. "Let's be real, this place wouldn't even exist if it weren't for you and Dad."

"Thank you, again, sweetheart. I think I really needed that."

I kissed her cheek and grabbed my bag. "Love you, Mom, and I especially love your baking." I swiped another muffin and headed to my cabin.

My phone vibrated just as I got home. I sighed heavily. It was a struggle to balance everything going on with my life and work. I read the screen.

Sophia: I'm working tonight, talking to my friend, she thinks she saw ninja turtle guy. Can you stop by?

Oh, shit. The message had been sent thirty minutes ago. I rushed inside my cabin and dumped my things on the table and quickly sent off a text.

Bree: Hey, sorry just saw this now. Have you spotted him yourself?

I quickly called Brad, but it went straight to voicemail. I left a brief message, then sank into a chair as I thought about how to handle this situation.

Sophia: Yes, he's here.

I was immediately nervous and excited at the same time. This was our chance.

Bree: What do you notice about him? What's he wearing? Can
you tell me where he is in the club? Who's he watching?
Sophia: He's watching the girls in sexy dresses like the kind you
see in Vegas.

I channeled my inner Brad and thought what he would say at
this point.
Bree: Can you tell me what he looks like? I tried again, but no reply.

Bree: I'm coming. I'll text you when I arrive.

I eyed my closet, then went through my dresses. My eyes landed on
a black dress from my Quantico partying days, and I decided it would
be perfect.

Bree: Sophia keep your distance but if you can get his face on
camera that would be huge.
Sophia: I'm trying to get his face for you. I'll show you as soon
as you get here.

I rushed to get ready.
"Damn, girl," Lainey said as she caught me on the way to my truck.
"Who's the lucky guy that gets to see you in that tonight?"
"Nope, too much." Charley suddenly appeared and pointed at my
exposed cleavage. "Back inside you go."
I rolled my eyes at him. Charley was as bad as my twin.
"Tell me that's for Bradley." Lainey grinned.
"Sorry to disappoint." I yanked open my old truck door and
hopped in. "But this little baby is about to catch a killer."
"Hang on." Charley held my door open. "Come again?"
"Our one and only suspect has been spotted at the club, so I'm
going undercover to see if I can catch his attention."
"Does Bradley know?"

"He will once he looks at his phone." I yanked my seat belt across my body. "Besides, the place is crawling with police, and I fully plan on calling Cap right now to get him to alert the guys."

"I don't like this." Lainey looked at Charley.

"Me neither." He shook his head, then looked up at the sky. "She won't listen to us."

"I'm right here."

"Maybe we should call Bradley ourselves?" Lainey pulled out her phone, and I slammed the door closed but rolled down the window so it didn't seem rude.

"Seriously, guys." I laughed. "I'm not reckless and never have been." I skirted around the few times I had been. "I very much like my life and won't risk it for some loser. I got this." I started the old engine, and after two tries, it roared to life. "Believe it or not, this isn't the most dangerous thing I've done."

"Don't tell me those things." Lainey held up a hand. "Shit, just check in, okay?"

"We really need some help with this case," I tried to explain.

"Don't you have someone else who could go? I get people to do things for me all the time." Charley shook his head, and I could tell he wasn't happy about me going.

"I promise, I'll be careful." I waited for them to step back so I could swing around the loop in the driveway and head into town.

The club was in full swing by the time I arrived. Nelly's "Hot in Herre," to my surprise, was blasting from the speakers, and a sea of people danced away to the beat. I couldn't reach Cap on the way in, but I did leave a detailed message and made sure to show my ID to the bouncer and the police and let them know my intentions.

"You're working with Detective Stone, right?" one of the officers asked.

Bree: I'm here, where are you?

"Yes, we are." I tried to recall what he had just said.

The officer was undercover in street clothes, and he shifted his belt in a poor attempt for me to look down at his crotch. "He's a lucky man."

"More like *lucky me*," I tossed back and headed into the crowd to see if I could spot Sophia. I did a quick once-over of my dress in the mirrored wall on the way down the stairs. My dress was open in the back and had a thin lattice detail down the front. It complemented my cleavage, and I felt nerve-rackingly sexy. Once I joined the crowd of other women who were dressed much like I was, I felt I didn't stand out as much and took a breath to reassure myself.

I glanced at my phone and saw no missed calls or messages, but it was getting close to 1 a.m. *Sophia, where are you?*

The dance floor was much too crowded to spot anyone. I felt like a ball in a pinball machine, being bounced around by the crowd. I glanced at the time again, and, worried, I moved to the bar, where I flashed my ID at the bartender. He recognized me, as we'd met before with Brad, and I asked for a mocktail. I knew not to drink on the job. I wasn't going to risk anything being thrown out or used against me in court.

"On the house," he yelled, and I mouthed a thank-you. I kept my place at the bar but turned to face the club and scanned all the faces around me. There was no sign of Sophia. *Come on, you sorry excuse for a murderer, where are you?* Out of the corner of my eye, I felt someone watching me. I tried to take in what I could see, but it was tricky, as the place was so packed. Dark hair, taller than me, slimmer build. After a few moments, I sucked on the straw and made a face like it tasted funny. Slowly, I turned toward the bar, but as soon as I did, the man I'd tried to get a look at turned away from me and faded into the line of people farther down the bar.

"Okay?" the bartender asked. I nodded and made a movement with my eyes that I might have spotted something. He stepped back and switched the way he was accepting orders, making sure not to head the way I motioned. Smart man. Someone tipped over their drink on the bar, and I heard a girl's voice as she apologized. She was only three people down, and when I glanced that way, I caught a man's hand as it reached out to right the girl's drink—and I spotted the green nail. I froze for a millisecond before I stepped back and saw a guy heading for the exit.

"Hey, man." I hit his shoulder, and he whirled around with a nasty expression. "Sorry, but I think you have something on your hands." I reached down and lifted his hand to see his nails were clean.

"What the hell?" He snarled and ripped his hands away.

"Sorry." I stepped back. "My mistake."

An earth-shattering scream tore through the place, and instantly, something cold ran through me. I beat my way through the crowd as other officers and bouncers followed suit. I followed the sound of sobbing straight into the room marked EMPLOYEES ONLY and saw Maria on the floor holding Sophia. My mind immediately went to Shelly and Maggie. It was obvious Sophia was dead.

"No one leaves!" I shouted at the bouncers and police to bar the exits. I checked Sophia's pulse on her wrist even though I knew she was gone.

"Is she alive?" Maria sobbed.

I looked up at the officer I had spoken to earlier as I shook my head. He spoke into his phone as the weight of what had just happened sank in. I reached over and hugged Maria, who had completely fallen apart. I didn't blame her.

"Come on." I helped her to her feet and walked her back out to the dance floor. The music had stopped, and officers were asking people to remain calm as they attempted to herd them into groups against the walls. In the moments after the screams, I knew there had been time for a lot of people to escape in panic. Hopefully, the cameras would help identify any of those who had run through the doors.

The officers were asking anyone who had footage or pictures to send them to a designated email address, while they pleaded for calm.

"Bree?" Brad and Kennedy came rushing in with their jerseys on. Clearly, they got the call while playing hockey, given that they were sweaty.

"I'm fine." I left Maria's side and waved them away from the others. "I know he was here, but dammit, I didn't get a good look at him."

Brad moved in front of me and looked me up and down. "Were you trying to be his next victim?" His voice had an edge to it. "That dress would certainly draw his attention."

"Yes, that's exactly what I was trying to do—I was trying to prevent someone else from being killed, Brad."

"Okay," he said, lowering his voice as he looked around, and that's when I saw Cap arrive. "And what exactly were you going to do once you caught his attention? Tell him to wait while you wave over an officer? Christ, Bree, you don't even carry cuffs!"

"Hey," the officer I had been dealing with called to Brad as he did a gawking sweep up my front. He got a hard look from Brad in return. "Did your rent-a-cop recognize anyone?"

"What?" Brad spoke sharply.

I fought to hold my temper back. "I'm a consultant with the SPD."

He smirked. "Cute."

Brad went to move, but I put a hand on his chest and shook my head. "We have more important things to deal with than this small-minded officer who clearly doesn't have respect for females."

"Whoa." He held up his hands when another officer shot him a nasty look. "Don't make this a thing." He spoke over my head to Brad, "I was just asking if anyone stood out since she was on the dance floor, and over there"—he pointed—"toward the bar. I mean, maybe she saw something."

Brad pressed his lips together, trying to hold back his words, then looked at me.

"I thought I saw his fingers, but maybe I didn't."

Poor Maria sounded confused as she tried to get through her statement to Kennedy.

"What a fucking nightmare." Cap's tired expression spoke volumes. "I've got the bureau so far up my ass I can taste what they had for dinner." He looked at me. "Sophia was strangled."

"What!" That completely blew me out of the water.

"I need to get all the details, but I don't get why the killer would change his method. Maybe she caught him off guard, and he panicked."

"Holy shit." Brad ran a hand through his wet hair. "Do you think this could be the work of someone new?"

"Look, Bree." Captain's chest rose and fell. "I appreciate what you were doing here. I also applaud the way you let everyone know what was happening."

I eyed Brad. "Thanks, Cap."

"I disagree."

"Well that's your opinion." I rolled my eyes. I understood it was a big risk, but I saw what I saw. "Cap, I do think I spotted the green-thumb guy."

"Really?" That seemed to perk him up. "All right, fill me in, and then let's get through all these people as fast as possible."

After I filled him in, I gladly accepted the coffees that were offered to us as Cap moved away a few steps with his phone in his hand.

"Do me a favor"—Brad puffed out a breath—"wear this for me." He held up his jacket. "It's distracting." He looked around as I slipped it on without argument. "All right, let's do this."

We worked well into the next day. People's faces started blurring together, which might have been due to my lack of sleep. Kennedy made sure we all got fed around midafternoon, but it wasn't until six o'clock that night that we were officially finished with the interviews, fingerprints, DNA swabs—the list went on. In the end, though, we got nothing. No one saw anything out of the ordinary. We still had a little more footage to go through, but it seemed highly improbable that we would get anything useful. After all that, we had a dead young woman and a heartbroken best friend.

"Don't carry Sophia's death on your shoulders." Kennedy gave me a pat and looked at me. I felt he mistook my exhaustion for sadness. "Sadly, leaning on a potential witness is a risk we take to solve a case. It's not the first time someone tried to help and got caught in the crosshairs."

"I know." I nodded. I really was tired, but there was a little piece of me that wondered if I had played a role in what had happened. I wished I hadn't asked her to try to get a photo of his face.

"Good." He gave my shoulder a light squeeze and flagged down his partner, Ellis. The great thing about Kennedy was that he said his piece and that was that.

Lainey: Just know I'm here if you need me.

Lainey and Charley must have called me twenty times. She needed to be sure I was all right, and I'd assured her I was fine. She hadn't been happy, but I'd explained I had a few more things to deal with before I could go home.

I leaned against the wall and fought to keep my eyes open while Brad spoke to Mr. Longboard, the owner of the nightclub, to try to convince him to keep it closed until the killer was caught. There was no way he was going for that.

"Prick," Brad hissed as he sat down next to me. "He refuses to close. Profit is more important than people's lives."

"Then the next death is on him." I yawned.

"How was your coffee date with Hayne?"

My mouth dropped. *How did he know?*

"Oh, he made sure I knew about it." He looked down at me and was about to say something else when his phone rang. "Damn, one second." He stepped away, and I guessed it was Sherry. I was sure she'd gotten wind of what had happened and knew I'd be with him.

"Damn, Sherry has been blowing up his phone continuously. Sometimes I think she totally forgets we have a job to do," Kennedy muttered. "So how was your date with Hayne?" He grinned.

"It was far from a date. Did Brad tell you that?"

"No, I was there when Hayne made sure Brad knew."

"Shit, Bree, I have to go." Brad slipped his phone into his pocket. "Here." He pulled out a set of keys. "Sleep at my place—you're too tired to drive home."

All I could picture was him and Sherry coming back to his place with me there. *No way.* "I'm fine. I'll text you when I get home. I need a shower, change of clothes, and a large pizza all to myself." I pushed off the wall and gave my neck a stretch.

"I have a shower, I have clothes, and I can have a pizza sent to my house before you even get there."

He walked me outside, and I shrugged off his coat, and he hesitated. "Brad, let's not poke the bear. Clearly, Sherry needs you right now, and I'm fine." When he huffed out an exasperated breath, I raised a brow. "Thank you, but I'm good." I handed his coat to him.

His mouth pursed as he studied my outfit again, then he brushed his hair back from his eyes. "I'm sorry. Okay, let me deal with her, and I'll check in on you later. Ray!" he called out to the older detective. "I want you to walk Bree to her truck."

"All right." Ray didn't look pleased, but he just shrugged.

I shot Brad a slit-eyed look.

"My place or you let him walk you to the truck."

"I don't think he likes me," I said quietly as I pulled my purse over my arm.

He checked the time. "You'll be fine. Just call me when you get home. Okay?"

"Yes, sir." I rolled my eyes, then he leaned in with a grin.

He let his lips linger at my jawbone, but to anyone else, it would look like he was speaking to me quietly. "That's my girl."

His three simple words sent my libido into overdrive. My skin heated, my chest heaved, and my thighs clenched together. I felt sixteen again. But as quickly as the thrill went through me, flickers of Sophia's lifeless body pushed through, and our moment quickly faded.

"Call me later." He tapped my bare thigh as he pulled back. I blinked and tried to gather myself from the grief that had taken over me. "Night."

I watched him race off in the opposite direction of my truck with the phone to his ear. "Night," I managed to whisper as I clung to the thrill that ran through me.

Ray walked over to join me, and I took a deep breath of chilly air and folded my arms. I wished I'd kept Brad's jacket. Mine was in the truck along with my warm boots.

I fought for something to say. "I forgot how quickly the sun drops this time of year." Ray wasn't good at small talk. He barely got words out before he questioned someone.

"So, you think you saw him?" Ray grunted in the normal cranky voice he used with me.

I nodded. "Yes, I do, which is why I want to see all the footage, not just what the owner offered us."

"There're protocols in place."

"And I understand that," I said and tried to curb my frustration. "I'm just saying I hope that something shows itself before anyone else dies."

"Does this mean you'll be sticking around town?"

I looked over at him. "Would that bother you?"

"What bothers me is Cap bringing in someone with no experience and no education or understanding of the justice system just so we can bend the rules a little." He made no move to start walking.

"My truck isn't far. Can we go?" I was frozen, and now he'd pissed me off. "And to address your comment, first, I *am* educated and have a very good understanding of the justice system. Second, from what I hear, you have quite the reputation for bending the rules from time to time as well."

"Stone tell you that?"

"No." I would never toss Brad under the bus. "But people talk."

"Yeah, well, don't believe everything you hear."

I chuckled. "Shouldn't that go both ways?" I winced as my feet throbbed. Wearing heels for so many hours was a bad idea. I groaned as we made our way through the parking lot and onto the street. "Ray, you seem to have had a problem with me since the day I arrived. Why is that?"

"The guys don't need the distraction. We need to stay focused—not showing up at a club to find our *consultant* dressed like a pinup girl in some sleazy tattoo parlor."

"Wow." I laughed in disbelief. "Please don't sugarcoat your answer."

"I never have, and I ain't startin' with you."

I turned to face him dead on, tired of his attitude. "Fine, have a problem with me, snicker behind my back about how I dress. I had to play the part of a female looking to blow off some steam. I did everything by the book, just like you would have if you were undercover. I know I was close to luring him out."

"But you didn't lure him out," he said, and I saw red. "Fuck." He suddenly held a hand up in my face as he answered a call. Wow, he was rude.

I stepped back with a curse of my own.

"Yeah, all right." He hung up and looked over his shoulder in the direction we came from. "I forgot something."

"As much as this conversation has been the highlight of my evening, please go." My voice dripped with sarcasm as I waved him off. "My truck's just around the corner in the parking garage."

"Don't have to tell me twice." He turned on his heel and headed back toward the club.

"What an asshole." I felt the exhaustion kick back in as I rounded the corner and headed through the parking lot. Normally, I'd make an extra effort with people to try to make them see me for who I was, but Ray could suck it. I didn't think he even wanted to see me any differently. He'd made up his mind about me. "Stubborn ass." I shook the stress from my body as I thought of the comfort I'd soon have in my favorite jammies. The idea of curling up in the back of my pickup also appealed.

A ripple of fear suddenly went through me as my ears picked up a sound. I focused on the footsteps that I could hear behind me. I turned, but no one was there. "You're fine, Bree." I needed to keep my head focused, or it could spin out to dark places. I pulled out my keys and threaded them through my fingers. *Solar plexus, instep, nose, and groin.* I chanted the SING self-defense moves repeatedly. I'd taken several classes over the years, and though I wasn't the best at self-defense, at least I tried and knew the basics. My biggest hurdle was always my mental state—anything remotely terrifying brought me right back to that day at the river and the way his eyes had paralyzed me. One of my teachers told me my head would be my downfall if I were ever attacked. Maybe he was right, but therapy just wasn't for me.

I kept my quick pace and even contemplated removing my shoes to stop their echo, but that would mean having to slow down.

Again, the sound found its way to me, and my fingers flexed around my purse strap. There was no need to panic. I wasn't the only one parked here. A car from above came rolling down, looking for the exit. They slowed when they saw me, and I fought the urge to flag them down. I didn't want to be alone in the garage.

Finally, I spotted my truck and breathed a sigh of relief, but it was short lived. I heard a sudden quick footstep behind me. With terror coursing through me, I forced myself to turn around. Then, like in my nightmare, I saw a figure step out from between two cars. My entire body went cold as the person, dressed in jeans and a dress shirt, with some sort of rag over his face, took a step toward me. His ball cap cast a shadow over his face, so I couldn't see his eyes. My knees felt weak.

"Bree Jaminson," he called out. My mouth went dry, and my hands shook. "I thought it was time we met."

No.

"You're so much prettier than your videos." The ringing in my ears made it hard to think.

"How." I struggled to get my words from my brain to my lips. "How do you know my name?"

He lifted his head, and for a split second the light above him revealed his eyes. The wrinkles around them seemed like he smiled, but then they were masked by the shadow again. He pulled his hand out of his pocket, and I saw the stain on his thumb. "I know a lot more than your name."

"Who are you? What videos?" I tried to buy myself a moment to think while my brain spun out on me.

His head tilted. "I think you already know who I am." He took a step toward me, and I lost it.

Fight or flight kicked in, and I flexed the keys in my palm as I counted in my head. *One, two, three.* I took off running toward my truck, my heels pounding the pavement as I fought for traction. My fingers shook when I desperately tried to insert the key into the old truck door.

I glanced at the reflection in the window to make sure he wasn't coming up behind me. Finally, I yanked the door open, hopped inside, locked the door, and started the beast's engine. I didn't look for other cars—I just pulled out and tore toward the exit, then checked my mirrors, but there was no sign of him following. My heart beat out of my chest as it looked for some kind of escape, and it only slowed when I got out of there and into a more populated area. At a stoplight, I pulled out my phone with shaky hands and called Brad. It went straight to voicemail again. *Damn.*

I jumped when the car behind me beeped. I looked at it in the mirror and then saw the light had changed. My foot moved to the gas, and I waved as I headed toward the highway. No streetlights lined the roads, and I realized that meant I got a nice panoramic view of the night sky. *I no longer want that.* "Breathe, Bree." I lifted a hand from the steering wheel and saw it was trembling.

A truck came up on me quickly and rode my bumper. I tapped my brakes for him to go around if he wanted to pass. "Christ, is there something in the water tonight?"

I waved for him to go around, but he stayed glued to my bumper. *Oh no, it has to be him!* Then, like that night Brad and I were followed, a giant light bar was turned on, and I was blinded. I quickly tilted my mirror and stepped on the gas.

"Ah!" I swerved to the side as I tried to blink away the black spots. Goose bumps broke out across my skin. My foot pushed harder on the gas, and my old truck fought to pick up speed. "Come on, girl," I begged as I squinted at the lights behind me. This guy was psychotic! He sped up and matched my speed without hesitation. I swung over to the opposite side of the road, and he followed. I moved back, and he mirrored me. I grabbed my phone and tried Brad again. "Come on, come on! Fuck!" His phone must have been turned off. "What detective turns off his phone!" I shouted in anger. I needed something to control my fear.

Bang! The truck hit my bumper, and I was thrown forward hard against the wheel.

I screamed and tried to get the truck under control. *Screw this!* I called 911.

"911, what's your emergency?"

"I'm Bree Jaminson, with the Sheffield Police Department." I sobbed out my words, I was so happy to get a real person. "I'm on the highway heading south, and there's a truck behind me—" *Bang!* I was hit again, and my phone went flying to the floor. "Don't hang up!" I pleaded. "It's the same truck that ran us off the road once before!" I tried to give as much information as I could in hopes the dispatcher could still hear me.

The truck behind me suddenly pulled back, and I took that moment to unclip my safety belt, duck down, and grab my phone. I hit gravel and shot back up just in time to miss taking out a speed limit sign. I swung back onto the road and was again blinded by his light bar. When I looked at the screen, I saw the call had disconnected. "What do you want from me?" I screamed and hit the dash just as he hit my bumper again. "Stop!" I cried as I fought the wheels to stay on the pavement. "Please just stop!" Tears poured down my cheeks, and my vision blurred. I quickly tried to dash them away with my hand, but the moment I took my hand off the steering wheel, he hit me again.

My phone lit up, and I saw it was the 911 dispatcher calling back.

"Hello!" I was careful to hold the wheel while I gripped the phone. "Hello!" but I couldn't bring the phone to my ear and only managed to hang up. Frustrated, I let out a scream and almost dropped the damn thing as it rang again. This time I managed to hit the speaker button.

"Bree, are you okay?"

"Dale? Oh my god. Listen." My lips shook as I tried to think straight, reminding myself I was talking to my ex. "Dale, I'm being chased. There's this truck that ran us off the road." The rest of the words jammed up in my mind. "It's him again. I need you to call the police for me." I cried as the truck got closer, "I think he's try-ing to kill—"

Everything happened so fast, I never had time to react. The truck clipped my bumper again, and I went into a tailspin across the road. I saw the big rock as I hit it and was launched into the air. My phone went flying out of my hand as the truck dipped forward, and I hit what felt like concrete. The last thing I saw was a blinding white light before it all went dark.

"Ooooh," I moaned as I came to. Pain shot through my head, and I touched something wet on my forehead. I opened my eyes to look at my fingers and saw blood.

Everything came at me at once, and I saw I was underwater in my truck. I tried to clear my head, but it was difficult to see, and I realized I had hit the windshield. A whole new level of fear came over me as I assessed the situation. I was now sinking into the lake in my truck, but my window was still above the water line. I reached to roll it down when bright lights lit me up like a Christmas tree.

"No!" I cried as I realized he was there, parked on the side of the road, waiting for me. My head pounded as I watched the water rise around my feet.

"Wait." I felt around for my phone but saw it on the floor under the water. I wondered if it was still connected to Dale. I leaned forward and felt the truck tip. "Whoa!" I quickly sat back as I realized it was better to hold still. The water was up to my waist, and I tried hard not to think about what else might be in there with me. "You got this," I yelled at myself. "Think!" But then I broke—everything that I had been holding onto came rushing out in one big wail of a cry. The harder I sobbed, the more it felt like my head was going to explode. The water reached my chest, and I knew I had to fight if I was going to survive. I tried to steady my breathing.

I could still see the lights of the truck that had forced me off the road. I figured he was waiting to see if I'd suddenly appear.

"Don't die, don't die." I thought hard about everything I could remember from my training and books I'd read, trying to come up with an idea. I tipped my head back as the water covered my shoulders and sucked at the last pocket of air that was left. I had to wait for the truck to fully submerge.

Everything went quiet as I sank farther into the unknown, and I knew I didn't have much air left. Finally, I had no choice left, so I rolled the window down slowly to let the pressure equal out around me. Then

I wiggled out of my seat and through the window and pushed off the roof to help speed up my swim toward the surface.

I couldn't see any lights, and I prayed he'd given up and left. Everything was so black. I tried to angle my swim so I didn't come up right above the truck. My lungs begged to breathe, and a few times I had to cover my mouth to stop the uncontrollable action. I wouldn't die that way. I refused to die before I knew the face of the man who haunted me.

My legs cramped just as I felt the surface with my fingertips. With one last effort, I kicked with all my might and broke the water line. I sucked in a mouthful of air and water, then coughed and went back under, but I managed to resurface again. I looked desperately around. *Is he trying to wait me out? Does he see me? Does he know I'm alive?*

With the last of my energy, I began to swim toward the shore until I could touch it.

"Bree!" Brad's voice came from somewhere, and I fought to stay with it as the rocks on the shoreline dug into my aching body. "Bree, where are you?"

"How do you know she's here?" someone asked.

"Her location says she's in the fucking lake!" Brad barked at someone, then I heard footsteps get closer. "Bree!" I could hear him again. His desperate call forced me to focus, and I tried to answer back, but all I could do was cough and sputter.

"Bree! Over here! She's here." I heard him shout, then felt him drop to his knees beside me. "Holy shit! Get the medic over here," he hollered again as he rolled me onto my side. "Hurry, she needs help!" he yelled, and then there were people above me. Things went in and out for me then. I couldn't take the confusion, and, exhausted, I fell back into the comfortable darkness.

One moment, Brad was there, and the next, I wore a neck brace and was being lifted onto a hard board with a mask over my mouth. I came to again and felt a needle stuck in my arm. There were bright lights everywhere, and Brad was back.

"I need to know if she's okay," Brad's voice pleaded with the paramedic. "I know time's important here, but please, Kelly, is she okay?"

"Her head hit something hard, Stone. Let's just hope it's only a concussion, but I can't rule out something worse until she has a scan. I'm also concerned about her lungs and the possibility of a secondary drowning. She's still got water in there. She needs to be at the hospital, not in the back of my rig. Now get out, and let me do my job." She pressed a wad of gauze against my forehead and taped it.

I reached out for Brad's hand and tried to let him know I was okay. He looked down at me and squeezed my hand.

"You hang in there, Bree. Don't you die on me." His voice cracked.

"Stone!" Cap's voice cut through our moment. "We've got a location on the truck! Let them deal with Jaminson so we can get this bastard!" Brad pulled his hand from mine as the last voice in the entire world I wanted to hear spoke up.

"Go, Bradley. I'll ride with Bree, so she won't be alone, and if anything changes, I'll call you."

I begged Brad with my eyes, but he looked away.

"Come on, man, you can't do anything anyway." I couldn't see Kennedy, but I knew it was him. "Let's get this guy."

"Bree, I'll be back soon. I promise you. I have to go." He squeezed my hand again, and it lingered there for a moment.

"I got her." Brad's face was replaced by Sherry's. *Is this a nightmare?* She smiled down at me. Then the ambulance doors closed with a bang, and Sherry settled in next to me. The EMT started taking my vitals as someone banged on the door, and we were off with the sirens blaring. I closed my eyes as the sound became too much.

"I need you to stay with me, Bree." Kelly squeezed my arm. "I need you to fight the urge to sleep." I didn't like that idea.

"Bree?" Sherry loomed over me. Her eyes mocked sympathy. "I know Brad and I are divorced, but you should know he struggled with a deep depression for several years. He just didn't seem to care about anything, and it drove a wedge in our marriage, and at some point, I just couldn't take it anymore, so I ended it."

I couldn't believe she was taking advantage of my vulnerability to talk about her relationship with Brad.

"But he still needs me. He's always needed me, and I think that point was made clear when we got married."

"All right, that's enough, Sherry. I've got a job to do here, and I think you've said your piece." Kelly leaned in and began to feel around my body. "Bree, does it hurt anywhere? If anything does, just let me know." I flinched when she touched my left side. "Okay, that's a yes, sorry."

"I'm sorry you're in pain, Bree," Sherry continued and ignored Kelly when she gave a loud huff. "I'm not trying to be a bitch. I'm just saying if you're going to start something with Bradley, just know I will always be a part of his life. So, we're going to have to find a way to get along."

The topic of Brad and Sherry was becoming too much. The heartbeat on the monitor slowed as I slipped off to a dark bliss. Good. I needed to be alone and not trapped in this steel box with Sherry.

Beep, beep, beep. I woke to a horrible beep that felt like a sledgehammer to my head. Nope, I wasn't ready to be back here. I closed my eyes again.

I heard the sound of people in the room whispering.

"A witness across the lake said the asshole kept his light bar on her truck until it sank." It was Kennedy's voice, but I was too tired to open my eyes.

"Concussions are a tricky thing." I didn't recognize the man's voice. "The brain decides if it can repair itself or not. It's just a waiting game."

"Thanks, Doctor." I heard my mom's voice, and I pushed through the darkness and forced my eyes to open just in time to see her turn and look at me. "Bree?" She leaned over the bed and started to cry. "Oh my god, just wait, let me grab the doctor."

Dad moved into my line of vision and smiled at me warmly. "Welcome back, kiddo."

The door opened, and the doctor came in and began to shine a light in my eyes. After a few questions he seemed satisfied and had a quiet word with the nurse, then began to write on my chart.

"You had some water in your lungs, so your throat might be sore. Just give it a few tries and see how you feel." The nurse held a cup and straw to my lips, and I took a few sips.

"Bree, can you tell me where you are?" the doctor asked.

"Hospital," I croaked out.

"Very good. Do you remember what happened two nights ago?"

Two nights ago? Holy shit, I've been out for that long? I nodded.

"Okay, what happened?"

"I was pushed off the road and into the lake." I was surprised by how much my head hurt as I spoke.

"You weren't wearing your seat belt, so you hit the windshield." He gave me a disapproving look, which got my back up immediately. "You're lucky you survived at all. A hit that hard to the head should have kept you unconscious until you drowned."

"The truck"—I licked my lips—"hit me, my phone went flying, and I tried to grab it. Belt needed to come off so I could reach it." Good Lord, I felt exhausted from three little sentences.

"Okay." He nodded and wrote something else on his tablet. "If you feel well enough, your friends at the SPD want to question you on what happened."

"Can't it wait?" Mom pleaded, but Dad placed a hand on her arm, and she nodded. She knew I had to do that. "She's just been through so much."

"First seventy-two hours," I croaked out.

"That's right." The doctor gave me a nod. "The first seventy-two hours are most critical in cases like hers."

"It's okay, Mom," I whispered and tried to be strong for them all. "I can do it." I felt around for the button and raised the bed to sit more comfortably. I spotted Patrick and Lainey in the corner. They both looked concerned. "I'm fine, really," I assured them as Lainey moved to touch my hand before she eased herself onto the edge of the bed and sniffed.

"We were so worried, Bree." Tears fell down her cheeks. "We just got you back, and then . . ." her voice trailed off. "I thought we lost you."

"I'm still here." Every word took so much energy. "See?" I squeezed her hand as I looked around. "Where's Charley?" Where there was Lainey, there was Charley.

I loved my twin brother, but over the years after what happened at the river, I'd pulled away, and he'd let me. Lainey had always been on my side when I was young, but I'd never felt I could confide in her. I always knew she told Mom everything, and I wanted to live a different life from what she seemed to picture for me. When Charley came into the picture years ago, there was something about him that drew me in. I guess it was what Lainey saw in him—he was thoughtful and always made time for the family. Maybe it was because he didn't have any siblings of his own and adopted all of us to fill the holes.

I leaned back in and tried to relax and hoped he'd walk through the front door, because I needed him at a time like this—he was my rock and always seemed to ground me.

"Oh, Bree, his mom's sick. But as soon as he heard, he looked at booking the next flight home."

I shook my head then. "No, Lainey, call him. I'm fine. His mom needs him more."

She laughed and dried her cheeks with the back of her hand. "Her dementia is getting worse, and as insensitive as it sounds, I don't think she'd even notice if he did leave." She drew in a deep breath.

"Sweetie," Dad said and linked arms with Mom, "the police are here."

"Oh, Bree"—Lainey held up her phone—"Dale called like a hundred times." *Oh my god, Dale!* I forgot he had called me during my attack on the road. "I hope you don't mind, but I texted him back that you were in the hospital. I told him to stay put and that we'd update him when we know anything."

"Thank you." I gave her a light smile. The very last thing I needed was Dale showing up and panicking over what had happened. The man had been through enough. I looked at Dad. "All right, I'm ready." He and Mom walked out of the room with Patrick and Lainey. Alone, I waited for Cap to come in.

To my utter disbelief, Ray was the one who came in to question me—after curtly informing me the truck had evaded capture. He was, of course, an asshole and questioned my judgment on most of my actions instead of just taking notes on the events that took place. By the time he left, I felt wrung out and pissed. As much as I wanted to report him to Cap, I knew better than to snitch. I needed to win Ray over myself, somehow.

"Nice to see you up." Brad was suddenly in the doorway, arms at his sides, fingers rolled into fists. "Welcome back." I felt my heart squeeze when I took in how handsome he was, and now I had to pull myself away before I let myself fall for him again. Tall, dark hair curled under his ears, dark eyes to match, lean and fit in a way that would make any woman stop and admire his features. He crossed the room, pulled up a chair, and sat next to me. "You hit your head pretty hard."

"Yeah." I touched the stitches that ran along my hairline. "Could have been worse."

"Yeah, you could have died." He coughed into his hand and gave me a pissed-off look. "I told Cap you should maybe step back."

"You did what?"

"This is getting real, Bree. You really could have died."

I waved a hand around as I tried to form a sentence. I was so pissed. "Who gave you the right to do that?"

His thumb swiped his nose as he fought to keep his voice down. "I'm lead detective, which gives me the right to pull people off the case. If you were anyone else, I'd still do the same."

"I packed up my life in New York to come here." I glared and ignored how much it hurt to talk. I took a sip of water. "I came as a favor for Cap, so if he pulls me, fine, but I don't take orders from you."

His fingers tapped the bed rail as he absorbed my words. "I'm only trying to protect you."

"Not yours to protect," I ground out. More of what Sherry had said in the ambulance seeped back in. She clearly still had feelings for him, and I realized he was trying to balance her and work—and me. It was all just too much. I turned away as his phone vibrated. He cursed when he read the message. He tucked it away and stood over me.

He leaned down close and whispered, "I will always protect you." I felt tears prickle my eyes. "I'll check on you later," he said as he straightened up and walked out of the room.

Once I was alone, I thought hard about everything. If I ever let Brad in, then Sherry would always be in my life too. Not to mention the fact that I was being targeted by whoever it was who ran me off the road. I had my job and my happy life back in the city. I went over and over it, but my body felt like it had been hit by a truck. Oh wait, it basically had been. I let the pain in then and silently sobbed into a pillow.

Chapter Eleven

BRAD

Seven days had passed since Bree had been run off the road—and five days since we'd spoken. I had called and left messages, but she'd never returned any of them. I knew she was pissed with me trying to pull rank, but she'd almost died, and for what?

I hopped into my car and headed toward the station. My phone buzzed. I saw it was Sherry, and I declined it, only to have her call again. I hit *answer*. "What!"

"Hi, honey, no need to be so short with me. I'm only calling to see how Bree is doing."

Will the woman never listen? I thought I'd gotten through to her at the restaurant. I'd only met up with her because I'd wanted to talk to her about Ginger. I knew she only liked to have her as a link to me. "Last I heard, she was fine." I pulled into my parking spot and took a deep breath.

"I'm pleased to hear that. Now, Bradley, I heard you at dinner, but I'll never stop caring about you. I also just want to make sure that Bree being back doesn't trigger some dark memories for you."

"I'm fine—back off, Sherry. I just got to work, and I have to go." Before she could speak again, I hung up and got out of my car.

When I went inside, I heard some commotion and saw Ray laughing and talking with some of the guys in the main work area. He'd been avoiding me. For his sake, I was glad, because I'd wanted to rip his throat out for leaving Bree alone.

"Ray." My tone was sharp as I walked toward him on the way to my office. The guys he had been with suddenly got busy, and one scooted away toward the copy room. It immediately grew quiet. "A word?" I stepped aside and motioned for him to join me privately.

He reached for his duffle bag that hung over the back of a chair and swung it over his shoulder. "Gotta be somewhere."

"This'll just take a sec." He stood his ground, and I gave him a chance to save himself from embarrassment in front of the others, but he either didn't care or didn't think I'd say much in front of everyone. "All right, here then." I tucked my hands into my pockets and leaned against the wall for fear I'd punch the guy. "When we were partners, I had your back no matter what. I listened, I learned, I became a better detective with your guidance."

He scratched his nose. "Then you ditched me and left," he growled.

"I did, yes." I nodded. "But only because I began to disagree with some of the things you did, but I always had respect for you, Ray, until now." A few of the guys whispered something, but I didn't react—this was between Ray and me, and he'd been the one to make the conversation public. "I didn't pull rank often when I became lead detective, but I did tell you to walk one of our fellow employees to her truck. Instead, you left her alone, and Miss Jaminson was almost killed. You totally disregarded her safety and left her vulnerable."

"If the killer wanted to get to *Bree*, he would have—with or without me." Ray rolled his eyes at the others.

"Maybe, but I guess we'll never know, will we?" I stared hard at him. "I spoke to the chief. I told him you disobeyed a direct order, and that decision left a fellow employee in the hospital. He agreed with my concern. You're suspended for the week."

He blinked at me in shock. "What the hell? That'll go on my record—"

I cut him off. "You need to understand the gravity of what happened."

"Gravity?" He spat. "That's absurd! If she hadn't been dressed like a damn whore, she'd have had no problem getting to her truck. Whose fault is that!"

I saw red.

I didn't even think as I pushed off the wall and went for him, but then Kennedy was suddenly in my face.

"That's exactly what he wants, Stone"—Kennedy held me back—"for you to get written up along with him. Don't let him suck you in."

"Ray!" Cap barked across the room. "You got an order. I suggest you take it. If you disagree, call the chief."

Ray lifted the bag he held and shook it. "Yes, sir." He held my stare for a beat, then left.

"You good?" Kennedy stepped aside.

"Yeah." I was furious and knew I had to get out of there. "I've got somewhere to be." I grabbed my coat and headed out to my car.

"Detective Stone." Officer Smith caught me as I opened the door to toss my jacket into the passenger seat. "I just heard from Bree. She thinks she may have found something."

"Something?"

"On Maria's footage. I guess it was dropped off to Bree the other day, and she's been combing through it."

"I see." I checked my phone and saw no missed calls or messages. "I'll swing by and see what she's got."

"Cool." He held up a hand, and his young face brightened. "Tell her I hope she's back soon."

"Yeah, sure." I slipped behind the wheel and threw a wave at Hank as he pulled in with his UPS truck. Maybe the coffee maker I ordered had arrived. I figured Bree would appreciate that I was feeding her addiction. I headed toward her place. I had a couple of stops to make along the way.

By the time I arrived at Bree's cabin, it was dark, the temperature had dropped, and the warm glow from the windows was comforting. It was only early in the season, but it felt cold enough to snow.

I knocked and heard her move around. A moment later, the door opened, and I took in her sweatpants that sat low on her hips and the crop top that barely covered her bra. Her hair was down and wavy, and she was makeup free. She was unbelievably gorgeous.

"I come with a peace offering." I held up her favorite coffee and a bouquet of bright-orange Chinese lanterns.

She hesitated and chewed on the inside of her lip before she stepped back and let me pass.

I set both items on the table and snagged one of Bree's mom's cookies—they were legendary when we were in high school.

"You're looking better," I said when she stayed quiet. "How's the head?"

She eased onto the couch and covered herself with a blanket, even though it was toasty warm inside the little storybook cabin. "Better."

"These are really good. Did your—"

She cut me off. "What can I do for you?"

I swallowed the rest of the cookie and brushed my fingers clean. "I can't come and visit you?"

"Or did you visit because you spoke to Adam?" She folded her arms, which drew my attention to the bit of lace that now showed. God, she had great breasts. "Yeah, okay." She mistook my silence for something else. "Maybe it's time you left." She got up as if to see me out.

"What? No." I blocked her path to the door with my body. "Yes, I spoke to Officer Smith, but I was on my way over regardless. I want to know what you found." She stared straight ahead, not meeting my gaze. I'd seen Bree ticked off before, but I'd never seen her like this. She seemed sad more than anything else. Maybe Sophia's death played with her head. "You've been dodging my calls all week, and I wanted to make sure you're all right. If it wasn't for Patrick or Lainey, I'd think you left town again."

"You came, you saw, I'm fine." She looked down, and I used the tip of my finger to raise her chin so I could see into her eyes.

"You don't seem fine."

"Well." She clenched her jaw.

I studied her. "What's going on in that pretty little head of yours?" A flash of emotion flickered across her face, and her eyes went glossy. "Hey, Bree, speak to me." I moved closer, but she stepped back. I closed the distance between us and used the couch to trap her. "Bree?"

She looked away as she sank to the couch. She gave me a painful expression, and I stepped back, confused.

"I've been going through Maria's footage," she said quietly, totally ignoring my question. I sat across from her and took a deep breath. "The last thing I said to Sophia was to try to get a picture of *his* face." She looked stricken. "It's probably what got her killed." Her voice cracked, but she swallowed and went on. "Maria and Sophia had been trying to do what I asked." She opened her laptop. "I didn't catch it until now, but Sophia mentioned that she started to back up her files to an iCloud account. It got me thinking, and after a phone call to Maria, it turns out that they share the same account." She turned the laptop toward me. "It's just the first few minutes, but this is right before she's killed." The video started, and in a quick flash a hand could be seen. It looked like it unclipped the camera from her, then it swung upward and flickered off. She replayed it a few times.

"So, the killer knew how to remove the GoPro camera from the holder and turn it off before it showed his face?"

"Yes, and when I called Maria an hour ago to check in on her, I asked about the mechanics of the case the GoPro sits in. She said they were a real struggle to work with and you'd have to know how to open it to have removed it as easily as this person did."

"Really?"

"Not only that, but look at his wrist." She backed up the video and pointed at a zigzag scar. "It looks fresh. I know it's not much."

"But it's a start!" I nodded, impressed, but wished she hadn't been making calls and would just rest. "Can you send that to me?" She nodded. "Okay, Detective Bree, anything else?" It was just this attention to detail that made her so valuable.

"I saw one more thing, and I still have five more hours to go."

"And what about the doctor's orders not to watch any kind of screen while you heal from a major concussion?" I knew my voice betrayed how frustrated I was, and I didn't like it.

"Between Maria and another girl, there's fifteen hours of footage." She looked at me for the first time. "I've been locked in this cabin for five days. You do the math and see if I'm overextending myself."

I rubbed my face with both hands. "Fine." I dropped my arms, knowing she was too stubborn for her own good. "What else did you see?"

She shifted over so I could join her. I sat and watched her pull up a file on her computer that had little snippets of footage. "This here"—she pressed *play*, and I recognized Maria's bracelet as it came into the shots as she handed out samples of beer—"is when she first spots him." She pointed at the back of a man's head. "Watch when he touches this guy's shoulder." I could see his hand, and sure as hell, he had a green outline on his thumbnail. "And here." She started another clip, and he was walking through the crowd but was smart enough to keep his head down for all the cameras. He even evaded their body cameras, keeping his face tipped away. "And here." She pointed at the new clip, where again, he used his arm or hand to block the view of his face.

"Well, we know he's Caucasian, roughly five eleven, under two hundred pounds, brown buzz cut. That's good, but, Bree, please give me the rest, and I'll look through it. You need a break."

"I got it." She closed her laptop and leaned back with a sigh. "I'm going crazy here, and now that I know I still have a job, thanks to

Cap"—she eyed me—"I just need to get through this weekend and then I can get back to work."

I leaned back, too, and tucked a hand behind my head and looked at her. "I spoke to the chief of detectives, and he agreed with my concerns and gave Ray a suspension." I figured I'd tell her now rather than have her hear about it later.

"Why?"

"He left you. I asked him specifically to walk you to your truck."

She closed her eyes and let out a controlled breath. "The last thing I need, Brad, is a target on my back. He hates me already."

"I gave him specific instructions, Bree. He knew what I told him to do."

I really liked that sexy fire she got whenever I was bossy with her. I could see it in her face.

"You think you can order me around and I'll listen?" She was mad.

"When it comes to work, yes." I couldn't resist poking a little more. "And when we're alone."

She raised a brow, then her expression fell. "We shouldn't be alone together."

"I disagree."

I breathed in her freshly washed hair and felt my pants tighten. Shit. I needed a distraction, so I grabbed the remote and turned on the TV. A movie that had been paused was on, so I hit *play*.

"Not that." She tried to grab the remote, and a second later I saw why. I read the title at the bottom.

Through My Window? Now that piqued my interest, and I blocked her arm when she tried for the remote again. "Wait, I haven't seen this before," I teased as the guy on TV accused the girl of stalking him.

"Okay." She pointed at the screen. "Let's watch it. If you don't mind that it's dubbed."

"I don't mind."

"Good." She wiggled down under her blanket and tried to look relaxed. Ten minutes in, I wished I had put an action movie on—really anything but the sexual tension that played out in front of us. I sneaked a glance and saw her neck was strained. We were both feeling it. My head started to run with memories from when we were younger and how there used to be an unspoken spark between us. We'd never addressed it. In fact, most of the time, we'd ignored it, but there were a few occasions where we'd given in to the moment, and then the world would pull us apart.

I glanced at her. Something was really off here. Maybe I needed to go slower.

"I should probably go." I snagged my phone off the table.

Bree paused the movie and quickly stood. "Yeah, it's probably a good idea." She walked me to the door, her smell lingering in the air. She opened it, and I reached above her head and pushed it closed again as my head battled with itself. "I wish you would talk to me."

"Brad." She slowly turned. I saw her fight tears. She covered her mouth. "I can't do this."

I ran the back of my fingers down her cheek. This was the woman I wanted. I needed. "Okay," I assured her, "but Bree, what are you feeling?"

"It doesn't matter what I'm feeling."

"It matters to me."

"It shouldn't." She looked away, and I knew she was closing up on me again. "I need to find where I fit." Her glossy eyes looked at me.

I needed to say something. I hated to see her so confused.

"I felt so dead inside for so long." I looked out the window. "Then you came back, and it felt like just your being here mended something." Her chest heaved, and I looked down at her and saw tears leaking down her cheeks. "Hey, I'm sorry. I didn't mean to upset you."

"You didn't, but you and Sherry have got such history." She opened her mouth to say more, then closed it again.

Of course, she got the wrong idea of why I was out with Sherry. "We do, but my heart certainly isn't with her anymore. The only reason I met with her the night you were hurt was because I want full custody of Ginger. She's not making it easy on me, but I see it for what it is. She's jealous you're back."

I'd made the wrong choice years back when I'd chosen Sherry. I'd turned to her because she'd made me feel safe. I had to make Bree see it wasn't that way now.

"That explains the ambulance talk."

"The what?" My hackles went up. "Did Sherry say something to you?"

"Never mind." She tucked her hair behind her ears, and I could see the sadness in her eyes. "Brad, I think we just need to keep that line drawn no matter how tempting things get."

"So where does that leave us?"

"Friends," she said weakly, "coworkers, I guess." Pain showed on her face, and I wanted to reach out and touch her, but I also had to respect her wishes. She needed space to figure out what she wanted. For now, at least, I'd have to give her the time.

"I'll see you soon."

"And I'll let you know if I find anything else." She gave a smile, but it didn't reach her eyes, and I stepped back so she could open the door. "Bye, Brad."

The ride home was painful. My head was so messed up. My relationship with Sherry had been so important to me when I was younger. She had been my anchor through everything that had happened. The terrible aftereffects the murders at the river had left me with and the constant unwanted attention afterward had almost swallowed me whole. I felt guilty for checking out on her, and I know I was the one who'd pushed our marriage to where it was, even though she was the one who'd left. Things got dark, and I couldn't find my way out. She told me either I did things her way or she wanted a divorce, but I wasn't willing to spend the rest of my life like that. I needed peace, and going out all the time wouldn't bring me any.

The time away from life with Sherry had done me good, and I'd started to come around. Then when Bree returned, something inside of me that had been missing switched back on.

While I sat at the stoplight at the entrance of town, I spotted Bree's old Chevy truck parked by the fence in the impound lot. I quickly switched lanes, flashed my ID at the gate, and was waved through. I was pleased there was even someone willing to let me in this late. I hadn't seen her truck up close yet, and I needed to brace myself for how it might look. Cap said the guys would check it out as soon as they could, but I wanted to see it for myself. I pulled up alongside it.

"Is she yours?" one of the employees who was rubbing grease off his hands with a dirty rag asked me.

"No." I ran my hands along the dent on the bumper. "It's my partner's."

He whistled. "Your partner okay? I heard they fished it out of the lake."

"She's okay." I opened the passenger-side door and saw the damage the water had done. "Lucky as hell but okay."

"Happy to hear that." He scratched his head.

"Me too." I ran my fingers over the broken windshield where her head had hit. I couldn't even imagine the fear she must have gone through when she came to and found herself in the middle of a lake, taking on water.

"At least you got a lead."

I pulled my hand away from the windshield and looked at him. "Lead?"

"Well, yeah." He pointed at something, and I hurried over to his side. "See this?" He scratched at a black mark on the tailgate, then flipped his finger over. "I tried to tell the officer that came by before what I discovered, but he wasn't too interested." He rolled his eyes. "Seems I'm not someone people want to listen to."

"Yeah, well. I'm listening."

He smiled. "All right." He wiped his hands free of oil. "Well, this paint came from a Ram." He flipped the tiny flake of paint over. "Back in 2021, Ram discontinued the color sky gray." He showed me the other side. "Seems this guy wanted black. He'd have gone to the manufacturer and got the new 2024 black that just came out and got her repainted. If you look real careful, you can see it has a sparkle to it."

That all lined up with the black Ram that had come at us before. "Okay, what else?"

"My best guess then would be a 2021 with a lift kit, given where this scratch is." He pointed to Bree's truck as I scribbled down the information.

"Anything else?"

"Yeah, actually." He dug in his pocket and pulled out his phone. "My buddy, Ricky, he's batshit crazy, but he said he was out night fishing and heard the crash. He was about a mile down from it and said he noticed the truck as it whipped by him. He caught a pic."

I moved to see his phone screen. "Seriously?"

"Yeah." He pointed. "See right there? 'ACD.' Last three letters on the license plate."

Yup, that's the same plate that I called in the day we were run off the road.

"Did you take this to the police?"

"I was going to show that other detective, but like I said, he didn't seem interested." He gave a shrug. "He said everyone's an expert, or some shit like that. So, screw him. If he didn't want the tip, it was fine with me."

I ran through my head who was on call that day. I turned to him. "Tall, hair kind of like mine, big smile, skinnier build?"

"No, older, weathered-looking, shitty attitude."

Fuck me, that's Ray. "Any idea what he was doing with the truck?"

"He just said he needed to see it. Flashed his badge and waved at me to hang back while he rooted around. I didn't see him take anything—he just seemed to look it all over."

"I see." I headed over to the front passenger seat. I didn't think there'd be much that could be saved, but Bree had a few things I'd wanted to get for her. The truck was toast, which was too bad because I know how much she loved it. I removed the guardian angel clip that she had fastened to her visor and the stack of bracelets on the gearshift. I put them in a bag I found on the back seat that looked like it had a few outfits inside.

I moved on to the glove box, where her truck insurance and owner's manual were all stuck together like paste, so I tossed them aside. "Ouch, dammit!" I jerked my hand back and saw a small bead of blood bubble out of my finger. I bent down to look carefully inside and found a small knot of barbed wire tucked in the far back corner. A cold, damp chill raced down my back as I studied the little twist of steel wire with its sharp red tips. Why would she have that?

"That's odd." The man looked over my shoulder.

I tossed it into the bag and moved her things into my trunk. "What's your name?"

"Rudy." He offered me a hand, and I shook it. "Rudy Vamp."

"Well, Rudy, how would you like to make a few extra bucks?" People like Rudy were invaluable resources to the job.

He pulled out a smoke from his breast pocket. "I never turned down cash."

"Anyone that comes to see this truck, I want to know about it. You send me a photo, a video, or just call, I don't care. If they even glance at it, I want to know. If you hear anything at all about it outside of here, or your buddy remembers anything else, I'd like to be the first to know." I handed him my business card. "Don't care how small the detail is."

"Copy that." He added the card to his cigarette pack and put it in his pocket. He blinked as smoke blew into his eyes. "I got some friends that might know some stuff—I'll see what I can dig up."

"I'd appreciate it, Rudy, and I'll make sure it's worth your time." I closed the trunk. "Call my cell so I have your number too." He did, and I quickly programmed his information into my phone. "We'll talk soon."

"Yeah." He waved as I headed back out to the road. It was getting late, and I was hungry. By the time I stopped at the market and then got home, it was close to eight fifteen. I hated to eat that late, but I couldn't face another cold pizza.

I opened the door to find Ginger sitting impatiently, sock in her mouth, with a full-on bum wiggle as she waited for me to come in.

"Well, hi there, my big girl." I bent down, and she made her way over with excitement. I saw Mom's note on the counter explaining she'd run into Sherry and insisted on taking Ginger back to my place herself. I appreciated what she did. Sherry was the last person I wanted to see. "Come on, girl, let's go eat."

I fell asleep on the couch and didn't wake up until morning. It was the first good night's sleep I'd had in a while. Cap's call woke me up. I must have forgotten to set my alarm, and that was unusual for me. I squinted at the time and saw I was insanely late for work.

"Hey, Cap, sorry, I overslept," I offered as a greeting.

"If you got sleep, you've got one up on me." He yawned. "Please tell me you and Bree have something for me to report back on?"

I rubbed my head and tried to think straight. "We think we found him, but he's smart and knows how to hide his face from the club cameras and the body cams. But last night Bree had a few more hours to go through, so maybe she's found something by now. I'll give her a call and see where she's at."

"I'll ask her myself. She just walked in."

"Oh, okay." I leaned my arms on my legs and fought back the morning fog. "Let me shower and get changed, and I'll be in."

"Sounds good." He hung up, and I raced off to the shower. I grabbed my clothes and hurried to dress with Ginger on my heels. I didn't blame the pup for always sticking close to me. She never knew if she was staying here, going to Mom and Dad's, or being shipped off to Sherry. I wanted her here full-time or at Mom and Dad's. I hoped my talk to Sherry had fixed the issue. Now it was on to the next thing. I eyed the piece of barbed wire that lay on the table by the door. I snatched it up and headed out.

I hurried to the coffee shop to order Bree and me a coffee. I'd probably get stabbed to death if I showed up empty handed without a caffeine fix for her—and I still didn't know if the new coffee maker had arrived.

"Morning." Bree's twin brother, Patrick, smiled over at me from the cream-and-sugar table. "I heard you skipped out on practice this morning." I threw him a questioning look. "I ran into Kennedy." He chuckled. "He figured maybe you were with Bree last night."

"No, I was home." I paid the lady at the counter and joined him. "The night got away from me, but I won't miss the game."

"Good." He smiled. "Maxine's working late, so I figured I'd swing by and use the rink to keep me up."

"Happy to have you there." I'd known Patrick for as long as I'd known Bree. He was a great guy and had followed my footsteps by marrying his high school sweetheart.

"Hey." He stopped me when I went to leave. "Fuck." He rubbed his head. "I'm sorry, man, but I have to ask, is there something going on between you and my sister or not?"

My skin heated when my mind flashed back to when we'd kissed. Her lips had been so soft, and her kiss had been tender, but it had been laced with a hunger that I'd felt straight to my core, and her taste . . . her taste had been what I expected heaven to be like.

"No." I instantly felt like I'd betrayed him somehow by sidestepping that Bree and I had actually had a few very intimate moments. "I'm not saying there's nothing there, but a small town and an ex-wife is tricky to navigate."

"If you need me to run interference, let me know." He laughed. "My sister's been in love with you since I can remember. But don't tell her I said that, or she'll push me out of our drinkin' loft."

"Really? She told you that?" I beamed at his comment. Bree was often a closed book when it came to sharing her emotions, so to hear this made me excited. I'd been in such a heavy place with Sherry, and his comment only confirmed how wrong I'd been in my choice of woman.

"Not in so many words, but I know my twin sister." He tapped his heart.

Now I was even more determined not to let her go.

"If you really want to help, get her to stay and not go back to New York."

A knowing look went over his face. "Yeah, I'll help you there."

"I'm not sure where you're going with that, so I won't ask." I held up the coffees and walked backward toward the door. "Thanks, and see you tonight."

As I crossed the parking lot toward my car, Kelly's EMT rig pulled in across from me. She hopped out of the driver's seat with a grin and a wave. Kelly had arrived in Sheffield just after I made detective—she was a great paramedic and was trying out for the fire department. She and her partner, Neil, were both going for it. The city had developed a new program so EMTs and firemen could have the same training to help each other out in the field. It was a great plan, and I hoped they both made it.

"How's your partner?"

I shrugged. "Healing."

"Scary stuff." She frowned. "She was lucky she made it out at all with that hard a hit to the head."

"Yeah, I know." I twisted my mouth and contemplated if it was wise for me to ask. "Hey, Kelly, you've never sugarcoated anything since I met you, so when I ask this, please be honest."

"Shit." She closed her eyes. "Is this about Sherry and Bree in the rig?"

I nodded, my suspicions solidifying. "What happened?"

She puffed out her cheeks and let out a long breath. "For the record, and I know I sound like a jerk, but I'm not a fan of Sherry." She gave me a look. I knew most women weren't huge fans of Sherry—she just didn't get along well with other females. "Man, your ex really laid it on the line with Bree. I wanted to dump her out the back of my rig."

"And I wouldn't blame you." I waited for her to go on.

"She basically said to Bree that you and she had such deep history that if she was to date you, she had to be okay with her still being in your life. Something about how you will always need her. It was hella awkward, I can tell ya that."

"Shit." I twisted the coffee cup on my roof as I thought. "Sorry about that, Kelly. Sherry's feeling threatened since Bree's been back, and she's just making things messy. I'm trying to smooth it out."

"No worries. I do messy just fine." She smiled warmly, then turned to go.

"Wait, one thing."

"Yeah?" She turned back.

"How did Bree seem to handle it all?"

She pressed her lips together and took a few steps toward me. "Truth," she said and lowered her voice, "she just seemed sad." She made a wry face and studied me for a moment. "Maybe it was the accident, but she gave me a look at one point that made me connect to her in a way that I felt all her pain at once. It came from here"—she covered her heart—"not here." Her hand moved to her head.

"Yeah." My own chest heaved. Bree being in that situation with Sherry trying to mark some sort of territory over me was unacceptable. "Thanks, Kelly."

"Any time." She headed into the coffee shop as I took a moment to digest all of that.

I was in a constant battle in my head as I drove to work. What Kelly had to say made me want to wring Sherry's neck. No wonder Bree had shut down on me. I knew I had to clear things up with her, but I needed to find the right time.

I couldn't find Bree when I got to the station, so I shut myself in my office and started to comb through the recordings. One thing I knew for sure—I wasn't cut out to be an influencer: The way men put themselves in Maria's direction was almost revolting. I understood the whole chase thing when it came to women, but there was a line between chasing and downright stalking. Hour after hour went by, and the faces started to morph into one. I gave in and reheated Bree's coffee, then downed it myself. The caffeine was just what I needed to get my focus back.

Cap came in to see how things were going. "Long day," he commented after we chatted for a few minutes. Then the door opened suddenly.

"Afternoon"—Bree's voice found me as I started the last video—"sorry for being late." She took off her jacket and threw it over a chair. Where had she been?

"Jaminson, how was your doctor's appointment?" Cap asked, and I pinched my brows together at her.

"All clear." Her cheeks pinkened, and I could tell she wasn't being completely honest.

"Glad to hear it." Cap nodded. "Well, I'll leave you both to it." He left and closed the door. "What can I do?" Bree pushed up her sleeves. I didn't answer her, as something in Maria's footage caught my eye. I slowed it down and watched it again.

"Holy shit." I looked at Bree. "Look." She moved around the desk and leaned down to see the screen better.

"Is that his . . . ?"

"Face." I nodded excitedly. "He might know all the camera angles, but he sure didn't account for his reflection on the coatroom door."

"Okay." She squared her shoulders and grinned at me. Her slight wince let me know she was still dealing with some tenderness from the accident. "Let's get this son of a bitch."

Chapter Twelve

BREE

"Timothy James Ford Jr."—Cap read the results generated from the facial-recognition software over Brad's shoulder—"age forty-two, originally from Florida. He also had two priors for stalking."

"Last known address"—Brad pointed at the screen—"was three years ago. Waco, Texas."

"Great." I sank into the chair and rubbed the spot where the headache wouldn't let up. "Maybe we need to bait him?"

Brad cracked his knuckles, and I peered over at him. "You're kidding, right?" He sounded shocked. Both guys looked at me like I was crazy.

"Jeez." I dropped my hand from my head. "It was just a suggestion."

"All right." Brad closed his eyes as he thought. "I'll have the guys dig up as much as they can on this guy. Bree, you and I can start digging into the poison and where it's being sold."

"Payne, you and Adam search through any names that cross-reference with this asshole and tell me if anything comes up. We can't assume that Ford is working alone."

"Bree." Cap held up a hand to get my attention. "How about we get you into the shooting range this week?"

No way. I took a moment to readjust my bag on the back of the chair as I considered my answer. I had my reasons for not liking guns, not the least of them was having my own turned on me. "I'm good, Cap." I didn't have to explain myself.

"In this line of work—"

"I know, but I'm all good." I refused to make eye contact with Brad.

I gathered my things and spotted two empty coffee cups in the trash bin next to his desk.

"You were late," Brad said, reading my thoughts, "and it turns out I actually do like your drink order."

"You drank my coffee?" I pressed a hand to my chest.

"Yup, actually, I did. Better than tossing it down the sink." He grinned evilly at me.

"You're a monster," I teased as I checked the time and saw it was just after 1 p.m. "No worries—we can always stop by and grab a replacement."

Brad shook his head as he held the door open. "You have a problem, Bree. You know that, right?" We walked together toward bookings. It was the noisiest part of the station.

"Bradley," a voice called, and we turned around. "This just came in."

"Thanks, Hank." Brad's brows went up as he happily took the box from him. "You remember Bree Jaminson?"

"I sure do. Nice to see you again, Bree." He clicked his scanner at the bar code on the package. "Well, I got a busy day. You enjoy that." He gave a quick retreat and headed for the front door.

"All right"—I turned to Brad—"what's in the box that's got you so excited?" He looked like the Cheshire cat.

"Something to feed your addiction."

"You bought a coffee maker?" I raised a brow. I was touched that he'd thought of me. Of course I had to give him a little shit for it. "You know it's not just about the brew. It's about the kind of coffee, the creamer, the sugar treat that goes with it."

"Oh, trust me, I didn't think it was that easy," he joked and waved at me to follow. We headed for the lunchroom, and he put the box on the counter. "Okay, we'd better go. I'll set this baby up later."

"Are you two on your way out?" Officer Smith called as we were about to go out the door.

"We are. Have you got something?" Brad's eyes lit up.

"No, sir. I just wondered if you were going to the game tonight, Bree?"

"Ahh, I wasn't aware there was one, but maybe yeah."

"Cool, I'm hoping to make it too." He shot Brad a quick glance before he excused himself.

We continued toward the doors. "You know he worships the ground you walk on, right?" Brad shook his head and unlocked the doors to his car.

I reached for the glove box to grab a Kleenex, and my eyes landed on the TASER, and I shuddered. Brad gave me a look, and I slammed the glove box shut. He stayed quiet as we worked our way across town, knocking on doors to any business that might sell plants or gardening stuff. Something seemed to be on his mind, so I let him be. The next nursery we headed for was known to sell exotic plants. I left him to his thoughts as I researched the poison moss more.

There were a few cases where people had accidentally ingested the moss and died within minutes. Animals knew to stay away from it, apparently, but some out-of-town hikers who'd gotten lost and gone searching for food hadn't been so lucky. It had turned out to be their downfall when they made tea with it.

We parked, and I tucked my laptop away as Brad opened my door and offered me a hand.

"Thanks. Hey." I pulled on his arm. "Are you okay? You seem off."

"No, I'm good." He nodded for me to follow.

"Then why are you so quiet?"

He pulled out his badge as we headed inside. "Just have some things on my mind." He flashed his ID to the clerk. "Good afternoon, I'm

Detective Stone, and this is my partner, Jaminson. Are you the owner of the shop?"

"I am, name's Paul Wiseman." He looked worried as he set his spray bottle down. "Am I in trouble?"

"No." Brad smiled at him. "But we're trying to locate a possible customer of yours." He pulled out Ford's photo. "Does he look familiar to you?"

"I mean, he kind of looks familiar, but he might have one of those faces, you know?" He studied the photo for a moment. "Can you send me his photo? And if anything comes to me, I'll give you a call."

Nodding, I stepped up to the counter and AirDropped his photo. "Any chance you could look up a name for us?"

"Sure." He turned his computer screen so we could see it. "What's his name?"

"Timothy James Ford." I watched as he typed it in, and the screen gave a little shake as if to say, *No one used that name.*

"Try just Ford," Brad suggested, and a list of names came up.

"No Timothys." The clerk shrugged. "Hang on, I'll try something else." We watched as he tried different variations of the name. "I'm sorry, nothing is coming up."

"It was worth a try." Brad shrugged, and we went back outside, where he checked the time. "That's all the nurseries in town. Why don't we grab a late lunch and regroup?"

"Sure."

Brad took us to a mom-and-pop sandwich shop, and we sat outside and ate at one of their picnic tables to enjoy the warm sun while it lasted. The heat felt nice on my back. A cool breeze made it perfect. I chomped happily on my smoked meat on rye. This was my absolute favorite time of year.

"Can I ask you something?" Brad's voice was muffled as he spoke around his mouthful of sandwich. I shrugged, unsure I wanted to commit in my happy moment. "Why won't you take Cap's offer and get yourself a gun?"

I stopped chewing and slowly put my sandwich down. "I can do my job without one. Not gonna start now." Brad studied me, then shook his head as if frustrated.

"You sure know how to shut down a conversation."

It immediately ticked me off because he was right. "You carry, so why should I?"

"Because of times like the nightclub where you could've been killed. What if he approached you? Or pulled a gun on you?"

I shrugged and pretended all that stuff didn't run through my brain that night. "You paint me as reckless. I made sure all my bases were covered."

"No," he said, then paused. "They weren't." He made an irritated noise deep in his throat. "Fine. If you won't tell me about that, can you at least explain this?" He reached into his pocket, then stopped as something caught his eye behind me, and he went still.

"What?" I looked around. I didn't see anything or anyone out of place.

"Come with me." Brad tossed the rest of his lunch into a trash can, and I followed. I wondered what he was up to in that sharp brain of his. He held up a hand to a car as we crossed the road, and he led me up the front steps of the familiar church. "Father Mark." Brad's whole demeanor softened as we approached the tall, red-headed man in a collar. The man smiled as he balanced the pile of hymnbooks he carried and reached out his hand for a shake.

"Detective Stone." He smiled warmly at Brad. "What brings you by this time of day?"

"You remember the Jaminson twins?" he asked. I stepped around Brad, feeling like I was in Sunday school again. "Well, this is Bree. She's come back to do a bit of consulting for us."

Father Mark's face lit up, and I could feel his love when he stepped forward and gave both of my shoulders a friendly squeeze. "My goodness, look at you, Bree." I tried to smile, but I still had some deep-rooted issues I needed to deal with before I'd ever feel totally comfortable here. "Are you back?"

"For now."

Brad shot me a look, which I pretended not to see. I had pushed back on the church after what happened at the river, and I knew some of the locals secretly judged me for not wanting to share every detail of what happened to us, every single Sunday.

He stepped back when an older lady appeared, and it was obvious she wanted a word with the priest. "Well, we've missed seeing you here. I sure hope to see you in the pew with your family this Sunday." I offered a small smile and a nod. I didn't want to commit or lie.

"Sorry for jumping right to business, Father, but would you mind if I spoke to the man in charge of the gardens?" Brad pointed outside.

"Of course not." Father Mark spoke to the lady and told her he would be right back. He waved for us to follow, and we went out a side door. He approached a man who held a leaf blower and said something we couldn't hear.

"You know you should really make a decision," Brad said.

I knew he was referring to whether I was staying or not. "I was hired to work with you on this one case, and once we get this guy, I might be out of a job, so . . ."

"Detective Stone, Ms. Jaminson, this is Mandell. He and his small company do a wonderful job of keeping our grounds looking fantastic." Father Mark smiled at the man as he introduced us.

Brad flashed his badge, and I pulled mine out, but Mandell didn't even glance at them—he just stood rigid and looked uncomfortable.

"Hi, Mandell," Brad said and smiled warmly. "We won't keep you long. I just need to ask you a few questions about your job. How big is your company?" The man's eyes widened, but he didn't answer. It was obvious he was nervous. "Look, what I really want to know is do you ever work with international plants? Moss, to be more specific?" Again, the man simply swallowed and looked helplessly toward Father Mark.

"It's all right, Mandell. You can talk to them," he gently said to the stricken man. "They're friends of mine. They just want to talk."

Still no response, so Brad reached into his breast pocket for his notepad. "All right, look, Mandell, I don't care what's going on with your company or if you have papers to work here legally. Right now, all I'm looking for is a specific type of moss called"—he looked at his pad—"butterfly root moss. I've checked all the nurseries in town but can't find anywhere that sells it, so now we're checking with wholesalers and landscapers. I just wondered if you might be able to point us in the right direction. I need to know where you could buy it."

The man glanced at me, and I gave him a nod to show it was okay. He licked his lips, then spoke. "That can be bad stuff if you don't use it right. I don't use it."

"That's okay. I get that," Brad reassured him. "Do you know any-one who does?"

"No, but I know that Mano's Supply carries all kinds of strange things like that. Maybe check there." He lowered his head, and Brad didn't push it any further.

"Thank you."

We headed back inside, and Father Mark looked at me carefully. I shifted my weight and wished Brad would say it was time to go.

"I see you, Bree, and all that you carry inside," Father Mark said.

"I'm sorry that you see that, Father." I looked away from him and studied the inside of the lovely old church where I had once been so comfortable. After everything happened, I was constantly talked about. I'd heard the whispers in school from my peers, but it was the church that was the worst. Church meant well-meaning adults trying to get me to talk about it. Parents, aunts, uncles, even old biddies who had nothing better to do than wonder about what it was like to see those women, face their killer, how I felt.

My mom would ask them to please stop, and every so often, Dad would say something, but none of it helped. What happened that day at the river had made me an object of curiosity. I felt like an outcast.

Then there was Brad, who'd just sit there with Sherry and her family. He didn't seem affected by all the attention—at least I never saw it.

"If you plan on staying in town, which I hope you do, come back and walk tall through those doors." He pointed to the big wooden doors. "Show people you aren't that child anymore. You are a confident woman, and you're here for your future and for him." He pointed heavenward.

"I'll think about it." I looked at Brad for help, and thankfully he got the hint.

Brad pulled out his phone and read something off the screen. "Sorry, Father, we have to go. Thank you so much for your time, and I'll see you Sunday."

"Happy to be of service." He looked over at me. "If Sundays don't work for you, Bree, I'm here seven days a week." He smiled and winked.

I forced a smile and followed Brad back to his car. Once out of hearing range, I glared at him. "Thanks for that."

"Anytime." He slipped in behind the wheel, and I cursed before I joined him.

I waited until we were on the road. "All right, so how far is Mano's Supply anyway?"

"South end of town." He looked at me like he wanted to say something, but didn't. That was the third time he'd done that since we'd left the station. I wanted to ask, but at the same time I wasn't sure I wanted to know what was on his mind. It was probably more questions about my sanity.

I kept my eyes locked on the horizon as we drove and left him to his thoughts. When his phone rang loudly, I jumped. His finger hovered over the *decline* button on the dash, then he seemed to change his mind and hit *answer*.

"Hey, how's your day going?" Sherry's high-pitched voice was like a needle to the eye. I kept my gaze locked on the horizon.

"Bree and I are actually just about to get out and question someone." Brad tried to sound normal, but I knew him well enough to know he was uncomfortable, by the way his hands flexed on the wheel.

"Oh, you're with Bree?"

"Yes, I'm at work."

"Oh, hi, Bree. I hope you're feeling better."

"What do you want, Sherry?" Brad's voice was cold.

"I was just calling because I was going through one of the boxes that I took from the house and realized it was your old hockey stuff." She blew out an exaggerated loud breath. "I wasn't sure if you wanted it or if I should burn it." She made a *yeech* sound and laughed as if she'd made a joke.

Brad shook his head and quietly cursed.

"Sorry, Bradley, but you know the smell is the one thing that I can't get past."

"Leave it on the porch, and I'll come by and get it later."

"Or I can drop it off." I rolled my eyes at Brad. It was so obvious she'd taken the box on purpose.

"No. I'll come by later." Brad ended the call by jabbing the button hard.

I was relieved when Brad parked, and the moment he stopped outside the store, I hopped out and took a big deep breath and righted my head.

"Bree." Brad looked at me over the roof of the car. "I know she went at you in the ambulance. I talked to Kelly."

"You know what?" I plastered on a smile. "I have a really good feeling about this interview. Let's go see if my gut's right." I turned on my heel but heard him sigh as he slammed the door and followed.

"Bree." I ignored him and headed inside, where I spotted a man behind the counter. "Bree, please."

"Hi there." The man smiled at me. "What can I do for you today?"

I looked around as I approached him, Brad right on my heels. "I was told that you're the man to come to if I needed some international greenery." His face brightened at the thought of a sale. Brad leaned forward, but I stopped him from showing his badge. He didn't question me—he just stepped back. This was, after all, what Cap had brought me in to do. By the look of this man, I felt he'd get spooked if he smelled law enforcement.

"You a cop?" he asked me, suddenly cautious.

"No, are you?" I bantered back with a smile.

"Not the last time I checked." He grinned, and his gaze shifted over to Brad, who decided he should look around. "You might be a woman, but you have that look."

"Do I?" I looked down at my outfit and thought I looked more business casual, but okay, I'd take law enforcement too. "Well, if it helps, by law, if I was a cop, I'd have to disclose that information, so." I shrugged. "My uncle's an officer, though, and I'm a good listener." I beamed, and he joined in.

"All right, what kind of plants are you looking for?" He tapped some buttons on his computer, and I leaned over the counter and watched his throat contract. *Perfect.*

"It's some kind of moss from the Netherlands. It's thick and kind of drapey. I believe it has a funny sort of smell to it." I acted like I was lost on the details. "My sister told me about it, said it was great for keeping the raccoons away." He looked at me carefully.

"Are you a fan of PETA?"

"You mean the animal rights group?" I played along. "If you're asking if I'm worried about one of those rodents keeling over, don't be. They're like a parasite—they never friggin' leave."

He smiled, and I knew I had him. "Great answer." He clicked away on the keyboard. "I do have some butterfly root moss that shipped in last month. Hmm, yup, looks like I have some left out back."

"How much do you normally get with each shipment?" I asked casually. "Is there a high demand for it here in Sheffield? I mean, how many raccoons are there?" I laughed.

"No, actually"—he chuckled—"seems it's become quite popular lately. The last guy who asked me to get it in for him took the first bunch but never came back in for the rest. No skin off my nose—he paid up front. So, you're in luck."

"Lucky me." I grinned as I tried not to show I was excited by what he'd just said. "Would it be too much to ask for the names of the people who ordered it?" His mouth dipped, and I quickly recovered. "It's just such a different plant that maybe I could learn from them how they use it. God love my sister, but she also suggested setting up beer cans with pennies inside around my property. With my luck, I'd just have kids knocking them down to swipe them all." I laughed and touched his arm and was happy when his smile returned. "Come on, it'd sure be helpful. Can you tell me?"

"By law, no." He looked at my hand, still on his arm, and casually turned the screen a little toward me. "Just give me a moment and I'll grab what's left."

"Thanks." I waited for him to leave, then focused on the spreadsheet on the screen.

"You can't do that," Brad muttered as if it were a knee-jerk reaction. "You don't have a warrant."

"Insert Bree." I grinned.

"Hurry," Brad warned as he watched the door.

"No." I tapped away on the search bar. I went for sarcasm as I ran my finger down the list of at least fifteen names. "I plan on taking my sweet time so that he can catch me. John Quinn, Ross Smith, Peter Fredericks, Oscar Moore, Brian Lipton"—then my heart stopped as I came to *Timothy Ford.*

"Hello, there." I quietly whistled, and my eyes went to Brad's. "What?"

"One sec." There was a *notes* section. I quickly clicked on the drop-down menu.

He'd ordered a half pound of butterfly root moss two weeks before the first murder, and the shipment arrived four days before the day Shelly White was killed. He'd paid in cash and had rushed delivery. Two asterisks were at the bottom with a note that read "strange." I quickly hit print. I grabbed the sheet as it exited the printer and shoved it into my pocket. I clicked back to the original screen as I heard him coming back. I didn't want to take any chances.

The store clerk set the box down on the counter and opened the lid. "This is all I have left—it's fifty even." I handed him my card, and as he ran it, he took note of my name. "Bree Jaminson, sounds like a country singer."

I tossed my head back and laughed. "If only I had a voice, maybe I could give up my day job."

He chuckled and closed the box. "I'm supposed to warn you, this stuff is just for planting. It's not supposed to be used for anything else." He eyed me and shrugged. "I have to say that," he repeated. "The less you touch it, the better." He lowered his voice at that part and winked.

I worked up the nerve to pick up the bag and met Brad at the door. "Oh, and miss?"

I turned to look his way. "Yeah?"

"You should wear gloves. That stuff'll stain your hands like you just strangled Kermit the Frog."

"Gloves it is." I stepped outside, and Brad took the bag and set it safely in a box in his truck.

We drove around the corner and stopped next to a Jack in the Box food joint. I handed Brad the paper to show that Timothy Ford Jr.'s name was there. "He's guilty. I just know it."

"You were incredible! Great work, Bree." Brad wrapped me in a hug, and we both stilled as we felt that familiar crackle of energy between us. I slowly leaned back and slid my hands over his shoulders and down his arms, completely engulfed in his scent. He turned his head into me and brushed his lips by my jawbone as he pulled back. He let out a frustrated sigh, and I blinked away all the delicious thoughts that came with Brad Stone.

"Now." I cleared my throat and forced myself to find my voice. "We just need to find the son of a bitch and hope he hasn't skipped town."

"Yeah." He leaned back and mouthed something silently. Then he said aloud, "Let's go tell Cap." We headed for the station.

"I knew it. I knew you two would figure this nightmare out!" Cap was beside himself that we had something to bring to the higher-ups. "And Bree, great job on getting the list."

"I appreciate that Brad let me take lead when he saw the guy wouldn't respond well to the badge."

"That was all Bree." Brad grinned. "Hey, Cap, you should consider bringing her on full-time—we could sure use someone with her talents." I raised a brow at him, but he wouldn't look over at me. "Who can step over the line for the right reasons."

"I'm working on it, trust me." Cap grinned, over-the-moon excited. He held up the paperwork. "Now we've got proof that he bought the plant. I'll send Kennedy for a warrant, and we'll get it logged properly so it can't be thrown out in court. You two go work some more magic."

"Oh my god." Adam ran into the room waving a piece of paper. "You got him. You got him. A guy named Paul Wiseman just called. He said you talked to him in his shop." He glanced at Brad and me with a big grin. "He remembered that customer you asked him about, Timothy Ford. He said that he came back—and are you ready for this? He was driving a Ram truck with a giant light bar."

"Son of a bitch." Cap jumped up. "This day just gets better and better." He rushed out and left the two of us alone in his office.

I took a deep, steadying breath. As I focused on the present and checked the time, I saw Maxine had called. We were supposed to meet Patrick and go for dinner. Patrick was going to stick around town to wait for her to get off work, then he'd drive us both home. Maybe something had changed.

"I'll see you later." I gathered my things and turned to leave, but Brad stood in my way. "What?"

His jaw ticced, and his eyes narrowed in on me almost as if he were mad. "We need to talk."

Another call from Maxine pushed through, and I held up my phone. "Can it wait?" He didn't answer, so I moved around him and headed outside with my phone to my ear.

"Hey, Maxine, sorry I missed your call before."

"Oh, Bree, I'm so sorry. There was this accident on the lake, and three dumbass boys who thought drinking and high-speed chases were a wise thing to do found out the hard way they aren't, if you know what I mean." She groaned. "I'm exhausted, but I have to help in surgery again tonight. I let Patrick know. It's an all-hands-on-deck situation. I told him you could get a ride home with Bradley. I hope that's true?"

"Absolutely, I can get a ride. Don't be sorry! I'm fine to grab something to eat, and I'll touch base later if for some reason I can't get a ride home." I wasn't concerned.

"You're the best—rain check on dinner?"

"Absolutely."

I turned around to see if Brad was still there, but he was gone. I figured he had already left for the rink. I felt my stomach growl and decided to go grab something to eat.

Lonny's still made the best pastrami sandwiches in town. When I stepped in the door, I decided on takeout. As much as I would have liked to stay and eat, the place was packed, so I decided to take it with me and visit the rink instead. I knew from Patrick that Brad's usual game was around this time. I'd often gone there to watch games or practices while I ate when I was younger. I loved the atmosphere and the camaraderie, and it didn't hurt that I'd get to see Brad play. Deep down I knew I hoped to get a ride home with him.

Patrick: Maxine is working AGAIN tonight. I dropped off the keys for her and dad came and got me. She said you can get a ride with Bradley. Tell him I'm sorry to miss his game but I'm spent from waiting around.

I knew he had been looking forward to the three of us having dinner, but Maxine worked at the hospital, and with that came a certain level of responsibility.

Bree: Will do. See you later.

Once I was at the rink and settled on the bench seat, I eyed my sandwich, unwrapped it, and dove in. I moaned as I bit into the spicy meat. I didn't care how I looked right then. I was starving, and the taste of the meat on Lonny's homemade rye bread with its hint of dill from the half-sour pickle was just what I needed.

"I wish a girl would look at me the way you look at that sandwich," Kennedy joked as he climbed up and sat next to me and started to tape his stick. I read the label. *Savage.* I remembered that brand—Brad used to use it all the time.

"She would if you tasted this good," I blurted, then blushed at how it sounded. "You know what I mean."

"I do." He laughed hard, and it drew the look of some of the guys on the ice.

He stood up as the ref blew his whistle and shook his head like he didn't agree with the call. "So, what brings you here tonight?"

I wrapped the rest of the sandwich up in its tinfoil to keep it for later. "My brother was going to pick me up. We were supposed to meet up with Maxine for dinner, but she got called into surgery. So, I'm just hanging out here. It's a safe place to be until I figure out my way home."

"Well, if you still need a ride after the game, I can take you."

I took a sip of my water. "Thanks, Kennedy."

"At the risk of overstepping, I have to ask you something."

I lowered the water bottle from my lips. "Okay."

"Did you leave town because of what happened at the river that day and you couldn't get past it, or because Brad asked Sherry to marry him?"

"Christ, Kennedy, ask a girl for dinner first before you jump right in," I joked, but really, I was stalling until I could figure out how to reply.

"Sorry, I guess you don't have to answer that," Kennedy said.

I twisted the top onto the bottle and tucked my cold hands into the pockets of my long coat. "Both, I guess," I confessed.

"You still care about him, don't you?"

I lowered my head and felt that pang in my chest that I felt whenever I let myself go there. "Does it matter?"

"Actually, it does."

"What does that mean?"

His face twisted like he was debating something. "Fuck it." He turned toward me. "Brad's still stuck in the past—he never got over that shit either. Sherry was there before the murders, and he only married her because he thought she'd help clear the day from his head." A whistle from the ref drew our eyes to the ice. "I can tell ya, Bree, it didn't work. He spiraled down a darker path, especially once he heard you'd left town without even a goodbye."

"Yeah, that's a bad habit of mine." I thought about Dale and how I just ended everything without telling him the whole truth.

"I wish you two could see each other for what you are. You're running toward your future, scared to look back, and he's running backward, trying to find some kind of hope for what was."

"Well, two people who run in opposite directions aren't going to find the same ending." I shrugged.

"Bree, Brad went dark and stayed dark. Like shut down, barely spoke. He worked out way too much and stayed late at the office every day. The only thing that seemed to bring him any joy was this rink and when he got Ginger. You know when I saw him truly come out of it?" I shook my head. "Recently, when you came back."

"Kennedy—"

"It's like this light is back in his face. He's talking and smiling and—" He wriggled his shoulders as if they were tense. "Look, I don't know about you, but I miss my friend, and I've been seriously worried about him."

"I get that, Kennedy, and I know what a good friend you've always been to Brad, but what about my life and what I've built back in—"

"Sweet Lord, you'd think they'd add a little heat to this locker room–smelling rink," Sherry said loudly to another woman as they took a seat at the bottom of the bleachers.

"I really do have the worst luck," I muttered to Kennedy under my breath.

"What the hell! She never comes to the rink," Kennedy whispered back. His face was scrunched in confusion.

"Well, I'm back, and apparently I've made Brad appealing again."

He snorted and rolled his eyes. "She's always made it known that she hates this sport and everything to do with it."

I didn't think she'd spotted me, and I wondered how I could possibly get down and out of there before she did. I looked for an escape but saw no way to get by her. I pulled my coat up around my neck and tried to look as small as I could. Kennedy grinned at me, and I wanted to swat him.

"Well, regardless, she's here, and so am I. No matter what I do, I have a feeling this isn't going to end well."

"One can only hope," Kennedy whispered.

"Yay, Bradley!" Sherry shouted and clapped her hands like a groupie, and Brad got bodychecked by a guy as his gaze flew toward the stands. As he got up off the ice, he looked directly at Kennedy and mouthed, "What the fuck!"

"Well, well, well, who do we have here?" Hayne's voice caught my attention as he and Ronnie climbed the bleachers toward us. Sherry turned immediately to see the commotion as Ronnie sat next to me, and her look of distaste settled on me. I looked away so as not to give her the satisfaction of knowing how uncomfortable I was.

Kennedy stood and offered his hand to Brad's brother. "Nice to see you, Ronnie."

"You, too, man." Ronnie smiled at me. "How are ya, Bree?"

"Great." I smiled as Hayne went behind us and stepped down onto the seat next to me. It also wasn't lost on me that Kennedy didn't greet Hayne the same way he did Ronnie. In fact, the two of them didn't greet each other at all.

"We meet again." Hayne beamed down at me. "So about that Italian restaurant, as friends." He held up his hands to stop me from making a comment.

"You sure are persistent about wanting to eat together."

He squared his shoulders. "Yes, Bree, will you go to dinner with me?"

I felt Kennedy shift, then say, "Trouble."

"Bradley and I were talking, and we decided we were going to spend more time together. We're still pretty close," Sherry said loudly to her friend. Maybe Sherry would see I wasn't a threat if I left with Hayne. I was way past the enemies-in-high-school thing.

Kennedy nudged me. "Don't trust a word out of her mouth, Bree. The woman's a compulsive liar."

"And all the more reason to stay out of her way." I raised a brow at Kennedy. "You know what, Hayne, let's have that dinner." The moment the words pushed off my tongue, I instantly regretted them.

"Whoop!" Hayne yelled out, and I wanted to sink into the floor as people looked our way, including Sherry and her friend. Brad skated by right on cue and squinted when he saw me next to Hayne. His face was hard to see with the glare from the lights on his half visor, but he didn't look pleased.

Kennedy made a hand signal at Brad.

"What was that?"

"It's just something from when we were kids." He didn't look at me.

"You know what I remember from when we were kids?" I raised my chin as he met my gaze. "That you two barely had to speak to communicate. Don't start trouble where trouble doesn't need to be. I've made it perfectly clear to Hayne that this dinner is only about friends. If Brad thinks otherwise, I'll set him straight."

"I didn't start anything." He leaned in. "That was all you."

Suddenly, the whistle blew, and Sherry's angry voice could be heard over the crowd.

"Bradley Stone, you let him go this instant!" She was on her feet and shook her finger toward the fight that had broken out on the ice. I had to muffle my laughter at her outrage. Brad had an arm around a guy's neck as he got in a few punches. The fellow's helmet went flying across the ice. I was a sucker for a good hockey scrap, mainly because

I knew it stayed on the ice. These guys all knew the line not to cross. Even when Brad played for the school, he'd been the same way. He liked a good fight—but only during the game with the ref there.

"Interesting." Kennedy rubbed his chin. "He hasn't had a good fight in a while."

"Who's the guy?"

"Dillan Overbeck," Hayne answered for Kennedy. "He's a cop over in New York division. Good guy, but those two often get into it." Kennedy snickered something, and Hayne rolled his eyes. "So, Bree." He turned to me. "Ready to go?"

"Okay."

He stood and offered me a hand, and I let him pull me to my feet. "Great. Trust me, you're going to love this place. Just give me a sec. I'll be right back." He hurried toward the rink office.

"So, you don't need a ride home?" Kennedy threw me a worried expression.

"I guess not, but thank you for the offer." I gave him a hug. "Bye, Ronnie." I waved, then followed Hayne.

"Is that her?" Sherry's friend sneered as we reached the bottom.

"Yes, but don't say anything," she warned her friend as she watched me step down onto the rubber flooring. "Wait, Bree," she called out, and I stopped. My shoulders stiffened. *This can't be good.* Her smile fell as she approached me.

"I just want to make sure that you're okay. The last time I saw you, well, you were in bad shape."

"Well, considering I'd just been run off the road, had my head slammed into a windshield, almost drowned, and had a major concussion, I was in bad shape."

"Yeah, that was bad." She nodded a few times, and we both stood there in our awkwardness. "So you and Bradley have been working—"

"I have to go. Hayne is waiting for me."

Her eyes bugged. "A date? Really? Wow, that's great!" Her enjoyment was enough for me to turn and walk away, but I didn't give her that, nor did I correct her. "Go have fun." Her smile ate at my core.

I nodded, turned on my heel, and began to walk away. I saw Brad watching us from the centerline.

"Ready?" Hayne was back and held up his keys.

"Yeah, I'm ready." As the door closed to the rink, I heard the ref blowing his whistle furiously as another fight broke out.

We stepped out into the chilly evening and got into his car. I couldn't resist glancing back a few times to see if we were being followed. Thankfully, the restaurant wasn't that far, and when we parked, I drew in a breath of relief.

The place was a hole-in-the-wall downtown, in an area with a lot of nightlife. I might have been only twenty-nine, but I didn't miss those days of going out to drink and party. I had to admit I was happy to leave that all behind in New York City.

Hayne's attention was glued to his phone. He'd told me he was waiting for a call from work and that's why he'd chosen this place, since his office was right next door. I knew from our chat over coffee he was a medical-supplies salesman. I didn't mind if he had to take a call, as it would give me a little time to be alone with my thoughts. The case looped in my head, and I found myself picturing the murder board. Did Maggie or Shelly sit in a place like this with a date while their killer watched them? I wondered how long he might have stalked them.

"So, what's your deal with Stone?"

Wow, that brought me back with a jerk. I reached for my water to buy myself some time to think of a good answer. "What do you mean?"

He tilted his head and studied me. I felt my cheeks go hot. "I'd have to be blind not to see you have feelings for the guy." He sat back.

"I think what you might be seeing is just the strange bond we share. I know you've heard the story." I huffed and bit my lip. "Things like that can warp you. I'm sure you can get that, of all people—you've shared your PTSD stories with me. You and Ronnie have a strong bond because of it."

"We do, but I don't have feelings for him."

"Okay, then here's a question." I looked away, then decided to flip the tables on him. "If you think I have feelings for Brad—"

"I do." He smirked.

I shot him a look to tread carefully. "Are you having dinner with me as friends, or are you toying with Brad to upset him by taking his partner out for a date?"

"Stone can use a little competition. I've seen women fall at his feet just because he's good looking and the fact he wears a badge."

"So you do have an ulterior motive."

"I saw the way he looked at you. So, yeah, at first it was to get under his skin," he said and sipped his beer, "but you're an attractive woman and I thought maybe you getting to know me, you'll see that I'm not as bad as Stone and Kennedy make me out to be."

"At least you're finally being honest." But I wasn't about to let my guard down. Brad and Kennedy were wary of Hayne, and I knew to take that into consideration.

"I just want a fighting chance here."

"I'm here, aren't I?"

"You are, and I'm happy you're here." He smiled, then picked up his menu. "Let's order, shall we?"

Chapter Thirteen

BRAD

I could barely see as I drove home. My mind kept going over the fact that Sherry had shown up at the rink the one time in over a decade that Bree came. Then Hayne had taken Bree out on a date. I was furious with Hayne. He had a bad reputation with women for a reason.

I was more than happy when I turned into my driveway. I locked the car and dragged myself inside the house. My plan was to hit the shower and then bed, but once inside, instead of heading to bed, I stood in the center of the living room for a moment, then dropped into a chair. I sat there and let my head spin. My knuckles were sore from the two fights I'd gotten involved in at the rink. I was always up for a good fight, but when Dillan Overbeck had started to make comments about Bree leaving with Hayne, I had lost it.

I glanced to the photo of Sophia on the coffee table. That young woman would have had an entire life ahead of her. If only she had made safer choices. Frustration flared, and I snatched up the file to review it again.

I must have dropped off to sleep, because I jerked awake in a sweat, and my eyes went to the drawer across the room. I tossed the file onto the floor next to me, got up, and walked over, then forced myself to open it. There, tucked in a napkin at the back, was the small piece of barbed wire that I had found in Bree's truck. I studied it once again in the light. The tiny bits of red on the tips were odd. For the life of me, I couldn't imagine why she had it. I'd taken it to Wes to get it checked out, and it was just red paint. He couldn't find anything else on it. I wondered if someone had played a cruel joke on her.

"Fuck!"

Ginger jumped, startled by my outburst.

"Sorry, girl." I patted her head. "I need to deal with something."

I grabbed my shoes and keys and headed out into the chilly night.

I got to Bree's cabin within ten minutes with no traffic. I parked and hopped out. Her place looked empty, but I knocked at her door. I immediately got annoyed at the thought of her staying overnight at Hayne's. I knew she wasn't mine, yet, but I wasn't giving up. That weasel sure as hell wasn't good enough for her. Where the hell were they?

Ronnie had mentioned he didn't like the way Hayne treated women, in spite of their friendship. He schmoozed, got what he wanted, then chucked them.

I heard a car and stepped into the shadows. I wasn't sure I wanted to witness their goodbyes. *It'd better just be a goodbye.*

Hayne went around and opened the door for her and went in for a kiss. I saw Bree turn her head at the last minute, and he caught her cheek.

"Gotcha, good night, Bree." He leaned against the car. "Thanks for joining me for dinner and for listening to me talk half the night." He looked at his watch. "Wow, most of the night. I sure didn't mean to keep you this long."

"I'm happy to listen. We all have stuff we're dealing with." She yawned.

"Yeah, maybe next time you could share something so I don't feel like it's all about me."

"Maybe." She stepped back and gave him a clear signal that she was done.

He turned to get into the car, then looked back at her. "Call you later." She waved as he got back in the car, and she watched him leave.

She jumped when I stepped out of the shadows. "Holy shit!" She grabbed her chest. "What the hell, Brad!"

"We need to talk."

"Right now? I'm so tired."

"Yeah? You obviously were busy."

She rolled her eyes. "Look, Brad, what do you want to talk about? Can't it wait? I really am tired." She rubbed her arms as if she was cold.

"Something isn't quite right with him, Bree. I know he's a friend of my brother's, but I think you should be careful."

"Maybe," she agreed, "but I'm a big girl and can handle myself. I made sure he knew I wasn't interested in anything except friendship." She brought her chin up.

"And I'm sure he's looking for a *friendship* too." I was being an ass, but I couldn't help it. I'd aways been protective of her. Her eyes challenged me. "Anyway"—I held up my hands—"that's not why I came here."

"No?"

"Can I come in?" The cold was starting to set in, and I could see she was shivering under her coat. "I don't want to talk about this out here."

She dropped her head back with a heavy sigh, then turned and headed up the steps to her door. I followed her and noticed how cold and damp it was inside, so I made quick work of building a fire. She had disappeared into the bathroom, and I took a moment to check that her windows were locked.

She appeared a few moments later in loungewear. She tugged on a sweater, then gathered her long hair into a messy bun. As she slipped her feet into some slippers, she looked at me. I was glad that she was comfortable being casual with me. That had taken Sherry years to do.

"Can we make this quick? I'm barely able to form a thought here."

I took a seat and waved her toward the couch across from me. Then I leaned forward and set the piece of barbed wire on the coffee table, and her eyes widened. I saw her throat contract as she put a hand to her chest.

"Where"—she cleared her throat—"where did you get that?"

"Your truck."

"When?"

"Yesterday."

She glared at me, and I saw a familiar darkness go over her. I knew the look because I'd seen it in my own eyes in the mirror. I knew how it felt too. Since the river murders, it had never really gone away.

"You had no right to take that." Her voice was low and haunting.

I sighed. "You think I want it? Take it." I flicked my wrist at it.

She reached for it, but her hand quickly retreated, and I had to wonder why she had it and what kind of memory was connected to it.

"You should leave."

"I disagree." I wasn't going anywhere until I had answers.

"Brad."

I shrugged and stood, my body towering over hers as I looked down. I felt my temper build inside me, and I felt dangerously close to the boiling point. I knew I needed to relax. "Bree, stop pushing me away. If this is going to work"—I paused—"as partners, we need to be honest with each other. Starting with this."

"It's from him. *They're* from him!" she blurted and tossed her hands in the air.

"Him? The Barbed Wire Killer?"

"Yes, at least, I think so." At her words, a painful, deep chill spread through me, and images from that horrible day broke through my mental barrier. I'd always wondered where the monster had been hiding, but to think he could have been watching her all this time—that thought was enough to make me sick. I opened my mouth to speak, then her words repeated in my head.

"Wait, you said *they*, as in more than this piece?"

Her fingers twisted the side of her sweater, then she turned and crossed the room. She opened a drawer and took something out, then came back and set six pieces next to the one I had brought.

She slid each piece apart, leaving a space between them. She pointed to each one in turn. "One on the plane itinerary, all four tires at Quantico, and"—she slid the one I brought over—"one left in my mailbox." Suddenly, her story from the night at the dude ranch campout came screaming back to me. It had been about her.

"Yes." She seemed to read my mind again. "The trip itinerary story was about me."

"All right." I tried to place everything just so in my head.

"Each of these came when I seemed to be faced with a major life decision."

I studied the pieces, and they all looked clean and were cut the same way, and each had the red-dipped tips. I wondered who else would take the time to screw with her this way. "Do you think it was a message?"

"You're the detective. You tell me." She lowered herself onto the arm of the chair.

I closed my eyes and talked myself off the ledge as the logical side of my head kicked in. "Have you considered that someone might be screwing with you? Someone who you may have pissed off, like an ex-boyfriend or client? I mean, a simple internet search on either of our names would give plenty of unstable people a silver platter of ideas on how to hurt us."

"Of course I thought of that"—she ran a frustrated hand over her face—"but I make a habit of not making enemies, so . . ." She lifted a hand as if to say, *Your turn.*

"Okay." I nodded. But my mind spun. As unlikely as the idea might have been, was it possible she could still be watched by him? "I just can't believe, this whole time . . ." I stopped myself from saying something mean. "Bree, did you tell anyone?"

"I did. I told the local police in Virginia. I even shared the file on the Barbed Wire Killer, but they believed that it was someone at

Quantico who wanted to play a trick on me so I'd leave. They said given how well I was doing there, I was a target for that kind of behavior. I even called the detective who was on duty here in Sheffield, and I was dismissed again. He said that there were three murders in Kentucky a few years after the murders here and that though the case had gone cold, the killer most likely was picked up on a different charge and was now sitting in prison." She tossed her hands in the air. "I got shut down twice and had no one else to tell."

I stood. "Me, you could have told me. The one person who would have listened and helped." I took a pause and rewound what she'd said. I had heard of the Kentucky murders, and the lead detective on that case had sent over the paperwork to compare. In my and Cap's opinion, they had been extremely similar to the BWK cases, and they had never been solved.

She slid off the arm and took a step back like I was too close. "No, you didn't need that. You had enough going on. I wasn't going to meddle in your life."

"It's not meddling, Bree." I would have stopped time itself if she had told me she needed me in the past. "This could seriously be something. If this is him, it means he's still out there and apparently watching you! Doesn't that scare you at all?"

"Scare me?" She tossed her head back with a dark laugh. "*Scared* doesn't even scratch the surface of what my life has been since that godforsaken day."

I felt my temper rise. "You weren't the only one there, Bree. You're not in this alone." How could she not see that?

"But I am." Her face fell and twisted into a painful expression. "You had someone, Brad. You had Sherry. I didn't have anyone, and that's okay."

I felt a punch to the gut. How could she think she didn't have me? We had such a history together and a bond that was unlike anything I'd ever experienced with someone else, Sherry included.

"Back then I couldn't lean on you, or let you in, when we both knew where that could lead. You and Sherry obviously wanted to start a life, and my being here wasn't helping." She stepped back and opened the door, and I felt my heart sink into my gut, already bruised from her earlier comment. "You should leave."

"Bree, Sherry and I are divorced. We aren't together anymore."

"You might be done, but Sherry certainly isn't."

I gave a tempered sigh and stood in front of her and took her hand. "Please, I can't stand the idea that you've been dealing with all this for so long, all on your own." I wish she could hear me.

"Though it might not seem like it right now, Brad, I'm a strong woman and have been dealing with this twisted shit for years. My life is complicated, and so is yours. I just think we should take a beat and see how things go after we solve this case. I don't want to fight. I just want to sleep."

I squeezed my eyes shut in frustration. "I don't want to fight either." I softened my voice. "For the record you're an amazingly strong woman, Bree. Strongest I've met yet. I'm sorry that Sherry got to you. She's been a fucking pain in my ass lately." I leaned forward and liked that she didn't pull away. "If you want to take a beat, fine, but know I'm not letting you go that easily." I kissed her cheek. "I'm going to leave now." I stepped out into the cold and headed for my car. Now wasn't the time to push Bree. She was exhausted, and so was I.

I crashed at my parents' house. I needed time to think about how I could get Bree to see things the way I did. I must have slept the day away because the next thing I remembered was Ronnie smacking my leg from the other side of the couch. "Don't you need to get to work at all today?" He held a plate of food and stuffed a piece of steak in his mouth.

"What time is it?"

"Time for you to answer your damn phone. It's been ringing all afternoon." I waved off his comment and headed for my old bedroom.

My shower felt great, and after I changed, I saw I had a million missed calls from work. I grabbed the bag of food off the counter and yelled goodbye to Ronnie.

I stepped out into the cold night air and flipped up the collar on my jacket as I opened the car door. Just as the engine started, my phone rang, and I tapped the screen. "Stone," I barked.

"Hi, Detective, it's Officer Smith. I know you said anything to do with the nightclub case, to call, so that's what I'm doing."

"Okay, Adam, and . . . ?" I pulled out of the driveway and turned onto the main road.

"You know that Ram that we're pretty sure drove Ms. Jaminson off the road?"

"Yes, you mean the Ram with the light bar?" I just wanted confirmation.

"Yes, I've been following it now, sir, for the last few minutes." That perked my mood up. "I'm in my own car, so I don't think he'd make any connection to who I am, but before he does—"

"Where are you?" I interrupted as I pressed hard on the accelerator.

"I just left town, heading south."

"I'm coming toward you. Stay on him. I'll call it in, then I'll call you back."

"Copy that."

I turned onto the highway that led back to town as I dialed Cap's number. There was no answer, so I left a message. Then I tried Kennedy. He answered quickly, "Hey, what's up?"

I felt a rush of excitement. "Smith's found Timothy Ford's truck, and he's following him."

"No way!" I heard him grab his keys from the bowl by his door. "Where do you need me?"

"He's heading south out of town, and I'm heading in. I plan to cut him off, but we could use some backup. Who knows what he might have on him."

"I'm on the way. Did you call Cap?"

"Yeah, no answer."

"Cap just texted. He's on the way." Kennedy hung up, and I called Smith back.

"Adam, you still on him?"

"Yes, sir, though he's slowed a few times. It's late, and I think he might be wondering who I am."

I hit the wheel. The guy might be smart, but this was what we did. "Go around him, but keep him in view. If he turns, slows, anything, tell me."

"Yes, sir." I heard the blinker and his engine as it accelerated. "The windows are tinted, so I can't see inside."

"That's okay. I should be getting close. Just keep going." I pressed harder on the gas and was tempted to use my light bar, but the last thing I wanted was to spook him. Finally, in the distance, I could see headlights approaching. "Can you see headlights?"

"I do."

"Flash your lights so I know it's you." He did, and I knew I had the right vehicle. "Good. Now here's what's gonna happen. I'm going to let you both pass me, then I'll swing around and come up behind him. If he switches lanes, you do the same, and we'll block him in. Kennedy's on his way, and Cap's aware of the situation. And, Adam . . ."

"Yes, sir?"

"Any time you feel things aren't safe, you pull over. You hear me?"

He let out a long breath. "Copy that, sir."

"Good." I pulled back on my speed and waited for them to get closer. "Good. Just keep going like normal. Don't swerve or anything." I talked him through it. "The more normal we look, the smoother this will go."

The two vehicles passed me, then I took my foot off the brake to make sure my brake lights didn't show. Once they rounded the curve in the road, I pulled a U-turn and headed back toward them. "Okay, Adam, I'm behind him, and he's tapping his brakes. He wants me to pass."

"That's what he did to me."

I looked around and saw headlights way behind me. I guessed it was Kennedy. Suddenly, an arm popped up out of the window ahead, and the driver waved at me to go around. "He's getting nervous. I'm going to toss my lights on, so be ready." I flipped the switch, and my red and blue lights lit up the area around us. Instantly, the truck took off, but Adam was ready and blocked his path. He swerved back, but again Adam quickly blocked him. I grabbed the microphone and made sure I did everything by the book so there was zero chance a lawyer could find fault with me. I knew my dash camera was recording, so that would also work in my favor. "This is the SPD. Pull over."

Nothing.

I snagged my radio from the dash. "Dispatch, this is Detective Stone. I'm in an unmarked vehicle, and I'm following a wanted suspect going south on the main highway. Suspect is refusing to stop. I will be administering the PIT maneuver."

"Copy that, Detective Stone." The rush that normally came with this part of the job coursed through me.

I tried to contain my excitement at finally nailing this asshole. "Did you hear that, Adam?"

"Yes, sir. I'm ready when you are."

"Speed up so he doesn't clip you."

"Copy that." I heard his engine roar. "You're good to go."

I checked my surroundings and saw the coast was clear. Then I pressed on the gas and gunned it. I planned to bump his fender with my brush guard. He shot forward just as I was going to hit him. I got myself in position again, but this time he slammed on his brakes, and I flew off to the side.

"Shit!" I snagged the shoulder and fought to keep the wheel straight. My tires caught the rumble strip, and I was violently shaken. Suddenly, I was swung off on the shoulder when my wheel hooked in a groove. I was forced to drive next to him over the rough ground. My body bounced around like a rag doll. This wasn't good, considering how large his vehicle was compared with my car. I silently cursed the highway department for not keeping up the roads.

"Come on!" I fought to keep some kind of control. A speed limit sign up ahead was going to make or break this moment. The bottom of my car screamed at me to do something as it scraped along the nearly frozen ground. "Come on, come on!" I shouted at myself. I forced my foot to ease off the gas, and he took off ahead of me. I desperately swerved to get my wheels back onto the pavement. At the last second, I caught traction and skidded back onto the road. I zigzagged, trying to gain control, leaving a trail of rubber behind me.

Adam's voice pushed through the speakers. "You okay, Stone?"

"Yeah." I accelerated hard to gain some speed on him again. All excitement was gone. Now I was just pissed. "Get ready," I warned out loud. I acted like I was going for the right side of the bumper again, but at the last second, I switched to the left. He swung left, too, and I slammed into him, sending both of us into a twisting spin across the highway. Screeching tires deafened me, rocks and dirt flew all around us, but it was worth it when we came to a stop, and all I could hear was a screaming engine.

I tore off my seat belt and ripped my door open as Adam's car skidded to a stop ahead of mine.

"Cover me!" I shouted as I pulled my weapon and raced across the road where the truck had gone off the highway and hit a tree. "Hands up, Ford!" I yelled as I approached. I wasn't sure what I was walking up on. "Don't be dead, you son of a bitch." I carefully approached and felt Adam behind me. "You're not gonna get off that easily—" I opened the door and pointed my weapon. My stomach took a massive dive. "Who the hell are you?" I then called over my shoulder. "Smith, call a medic."

"Ahh." The man struggled to move, and my disappointment set in. I saw he'd been trying to type a text message. I grabbed the phone from him and read the text.

Zach Savage: Gumbo drive my truck to our meeting spot.

Me: Cops are on to the truck. I'll stall . . . was all that he'd been able to type in, but he hadn't pressed *send*.

Zach Savage, I repeated internally as it pulled at a memory from years ago. Huh . . .

"You got ID on you?" I felt around the man's pockets as he struggled to breathe. I felt his wallet and pulled out his license. "Rodger Gummy. Wow, that's quite the last name. I'd stick with Gumbo." Sirens could be heard in the distance. I checked the man over. "Can you speak?"

"No," he gasped.

"Well, that's a start." I wiggled a glove over my hand and felt his weak pulse. "Wanna tell me why you're driving Timothy Ford's truck and why you're texting someone named Zach Savage about us? Are you involved in those murders too?" His eyes widened and his mouth opened as if he were going to say something.

I felt around his stomach, and he yelped. "You've got internal bleeding. Looks like the airbag got you pretty hard. That's all I can see, but I'm no doctor."

His mouth opened, then shut again.

"I see you're wearing a cross." I gave him a little shake. "Hey, stay with me. Hey, Gumbo, you might wanna do the right thing with the man upstairs and tell me where Timothy is."

Saliva dripped from his chin as he turned his head ever so slowly to look at me. "This is"—he coughed—"far from over, Detective Stone. So many foxes." He smiled, then his head fell as he lost consciousness.

There had been a couple of times in my life when something had chilled me to my core. The river murders, the first time I'd witnessed my brother have a PTSD episode, and now this man's comment.

The medics arrived, and I stepped back to give them room. I tucked what I'd heard from Gumbo away to unpack later. I gave them as much information as I could as they took over.

"Stone," Cap called as he approached with Kennedy on his heels. "Did we get him?"

"No. It's not him."

"Fuck." He dropped his head as his face plummeted.

"Sorry, Cap." I groaned as we got close. I was just as pissed as he was.

"You good?" He looked at me, and I nodded. "All right." He put a hand on my shoulder. "Look, go home and give me your report in the morning. Let's make this as smooth as we can."

"I will." I wouldn't let Cap down, and he knew it. "But I got his phone—he was in Ford's truck and in contact with some guy named Savage."

"This is great, Stone. Good work. Now take a moment and shake it off."

"Copy that." I nodded without another word and hurried to my car. I turned the key, and once she purred to life, I headed to the city. My mind drifted back over the case, and my first instinct was to call Bree and fill her in, but I wanted to be respectful of her boundaries. I eyed the lake and felt my chest tighten as images of her swimming toward the shore flooded back to me. She could have died that night. The thought sickened me. I tried to force it away, but it stuck.

I didn't consider where I was headed. I just found myself at the bottom of the church steps. I think my soul must have known I needed guidance from someone higher up.

The place was empty, just what I wanted. I slipped into the middle row and drew in a deep breath and let my guard down. My eyes went to the beautiful stained glass windows, then I relaxed and bent my head.

I felt movement on the bench and quickly looked up. "Hello, father." My lips curved upward.

"Sorry to disturb you, my son. What a lovely surprise to see you again so soon. Are we sitting in silence, or do you wish to talk about what brings you here?"

I leaned forward and rested my arms on the pew in front of me. "I know I chose this life, one where I fight evil for the good. This case just seems different."

"How so?"

"This killer confuses me. The clues confuse me. It's a case like no other." I rubbed my eyes. "He's taken two lives now, and there is zero evidence of why. I get the sense he just enjoys messing with us. Why use a poison made from some crazy green moss?" I glanced at him. "Sorry, father, I shouldn't have revealed that."

"These lips are sealed as always." He patted my arm. "And now you're questioning why the Lord would allow such things." He raised his brows, and my mouth twisted at his comment.

"Maybe a little." I knew that wasn't fair. God didn't have control of everything. Demons were everywhere with their own agenda.

"The Lord takes who he needs, sometimes in the worst of ways. It's hard for us to understand. I can't say I understand why he'd take those two young women in such a way." He pointed to the ceiling. "I think of little Johnny Cleveland. Just playing one afternoon in his mother's greenhouse, and the Lord decided he needed him." He fingered the cross he wore.

Greenhouse? The word bounced around in my head. "I don't remember that. What happened exactly?"

"It happened in the next town over, Colville." He stopped to think. "Back in the sixties or seventies, I believe. He was playing with a friend and got into something, some kind of moss—I'm sure she said moss. Anyway, within seconds the little one was gone."

I looked up at the ceiling and felt something inside me shift. "Was the friend killed as well?"

"I don't believe so." He shook his head, then looked toward the door. "Forgive me, son, but I have to meet someone."

"Of course, thank you for the chat."

Something told me it was worth checking out. I called Cap.

"Stone, are you resting?"

"Cap"—I ignored him—"I want to check into something. Will you call ahead to the Colville PD and let them know I'm coming to look at some files?"

"I can do that. Want to share?"

"Probably nothing, but do you remember what detectives were working in the late sixties and seventies?" I knew his father had worked closely with the Colville PD back then.

"Sanders and Pera stand out the most. They both worked homicide. Sadly, both have passed."

"Okay." I repeated their names in my head.

"Keep me in the know."

"Copy that." I hung up and decided I wanted Bree along. Ten minutes later I banged on her door.

"Bree!" I called out. "Open the door."

The door flew open, and her face scowled. "Brad, for heaven's sake. What are you doing here?"

"Get dressed."

She leaned to the side and looked around me, then spotted the dirty side of my car from my earlier chase. "What happened to your car?"

"I'll explain. Just get dressed."

"Why?"

"We're headed to Colville." I told her a few details on the chase, but left out Rodger Gumbo's name.

Bree balanced her coffee in her hand as I held the door open for her. Once I showed my badge to the officer at the front desk and explained, she waved us through.

"Old files are stored downstairs, second door on the left. Knock yourselves out." She turned back to her laptop.

"Are you sure you're okay?" Concern was written on Bree's face, and if I hadn't been so focused, I'd have relished the feeling that she cared. "I can't believe you didn't tell me right away."

"I was trying to give you space."

She let the topic go and dumped her big purse on the table, then followed me through the rows of stacked boxes. "Okay, well what are the odds this isn't a wild goose chase?"

"You of all people understand a gut feeling." I scanned the scribbles of dates and names in marker. "I just think we need to check it out."

"All right, let's do this." She headed for the other side of the shelf, and we started to hunt. We stopped for a short break about an hour later to clear our heads but jumped back into it. Any clue that might give us something would be worth finding.

"Got it!" I yelled and pulled out a box and hauled it over to the table. I quickly went through the case files and pulled out the one I wanted.

"Oh shit"—Bree leaned over and held up a photo of young Johnny on a red bike—"he was so young." I looked away. No matter how many cases I dealt with, kids were the worst.

"Here it is." She moved closer as she read it out loud. "'Johnny Cleveland, age eleven, was playing with a friend in his mother's green-house when he inhaled something made from some kind of plant.' She swore she'd never seen it before and had no idea how he found it. There was an inquiry, but she was cleared."

"What do they say was the type of plant?" I waited for her to discover it.

"Um . . ." She ran her finger along the page, then stilled. "Oh my god, Brad." She pointed to the name. "'Butterfly root moss'! Do you think the mom might have something to do with our case? Like revenge on the girls or something?"

"I'm not sure of that"—I slid the file out of her hands—"but I'm interested to know why he died and not his friend." She stepped closer, and I tried to ignore the goose bumps her silky hair brought up on my arm as we both sifted through more paperwork.

"There's nothing here on the other kid, except that they kept his name out of it to protect him from the media."

"Mrs. Cleveland moved after her son's death"—she held up a hand-written note from Detective Sanders—"which is not surprising."

"No, it isn't. More times than not, the family moves to get away from the attention." I snapped a few photos of the file and sent it to Adam to dig a little more. "Let's go check out the place. It's not far." We tucked everything back inside the box and replaced it on the shelf.

The Clevelands' old house was on the outskirts of Colville. We parked outside the address and looked around. It was a rather dull-looking street. We approached the gate, and I pulled back the rusty latch on the chain-link fence and let Bree go first down the path toward the house. I scanned the windows for any sign that someone was home, but no car was in the driveway, so I wasn't optimistic.

"Ready?" she asked, and I reached over and rang the doorbell.

"Police department, anyone home?" I called out. I rang the bell again, then knocked loudly.

"Excuse me, Officers," a woman called from next door, "if you're looking for Mr. Gee, he won't be home until tomorrow. He's off visiting his daughter."

I stepped back to see an elderly lady holding her sweater tight around her.

"Good to know, thanks," I called and looked at Bree. "Go work your charm."

"Charm? You're one to talk." She chuckled as she walked toward the lady. I tucked that comment away for later.

"Excuse me"—Bree held up a hand—"can I ask how long you've been living here?" I lagged behind her a bit.

"Since I was a little girl. I moved here after my father got back from the war." The skin around her eyes smoothed as she smiled.

"So, you would have been here when little Johnny Cleveland had his accident?" The lady's face fell, and sorrow replaced her smile.

"Oh dear." She closed her eyes. "Would you like to come inside? I'll put some tea on."

I leaned into Bree. "See? Charm."

The warmth of the lady's house felt good. We sat in her living room and had tea placed in front of us. Bree warmed her hands and sipped the brew, but I let mine sit.

"What's your name?" I asked and pulled out my notepad.

"Jean Moddle." She leaned to the side and removed an old photo album from under her table. "I don't like talking about that awful day, but I'm also a believer that his memory shouldn't be lost."

"I agree." Bree spoke softly.

"Let's see"—she closed her eyes briefly—"it was a Sunday. Everyone was back from church, and the neighborhood kids were out to play. Johnny was a happy boy despite the fact that his father left when he was born. It was only him and his mother. She was a hardworking woman but found a love of gardening thanks to that greenhouse. It was there when she moved in."

"Did Johnny have any friends?"

"A few, my son included. But it was Reddy that was there that day." Her eyes drifted downward, and the corners of her mouth pressed in like she was uncomfortable. "That's not his real name, but he had these deep red cheeks when he got mad, and that's what the kids called him."

"Reddy," I repeated as I scribbled down the name.

Bree set her tea on the coaster. "What was Reddy like?"

"He was a little different from the others."

"How so?" That caught my attention.

She pulled her sweater tighter around her midsection. "I don't feel right talking bad about a child, but given what you're asking, I'll be honest." She stared at the wall. "He seemed nice enough, but he had a side of him that made me wary. I can't say I liked it when my son brought him over."

"Did he get angry a lot? Or was it something else?" Bree was onto something.

"No, it was just a sense I got. When things didn't go his way or he didn't like someone, he got this look. I noticed the boys would quickly give in to him. That look brought on a stone-cold chill, I tell you." She shivered. "I often wondered . . ."

"What did you wonder, Mrs. Moddle?" Bree shifted forward with interest.

"Oh, nothing, nothing." She waved her hands. "Don't mind the words of an old woman." She seemed to shake it off. "Anyway, after Johnny's accident, Reddy was in the hospital for a bit. I guess he got some of it too."

Bree shifted forward with interest. "What happened to him?"

"Some sort of nerve damage to his leg, if I remember correctly. He walked with a cane."

I thought of the bartender from the nightclub and remembered his hand shaking. He blamed it on being overworked, but now I wondered if it was something brought on by the poison. I made a note to look into it.

"How terrible." Bree rubbed her chest in sympathy.

"Mrs. Moddle, do you think Reddy had anything to do with Johnny's death?" I had to ask.

"I don't know. I'd like to say no, given he got hurt too. It's just that the boy had something wrong with him." She pointed to her head.

Interesting.

Bree stepped in. "You mentioned you have a son. Would you happen to have a picture of the boys? Maybe one of Reddy?"

"I do, actually." She started to flip through the photo book, and Bree threw a knowing glance at me; we both could feel there was something there. "Ah yes." Her eyes went glossy as she pulled out the photo and pointed to a dark-haired boy. "That's Reddy standing next to Johnny, and that's my son on the far right."

Bree held the photo between us, and something odd nagged at me. He looked familiar.

"And you have no idea what his real name was? Or maybe where he is now?"

"His family moved soon after as well. I think the other kids in town isolated him after that." She shrugged, then dipped her head to look at something. "I guess I do have his name. I see I wrote it on the back of the photo."

Bree flipped it over, and we both went cold. *What the hell?*

I drove Bree back home as she admitted that her head hurt. I really wished she'd rest and let herself fully heal.

"You rest, and I'll fill Cap in on what we found." I watched as she slipped her belt off.

"I wonder when he ditched the cane," she thought out loud.

"Yeah, I have many questions if we're right."

She hesitated as she reached for the door. "You'll update me?"

"Yeah." I nodded. I watched her leave and heard a text pop up.

Adam: I worked on the footage from Sophia's camera the night
she died, I was able to recover more footage.
Stone: Send me what you have. Great work.

I quickly called Cap.

"You find something?"

"I did." I hated where this was leading. "Cap, you won't believe this."

"Okay." He paused. "Let's hear it." I filled him in on everything as I drove to the station. Once I was there, Cap and I got together and came up with a plan. We texted Savage from Gumbo's phone.

"Now we wait." Cap smacked my shoulder, and I headed back to my car.

Later that night I paced the floor as I waited to hear back from Cap. When he called to say we had a response to our text to Savage, I had to sit down. Savage had thrown a wrench in our plan. We hammered out a new idea. I only hoped it would work. Feeling mildly better, I headed to bed.

The next morning, while I was in the kitchen, my phone rang again, and I saw it was Sherry. My mood plummeted, but I answered.

"Hi, Bradley. I know you're up and probably having your coffee."

"What is it, Sherry? I'm just about to leave for the office." I reached over and poured my coffee down the sink.

"I wanted to remind you about the fair."

Oh, trust me, I remembered. We had attended the fair every year of our marriage. Even at the worst of times, she had dragged me there.

"Seriously, Sherry, what's your angle here?" I was tired of her mind games.

"Angle? There's no angle. It's just that this is our thing, and I thought we were going. Oh please, Bradley, it would be so much fun."

"It was your thing, not mine," I reminded her. "Regardless, I have to work." That was a lie, but she didn't need to know that. She didn't need to know anything anymore. I thought of what Cap and I had planned for the fair and exactly how we needed it to happen. The last thing I wanted was Sherry showing up and screwing things up. "I heard it's going to be dead. I'd skip it and save your money."

I heard her sigh. "I see. Yeah, maybe I'll skip it." Good. "You know, I thought we could at least be friends."

"I thought we could be friends, too, Sherry, until you started messing with Bree's head. You crossed a line when you were with her in that ambulance. I put my trust in you that you were going to be there for her."

"Bradley, no, you misunderstood—"

"I gotta go." I hung up before she could say goodbye.

I had a meeting with the chief, but to my relief, he canceled, which meant I had a few hours free. I needed to do something with myself given the facts that Bree needed space and Sherry's sudden need for my attention was exhausting. I needed to work through our plan, and the last thing I wanted was Sherry in my head.

My mind went to Bree. I thought again about my decision not to include her in the takedown. I knew it was unfair, but I worried about her safety. She'd been through a lot but had never been through something like this. I shook it off.

I nearly made it out of my driveway when Officer Stanley called through.

"Mornin', Stone. I'm putting a gal through to you—name's Donna Jay. She works for Sea Foam Brew. Says she has something to share."

"Go ahead." I stopped the car and waited for her voice to push through.

"Detective Stone, my name is Donna, and I worked with Sophia before." Her voice sounded nervous. She paused, and I heard a small whimper. "Sorry, I still can't believe she's gone."

"I'm so sorry about your friend, Donna." I tried to be sympathetic while anxious to hear what she might have to offer. "Was there something you wanted to share?"

"Yes." She sniffed and let out a long breath. "I'm not sure who you spoke to or haven't yet, but I would investigate Jeremy Law—he's a brew rep with Sea Foam, and she used to complain that he followed her home a few times. He was always creepy with her and hated when anyone else would flirt with her."

Ah yes, I remembered he was on our list of people to check out. "Any idea where he might be?"

"Actually, yeah." She paused. "He's at the Velvet Nightclub right now. I work across the street when I'm not working nights there, and I can see him."

"I'm on my way." I eased out onto the road. "Whatever you do, don't engage, and don't let him see you watching him."

As I pulled into the driveway of what the media now called the Murder Club, my gut told me something was off. I could see the owner, Longboard, next to the building. He had his arms in the air and seemed to be in a heated conversation with a man who I assumed was Jeremy Law wearing a Sea Foam Brew jacket. I parked and watched them argue as I radioed in my location, then shot Cap off a message about what I had heard, that I was at the club, and that I was going to check it out. I activated the AirTag that was embedded in the inside of my jacket. Captain had asked us to wear them given how crazy this case had become.

As I stepped from my vehicle, Longboard suddenly reached out and knocked the man's clipboard out of his hand; it hit the ground not far from me, and Longboard looked my way, then shook his head and headed inside the club.

"Asshole," the guy muttered as I grew closer. He picked up the clipboard and started to walk down a narrow alley next to the building where his truck was parked.

"Good afternoon." I hurried to catch up with him. "Excuse me."

"What?" he snarled over his shoulder as he reached his truck. He started to load some boxes of beer into the back.

"Looked like you and Longboard had some words back there."

"Yeah." He spun around. "And what's it to you?"

I pulled back my jacket and showed him my badge. "It means a lot to me, and to a case I'm working on."

His face paled, and he pulled on his gloves with a huff. "You're a cop?" He lifted the dolly into the truck.

"I'm a detective workin' on the club murders." I grabbed hold of the end and helped him load it. "I want to ask you a few questions. What's your name?"

"Jeremy Law. Haven't you already asked all your questions? I've seen you here a few times talkin' to people."

"Yes, but I want to ask you a few questions. We haven't talked yet."
He shrugged.

"What's going on with you and Mr. Longboard?"

He tugged his winter hat down over his ears as I quickly sent his name to Cap to check him out. "He just canceled our contract. Said our brand reminded his customers of the murders and he doesn't want to let brew reps advertise in his club anymore." He used the back of his hand to wipe his nose like a child. "Guess we're in the media too much. I reminded him that any kind of publicity was good publicity, but as you saw, he disagreed, and there went my Christmas bonus."

"Well, given that it was one of your young reps who was strangled to death in the guy's club, I can see where he might be coming from."

"Maybe." He shrugged like the whole situation didn't faze him. He grabbed his clipboard again and started to study it.

"You know what I do find interesting?"

"What's that?" He didn't look up.

"The killer knew right where to stand to be out of view of the camera. Like he knew where the blind spots were."

"Watch any of their videos, not hard to find the blind spots." He snapped his gloved hands.

"Also, the camera strapped to Sophia's chest had this odd clasp on the bottom. It took us several tries to open one like it, yet with the timing of how fast he worked, the killer must have known exactly how to unclip the camera case and was able to take it off before anyone saw him."

He pinched the bridge of his nose. "And you think we're the only company that uses those kinds of clasps?"

"Maybe," I said and went for a lie. "What I found the most interesting was that during their struggle, the camera flickered back on just for a second." I noticed his pen stopped midstream as he wrote "rejected" over the canceled invoice. "I'd like you to come down to the station for a chat."

He flipped the clipboard shut. "Do I have to?" He quickly glanced at me. "I've still got deliveries to make." He shifted uncomfortably.

"Unless you have something to hide, Jeremy, it shouldn't take long."

"I guess I don't have a choice." He looked over his shoulder. "Look, I'm gonna be out my bonus, and I'm about to be on my boss's radar. Do ya mind if I just grab my phone and let the other bars know that their shipments won't be arriving on time? Maybe I can at least save my job."

I understood what the loss of a bonus and a paycheck could mean to a person and their family. I wasn't heartless. "All right." I nodded. "Make it quick, though."

I stepped back and nodded at him to go ahead. As he slipped around the driver's side of the truck, I noticed a bit of blue paint in a small dent on his bumper. I snapped a quick photo of it and the license plate. A text popped up and pulled my attention.

Captain: Kennedy pulled up that truck driver, Jeremy Law. He's got priors, I'd say get him down here.

Oh shit. I shoved my phone into my pocket and reached for my cuffs when something hard hit my back, and I went flying into the wall. Everything went black.

A loud engine noise pulled me from the abyss, and I blinked back the fog and quickly took in where I was. Country music played loudly from a set of poorly tuned speakers; every few seconds static took over the words.

My back lay against the cold steel on the floor of the truck. I tuned into my training and replayed everything that I could remember before I ended up there. Something wet was on my face, and when I tried to reach up to touch it, my arms jerked and bounced back. They were held in place. He'd used my own handcuffs to secure me. *Awesome.* Little did he know, Kennedy and I had spent endless hours finding ways to get out of handcuffs. I almost laughed.

"Hey." Jeremy banged on the grate just above my face. "You awake in there?" I didn't answer and kept still as I assessed the situation. There were boxes of beer bottles by the roll-up door, kegs were locked in place, and twine was thrown about everywhere.

Tink. Something hit my face. A screw had worked its way loose from the grate that covered the opening from where he was to the back, where I was. I awkwardly ran my thumb over the other screws and felt they were all quite loose.

"Hello?" He banged on the grate again, and I stayed quiet. Then his phone rang. "What?" he barked, and I struggled to keep still to try to make out the words. "Yeah, well I have an even bigger problem than that Sophia bitch." The music made the next bit difficult to hear. Then he paused as he listened to someone. I took that opportunity to peek out and saw we were on one of the country roads. Where in the hell was he headed? "No, you need to come!" His raised voice could be easily heard over the music. It was full of anger and frustration.

"Shut up, John! Just fucking meet me where I said and bring the guys—I don't want to go up against this one alone. He's fucking built and has at least two feet on me."

I knew I couldn't let him get to wherever that was. I'd be outnumbered, and he had my gun. I was as good as dead if I didn't take action fast.

Inching my thumb around the spare key in my shirt cuff, I managed to free it from the stitching and made short work of getting out of the cuffs. I stayed low and moved to the wall next to the doors.

"Shit." He had removed the safety release handle on the inside. "I guess you aren't completely dumb," I whispered.

We hit a bump, and the bottles rattled together, and it gave me an idea. I tore open a box and inched the cap upward, letting the carbonation slowly fizzle out. I emptied the bottle and tucked it in my jacket pocket. Then, keeping myself low, I crept back to my position by the grate. He suddenly took a left and headed down an unpaved road. I slammed down hard and groaned at the impact.

"About time you woke." He snarled and turned to look over his shoulder through the grate.

I stayed in place so he couldn't see I wasn't handcuffed anymore. I used the cap and started to loosen the screws around the grate. They came out easily, and the noise of the bumpy road and music covered any sounds. He suddenly looked in his rearview mirror with a scowl.

"Don't think of getting clever, Detective!"

"Wouldn't dream of it," I muttered and looked at him through the grate. "I used to drive trucks." I needed a distraction so he wouldn't realize what I was doing. "Yeah, back before this job I did deliveries, then I worked for a steel company." The third screw came free in my hand, and I pressed hard on the grate to keep it from rattling.

"I don't give a shit what you did."

"Maybe you don't, but I know what you did." I fought the last screw. "Why'd you kill Sophia?"

"What?" His face went red in the mirror. "I didn't kill that bitch."

"*Bitch*, huh?" I finally got a good grip on the screw and twisted hard. It let go, and the only thing that held the grate in place was my hand. "In my experience when a suspect uses terms like hate toward a victim, there's more to the story."

"Get out of my head!" He hit the wheel.

"Did she dump you? Is this a bruised ego?"

"Fuck you, Detective Stone!" He held up my license. "I know where you live. I know your age. And I know you were married."

"And I know you killed Sophia. What happened? Did she dump your pathetic ass? Why'd you kill those girls?"

"What? I didn't . . . Ahh!" He screamed and sped up. "You know you're dead, right? Like you aren't going to make it out of this alive."

I waited for the perfect moment, as I knew things were going to happen fast.

"If my fate's sealed anyway, why not tell me? What'd I miss?"

"Miss," he muttered. "What did *I* miss, you mean? Every time that girl was left alone, another man would hit on her. I got text messages to show proof she was a little whore. Then that night, two men this time trapped her in the coat room. They said something that upset her, and-and-and," he stuttered, "and I tried to help, but she never listens to me. I had to make her listen to me." His gaze moved up in the mirror and latched on to mine. "What choice did I have? She wouldn't stop shouting, and I needed her to shut up. I didn't mean to kill her, but she just wouldn't stop talking."

"So, you did kill those other girls, too, right?" *C'mon, give me something.*

"You think I killed the—" Suddenly, his shoulders went stiff, and he shifted in his seat. I saw a car coming toward us and waited for it to get closer.

It was time.

I let the grate drop, pushed my arms through the opening, and wrapped them around his neck. I pulled hard. I knew this was my one and only chance, as I couldn't risk him getting close to where his buddies waited.

The truck swung to one side and then the other. I struggled to keep a tight grip. It came down to him or me, and I wasn't about to die in a beer truck.

He tried to pry my hands from his neck, and the truck swerved crazily. I lost my grip when the truck flipped on its side. We hit hard, and I was thrown against the beer kegs.

A loud, high-pitched noise drove through my brain like a nail gun to the ears. I fought to open my eyes, and when I did, the light matched the intensity of the noise. I did a quick evaluation of myself, and all things considered, I was all right. I stumbled a few times but soon made it to my feet. The truck was a mess, beer was everywhere, and I felt the broken glass as I fought my way out. The impact had blown open the back doors. My legs were like rubber as I wobbled toward the front of the truck. I needed to see if he was still alive.

I jumped up on the wheel and looked down into an empty cabin.

"Shit!" Blood stains on the empty seat and bloody handprints told me he was injured. I looked around the ground near the truck. As the sound of sirens approached, I started to track his footsteps.

"Stone!" Captain yelled as he flew from his car.

"I'm fine." I held up a hand. "The fucker got away," I snarled, beyond pissed he gave me the slip. I was better than that. "He killed Sophia."

He nodded, then left to get things started. "I need a five-mile perimeter of this area," I heard him yell.

Kennedy came flying up with Officer Smith. The car had barely stopped before Kennedy rushed to my side. "They got him less than a mile back. You okay?"

"Yeah. They got him?"

"Yeah, he got past Stanley." He gave me an odd look just as Officer Stanley joined us.

He rubbed his lips as he looked me over. "Sorry, Detective, he got by me. I didn't even see him." I glanced at Kennedy, who shook his head at me.

"Go fill Captain in." I nodded with my chin toward Cap's squad car.

"Copy that."

When he left, Kennedy handed me a water bottle. "He didn't see him." He rolled his eyes as he repeated Stanley's words. "He could hardly have missed him. What'd he do? Step aside to let him pass?"

I turned to watch Stanley as he moved slowly toward Captain, and something odd passed through me. Stanley was young, smart, and quick. To think he didn't see a man running toward him made the hair on my neck go up. I hated to think badly about a fellow officer, but my gut told me that it was odd. But I had bigger shit to deal with first.

My phone rang, and I answered it without looking at the ID. "Stone."

"Hi, Detective Stone, it's Rudy Vamp. Remember me from the impound yard?"

"Yes, of course I do, Rudy. You have something for me?"

"Yeah, well I was going through that Ram and found something."

I held up a finger to Kennedy so he wouldn't walk away. "Okay, I'm listening." I tapped the screen and moved the call to speaker so he could hear.

"I think I might know who ran your partner off the road."

Chapter Fourteen

BREE

I was in heaven. A sound I had missed so much after I left home was the sound of a horse's hooves when they crunched the brittle leaves of autumn. It was a beautiful morning as Patrick led the way along a rarely used path near the lake. He explained he didn't want to run into any guests. It was obvious my brother was struggling with something, and when he had asked me to join him for a ride at breakfast, I had known it had to be important. Plus, Brad had a meeting this morning, and I knew I could spare a few hours for my brother.

"I miss seeing you in flannel," he teased. I looked down at my hunter green flannel jacket. I needed it at least until the sun warmed the day. My light jeans and white T-shirt weren't enough to keep out the chill. "It's a good look for you."

"Thanks." I steered Toby around a fallen log and wondered when Patrick was going to open up. It was a twin thing to sense what the other might be feeling, and in that moment, I felt he was all twisted up inside and needed to get whatever it was out. As someone who lived that way daily, I totally got it.

My history of working with runaway kids also had taught me how consuming mixed-up feelings could be. If not handled right, they could make things way worse. I needed him to bring it up first.

We came over a big hill to a clearing and stopped to admire the view of our ranch. I looked over at the Stones' property and Ronnie's cabin a little farther up the lake. People paid money to come here, but we got to live here. Since I'd been back, I had repeated that sentence to myself more than a few times to remember how truly lucky I was to have this place to call home. "Oh man, Patrick, I just can't believe what you guys have done with the ranch."

"Mm" was all he offered me.

"This time of year, it's like a watercolor coming alive."

Patrick adjusted his beloved cowboy hat that Dad had given him as a graduation present and squinted over at me. "I'm going to need you to pray, Bree." He pulled his chin in like he might lose it. "This is a hard one."

Everything faded away as his words filtered through. I nodded and gathered myself for what he might say. I tried hard to give him a moment to get hold of himself but finally had to ask. "Is it Mom or Dad? I know Mom was sick before. Is it back? Is it Dad? He never gets *sick* sick!"

"Bree, no one's sick."

So many things ran through my head. Shit, what if it was Charley? I knew he wasn't back from visiting his mother. Maybe something had happened.

"No one is sick," he repeated as if he knew my head was still there.

"Oh, thank God." I blew out some air and tried to calm myself. Then my brain pushed a thought forward, and I couldn't believe I hadn't seen it before. He and Maxine had been distant lately. "Maxine?" The muscles around his mouth tightened, and his eyes went glossy. "What's going on, Patrick?"

"I think she's seeing someone."

I couldn't help my reaction, but I tipped my head back and laughed loudly. It echoed off the hills and found us again. It made my asshole-sister moment that much worse. "Sorry, I'm sorry." I tried to pull myself back in, but it was a struggle. "Patrick, that woman is so madly in love with you, she trips over her own feet when you walk into a room—she texts me about you almost daily. I mean, come on, she lights up whenever anyone so much as mentions your name. You don't do that if you have a sidepiece. So," I said and swatted him with my reins, "why on God's green earth would you go there?"

He bit his upper lip the way he did when he was little, and I noticed he tightened his grip around the horn of the saddle. "There's this doctor."

"Okay, let me stop you right there. Maxine hates doctors."

"Normally yes, but this new guy started, and she's been gushing over how great he's been. And whenever he's in surgery, she's his right hand. She's missed dinner three times in the last two weeks because Doctor McSteamy wants her to work."

"Oh, man, turn off *Grey's Anatomy* and watch some true crime."

He rolled his eyes at me. He knew I watched more drama shows than he and Maxine combined. "I'm serious, Bree. I'm actually nervous for us. She's taking on extra shifts, barely can hold her head up in the evenings, and mutters about how she should just sleep at the hospital because it'd be easier than coming home. That shit plays on a guy. She walks around like a zombie. I suggested she take some time off to get some rest, but she wouldn't hear it."

"All right." He had a point. "I agree it looks bad, but we're talking about Maxine here. Look, Patrick, I've got the weekend off—why don't I swing by and see what I can find out?"

"You'd do that?"

"Of course I would. You know, besides Lainey and Charley, you're my most favorite couple, and I refuse to let anything happen to what you have."

He lifted his hat and ran his gloved hand through his short hair. "Okay, yeah, that would be good. I just don't want to be blindsided."

"Makes sense. Leave it with me, and I'll figure it out."

"Yeah, okay." He grinned and shot me a look, and I knew what was about to happen. "Race ya home?"

I didn't get to answer before he spun the horse around and took off in a full gallop toward the house.

"Such a cheater," I yelled out as I followed him down the hill and along the trail. Now I knew why he suggested I ride Toby. God love the little fatty, but he was slower than dirt and usually tried to stop for a snack at every tree branch. I got maybe five minutes of run out of him before he slowed and snorted like that was enough. "Damn, Toby, maybe we need to lay off the snacks." He turned his head and looked at me, and I could have sworn he glared. He reached up and grabbed a branch and began to chew. "I should've ridden Kevin. That porker can move."

A twig snapped, and I whirled around in the saddle to see what it was. "I swear to God, if that's you, Kevin, we're done. I'll fry you up so quick."

"I do love some morning bacon." Ronnie stepped out onto the path, and my heart slowed. "Sorry, didn't mean to scare you."

I smiled and looked around. "What are you doing out here?"

He broke eye contact with me. "Ah"—he lightly laughed as if embarrassed—"truth? I think I had an episode, because one moment I was in the kitchen making a sandwich, and the next I was under some brush with a stick trained on a rock." He smiled again as if he'd made a joke. Then he dropped his head and rubbed it in frustration. "It's pretty messed up when you fight for a country that won't fight back for you."

I slid off Toby and dropped the reins because I knew he wouldn't go anywhere. I moved in and gave Ronnie a hug. "I'm sorry you're not getting the help you need."

"I get some." He shrugged. "It's just not enough to really do anything."

"I can't even begin to imagine where your head goes." I put a hand on his arm.

"Can't you?" he challenged as he pulled back and motioned for me to follow.

I snatched up Toby's reins and looped them over my arm and walked with him.

"Your battle might look different from mine, but we're still both affected up here." He pointed to his head.

"Maybe." I hated that the topic was now me.

"I know you hate to talk about it, and so does Brad, but keeping that shit inside hasn't done me any good."

I knew he was right, but it didn't make it any easier to open up. "I hear that a lot." I chewed on the inside of my cheek and knew my next question wasn't cool, but I couldn't help myself. "Did Sherry ever ask Brad about that day?"

"She knew Brad never liked to talk about it, so she never pried. It made her a safe place for him to be, I think. He didn't have to think about the dark stuff. She kept things upbeat, easy." He scrunched up his face as he thought. "But that's not healthy—your person should be the one you can share your deepest fears with, not help you hide from them. I think that's why I was so happy when I saw you were home, because maybe you two could talk."

"I can't be that person for him, Ronnie. I'm a mess about it myself." I shook my head. If I couldn't do it with Dale, I certainly couldn't do it with Brad. It made it harder because he'd actually been there that day. "I've got Sherry jealous of me being around Brad. She sees me as a threat. In spite of their divorce. I think she wants him back."

"What?" he shot back a little too fast. I pulled in my chin as he looked at me funny, then his face fell like he was holding something back. "She might, but he sure as hell is finished with her. If it helps, he was finished with her before you came along. The only reason he's even trying to keep things civil with her is because we grew up here and everyone talks." He gave me a pointed look like I could relate.

"I get that."

He nodded. "So, you and Hayne, huh?"

I chuckled. "We're just friends, that's it."

"I'm glad of that. He's a great guy to do a tour with. He had my back just as much as I had his, and shit, did we see some things that would knock the church right out of you. But Hayne isn't really boyfriend material. He's more of a good time, if you know what I mean. Just be careful. We share the same demons, and sometimes I think he might be worse off than me."

"Noted." I appreciated the insight from him.

"Well, this is me." He waved a hand as we reached the edge of the lake. "God, Bree, it's so nice to have you back."

"It's nice to be back."

"I'll never forget my brother's face when you left," he blurted, and I went still. "Just, don't run off again like that without letting us know. You didn't just hurt him"—he pointed to my parents' house—"you hurt everyone."

I felt shame at the way I'd handled things that day. I'd been hurt, and my head had spun off its axle when I heard he was going to marry Sherry. Something inside me just broke, and it still wasn't fixed.

"Yeah, I hear you." I gave him a quick kiss on the cheek, and he gave me a little shove toward the path. I swung my leg over Toby and slowly began to head up toward the ranch. One of these days I had to concentrate on mending myself.

"You're slipping." Patrick laughed from where he stood on the porch.

I flipped him the finger, then jumped when Dad stepped in front of me. "Bree."

"Dad." I glared down at the fat little runt in Dad's arms. "Breakfast?"

"You know, if you were nice to him, he'd be nice back." Dad rubbed the porker's head.

I looked over at Patrick, who watched with amusement. "Maybe if *he* was nice, I'd be nice back."

"He knows you want to eat him," Patrick called over his shoulder as he went inside the house.

I grinned down at Kevin. "Good, remember that." I made a V with my fingers and put them to my eyes, then pointed at him as if to say I'd be watching him.

"Behave." Dad scowled. "Here." He held up a set of keys. "She's old, but her engine works, and she's got decent tires. It'll get you from A to B."

"Poppy's truck?" I held the keys up like they were for a new Lamborghini.

"Your truck is done, and you need to be able to get around."

"Dad, thank you, but I know how special his truck is, and honestly, I just haven't had the time to get a new car, but I can."

"And until then, Pop would want you to use his. Now, I need to help your mother with a few things, and you need to figure out what's up with your brother lately."

"I'm already on it."

"Good." He put Kevin down and slapped his thigh as he left, and the little bacon slab followed him.

I squeezed the keys in my hand and knew I had to take her out for a spin.

I started the engine and eased her out of the barn. I grinned happily as I drove down the driveway and headed for the hospital.

The ER seemed quiet, and I was pleased to find Maxine standing in front of the vending machine. She just stared at it as though she were stuck in some kind of trance.

"Max," I called out, but she didn't turn. "Max." I touched her arm, and she finally looked at me.

"Hey, Bree." She forced a smile, but the bags under her eyes told me she was well past exhausted. "Did we have plans?"

"Nope, but I brought food from Bailey's Diner." I swung the bag, and I watched a little life come back to her face.

"You're a good person, Bree Jaminson. Good people bring hungry people food, and I'm so hungry." She used her badge to let us into a small, unoccupied room, where we sat on an uncomfortable leather couch.

"I feel like I'm auditioning for a porn shoot," I joked as the fake leather squeaked beneath us.

"Try sleeping on it." She yawned and ripped the paper off the barbecue wrap. "Not that I don't love surprises like this, but is everything okay?"

I popped open the box and started on the salad before my wrap. I stabbed a crouton and decided not to bullshit her. She was clearly exhausted, and mind games weren't something she needed.

"Truth?" She nodded. "Patrick is scared you're cheating." *Subtle, Bree.*

"What!" Her face fell, and tears flooded her eyes.

I held up a hand. "I laughed when he said it, but I have to ask, are you okay? Because for Patrick to bring up something like that is big."

"I'm not cheating—I love your crazy brother."

"I know that," I assured her with a squeeze to her arm. "That's why I laughed, but you do seem off lately, and I just need to know you're okay."

She took another bite of her wrap and closed her eyes like food was all she could think about. "I'm really not sure I can tell you."

That was interesting. "Why?"

"Because Lainey made me promise not to say a word."

Of course, I should've known. "Okay, what did she tell you?"

"That things are tight at the ranch and a huge party that she was banking on to cover some of the bills canceled without notice. It set them back, then a pipe broke in cabin one, and the chimney in the main house is causing some concern. Charley can fix some of it, but he's not a plumber. I just took on some extra shifts to try to help out."

"Max, that's not your problem."

"Yes, it is, Bree. We all live there, and we all want to see the ranch succeed. It's on all of our shoulders, not just Lainey and Charley's."

I respected that, and since I'd been gone and not helping, I felt horrible. I knew things were tight but not to this degree. "I'm sorry, Max. I had no idea. But why can't you just talk to Patrick about this?"

She brushed a tear away. "Because he puts everything on his own shoulders and tells me not to worry about things. He works so hard at the ranch and was even talking about getting a second job. Bree, he works from sunup to sundown. It's the last thing he needs to do." How I wished that I'd come home sooner. "Your sister has great ideas, but they're costly. In time it will even itself out, but not when things keep breaking."

"Listen, I've got some money saved and will offer it to Lainey to help." I inched closer. "Thank you for being honest, Max, but I do think you need to do the same with my brother. Lainey and I haven't had much time to talk lately, and Mom would never breathe a word." She sniffed, but I had one more question. I hated to ask it. "Don't kill me for even asking this, Max, but Patrick mentioned some doctor, he calls him McSteamy." I chuckled, and she did too. "He's worried about him."

"He really needs to get into ESPN." She crumpled up the paper from her wrap. "Dr. Matt is just a young doctor that was open to me working under his rotation. He's new and loves being in the OR, and like I said, I'm taking as many hours as they'll give me. But the idea seems to be taking a toll apparently, and not just on me." She leaned forward and rubbed her head. "I'm so tired." She sniffed. "I just want a night with Patrick with good food, TV, and an early bedtime."

"Okay," I said, and she looked at me confused, "but you're not going to get that at the ranch. There're too many distractions. I still have my place in New York. Let me call my neighbor and get her to fill the fridge for you two, and you can enjoy a long weekend reconnecting."

"What about the chores? We can't leave everything on the others."

"I'll cover you. Just get the days off and spend some time with my brother so you guys are right again. I hate seeing you two like this."

"You'd do that for him?"

"No, but I'd do it for the both of you." I leaned in for a hug. "I'm sorry I didn't know about the ranch troubles. But I'm here now. Think of me as extra hands and extra income."

"Please, don't tell Lainey I told you." She leaned back, and I could see how hard these past few weeks had been on her, and my heart broke. She'd inherited the ranch struggles, and that just wasn't right.

"You have my word."

"'Kay." She left, and I tried to recover from that kick to the gut. My family needed me, and I hadn't been around enough to see it.

I had texted Brad a few times looking for an update on our possible new suspect, but he told me nothing had come back. I really hoped we were looking at the wrong man.

As I drove through the streets of Sheffield, I let my mind wander. I'd spent years studying the Barbed Wire Killer, and I'd always come up empty. He was meticulous and smart. There wasn't one shred of evidence of who he could be. He was a ghost to everyone, an afterthought by now, but to me he was still very real, and the thought that my life was like a game of chess for him burned hot inside me.

I parked and blinked at where I had ended up without even realizing it. The café had the best cup of coffee in town. I thanked my subconscious and went inside.

I ordered, paid, and carried my cup over to where the cream was. A man moved in beside me and smiled at me as he ripped open two sugar packets and poured them into his cup. He skipped the cream and stirred. I couldn't help but recognize that it was just like Brad's order. I let my mind go there, and I wondered what he had been up to today. My heart wanted him—I knew that—but I kept going back and forth in my head about my life in New York City. I loved my job. I'd worked so hard to get where I felt I was really giving back. It had brought me so much joy and filled something that had been desperately missing in my life. Being back in Sheffield brought back that constant, deep-seated fear in the pit of my stomach. If it weren't for Brad, I'd never consider moving back here.

"God, it's good to see you." Suddenly Charley wrapped me in his arms and squeezed me tight.

"You're back." My voice was muffled by his shoulder.

He leaned back and held my chin up to study my face. He squinted as if to read my mind. "Sit with us?"

"Sure." That was odd. I followed him to a back table where it was quiet, and my sister waved at me as I approached.

"Hey, Lane."

"Hey, baby Sis." She gave me a hug, then looked at Charley like I'd missed something. "I'm going to order a few things for our guests. I'll give you a few minutes alone."

"Okay." I was clearly missing something. I held the hot coffee between my hands for warmth.

"I need to apologize, Bree. I wanted to come home the moment I heard what happened to you, but my moth—"

"Charley, where is this coming from?" His worry came from left field.

"You're upset. I can see it. I'm upset, too, and your sister needed me."

I cut in again. "So does your mother. I'm fine, Lainey is fine, even that jerk of a pig is fine . . . for now," I added for good measure and grinned. "Charley, we're all okay."

"Then what's with that face that I just walked up on? Because that was a serious face you were wearing."

"Nothing," I answered too quickly, and he tilted his head like I wasn't fooling anyone. "I'm just . . ." I stumbled to find the right words. "Okay look, I don't know where I'll be after this case, but Robert brought me on, and I feel like it's taking a lifetime to solve it."

"Are you doubting your skills?" He made a face like I was being ridiculous.

I leaned back and let out a long, steady breath. "I know how teens think, but this guy's got us stumped. He's so smart. Just too good."

"Which is stirring up old feelings on a case you couldn't solve. Maybe that's clouding your mind."

I gave a light shrug. "Maybe."

"Bree"—he twisted his paper cup between his hands—"Lainey wasn't the only reason Robert brought you on board. He knows you. You're a smart cookie, and you're relentless."

"Thanks, Charley, but—"

"Look, maybe you just need to get out of your head, step back, do something fun so you can unclog your thoughts and see what's right in front of you. All the clues are there. You just have to look past the noise."

"Yeah, fun. That does sound like something I should do. Maybe you're right."

"Of course I am." He grinned as we stood. "Can I ask you for one more favor?"

"I'm listening." I tilted my head at him.

"Ask Lainey out for a night. She's been working overtime, and frankly you both could use it."

He was right, and I needed to focus on the family more. "Yeah, I'd like that." I looked up at him. "I forgot how much I needed you guys in my life."

"Lonely out there, isn't it?"

"Very." I pushed the pesky tears back as we headed outside.

"Bree?" A male voice came from behind us.

"Go have fun." Charley waved before he headed toward his car, where Lainey was waiting.

Hayne jogged to catch up. "I was hoping I'd find you in town today. If it's not too late to ask, I wonder if you want to join me at the fair tomorrow night."

I couldn't remember the last time I'd been to a fair, let alone the one in our town. Charley's words echoed in my head about having fun, and I found myself nodding.

"You know what? That sounds like fun."

He handed me a ticket. "Good. I'll pick you up at seven?"

"Okay." I held up the ticket. "Thanks."

Once I was back in the truck, I sipped my coffee and pulled out my phone. I had a text message.

Brad: We found where Timothy Ford lives. I'm heading there now.

I couldn't type back fast enough once he texted the address.

Bree: On my way.

I thought for a second and switched to Kennedy's chat, knowing he'd most likely give me more details.

Bree: How did you get Ford's address?
Kennedy: After the chase, the Ram was brought to the impound lot. Brad got a call from Rudy, a guy who works there and found a gym membership under the seat. Cap made a call and got them to give up his address. It's him alright.
Bree: That's crazy, weird how things work out, but we'll take it. Thanks Kennedy, I'm heading over there now.

I added the address to my GPS and headed over.

Our number one suspect had a house on the outskirts of town, and by the time we arrived, SWAT and most of Sheffield's PD were in place down the street. I tried to ask a few times about his car chase, but Brad was so focused on this suspect that I had to let it go.

"Hey." He made the motion for me to roll my window down as he got closer. "Stay behind me, let me ask the questions, and if I tell you to do something, you do it. Understand?"

"Yes." I gave him a firm nod. There was no way I'd run the risk of screwing up for anything.

He held my gaze for a moment, and I saw something just below the surface.

"Want to tell me what's really going on?"

"I just"—he cleared his throat—"I just need you to be okay, so do as I say."

"I promise," I reassured him and stepped out when he stepped back. We walked up the driveway like we were a new couple looking to move into the neighborhood; at least that's the story we were spinning.

Brad threaded his fingers through mine as he knocked on the door. I hated and loved how much that simple touch did for me.

The door opened, and a lady who looked to be the housekeeper looked at us with a strange expression. "He's out back." She stepped aside without another word, and Brad wasted no time and pulled me with him through the house toward the back door. He let go of my hand as he stepped outside. I instantly missed the safe feeling his hand had given me. Timothy Ford's yard was well maintained. He had a large greenhouse set in the center of his garden beds. Brad pushed the door of the greenhouse open, and I followed hard on his heels.

At the far end of the greenhouse sat a battered Timothy Ford. His face had been beaten to a bloody mess, yet he seemed calm and raised his hands high into the air.

"Isn't this where you say, 'Hands up'?" He shrugged.

I noticed his hands had no obvious signs of a fight. His knuckles had no cuts or bruises. No defensive wounds. How odd.

"Detective Stone, welcome." He gave a happy smile, but his lip cracked when he did, and he flinched. "And PI Bree Jaminson, lovely to see you again." Brad kept his weapon on him as he took a step closer to me. I fought the urge to grab his arm. "I'm so pleased you made it out of the lake." His eyes lit up.

I grabbed Brad's arm to stop him from charging blindly toward the strangely smug man. Something was off here. "We know it was you who ran me into the lake."

"Of course it was." He was eerily calm. "You saw my face at the club, and that could have messed everything up. You needed to be dealt with, but . . ." He shrugged again and looked away as he touched his bruised cheek. I waded through a sea of Amazon boxes and thought he had a minor obsession with online shopping.

"I may have looked at you, but I didn't see you." I hoped that comment hit home.

"Yes, well, I suppose we both learned a lesson." He touched the cut on his lip, and I wondered who beat him up and if I could buy him dinner for what he did to Ford.

"Who did that to you? Was it Rodger Gumbo?" Brad's voice was sharp.

His lips twisted into a dark smirk. "Wouldn't you both like to know?" Then like a villain in a movie, he blinked away the darkness and grinned. "Just look at the two of you—you found me." He looked almost pleased as he held up his green-dyed thumb with a chuckle.

"Why?" The question dropped out of my mouth before I could stop it. "Why kill those girls?"

"Kill?" His face snapped back. "Oh no, no, dear, I'm just in awe of a much higher power. I'm a mere disciple of his work."

"Wait, so you didn't kill Maggie Deloitte or Shelly White?" I kept up the conversation, as I'd noticed Brad seemed to be looking all around the greenhouse, as he kept his weapon pointed at Timothy Ford. I took it to mean he wanted me to keep talking. He'd told me to stay quiet, which apparently, I couldn't do, so why wasn't he stepping in? "So, you weren't at the club when those girls were murdered?"

He opened his hands on the table he was sitting behind. "I didn't say that. I said I was an admirer, if you will. This entire thing is just"—his face wrinkled around his eyes and mouth as he beamed from ear to ear—"fascinating."

"Fascinating?" I repeated.

"We're so proud of you both." He pointed at my hand on Brad's arm. "You must be pleased, Stone?"

"Meaning?" Brad finally said something.

Ford leaned forward and squinted at Brad. "To have everything back to the way it should be."

Brad shook his head. "Listen, asshole, I'm not into mind games. It's time you put those hands behind your back. We're done here."

I gave his arm a squeeze to back off. I wasn't into mind games either, but he was talking, and that meant we might get something to hang him on.

"But you have green stains on your hands, so if you aren't the killer, and you obviously know who is, you're involved somehow." I looked around the greenhouse as it came to me. "You have the knowledge."

"Good girl." He beamed.

"Your hands are green, your name was on the nursery list, you knew where to be and at what time to see it happen," I said, and my brain spun with all the possibilities. "Which means you made the drug."

"Smart and pretty." He gave that weird, proud smile again. "I knew this was going to be fun. I knew I had to be a part of this."

My head started to piece the puzzle together, but there was a hole. "Did you send those letters to the girls?"

His smile widened. "I wanted a part in the game too." *Game?*

"That explains why the post dates were off," I muttered to Brad. If he wasn't the actual killer but wanted to play the game, as he put it, he could have been sending them after the girls were killed.

"Well done." Ford nodded, and I glared at him. He really did think this was some sort of twisted game.

"But why send one to Sophia? She was strangled. She wasn't poisoned." I could tell he wanted to gloat, and I hated to feed that, but we needed answers.

"I wanted to see if I could derail you, so I sent the letters. I thought the one I sent Sophia would really mess with you." He laughed. "I knew it was only a matter of time before young Jeremy would snap. He was obsessed with that girl, but she wanted nothing from him. So, in order to have a little fun, I got hold of his number and sent a few anonymous texts. I included some photos of her flirting with other men. As I expected, he snapped, and voilà." He waved his hand like he held a wand. Brad's sudden intense expression caught my attention. I wanted to ask, but I couldn't risk Ford closing up.

"So, you're saying Jeremy killed Sophia, and you had nothing to do with it?"

"Well, I wasn't the one that killed her. I just gave a little nudge, if you will." He looked pleased with himself. "It was all so easy."

"So her death had no connection to the murder of the other two women at the nightclub? That was just you playing Jeremy and screwing with us." I was incredulous. "And that was fun for you?"

He touched his injured lip and looked down. "Yes, well, it was until it wasn't." He looked up at me. "I crossed a line and paid for it."

"Paid?" Damn him and his twisted answers.

Ford leaned back in his chair and rested a hand on his lap while he tapped the table with his other fingers. "It's so frustrating, isn't it? Being so close to the answer that's been staring you in the face all along?" His voice was conversational, as if we had all day. "You know, now that I say it out loud, I suppose the two of you must be quite familiar with that feeling. Am I right?"

I felt a cold sensation wash over me. I knew he referred to the Barbed Wire Killer, but I wouldn't give him the satisfaction. I remained deadpan.

"You haven't even scratched the surface of this entire thing. So many foxes." He smiled, then he suddenly turned to look to the right as if someone was there. I looked where he looked and then—

It happened fast. Ford pulled a gun and put it to his own forehead. Brad yelled "Gun!" and shoved me to the floor.

"Don't do it, Ford!" Brad yelled as he pointed his weapon at the man. My heart pounded; this could go sideways in a hundred different ways.

Bang! Bang! I felt something heavy fall on top of me, and my ears rang. The acrid smell of sulfur filled my nostrils. Fear filled me as I scrambled out from under Brad's body. He must have thrown himself on top of me. Oh my god! Had he been hit? What had happened?

"Brad, Brad! Are you okay?" I desperately needed to know he was all right.

"I'm fine, I'm fine." Brad lifted me off the floor in one quick moment and checked me over. His hands were everywhere. "Are you hurt?"

"No. Jesus, that was scary." My words sounded far away. God, how I hated guns. I put my hands to either side of my cheeks and slapped myself in hopes it would help clear the panic I'd felt that Brad had been shot. I saw Ford's bloody head.

I couldn't believe how quick Brad's reflexes were. I hadn't even seen Ford go for his gun. A second later, SWAT stormed the greenhouse and cleared the scene while my heart was still wedged in my throat.

"C'mon." Brad pulled me to my feet and whisked me outside.

"The asshole shot himself!" He shook his head in disbelief at Kennedy and Cap as they rushed up. "I tried to wing him, to stop him. Dammit! Now we won't get any answers." He smacked his leg in disgust.

He walked me right to a squad car and sat me inside and closed the door. He turned his back as he spoke to the guys. I couldn't hear anything, and the damn car doors wouldn't open from the inside, so I couldn't get out. I wondered if that was Brad's intent. *What is he up to?*

Once the guys left, he opened the door and bent down. "You okay?"

"I am." I really wasn't, but I was good at tucking away the things that scared me. "What was that all about?" I pointed to Cap and Kennedy.

He looked away. "Nothing." I wanted to push, but I could see he was still reeling from what happened. "Brad, you asked Ford about someone named Rodger Gumbo. Who is that?"

He started to fill me in about how Gumbo was driving the truck and how he was texting someone named Savage. "I'm not sure how he was connected to everything, but I'm still working on that. He's been in and out of surgeries. The doctors said it doesn't look good. The chances of us getting anything from him are slim to none. I'd be surprised if he made it another day."

"Wow, okay." I still couldn't believe Brad had a full-out chase and made it out unharmed. "I asked Kennedy how you guys found Ford's address. Lucky break."

"It really was." He shrugged, then looked over his shoulder at someone. "You sure you're okay?"

"Yeah."

"Good, you should go home. You're putting your head through a
lot lately."

"I'm fine." I wished he'd stop worrying.

"Look, I've got something to deal with. I'll call you later, okay?"

"Brad." I snagged his hand so he'd stay put. "Why do I feel like
you're hiding something from me?" I didn't miss the way he lifted his
chest. I'd seen kids do it when they were about to lie. "Oh shit, Brad,
what's going on?"

"It's nothing. Go home, Bree. That's an order." He leaned in and
kissed the top of my head, then turned away.

Chapter Fifteen

Brad

I tapped the file against my leg as I studied Jeremy Law. The kid could have had a future with Sea Foam Brew if he hadn't become obsessed with Sophia. Now she was dead, and he was probably going to jail for life. He sat in the interrogation room, looking pale and tired, but he still had a cocky tilt to his head. A day in prison hadn't been enough to shake him.

"He seems pretty confident." Officer Smith stepped closer to the two-way mirror. "If it was me sitting there shackled to a table, I'd be sweating through my jumpsuit. 'Specially if I was about to see the detective that I kidnapped and tried to kill."

"Mm," I grunted in agreement, "he thinks I can't find any evidence to connect him to Sophia's death. He'll serve time for what he did to me, but slap a murder charge on him and I bet he'll crumble."

"Do you have something to actually connect him to Sophia's death?" He pointed to the file I held.

"He confessed, and you recovered more of Sophia's tape, and Ford gave me something. I can work with that."

"But that's not really enough, is it?"

"It will be soon enough, when I make him slip up." I pushed down the handle of the door and stepped into the room, leaving Adam to watch. In my experience I had found that guilty people sometimes gave things up while trying to cover their tracks. Since I didn't have much to go on, I needed him to slip up. But first, I needed to know one thing.

"Detective Stone." The corners of his mouth tugged upward. "We meet again."

"Indeed, we do." I pulled a chair out and held down my tie as I took a seat.

"Glad to see you're no worse for wear since the accident."

I kept my eyes on the folder and ignored his dig. I took a moment to think about the angle I was going to use. "I'm going to jump right in here, Jeremy. I got a call from a man named Timothy." The skin around his eyes tightened, and his head tilted ever so slightly. *Interesting reaction.* "He told me you guys were in the same grade at the same high school. Also seems he provided you with a solid alibi for the night Sophia was murdered." I lied, but I needed to see if he and Ford knew one another. If he didn't, Ford was telling the truth.

Nervousness showed in his microexpressions, but hope made his eyes widen and his pupils dilate.

"Well, see, like I said, I didn't kill Sophia."

"That's not how I remember the conversation." I held his gaze.

"You did get a hard knock on the head in that crash. You may've thought you heard me say otherwise, but you can't prove a thing." His smug smile only increased my hatred for him. "Besides, you said Timothy gave an alibi for me, so what are you doing here besides making me skip lunch?"

"Hmm." I nodded a few times. "What's Timothy's last name?"

Jeremy's cheeks squeezed under his eyes. "God, it's been years."

"And yet you met up with him only weeks ago." I let him stew on that for a sec. Then he scratched his nose as he bought himself time. "Let me refresh your memory. It's Gumbo."

"Yes." He pointed at me. "Gumbo, Timothy Gumbo. It's such an unusual last name that I always forget it."

"I see." I pulled out three photos and placed them in front of him. Timothy Ford, Rodger Gumbo, and my brother Ronnie stared up at him. "Which one of them is Timothy Gumbo?"

He slid his hands off the table and hid them from view. The muscles in his jaw flexed as he tried to pick the right person. I was surprised when he went with the youngest man in the lineup. "Middle photo."

I pressed my lips together and knew in my gut he had no idea who any of the men were. I couldn't help but look up to the window at Adam. I imagined he was smiling too.

"Are you sure?"

He leaned back and plucked the photo off the table to study it. "Yes, see that right there? That's a tattoo." He pointed to the middle man's collarbone. A tiny swirl of a tattoo showed from where the shirt was pushed back slightly. "He got that his senior year."

My heart gave a quick leap.

"What?" He caught my change in mood.

"You just gave me what I needed." Now I was the one who wore the smug smile.

The veins in his neck flexed as he looked at the photos again. He was panicking. "You got nothing."

I pointed at Ford's photo. "Timothy *Ford*." I moved my finger to the far-right photo. "That's Rodger Gumbo, and this guy right here"—I tapped the middle photo—"is my older brother, who, by the way, got that shoulder tattoo while overseas protecting the very country you live, well *lived*, free in."

"Okay, so I screwed up. He looked like a man I went to school with."

"No, sorry, you just outed yourself." I gathered the photos. "I know you have no idea who the two suspects are that we've connected to the nightclub murders, but I do know that you killed Sophia and why you did it at the club. You hoped we'd think it was the original killer."

"You got nothing," he repeated.

"No?" I stood and pulled out two more photos from the file. Thanks to Bree and Adam's magic with the iCloud account, I showed him the extra footage from the night she was killed. "This was taken the night you killed her. You knew how to open that clasp to take the GoPro off. That's not an easy thing to open." I set another photo down. "This is a still shot from that footage, which revealed this mark on the wrist." I ran my finger along the jagged cut before showing him the next photo. "This is you at a gas station the night after." I smiled at him. "You see that right there? See how your sleeve pulled up your arm as you handed the clerk the cash? That jagged zigzag scar." I grabbed his arm and flipped over his wrist to reveal the same scar as in the two photos. "You cut yourself on a keg a week before you killed Sophia." I slapped down the hospital report of his stitches. "Maybe next time you decide to kill, think of any identifying marks that could out you."

"This isn't fair!" He slammed his hands down. "She played me!"

I leaned down. "No." I chuckled darkly. "She wasn't the one that played you." I stabbed a finger at Ford's photo. "He did." His face twisted in confusion as he studied the next couple of photos I put in front of him. They were of the text messages that Ford had sent Jeremy. "He saw your obsession with Sophia. He got your number and started to feed you photos of her flirting." I pulled out his phone records and pointed to the highlighted number that had texted him numerous times. "He saw you were weak and decided to see if he could make you snap. He totally played you into killing Sophia."

"She was such a bitch!" He looked stricken as his world crashed around him. "I want to make a deal." His tone was low and defeated.

"Deal?" I laughed. "There's nothing more that I want from you. There'll be no deal. I hope it was worth it to you, because from now on you'll be living behind bars." I reached for the door but stopped myself. "I'll be sure to spread the word that you're single. Now who's the bitch?"

His jaw sagged open, and I hoped Sophia enjoyed that one. As I exited the room and the door slammed behind me, I saw Adam's face light up with joy. My phone vibrated in my pocket.

Cap: Sorry to do this at such a busy time, but I need you in Florida ASAP. I'll email you the details.

I closed my eyes and tried to remember this was all part of the job. I sent back a quick text.

Stone: I'll watch for the details.

"That was impressive." Adam beamed after I tucked my phone away. "Now what?"

"Now we move on to the next takedown."

"It's hard to let a serial killer dictate where a takedown will be. I'm worried it's such a populated place."

"Yeah." Smith whistled. "Do you think he's onto you? Or does he really think it's his friend, Gumbo?"

"No clue, but we're going to go with it."

"I know you have an idea who it is." He looked hopeful I'd spill it.

"Sorry, Smith. It's just an idea." I followed him out, and as the door closed behind us, I added, "And I really hope I'm wrong."

I cleared my thoughts as I sat in my car. I needed the quiet to regroup. The last few weeks had been a whirlwind. Kennedy waved from where he'd parked, then rolled down his window.

"Are you ready to catch this sick SOB?"

"Damn right, I am." I gave him a thumbs-up.

Later that night, as I sat in my car in the parking lot, I filled my cheeks with air, then blew it out hard as I steadied myself. I prayed that all this would come together as I hoped. I glanced at my watch and knew I had fifteen minutes. I bit my lip as I thought about Bree and how angry she was going to be at not being part of it. I picked up the report of her accident at the lake and thumbed through it. I had the same sick feeling as when I'd first read it. What if she had drowned? What if he got his hands on her? I'd always cared for Bree, and now she was back in my life, and I wanted a chance to do something about it. It made me want to protect her with every fiber of my being. It was why I'd decided to keep her out of the plan. I wanted her home safe and sound. I slammed the car door and headed toward the ticket stand.

I zipped my jacket up to my chin when a cold breeze sent a chill through me, and I got my head into the plan. I flashed my badge and was quickly waved through the fair gate. I was glad Cap had gone along with my idea. As I looked around at all the people enjoying their taffy apples and caramel corn, my mind went back to Timothy Ford. If there really were so many foxes, then I was on my way to catching another one—and I was sure this was the last place he'd think we'd strike. I looked around, then squeezed the button of the radio in my hand. "Cap, I've got eyes on the south entrance." I scanned the crowd again.

"Copy that, Stone. I've got eyes on the west."

"Kennedy, are you in position?" I glanced up at the haunted house, where he had a bird's-eye view of more than half of the place.

"Brad, check your nine o'clock." I caught his tone and turned and held my phone up as if I were reading something on the screen. I raised my eyes and saw Bree and Hayne.

"Shit, shit, shit," I muttered. What the hell? I wanted her home. Why was she at the friggin' fair? I'd been avoiding her calls all day. I knew she'd been wondering what I was keeping from her, and if I dared to try to explain that I wanted her to stay home, she'd fight me on it. "I don't want her here."

"Good luck telling her that." Kennedy chuckled. "I guess Charley didn't get your message to run interference." I should have called him instead of texting.

Hayne motioned her toward a ring toss game, and I heard her laugh and clap as she tossed the ring and it landed over the neck of the bottle. She must have felt my eyes on her, because she suddenly turned and locked eyes with me.

I don't want her here, I repeated in my head as she came closer. When she got near, I saw her face and realized she was pissed.

She looked pretty in her tight jeans, and the black shirt she wore was swooped low in the front. Then her perfume found my nose. It was the kind that turned off all rational thinking and . . . *Stop.*

"Are you purposely avoiding my calls now?" She narrowed her eyes at me.

"Sorry, it's been a day." I kept it vague.

She tucked her hands into her pockets. "I thought we were supposed to be partners." When I didn't respond, she studied me. "Are you all right? What aren't you telling me?"

I searched the faces around us. Someone caught my attention, and I shifted my gaze there. Bree moved to stand next to me. She followed my line of sight.

"You seem on edge."

"Yeah, it's all good. I just have a lot on my mind."

"Yeah." She lightly chuckled. "I get that."

I knew she did, and I felt some comfort in her answer. I glanced at Hayne, who kept his distance. "So, you and Hayne seem to be spending some time together." I was digging. She knew it, and so did I.

She held up a finger to Hayne to let him know she'd be another moment. Then I could tell something caught her attention. "Why are Ellis and Adam over there?" She squinted in a different direction as my stomach tightened. "Are you working? Is that Cap?"

Shit. I needed to do damage control. I'd made a mistake in not including her.

"Hey, look at me." I moved in front of her. "Don't be pissed."

"I can't promise that." She folded her arms and glared at me. Guilt burned in my gut.

"Look, I'm really sorry, Bree, but—"

"Oh my god. You're here, right now, to get him!"

"Yes."

She looked hurt, and I didn't blame her. I already felt shitty about my decision to leave her out of it.

"Once again, I thought we were partners."

"Look, I promise I'll fill you in more later, but in short, we used Gumbo's phone to contact him, and he chose this place to meet up."

She pulled her chin in and pinched her brows together. She was really mad. "And you weren't going to share that with me? Brad, I went with you, and we discovered that name together. I was brought in to help solve this case. Why am I being shut out now?"

"Keep your voice down." The last thing we needed was to call attention to ourselves. "Look, I'm sorry, but—"

She raised her hands, then dropped them. "Who made the call to keep me off this?"

"Me." I knew she wasn't going to like that one. "Wait." I stopped her from leaving. "Bree, you're not even healed from your concussion. You haven't had this kind of training, and I can't risk this guy getting his hands on you."

"That's not your decision to make."

"As lead detective, it is."

"Everything okay here?" Hayne was suddenly by her side, and I had to push my frustration back.

"Yeah." Bree dropped her hands. "Just give us one more minute."

"Sure." He gave me a strange look but held back.

"Look," I said and gently took her hand, to pull her attention back to me, "please, I beg you to go home."

"No."

This woman was going to kill me. "Bree—"

"Bradley!" Sherry's voice made my stomach drop. "What the hell? You couldn't take me to the fair, but you took *her?*"

This was going south fast, and I didn't know how much time I had left before this guy showed up.

"Why the hell would I take you to the fair, Sherry?" I was beyond finished with her.

Bree stepped in. "Sherry, you're wrong. I'm not with Brad. I'm here with Hayne. I just walked in on this. He's here for work, and I'm not involved." I felt that dig, and it stung.

"You're working?" Sherry seemed skeptical.

"It's true," Kennedy piped in over the radio, "and, Bradley, get in the game here, man. We need all eyes on this crowd."

"Stay off the damn radio." Cap sounded pissed. "This isn't friggin' *As the World Turns*."

"Sorry, Cap." As I spoke I pitched the bridge of my nose. "Sherry, please go, for your own safety."

Anna came up and tucked her arm through Sherry's. I saw the nasty glare she threw Bree. "I think we're done here. Come on, Sherry." For once I was happy her friend Anna was there. I needed Sherry away from me.

"Kennedy." I didn't have to say more. He knew I wanted him to keep eyes on Sherry. It would be just like her to circle back.

"On it."

I turned to Bree, but she held up her hand to speak first. "I know, you need to work on *your* case, and I need to get back to my night." She moved past me, but I caught her arm discreetly.

"Just do me a favor, if you see anything off, just call me, don't engage. If I'm right about who this is, he'll try and kill you."

"Apparently, so did Ford, but I handled myself well in that situation. Don't you think?" She was right. She'd been great, but this was different. "All the more reason we need to get this guy tonight." She then shook her head. "Oh wait, sorry, not *we*. I'm not a part of this." She glared and pushed past me. "Have you asked yourself why he'd pick such a public place to meet? Maybe he's onto you too." Her face spoke volumes as she looked around. She was right. I had thought about that, but we needed confirmation that it was indeed him, and if it was, we were coming for him.

"Good luck on your case, Detective Stone." The fact that she called me Detective Stone hit hard.

I took a deep, calming breath and tried to get my head back on the job.

Kennedy took a chance with Cap's temper and used the radio again. "Yeah, she's pissed, dude."

"Can you blame her?" I radioed. "Sorry, Cap."

"Possible suspect entering the north gate," Ellis chimed in over the radio, and I snapped back into work mode. "Black hat, green jacket, jeans. Stand by for confirmation."

"Kennedy." I looked around. "Where's Sherry?"

"Ferris wheel."

I went over and ducked under the rope. "Hey, man." I flashed my badge at the worker. "See those two women up there?"

He stepped back and leaned to look up. "Yeah, pink seat?" He pointed to the stripe on the bottom of the bucket seat.

"Yeah. Do me a favor and keep them on this ride until I get back." I handed him a fifty. I couldn't risk one of Sherry's jealousy moments ruining everything.

"Sure thing, boss."

"Kennedy, do you have eyes on Bree?"

"Coming up on your right."

Hank appeared and blocked my view of where Bree was headed. "Bradley, finally taking some time off?" He smiled. "Nice to see you out enjoying yourself."

I stepped back, then smiled warmly. "Hey, Hank. Not surprised to see you. I know you rarely miss a fair day."

"True, Michelle and I never miss it." He gave his wife a side hug.

"Nice to see you, Michelle." I smiled again as my radio crackled in my ear. I fought to not react to it. I desperately wanted to know where Bree was.

Hank seemed to catch the moment and gave a quick wave. "Well, I'm sure you want to get back to your evening. I'm sure it'll be more eventful than ours." He huffed a laugh. "Us older folk are on our way to buy cotton candy so we can later regret it."

"I hear the blue is the best." I'd actually never tried that spun sugar coma, and I never planned to. "You two have a great night." As I turned, I heard Kennedy let go of his breath over the earpiece.

"No one move until he hits his mark," Cap spoke. "We need to be a hundred percent sure he's our guy. There's no goddamn way we're gonna blow this case because someone else answered that text."

"He's walking, he's walking," Ellis whispered. "Okay, Stone, start heading that way. Bostwick and Stanley, you two go get into position."

"On it." My adrenaline spiked in anticipation. I had mixed feelings about the whole thing, but it was what it was.

"Kennedy?"

"Fun house." I didn't have to ask again. He knew I meant Bree.

The radio crackled again as I kept a steady pace toward the mark. Cap's excited voice broke over the radio. "We got positive DNA off Maggie's dress. You were right, Stone! He got sloppy." A part of me didn't want to believe that it was him, yet here we were. "Keep your eyes peeled. He'll be jumpy, and he may not be working alone. Everyone hold your positions and be ready. There're a lot of people here."

"Copy that, Cap," I answered for all of us. I'd convinced Cap to go with my suspicions even before the DNA results came back, but it was good to have it confirmed before we moved in. I scanned every face as I moved toward a concession stand. "Let's also assume he's carrying." I paid for some popcorn and opened my phone like I was anyone else waiting for someone to get off a ride. I popped the salty goodness into my mouth and kept my eyes on the crowd under the rim of my ball cap.

"Stone." Kennedy's voice alerted me something was wrong. "I have eyes on the suspect—he's now entering the fun house." *Bree!* I tossed the popcorn and raced off in that direction.

"Ellis and Adams, head that way," Cap ordered.

Hayne felt me approach and rolled his eyes as I came up next to him. "Where's Bree?" I blurted.

His face dropped, and he licked his lips like he was holding back what he really wanted to say. "Come on, Brad, you're killing this for me."

"Hayne, I'm here undercover, and I need to know where she is."

He cursed, then shook his head, annoyed. "Inside—" I barely heard the rest as I raced around the front. The suspect had already gone inside. I pushed through the small lineup and flashed my badge.

"This ride's closed until I clear it," I instructed the guy at the door.

"Okay." He shrugged.

I lifted the radio and spoke quietly. "I'm in the fun house. I've shut it down. No sign of him yet."

"Copy that. I'm moving your way," Kennedy replied.

"This is unlike any fun house you've been in before." The recording started as I entered the first room. "These are the rooms you dream about at night. The doors to all your fears have been left open."

I took a moment to let my eyes adjust to the dark room. It looked like it had been bombed several times. Dirt and fake broken cement blocks were everywhere, and the floor was slippery as I tried to hurry my way through. I imagined he would be a few minutes ahead of me. I hoped he'd be affected by the stuff inside the house enough to slow him down a bit. I stepped into the hall and was forced to take a sharp left. The music helped muffle my steps but also muffled his. I ducked when something shot out at me, but it stopped just inches from me. A swinging sandbag seemed to come from nowhere and almost hit my side. I knew they were just full of stuffing so they wouldn't hurt if they were to reach you. They were just to make you jump.

"Ahhh!" someone screamed up ahead, and I picked up my pace but stopped when I saw the girl. A boy laughed at what had just made her scream. Strings of marbles were used to skew the lighting. I reached up and pulled some off and tossed some in their direction.

"Hey," I mouthed as quietly as I could, then put my finger to my mouth as I showed my badge. Both kids froze. "Go back out the way you came." They didn't even question me, and the boy grabbed her hand, and they dashed back toward the front entrance. I tucked the marbles I still held into my pocket in case anyone else was up ahead.

I stepped into the next room and caught sight of his jacket just as the door slammed shut. "Welcome to your worst nightmare, where not everyone is as innocent as they seem. Can you spot them?" The recording gave a spooky laugh, then a strange smell was pumped in from somewhere.

"What the hell?" I scanned the fake dead bodies thrown together everywhere and thought how sick people were to use these kinds of ideas. I was all for scary stuff, but whoever the creator was of this house had clearly re-created a mass murder. It was gross. They had crossed the line from being fun and scary to disgusting and inappropriate. There was enough bad stuff like this on the news every day, and people didn't need more.

I put a hand on my weapon when the light went off, and a black light clicked on. Five letters lit up in neon pink. *IYKYK.* It stood for *if you know you know.* I hated that we lived in a world of acronyms. The lights flickered, making it harder to see. It wasn't hard to figure that the object of the game was to solve the puzzle. I studied the scene, then moved around each victim until I spotted a young shooter. I pulled the replica of a gun from his hands, and it shot up in the air, attached to some sort of retractable cord. Once it disappeared, the door behind me slid open.

"Gross." I felt like I needed a shower. That delay had caused me to lose my visual on the suspect. I only hoped he'd struggled with it longer than I had. The floor sloped at a steep angle, and I had to hold the wall to keep from—

Suddenly my feet were kicked out from behind me. I hit the floor and plummeted down a metal slide. The moment I hit a mat in the dark room, I quickly rolled to the side, then jumped to my feet and pulled my weapon at the same time. I heard someone behind me.

"So, you figured it out." The voice had come from somewhere beside me. I turned and aimed at the sound as I blinked to get my eyes adjusted. My heart sank at the sound of his voice. Even though I knew the truth, it still brought pain. That I had been so wrong about the man

I thought he was weighed heavily on me. But then the lifeless young faces of Maggie and Shelly came to me, and I felt a whole new level of anger. How was this man capable of being so heartless?

"I did. I know it's you, Hank," I yelled and used my voice to muffle the sound when I clicked on the radio. I wanted the others to hear us. "Give yourself up, because you've got nowhere to go." I was able to make out his silhouette as he moved and tracked him with the muzzle of my gun. The only light was a tiny red hue in the far corner of the room.

"Have you enjoyed my performance?"

"Performance?" I mocked. "I've seen better."

"I guess I should step up my game." He sounded amused. "Maybe we start with what I didn't finish at the lake."

"Funny, because right before Timothy Ford died, he took credit for nearly killing Bree."

"I suppose that's true." I heard him race off, and I followed but tripped over something on the floor. I fell but used the momentum to roll back up onto my feet. The next room was all mirrors. They were angled to disorient you, but at least there was better lighting, and I caught sight of him. I quickly jerked in his direction only to come face-to-face with a dead end. *Shit.* I had to think like this house of horrors. What appeared left wasn't left at all. The floor shifted under my feet, and I was turned in a different direction. "Why the fair?" I spun on my heel and saw that when the floor shifted, so did the mirrors.

"Why not?" His voice seemed to come from behind me. I slowly turned. "What better place than this for such a performance?" He laughed. It wasn't lost on me that he used the word *performance*. I wondered what else he had planned.

"Why, Hank?" I called as the lights spun. "I've known you for years, so why do it?"

"She's quite pretty, isn't she?" He spoke from somewhere different from before. I was thankful that he was still there and hadn't given me the slip. "I understand the infatuation."

"Were you doing this for someone else, Hank? I can't believe you really wanted to kill those poor girls. Or was it something from way back, maybe because of your friend? The one that died in the greenhouse when you were a kid?" I wanted to keep him talking. Then I quietly spoke into my radio. "I've got him with me in the mirror room," I said, filling the team in.

"No." He made a strange sound almost like a sigh. "I wish those girls were my subjects. I would have had a much deeper connection when their lives slipped away. I would have chosen something much more intimate."

"Subjects?" That was an odd word to use. "So, they were an experiment?"

"In a way, yes." I heard a door open and click closed, but I could see Hank in a small, tilted mirror, so I knew he was still with me.

"Dammit, get back here." I pretended I was pissed he'd left. I cleared my mind and refocused. Puzzles were a big part of my job, and I loved that part of it. I planted my weight firmly on both feet and watched how the plates moved under them. One movement to the left, two to the right, and another two to the left before the pattern repeated.

I could feel his presence in the room, like a dark chill that prickled at my skin. I'd known the man for years and never gotten a bad vibe from him. That played on my mind. *Focus.* The mirrors repeated the same pattern then in an opposite sequence. I counted the directions as I moved through the maze. I let the floor swing me around in a new direction, and I came face-to-face with Hank. He swung, and I ducked, and he yelped in pain as his fist slammed into a mirror. I jumped and fought the floor as it turned to change my direction. Two mirrors turned inward, and I was able to slip between them, grab Hank by the jacket, and haul him with me backward. Suddenly, we both whirled around in opposite positions, and I lost my grip on him as the lights went dim in spots around the room.

I prepared myself for Hank to reappear when the floor swung back around. I planted my feet, raised my fist, and was ready to drill him in his face when Bree suddenly appeared.

What?

"Brad?" She looked confused.

I reached out for her only to slam my hand into mirrored glass. This place was maddening.

"Brad!"

"Ah, look." Hank chuckled darkly from somewhere. "We have company."

I saw his reflection in two of the mirrors, but I didn't bite. I jumped to a different track and tried to see if I could catch her. The floor started to turn, and I forced myself to stand still and try to study the pattern.

"Ms. Jaminson, how lovely you could join us." I heard his feet scrape as he hit the floor. *Where is he?* "Tell me, how is your head?"

"Brad." Her voice was so quiet I hardly heard her, but when I turned toward the sound, she jumped onto my track, and I wrapped my arms around her to keep her with me. "Is that Hank?" she whispered.

I tilted her head up and nodded so he couldn't discover where we were. Her face hardened, and her eyes went wide with understanding. *You need to get out of here,* I mouthed.

How? she mouthed back.

I looked desperately around for the exit. I hoped I could get her out so I could focus on Hank. I didn't want him to catch us both together— it was too dangerous. I knew we needed to split up, but the thought of letting her out of my sight didn't sit well with me.

Whoosh. A knife sliced through the top lining of my jacket, just missing the skin of my arm. Before I could react, he was gone again. My heart pounded. It could have been my neck.

I held my hand up to Bree as if to say, *Stand still,* then bent down to remove my Hellcat backup gun. I took her hand and pressed her fingers around the handle. She shook her head and tried to push it back into my hand.

"No," she hissed. "No way."

I silently cursed but knew I couldn't force her to take it. I realized it might be more dangerous if she had it but refused to use it. "Stay close," I warned, then tuned back into the room.

"People who can't find their way out will face the clowns." The speaker cackled out a warning. Bree put her hand in mine. I knew she wasn't a fan of clowns. Most adults hated them, and I was no exception. I hated masks of any kind.

"Boo!" Hank appeared and threw a punch, but I blocked it easily as I shoved Bree away onto a different track. Her mouth opened as she disappeared from view. I turned, grabbed Hank's arm, and twisted it behind him, then pushed him forward. He used that moment to jerk sideways and jump onto a different part of the moving floor. He was slippery but clearly not a fighter. I changed my mindset and played his game. I'd outsmart the son of a bitch.

"Unlike you, Bradley, I wasn't an athletic kid." I knew he knew a lot about me. I never questioned his UPS route before, but now I questioned everything. Memories of him showing up with his UPS boxes at the rink or the office flooded my head. I remembered the talks we'd had when I'd pick up skates he'd sharpened for me before a game. I couldn't believe I'd never once seen this side of him.

I spotted the exit then and closed my eyes to try to memorize its position.

"I rather enjoyed the math club at school and, on some occasions, science camp." He laughed. "Just wasn't the sporty type. I did have some interesting friends, though." He lunged forward with the knife, and at the last second I jerked sideways and sent him into the wall. He stopped moving and disappeared as my shot missed him completely. I realized that meant there was a border along the wall that I could use.

Once close enough, I jumped off and was able to take in the layout of the room. His shadow bounced around the ceiling, and I ripped off my coat and wrapped it around my hand just as he appeared in front of me again. I deflected the next thrust that came at me and knocked the knife from his grip. I grabbed him by the collar of his jacket and pulled him into me. *I've had enough of this fucking room!*

"I knew you were quick." He grinned. I had a quick glimpse inside the window of his soulless body and was shocked at his lack of feeling. I felt his hand leave my arm as he removed something from his coat pocket. He held up something that looked like a tiny plunger and aimed it toward my face. *No!* As his fingers flexed to release what I could only imagine was the drug that had killed the girls, I held my breath and sent him backward into the mirrors. As he stumbled, I was able to grab his wrist and bend it to the side. I prayed he hadn't been able to release the toxic substance.

"Ahh!" he yelled, and I jammed my foot into the side of his knee. I felt a crunch, and he twisted as he hit a turning mirror hard. He was knocked out for a second. I saw the tiny plunger on the floor and saw a little puff of green powder get released from the plunger. I desperately wanted to gasp for a breath, but I held it as I kicked the plunger away and quickly secured his wrists in zip ties.

"Oh my god, I hate this place!" Bree lunged onto my platform and steadied herself against me as I slapped a hand over her mouth and madly made a motion to not inhale. Eyes wide, she nodded her understanding and smacked her own hand over her mouth to replace mine. Hank started to come to, so I grabbed him, and with Bree hard on my heels, we made it to the exit.

As we crashed through the door together, we almost collided with Cap and Kennedy, who waited with their weapons drawn. They both went for Hank together as Bree and I gasped for air. Once they realized I already had him secured, they pulled him to his feet.

"Aww, fellas, you missed all the fun." Hank laughed like a crazy person at Cap and Kennedy. "Stone was pretty amazing."

I started to run at him, but Kennedy grabbed my shoulders. "You think this is a game?" I yelled at him.

"No." He smirked with bright eyes. "I *know* this is a game." I brushed off Kennedy's hold on me and nodded at him to show I wasn't going to do anything.

"Get 'im out of here!" Cap growled. He handed him over to Stanley, who pushed him into the back of a squad car. I tried to catch my breath as I studied Bree. "Are you okay?"

"Yeah." She nodded with her hands on her knees. Hayne appeared then and hugged her and asked if she was all right. I looked away.

"You good?" Kennedy checked me over, but I held up a hand. I needed a moment. I was terrified we might have inhaled some of the drug.

"Plunger. Drug." I pointed behind me, and Kennedy ordered Ellis to get someone in to look after it. She took off, and I saw her pull gloves on as she ran.

"Shit!" He immediately called for medical assistance. "We need to get you two checked out fast."

"Where's Hank's wife?" I choked out.

"We got her, though she seems totally in the dark on what's going on," Cap answered as he inspected me. "Let Kelly look you over," he ordered. I figured by the time the ambulance arrived, we'd have expired anyway, but I still gave a sigh of relief once Bree and I had been cleared. As I stepped away from the ambulance and raised my thumb at Cap, I heard a shriek.

"Bradley!" Sherry's voice came from high up on the Ferris wheel. She must have spotted me. "I'm up here! I think this thing's broken. Get me down!"

"And then there's Sherry," Kennedy muttered. "I forgot you trapped her up there." He chuckled darkly, and I smirked for a moment along with him. The two of them had been close once. Sherry could be a lot at times, but before our divorce, he'd stopped talking to her completely. I'd never asked, because I'd figured he'd had words with her over something I probably didn't want to know.

I spat on the ground and considered myself damn lucky I'd clued in before we breathed that stuff in. "Adam, tell the workers they can let 'em down now."

"Sure thing, Stone." He raced off as Bree came forward. I reached out and grazed my fingers along her cheek, and for a tiny moment she leaned into me. Then she stepped back, and the moment was gone. I ached to hold her in my arms and bury myself in her. Her eyes were wide and glossy as she looked at me. I could see the pain in her eyes, and I knew she wanted it too.

"I guess you didn't need my help, after all." She tucked her hands into her pockets. "Thanks, though, for helping me back there. I hope you know I was keeping my distance."

"Of course, and I know that." I drew in a deep breath. "I'm glad you're okay. That was a little dicey." I pursed my lips and blew out some air. "Actually, Bree. I was dead wrong to shut you out of this, and I'm very sorry." I snagged my hat from the ground and dusted it off, needing something to do with my hands. "Why don't you come down to the station and help me question him?"

Her eyes lit up. "Yeah, I'd like that. I'll let Hayne know."

"Yeah." I looked at Cap, who grinned at me.

"Good job, Stone."

"Thanks, Cap."

"And for what it's worth, I'm sorry it was Hank." Cap rubbed his neck as he spoke. "It's not sitting right with me either. The man's been around since we were in high school."

"Yeah, it's a mind bender for sure." I felt the weight of it. I was just glad it was finally over, and I hoped we'd get a few more answers for the victims' families.

"Ready?" Cap asked, and I saw Sherry and her friend Anna watching me from the popcorn stand.

I righted my head and focused on what I needed to do next. "Let's go."

Bree went with Kennedy to the station, and we met later outside the interrogation room.

"Don't worry." She tucked her hair behind one ear. "Kennedy gave me the rundown. I take my lead from you, and I don't offer any information that doesn't need to be mentioned."

"Good." I left my hand on the doorknob for a moment as I looked at her.

"Wait, Brad, I have to ask. How did you know for sure it was Hank? I mean, it had to be more than the picture as a child. You said something about Gumbo."

I rubbed my jaw, still bothered by the fact I'd never suspected the man who was in my face almost daily. "Remember how I told you Gumbo texted someone, but the text never went through?"

"Yeah."

"He was texting someone named Zach Savage."

She shook her head like she didn't follow.

"There's this elite hockey-tape brand from Finland—great stuff— and the brand is called Savage."

"Oh right, I remember it's the type you always used." She nodded.

I was impressed she remembered that. "Yeah, but it's expensive, and guess which store in town was the only place you could buy it? Hank's hardware store. And later, because of the demand, he sold it to the rink where I play, and he started sharpening skates. Some of the guys called him Savage." I couldn't shake the feeling inside. "This sounds crazy, but I swore he used that name on purpose."

"Yeah, but what are the odds you'd catch it on that phone, that text, and at that time?"

"One thing I've learned from being a detective is there is no such thing as coincidences. My gut steers me, and it's screaming that something is off here. There's even more going on. So many foxes, remember?"

"Well, let's go see what we can find out."

"Yeah." I opened the door, and we could see Hank hunched over the table like his head hurt. Good, I hoped it hurt like a bitch.

"Detective Stone and PI Jaminson." He winced in pain as he turned to address us. "I was hoping to see you both in better light, and here we are." His odd smile didn't match his friendly tone, and it made the hairs on my arms stand up. I barely recognized the man.

"What happened to *Bradley*?" I asked him as I pulled out a chair for Bree and settled into the one next to her. "When did things get so formal, Hank? I've known you half my life." I looked down at the file I'd brought in and took my time reading from it. I clicked my pen after I was done and looked at him. "I guess I should really call you Zach Savage."

For a brief moment, I saw the old Hank, but then the creepy smile came over his face again as he nodded slowly. "I wondered if you'd catch that." He studied me a moment.

"I did, and it got me thinking. Then when I was at Ford's house and saw all those packages. I mean, you do get around a lot with your truck. Was he ordering stuff so you had a reason to go to his place?" I waited for him to speak, but when he didn't, I went on. "When we put it together with a photo we found of you when you were a kid, things really clicked into place. I'm so sorry you lost a friend at such a young age, Hank. That can have an awful effect on a person, especially a child."

"You figured it out." He sidestepped my emotional comment, then breathed in deeply as though he enjoyed the moment. "That was how I met Ford. He had an obsession with online ordering. I began to see potential in him."

"Potential?" I laughed.

He switched topics. "To be in the presence of both of you at this point makes me feel honored."

"I guess you had us all fooled for a long time. I don't know why you'd suddenly feel honored to be with us, but for such a fan, you had no problem using this on me." I dropped the evidence bag with the plunger inside on the table. Bree slid her hands from the table and put them between her knees.

"Did you test it for poison?" Ford asked.

Wes is in the process of doing that now.

"It was the poison you inhaled as a child that caused your limp, wasn't it?" Bree chimed in. Hank's eyes swung to her. Instantly I felt protective and leaned forward so I was closer to him than she was.

"Smart and beautiful," he praised. "You always were a bright girl. I'm pleased to see you two figured that one out too." I shook my head, dumbfounded.

"When did you get rid of the cane?" I asked.

"Let's see." He seemed to think about it. "It was around the time I started college. I felt it aged me and drew too much attention."

"Mm-hmm." He certainly had proved he was good at blending.

"I'm glad you survived Ford's little rendezvous at the lake. He was angry at the time." He shrugged apologetically at Bree.

"That makes two of us," she said, voice dripping with sarcasm.

His expression wavered slightly. "I know, that was wrong of him."

That was an odd comment, but Bree beat me to the punch. "That's a strange thing to say." She pinched her brows together. "Most people learn that hurting someone is wrong at a very early age."

"Yes, well." He didn't seem to like her comment. "We aren't all the same, are we?"

I slid the three victims' photos in front of him and waited a beat before I pointed at each one. "Shelly White, Maggie Deloitte, and Sophia McKinnon. You have anything to say?"

He waved a hand straight up through the center of the photos, then jerked it back like he remembered something. Then he pushed Sophia's toward me.

"That's not one of mine. I don't use such barbaric methods to kill—there's nothing poetic about it."

"Right." I tucked her photo under the file. Further confirmation of Jeremy Law's guilt. "All right, so these two were your victims. You have anything to say about them?"

"It was necessary. Tragic though it may be." He lifted a hand as if it had been nothing. How could I have missed such darkness in someone I'd known so long? I'd always liked the guy.

"Is that what you want me to tell their families? That it was necessary!" I looked at him like he was nuts. He obviously was.

He spun a rubber ring on his finger. "I want you to tell them that their children were part of something much bigger than they could understand."

"Explain it to me. Make me understand, and how does Gumbo fit into all of this?" He looked down at his hands.

"He's merely a pigeon." He shrugged.

"Ha!" Bree surprised both of us and smacked the table. She gave a dark laugh and turned her chair to look at me. "He killed two innocent women with basically an eyedropper so he could simply puff and run. Nah, he's nothing more than a coward."

"I'm a lot of things, Miss Jaminson," he said quietly, "but I'm not a coward."

"He's a coward and a pathetic excuse for a man." Bree ignored him, and it seemed to anger him. I nodded for her to keep pushing that angle.

Hank began to breathe hard, and his expression changed suddenly to one of anger. "Give me five minutes alone with you and I'll show you just how—"

Bree moved so fast neither of us saw her snap one of his fingers. His hand jerked back, and his pinky looked dislocated.

"Ouch!" He snarled at her. I was impressed.

"Watch what you say," she warned. "I've got nine more to play with."

"Psycho bitch." He babied his hand.

"No, no, no, *pretty* psycho bitch," she said. "At least that's what you implied that night you approached me in the parking lot. Right? I know it was you. Because of the way you stand. I forgot about it but noticed it at the station that day. You lean your weight on your right side. I just didn't catch it until now."

"She is good." Hank's anger disappeared as quickly as it came, and he smiled at me.

"I believe you also said prettier than my videos that night in the parking garage," Bree went on. "So, what the hell does that mean? Were you creepin' on me?"

I sneaked a glance at Cap, who was behind the two-way mirror. Why didn't I know about that conversation?

"You know what I wonder about, Stone?" Bree looked at me.

"What?" I played along, but it felt odd for her to call me anything but Brad.

"We have all the video footage of the murders, even the moment where he sprays the girls"—she turned to the two-way mirror as she bluffed—"thanks to the IT guys. Working backward with the girls' time of death, and now knowing Hank is the murderer, one thing bothers me. He never watched them die. Why is that?" She continued to direct her words to me and ignored Hank.

"Perhaps he didn't want to kill them," I answered. "Real killers drag it out and make their victims suffer."

"No, they didn't suffer," he muttered.

Bree glared at him then and laughed. Hank jerked his handcuffs, and I saw Bree's face harden. "How would you even know if it was painful or not? You didn't watch. You're still here, very much alive."

"No, because—" He sighed and shook his head slowly. "If only there was more time."

"What?" I swung my hand around. "Go on, defend yourself."

"I want my lawyer now."

"Right." I shook my head unimpressed. "You can't defend yourself because you have no idea."

He grimaced as if my words hurt him. He swung his head to look at me. "Killing someone with a simple poison is lazy. There's no art in that, no creativity." I didn't react. "Ford's powder process is flawless, better than what Johnny got into. The trick is making sure that every piece is a tiny flake, nothing that can get caught up in the lung or nasal cavity. It's smooth like butter going in. After it's in your system, it releases the poison that stops certain parts of your brain while it attacks other parts. They're like a drunk walking as they fall into a sleepy death. There's very little pain." He seemed pleased by that. "The club was the perfect place. Always packed, everyone on top of one another. It's so simple to puff a little powder that you can barely see. The girls looked drunk, and no one's the wiser."

"We found traces in their nasal cavities and lungs. The process wasn't flawless." Bree turned her nose up at him. "You're disgusting."

I cleared my throat. "However you look at it, Hank, or Zach, or whatever you call yourself, you seem happy enough to do the dirty work for the devil."

"I'm not a monster, Brad. I'm simply doing what was needed." He grabbed the marker that was tucked in my folder, swung the file folder around, and wrote, *six–nine*. "I can't give you any more than that." He pushed the folder back and rolled the marker to me. "But you'll be getting more."

"And men accuse women of playing games." Bree rolled her eyes. She pointed to the number he'd written. "Whatever this is, we're not playing."

"I want my lawyer."

"Right." I nodded and pretended to jot down some notes. "Oh, one more thing. Just before you blew their life away, did you ever look straight into their eyes and think, *I'm about to end everything you've worked so hard for and destroy everyone you love just because I'm a sick, twisted man?*"

"As I said, I killed them, yes. It was necessary." He moved his gaze over to the pictures again. "A means to an end. I'm just part of the whole. Such a pretty girl." He touched Sophia's photo. "Like I said,

I had nothing to do with that. It was unfortunate but did provide an interesting twist."

Bree huffed.

"I want my lawyer," he repeated.

I nodded a few times. "Yeah, it'd better be a really good one." I gathered up my things. I left the photos of the dead women face up in front of him, but he didn't bother to glance at them.

"Mr. Hank Brown?" a voice asked. His lawyer had arrived. She carried a briefcase and an armful of paperwork and sat down in front of him. "Sorry I'm late. I had meetings across town." She handed him a pen, and I noticed Hank hesitated before he took it. She put the paperwork down, and I scanned what she had. I noticed the file number, but she flipped it over when she caught me looking, and I frowned.

"Do me a favor and sign here and here." She pointed, and I noticed Hank stayed quiet.

Everything happened in slow motion. Hank's gaze moved up to mine, he jumped to his feet, and he shoved the table forward, sending Bree and me backward in our chairs. We both hit the floor, and I scrambled up quickly as he held up the pen. His thumb spun something around the top, before he swung an arm around his lawyer's neck, pulled her in close, and then jammed the pen into her shoulder. An audible click sound could be heard as a tiny puff of green powder released in their faces.

"No!" I cried, not wanting our last suspect on this case dead. I shoved Bree behind me without a second thought.

"What the hell!" His lawyer cried, then she started to cough before he released her, and she dropped to her knees. I went to help then, but he raised a hand, and I froze.

Hank struggled to keep his composure as he kept his focus on me for another brief moment, then he started to shake and turn blue as he clutched his throat. I saw the life drain from his eyes and knew he was gone. I couldn't believe this was happening. Why would he do this?

I whirled around and grabbed Bree's hand, and we quickly shimmied back against the far wall. So many things flickered through my head, but the biggest one was making sure Bree was safe. I glanced over and saw that her expression matched the horror in my own. We knew exactly what had happened. I pulled her up as the guard opened the door, and we dashed out.

Once we were outside of the room and I knew we were safe, I grabbed Bree's head and made her look at me.

Her eyes were wide. "I'm good. Are you good?"

"Yeah." The grip around my heart loosened when I saw she was all right. I slowly let her go as the enormity of what had happened sank in.

"Detective Stone"—the guard removed the piece of cloth he had covering his mouth—"they're both dead."

I squeezed my eyes shut and cursed internally. What a fucking shit show! I fought the urge to punch the wall and instead kicked a chair down the hallway, making Bree jump.

"Sorry."

She ran a hand through her hair. "Okay, so was the lawyer in on it?"

I didn't answer her as my anger spiked to a dangerous level. Once again, we were left with so many unanswered questions.

As we stood there in the aftershock, Cap and Kennedy ran toward us. They'd been watching through the two-way mirror.

"What the fuck, Stone?" Cap shouted as an alarm went off. "How am I going to explain this?"

"He shoved the table at us. He made sure we didn't inhale it. Shit, he even stopped me from helping the lawyer! He wanted me to know what he was doing when he held up the pen right before." I looked at Cap. "Why would he do that? Why let *us* live? Why take down the lawyer? Was she in on it too? I mean, she did give it to him." My head spun in multiple directions as I ran my mouth. "They both went down so fast, way faster than the girls did."

"What a fuckin' mess," Cap said as we looked through the small window at the two bodies that lay on the floor.

How could such a monstrous event happen? It made no sense to me. I was so twisted up inside by the entire thing that I couldn't focus. I was usually good at separating myself from a suspect, but this was on a whole new level.

"Clearly he had demons." Cap gave me a sad face, then rubbed his mouth as he turned to the guard who was quietly speaking with Kennedy. "Get someone in here to clear the scene."

"Yes, sir."

Later, after endless questions and many cups of coffee, Bree came in to gather her bag and coat.

"You need a ride home?" I turned off my laptop and tucked it into my bag. I'd been studying everything Hank had said to us for the second time. None of it made any sense, and I was dead tired. Bree pulled at the sleeve of her jacket like she, too, had something on her mind. The last forty-eight hours had been wild.

"You know what really bothers me?" She must have been mid-thought. "What were those numbers he gave us? They have to mean something."

"Yeah." I shrugged. "I'm just too tired to care at the moment. At this point I'm just glad a killer is off the streets, the families got closure, and the department has stopped breathing down our necks for answers. Those numbers can wait for another day."

"I guess so. That was a long night for you. Are you going to stay in town?"

"I have to stop by my parents' place."

She tapped her nail on the side of her purse buckle, and I could tell something was on her mind. Her chin jutted out and her eyes formed into slits as she looked at me. "For the record"—she crossed her arms—"I'm seriously angry at you for not bringing me in on this. I really am, Brad. I feel like you didn't trust me."

"I know." I went to explain but couldn't find the words. Sheer exhaustion had a tight hold on me.

"I'm not sure why you did what you did, and we have to talk about it before we move on." Her hurt expression brought acid to the pit of my stomach.

"I hear ya, but I had my reasons at the time."

"Which were?" She put her hands on her hips, but I saw she fought to control her emotion. I had to give her credit. If the situation were reversed, I know I wouldn't have handled things nearly as well.

"Maybe I was wrong. I don't know, but I'm really sorry, Bree. I think we need to talk it out." I reached for her and put a hand on her cheek. "Can we wait on it, though? I have to leave for Florida for another case."

"I'm not letting this go."

"I know."

She studied me for a moment, then sighed. "Guess I need to find a ride home."

"I'm going that way first. I can take you."

We started to walk toward the door. "So, Florida?"

"Cap asked me to help a fellow detective out on a case. Their perp did some stuff here before he moved to Florida. Long story." I paused. "I really need some coffee."

Her lips twisted, and she made a face, then chuckled.

"What?"

"Just you."

"Me?" I followed her out of the office.

"Yes, you. Acting like you love coffee the way I do."

I scoffed at her. "I do like coffee."

"Yeah, but not like I *loooove* coffee."

"I do."

"You're such a fucking liar." She elbowed me playfully, and I laughed to add a bit of fuel to the shit giving.

I mimed being shocked by her language. "Breanna Nina Jaminson, such a foul word you just used." I tossed an impressed look her way.

She opened the car door before I could get to it and waited until I opened mine. "Don't even get me started on how you settle for dealership coffee."

I stumbled. "They're not very good, but sometimes I just need a kick."

She buckled herself in. "Do you think that lawyer knew what was in the pen she gave to Ford?" Bree's voice was suddenly serious. "I bet she didn't. I mean, he grabbed her neck and pulled her in before he set it off."

"I dunno, but from what Hank said, it sounds like he was working for someone else, part of something bigger. We can only guess, but maybe that person ordered her to give it to him. She lost her life for it, right alongside Hank. Makes you wonder, though, doesn't it, if there's someone else calling the shots, why isn't he doing the dirty work himself?"

"True." She sighed. "The world's better off without Hank or Ford, that's for sure."

"Well, I know one thing." I looked at her. "If I see even one little puff of powder anywhere, I'm hightailing it out of there."

She laughed.

We laughed the entire way out of town as we came up with more and more funny lines to describe getting the hell out of a situation. That was what Bree was for me, someone who could take the bad and find a way to live with it. Humor was our way to cope, and it worked for both of us. At least for most things.

When we arrived at her cabin, she gathered her things but stopped when she reached for the handle. "I meant what I said today. Thank you for saving me, twice."

"I will always protect you."

"I'm still pissed," she added.

"I know."

She pushed a smile onto her lips as she reached for the door, then pulled her hand back. "Brad?"

"Yeah?"

She leaned in and pressed a gentle kiss to my cheek, her soft lips sending a wave of warm goose bumps across my skin. The delicate trace of her perfume lingered in the air, sweet and intoxicating. It made my head feel blissfully light. As she slowly pulled back, her eyes caught the soft glow from the cabin lantern, and they sparkled like stars in the night. "Thank you for the ride."

I licked around my dry mouth and somehow formed a sentence. "I'll see you in a few days." I waved at her as she walked away. I took my time to relive the moment before I drove away.

Once I hit the city limits, I heard a text come through. I pulled over and dug my phone out of my bag.

Captain: Change of plans. You're not needed for the case. The guy took a deal. Take the day tomorrow and we'll see you next shift.
Brad: Copy that.

I let out a happy sigh and leaned my head back against the headrest. *Thank God.* I hadn't been looking forward to the trip. Glad I hadn't gotten far, I was about to pull a U-turn when movement caught my eye, and I noticed a woman who looked mighty familiar run up to a man and wrap her arms around him, then they started to kiss. He grabbed her ass and whirled her around. I pulled in my chin and laughed.

"Well, shit, look at you, Sherry." To think she'd been putting me through the ringer with Bree, and there she was with another man. A newfound lightness came over me then, followed by a wave of clarity as I rewound the last few weeks of encounters with Bree. I had to let the past go and make a new life for myself. For years, my heart had whispered the truth I was too afraid to hear. But now, I was ready to listen.

I turned the car around and headed back the way I had come.

The lights were on in the cabin, and smoke piped out of the chimney. She was still up. I climbed the steps to her porch and knocked.

The door opened a crack, and she peeked out, and when she saw it was me, she opened it all the way.

"Brad? What are you doing here? Is everything all right?" She looked gorgeous in her silk pajamas. I loved those pajamas. I didn't answer her.

"Bree." I took a deep breath and went with the truth. "I was lost after what we witnessed that day as teens. I panicked and used Sherry as a crutch. Then I ran our marriage into the ground because I never really got proper help for what happened. I still shut down and go dark, totally unsure how to dig my way out of it." I took a breath as she stood there. "But the difference is, now that you're back, you've woken something inside me that I'd run from since the day we met."

She blinked. "Brad."

"Let me get this out." I shifted my weight to buy myself a moment. "You've been trying to tell me that you have a life back in New York City, and at first I didn't listen. You were home, and that's where I wanted you to be, but that's not fair. You left because you had to, and I stayed here because I thought I had to.

"But I want you to know that I hear you, and I want you to be where you feel the happiest and safest. I just need you to know that I've been in love with you forever. I was just too scared to make a move, and now you're back, and it's like someone is giving us a second chance." I sucked in a deep breath. "I don't know about you, but when we're together, everything just feels elevated and right.

"Wherever you need to be, Bree, I'll figure it out. I just want to be with you."

A tear rolled down her cheek, so I grabbed her around the waist and pulled her in for a kiss with everything I had inside.

"Brad." She struggled and pulled back a little as she studied my face. "I want this too"—she smiled through her tears—"but if we're doing this, we both need to get help." She wiped her eyes with the back of her hand. "We need to take this slow. I can't open myself up to you only to have you push me away again. I almost didn't survive the last time you did that."

"I promise." I flexed my hands and slipped them under her silk top.

"All right, then." She shivered. "Do you want to come in?" She looked at me with her head tilted to one side.

I pulled her in again, and she molded to me. "I need you." I walked her backward inside and kicked the door shut. This woman was everything I needed in my life. I pulled off my coat, and she clawed at the buttons of my shirt. I stripped it off as hot desire built up inside me. She found a way out of her silky top. I forced myself to slow down. "I want to do this right, Bree, but just for tonight, can we—"

"Brad?" She huffed her exasperation. "Tomorrow's for talking. Tonight, just take me."

The morning sun beat through the windshield, offering nothing to help warm the chill in the air. I started the car and glanced at Bree, who sat beside me, already eyeballs deep in some paperwork. I smiled as I looped around and headed toward town. We had gone a few rounds the night before, and, if I was being honest, I wished we had accepted Cap's offer to take the day off. He obviously didn't know Bree. She'd insisted we show up at work. We'd promised to take things slow and to keep whatever it was between us to ourselves. The label Bree had put on it was "getting to know one another." To me, we were in the early stages of dating, but I wasn't going to point that out just yet.

When she reached for her water bottle, I snagged her hand and kissed the back of it while I relished in the fact that I could. I thought I had gotten my fill of her through the night, but my body already was making plans. I shifted and tugged at my crotch at the stoplight, and she grinned at me. Then looked down at her lap again.

Bree had the victims' files spread out and kept flipping through the photos. I squinted at one of the pictures because I hadn't seen it before.

"Where did you get that one?" It was of Shelly White's bedroom.

She held it up so I could see it better. "It's one of mine. I've learned over the years that I miss a lot of stuff. I'm not blessed with a photographic memory." She smiled playfully and poked me in the shoulder. "You'd be surprised by how many times I've found kids just because of my photos. Things you might not see at first." She pointed to a Christmas ornament in one of the pictures. "For instance, CSI wouldn't have any reason to snap a photo like this. It's a simple ornament, but for me, it's a lot more. Remember, I found Shelly's TikTok account on her iPad. This was hanging in full sight, but if you look closely at the picture, you'll see it's from her secret lover, the professor. She showed me a zoomed-in photo with a heart and his name written underneath it. I wonder how many times Oliver the ex-boyfriend from the gym looked at it and just thought it was cute."

"Good catch."

"Thanks." She tucked the photo back in its place and closed her eyes.

"We still have a lot to wrap up with this case. Not the least of it is why the hell Hank did what he did. We need a search warrant for his house. I'll get on that first thing."

"Okay, I'll start by talking to his wife if you like. I'm sure she must be shocked over it all."

"All right, sounds good." I nodded. "I made a promise to myself that I'd give every case my all. Lord knows I could use a win after staring at that cold case for the past decade." I knew Bree still struggled daily with what had happened at the river, and to be truthful, so did I, but I channeled my nerves and stress with hockey and my work. I didn't want it to run my life anymore. It was high time she found better ways to deal with it too. It wasn't a good time to discuss that, and I didn't want her to shut down on me, so I changed the topic to something . . . fun.

"How'd you sleep, given the extra exercise you had?" I smirked.

"I was dead to the world until about three in the morning, when my nightmare came to visit." She gave a small shrug.

I decided not to comment. There was no easy fix to that, but we'd both agreed we'd start seeing a therapist.

She changed the subject. "Do you ever look at a case and just know you're missing something?"

All the time. "Yes, often. I think it's a sign of a good detective if you care enough to open the file after the case has been solved." I parked, but she stopped me from leaving.

"Brad, it's time to talk about why you kept me from Hank's takedown."

I knew she was right, and I only hoped I could make her understand where my head had been. "Truth? You're still not healed from your accident. You still get headaches. I know from years of hockey that stress is the worst thing when you're trying to heal from a concussion." I put a finger on her lips when she went to speak. "I'm sorry, but before you say anything, I need you to understand my thought process. Okay?"

She pursed her mouth but settled back.

"But, the main thing is, and I know this is going to piss you off, you don't have the kind of training for that level of police work. Arresting a killer is vastly different from talking down a runaway teen."

She wrinkled her nose, and I waited, but to my surprise she simply nodded. "I understand that."

"And add to all that"—I threaded my fingers through hers—"I was scared he was going to hurt you, and I couldn't bear that."

"Brad," she warned, "you don't get to make those kinds of decisions for me."

"I know."

"And, you and I both know, we could be facing something even more sinister from the things we've heard from Hank and Timothy Ford. If they're to be believed. I need to know that while I'm here, you're not going to keep anything from me."

She was right. Something was still very off. I could feel it coming. Like a dark presence lurking on the sideline.

"Brad, promise me."

"I can promise I'll try." I pressed her hand to my lips. I didn't want to focus on the bad stuff. She groaned, and I nipped her fingers playfully. "I have you back in my life, Bree. I'm a protective guy, and you"—I tugged her forward—"are worth protecting." I snagged her waist and pulled her in for a small kiss.

I opened my door, then went around to open hers as she gathered up all her paperwork. She smiled happily up at me as we headed toward the station together.

"Drinks at Karva at seven. Everyone's going to celebrate the case," Kennedy called as he joined us on the stairs.

I put a hand on her bottom.

"Brad!" She laughed and glanced quickly around. "Someone will see us." When I didn't remove it, she swatted at me, and I caught Kennedy's sly grin.

"You're naughty!" She pulled ahead of me.

"Darlin', you have no idea."

Chapter Sixteen

Barbed Wire Killer

I used the side of my key chain to scratch the word *Karva* off the recycled coaster that came with my beer. I needed something to take the edge off what had happened, and I also needed to check in.

The low lighting and the way the lamps were located on the tables cast shadows around the room. It made it difficult to make out faces, and it worked in my favor as I rested a shoulder against the wall of the table. The place was a favorite with the locals, and not many visitors strayed to this part of town.

The door opened, and I spotted Bradley. Then, to my absolute delight, there was no Sherry trailing in behind him. The constant sour look she usually wore when they were with his friends rubbed me raw. I hated that bitch. I'd left her alone because Bradley was on the right course. Lately I had begun to doubt that, but now I could see I'd been right.

"Is that a matryoshka doll?" A woman had moved between me and the table I'd been watching. She pointed at my key chain. "Yeah, it is." She picked it up. "Does it open? I love how they nest. Or is it just one solid piece of wood?"

"It nests." I took a swig of my beer and tried to control my temper. I hated to be interrupted when I needed to be alone.

"Can you show me?" She moved to sit, but I hooked my foot around the chair leg to hold it in place. She jerked back when it didn't budge.

I snatched the key chain and glared at her.

"Wow! Okay, red flag much." She scowled, and I flicked my wrist for her to move on. "Asshole."

"Bye," I muttered into the head of the beer. I went back to watching.

I saw that Bradley kept his eyes trained on the door, then I saw why. Bree arrived.

"Well, what are you going to do?" a girl whispered loudly from the table behind me. "I mean, it's Brad and it's you—you're endgame." I strained to listen better.

"I thought we were, but now with that bombshell bitch back, his head is clouded."

"Do you think he saw you and Jim? You two can't keep your hands off one another."

"If he did, he'll get over that. I just need to make him see that I wasn't in the right headspace. Bradley needs me, not her." Sherry's whiny voice cut me like shards of glass. "I can't believe he had his hand on her this morning at the station. He's mine, and I just need to send Bree a reminder of that."

"How?"

"Well, she's been run off the road into a lake, and nearly taken out by a serial killer at the fair." There was a pause. "I read Bradley's files when he's not home—the perks of having the spare key and having that mutt stay at my place."

"Smart." Her friend must have tipped her beer back because I heard the slosh.

"So, Bree can handle a lot and doesn't scare easily. I just need to find something that will do the trick." They giggled together.

I stared down at the small face on my matryoshka key chain and pressed it hard into my palm as I listened to the nasty bitch.

I've put up with so much. I will not have Sherry ruin everything. I'm done.

I dropped the key chain onto the table and pulled out the matchbox from my pocket. I pressed my thumb to the end of the box to push it out of its sleeve. Three small knots of barbed wire lay innocently together.

It was time.

Acknowledgments

My mother, my partner in crime, and my best friend. I wouldn't be here if it weren't for you.

My husband, Nathan, and my kids, Brooke and Parker, who support me no matter how crazy things get.

My sisters, Erin and Gillian, who always have suggestions on my next book ideas.

And to all my readers, thank you for following me on this journey.

Cheers to a new story!

About the Author

Photo © 2018 Candice Dartez Photography

J.L. Drake is a bestselling author of contemporary romance and romantic suspense, known for her dark, gripping books with brooding heroes and passionate lovers. Her world of mayhem comprises multiple interconnected series of books that can also be enjoyed individually. Originally from Nova Scotia, Drake now lives in Southern California. For more about the author, visit her website at www.authorjldrake.com.